THE FASTER DRAW

Rage distorted the blond man's face. He moved frantically, scrambling with both hands at the scabbard on his belt. *"This is all your fault!"*

Kylene's legs and back were rigid, locked tightly to keep her horse unmoving, even while she balanced with one arm and patted at her side with the other. Her actions were very simple: she removed knives from their pockets and launched them openhandedly in the air. That was all.

Once. Twice, Three times. Four...

He spun about dizzily, then marionette-walked to the edge of the stream, to sprawl over the bank. His eyes and mouth were open in astonishment. Water covered most of his face.

The knife slice across his jugular vein could be seen very clearly in the water.

Books by Mike Shupp
published by Ballantine Books

THE DESTINY MAKERS

*Forthcoming

Mike Shupp

Morning Of Creation

Book Two of The Destiny Makers

A Del Rey Book
BALLANTINE BOOKS ● NEW YORK

Library of Congress Catalog Card Number: 85-91207

ISBN 0-345-32550-8

Manufactured in the United States of America

First Edition: March 1986

Cover Art by David Schleinkofer

This one for
Neeters

The First Compact

To end eternal war, it is agreed by the telepaths and normal men that never again shall telepaths establish a separate state and exercise their dominion over men.

This Compact shall be preserved by the thoughts and actions of both human races and witnessed by the ti-Mantha lu Duois.

The penalty for violation, in thought or action, shall be death.

The Second Compact

To end the Second Eternal War, the Great Compact is reaffirmed by the Teeps and the Normals. It is also agreed by the Teeps and the Normals that never again shall Teeps employ their abilities in the service of national states and thus exercise their dominion over men.

This Compact shall be preserved by the thoughts and actions of both human races and witnessed by the spirit of the tiMantha lu Duois.

The penalty for violation, in thought or action, shall be death.

Hemmendur's Solution

"We have observed that neither Compact prohibits the employment of the Teeps, in whole or in part, in any role whatsoever, by a single all-encompassing world state. I suggest to you that such a state must ultimately arise. By its nature, it will be everlasting and unopposable.

"I suggest as well that given that inevitability, we attempt ourselves to give birth to that state and shape its growth. If our intentions are worthy, our actions honorable, and our ambitions steadfast, we shall be successful, for we shall gain strong allies.

"Not the least of these will be the Teeps, who are entitled to a role in human affairs and for whom I propose a most sacred responsibility—which is to ensure that men exercise no dominion over men . . ."

Part 1: Portraits—Grisaille
Waterfall Kylinn R'sihuc, 44,938 L.C.

CHAPTER ONE

*O*ne hundred thirteen plus six hundred fifty-four plus five hundred seventy-one made—it made a demon-rapturing mess, Kylene thought rebelliously. She shoved aside the teaching machine that overhung her bed and slammed her writing block down in front of her folded knees. *Stupid machine stupid writing thing stupid stupid Algherans!* One set of characters for digits that came first in a number, and another set for those behind a decimal line. *Their dumb numbering system is as insane as they are.*

They expected her to learn dumb, meaningless symbols to manipulate in arbitrary ways, meaningless dates and silly names, an ugly, inelegant language and graceless script... Completely dumb! This so-called schooling was pointless and the Algherans who did not admit it were hypocrites. It was not fair of them to make her waste life this way.

Someday... She would make them all sorry someday. Footsteps approached, slapping noisily on the glass

catwalk that led to the Teep quarters. People were returning.

Stupid, lazy, fat people! She frowned, squinting at the
drab rows of beds through almond-shaped green eyes,
making wrinkles press painfully against the green lozenge
that had been fastened to her forehead. Thoughts from
outside could not be seen through the mesh that covered
her triangular doorway and earthen walls of the kennel,
but the tone of the babbling voices bore its own message.
The Teeps had been frightened by some action of the
Normals less than a tenth of a day before; now they were
happy after their entertainment, their cowardly little minds
filled with gossip and excitement as they traipsed back
from their brief holiday.

Even to her sixteen-year-old's perceptions, these people of the far future were worthless. And the Teeps were
the worst of the lot. They were always on holiday. None
of them cooked, none of them washed clothing, none of
them made sailcloth, none of them felled timber, none of
them planted crops. Useless people, to match their useless education, they deserved to be hiding under the ground
from their enemies.

And they deserved to see that because of their petty
tyranny, she kept to her studies while they were gone,
and never had any fun of her own, and had to keep her
mind shielded from them because she was concentrating
so hard. This was their fault, so let them see her hard at
work and miserable and feel guilty.

She bent to straighten out the bed cover. Admiring
briefly the pattern of freckles on her thin forearms, she
smoothed out folds in the too-long brown dress, tossed
vagrant strands of black hair over her shoulder, then
yanked the teaching machine into place again, pouting,
making sure as the others entered that they could see how
stiff and uncomfortable she was.

She sniffed unhappily as people passed by and down
the long corridor, but none of them said anything sym-
pathetic. They callously ignored her, so wrapped up in

themselves that she caught none of them looking at her
when she took her eyes away from the teaching machine's
screen, none of them smiling at her when she abandoned
the masquerade of activity and swung her leg idly at the
side of her bed to advertise her boredom.

Across the aisle, a heavy man with gray-touched hair
took colored paper squares from his wall cabinet and held
them toward a thin brunet man. *Fifty units, Salm. Don't*
spend it in one place. If you can find a place to spend it.

They chuckled together, their thoughts interwoven.

All in one place.
Fifty units isn't so much.

> A day's pay.

With no place to spend it.
You can afford this.
I should have bet you for more.

> You'd have gotten it too.
> Never thought the Ironwearer
> had much of a chance.

The Ironwearer.
Strong. Brave. Resolute.
Willing to be hurt.
It was inevitable.

> Foolish thinking.
> Herrilmin ha'Hujsuon
> was—is—the best man
> with a whip sword I've
> seen in three centuries.

And a sadist.

> Which is why he's good
> with a sword.
> Sadist and masochist—
> what a pretty pair.

Not sorry to see
ha'Hujsuon shamed.

> Only a Normal.
> Don't take it personally.

Not sorry to see
any ha'Hujsuon shamed.

> Only Normals.
> Don't take it personally.

I'm satisfied.
Even without your money.

> Ironwearer stupidity, you know.
> He didn't understand he could
> have left Herrilmin to
> die in the dueling square.

The Ironwearer.
He wouldn't have.
Soft-hearted.
Toward us, toward Herrilmin.
You heard him—
there, at the end.

> Mushy-brained.
> Like all the Normals.

Is he like the others?
His thoughts are strange.

> But he doesn't see minds.
> He's a Normal.

They don't think he is.
Even his friends
the few he has.

> No one likes Ironwearers.
> They do idiot things like—

She's listening.

> She's listening.

Thought screens rose. Spoken words lifted over turned backs.

"Next time you find something to bet on, remember me."

"Hard to forget betting you."

The men separated, pretending not to see Kylene's tongue.

None of them cared about her. She could be dying and they would just yammer about their stupid entertainments. None of them cared.

None of them care. Really, none of them care.

Her face a goblin's mask, Kylene stood slowly and went to the doorway. But even as she hesitated, the mesh resting on her forearm, to see if her departure would be noticed, she sensed only conversations that mirrored what she had observed: glittering surface thoughts without depth or concern.

This was the first formal duel to be fought in over five years, and probably the last for years to go. We've seen real history!

I never even heard of a fight that ended like that. It's awesome, in a way. Who ever thought to defeat a master swordsman by accepting a disabling blow? And you saw that strike he made in return?

```
                                              I
   (Trust                                    saw
         the Normals                         him
I                   to make spectacles       try
  really                out of their         to
      like                  stupid           stop
          red-haired  You're    politics.)   it.
               men.    both
The            sexier.  being   We've never seen them get
   other    is          very    so upset before, though. If
       one              silly,  they are fighting among
   other   hates        girls!  themselves, instead of
The         Teeps.              against the Chelmmysians—
                                doesn't it show they have lost
Hujsuons                        sight of their goals? I worry.
are
going                                        You
to                      Are                  always
be                   both of them            worry,
impossible.          still alive?            Jerlt.
```

I hope they both die! Kylene cast back at the dormitory.

There was a gratifying moment of silence. Then the responses came:

Kylinn acting like Kylinn acting like Kylinn acting like Kylinn

He				Cimon-taken
saved	I DON'T BELIEVE YOU!			little
your	HE LIED ABOUT THAT!			barbarian
life				brat

like Kylinn acting like Kylinn acting like Kylinn acting like

	That's		She	
Diapers	a	I	needs	by
need	noisy	HATE	a	the
changing	little	HIM!	good	tra'R'sihuc
	brat		spanking	

acting like Kylinn acting like Kylinn acting like Kylinn acting

Can't anything be		Unfortunately,
done to shut up	I HATE ALL OF YOU!	we're stuck
the little pest?		with the brat.

acting like Kylinn acting like Kylinn acting like Kylinn acting
I WANT TO GO HOME IWANTTOGOHOME
IWANTTOGOHOME I WANT TO GO HOME
Kylinn acting like Kylinn acting like Kylinn acting like Kylinn
I have a headache. I have a headache. I have a headache.

S I L E N C E

I have a headache. I have a headache. I have a headache.
        Hello, Cyomit. Hello, Cyomit. Hello, Cyomit.
Hello, Cyomit.   Hello, Cyomit.
        Hello, Cyomit. Hello, Cyomit. Hello, Cyomit.

Drop dead from the headache, Cyomit, Kylene thought, stepping out of the doorway to avoid contact with the smaller girl. *Little Miss I'm-so-cute. Show-off. I don't like you.*

I hate you too. That was Cyomit's greeting. *Both of you!* She stood in the entranceway, close to tears. *Both!*

Kylene sneered down at her, then shoved at the brown-haired Teep. "Get out of my way, baby."

"No!" Cyomit grabbed at her wrist and refused to release it.

That maniac, Kylene heard in her mind. *Embarrassing me in front of everyone. Treating me like a slave. Making people look at me.*

An image of the maniac was conjured from memory: a red-haired giant, inhumanly tall and wide, his broad face distended by grief, looming over her, uttering broken phrases that she could not hear clearly.

Then the image dissolved, reforming with another picture of the same man on his knees, his face raised to show tears and hatred as he pushed futilely at the chest of a dead blond man. Blood streamed down his sleeves and the back of his shirt. Arm-length metal knives lay on red-splattered concrete. His mouth opened soundlessly. His fear and pain were obvious as he stared at Cyomit.

Timithial ha'Dicovys, the man who called himself ha'Ruppir—the man Kylene had known as Tayem Minstrel. The man from the world that had existed before hers, the man who had given her empty promises of assistance, argued her fate with her on a hillside surrounded by wolves, kidnapped her from her homeland, left her captive among the Algherans, then scornfully abandoned her. So Cyomit hated him too. Good. He deserved to have enemies, even if Cyomit didn't count for much.

You, Cyomit sent back contemptuously. *You. You're his fault too. If he'd let the wolves eat you, I'd have a sister, but instead—you're the one who doesn't count for anything! You're the one so dumb you're learning out of baby books and have to be told how to put clothes on right. No one needs you, Kylinn.* A moment passed while the two teenagers glared at each other, barely conscious of the tension-rippled backdrop of other conversations.

She's not going to speak till I do, Kylene noticed. "Let me go, Cyomit," she hissed, her mind shielded so the girl would be forced to use speech. She knew that would embarrass Cyomit. "Take your pudgy little fingers off me, or I'll hit you. On your head."

"The tra'R'sihuc wants to talk to you, Kylinn." Hatred showed in the small girl's eyes, then blanked out.

"Come to the infirmary door immediately. Both of you." Cyomit's tone was stern, deeper than her normal shrill voice. Kylene recognized the Sept Master's voice.

"There's your madman," Cyomit hissed.

Kylene halted automatically in the corridor, waiting for the three men to vanish down the stairwell to the hangar area, cautious but hardly conscious of her action, scarcely hearing the smaller girl. *Home.* She was going home. Her nightmare imprisonment was at an end. *Home.*

The gray concrete underfoot; the stairwell gaping blackly, glistening darkly on one side where water trickled; the scuffing sound of her sandals; Cyomit grabbing her elbow lest they be noticed by the two elderly Normals who emerged from the hangar into the passageway; the Teepblinded men turning away with incurious eyes to enter the control room, from which mixed curiosity and amusement at their Normal antics emerged until the metal door closed—none of this counted, none of this was more important than the meaningless grab bag of clothing in her hands, the deserted loading dock, or the almost empty hangar.

Home. She was going home. Someone was going to take her home.

She went down the narrow steps to the hangar almost blindly, giving no notice to the huge, silvered ax head that floated at one end or the tall, unmoving Agent wearing green and black. She felt as if she were gliding across the concrete floor, with only the weight of the clothes bag bumping against her knees to let her know she was walking. *Home.*

That's him! Cyomit thought angrily. *Go to him.*

Kylene stopped abruptly. An Agent, she had been told. But surely not this Agent! She stared at the big redhead with dismay, and stumbled blindly across the hangar only after Cyomit shoved her.

"Hello, Kylene," Tayem Minstrel said when she reached him. His voice was low, apologetic. "You've grown a bit, I see. Still very pretty. May I help with your bag?"

He was being punished, she realized. His thoughts were hidden from her by the metal of the Teepblind that showed through his hair, but she knew that was why he sounded sorry. That explained why he was here. Even though he had won that stupid sword fight for the Project Master and still moved stiffly from unimportant injuries, the Algherans had decided to punish him for kidnapping her. It was a good joke.

Make him keep begging, she decided. She ignored his outstretched hand and stalked up the ramp to the side of the levcraft, then stood between the man and the closed portal so he could not reach it easily and had to jump up from the hangar floor to slap the switch that opened the door. When the hatch slid upward, whirring softly, she entered the vehicle without a backward glance while Tayem scurried around to the base of the ramp.

She had forgotten how huge he was.

Just inside was a second hatchway, which rose as she approached it, then fell behind her. As she passed over the sill, recessed tubes in the ceiling flickered on, casting a feeble red glow over the interior of the shuttle. Tayem's vehicle was not like any other Agent's, she had heard; she indulged an instant of curiosity.

Partitions made a compartment the width of the vehicle. The walls, which seemed black in this light, were rectangle-gridded by dark, glossy lines. *Lockers*, she recognized. *Or covered shelves*. She pressed idly on a few of the rectangles, but the covers would not move. *Probably empty anyhow.*

An opening in the back wall was an entrance to an unlit corridor. Nearer to hand was a door. She pushed against it, and stuck her head through to peer at a pair of oversized bedshelves wall-mounted under a sloping ceiling. The flooring was the same spongy material under her feet; a blank wall divided the space into two; lighting came from niches high in the walls. Living quarters; she would make Tayem stay out while she occupied them.

The section forward had to be the control area. It was mostly empty space, though more storage lockers lined the walls on either side; at the very front a pair of tall, dark blocks stood before a low, one-piece window that ran the width of the vehicle.

The window had not been visible from outside, she remembered. She moved forward, noticing that webbed straps dangled from the sides of the blocks, which were half ringed by low cabinets arranged between them and the window. The cabinet tops were unmarked and pinkish—perhaps in normal lighting they would be white or cream-colored—and sloped toward the center of the ring.

Dark panels pivoted down from the high ceiling as she advanced. Struts snapped into place to hold the panels facing the dark blocks. She could see no steering instruments, no way to control the vehicle.

It *was* very Tayem-like.

The man found her looking out the window at another shuttle, a clear-walled bubble sitting alone in the center of the hangar. He stared across the cabin at her until he noticed the direction of her gaze.

"Herrilmin's," he commented quietly. He took her forearm and pointed her toward the left block. "Come on, we might as well get moving."

She had not sensed his presence till he spoke. Nor had she expected to hear him display such emotion. She stared as if at a stranger, trying uselessly to make out his features in the semidarkness while he took the bag of clothing from her and stowed it in one of the wall lockers.

For although he had spoken calmly, his touch had betrayed him. She had sensed sorrow and despair in a measure such as she had seldom before encountered; Tayem Minstrel was very nearly in tears.

This could not be the effect of punishment, she realized.

But she had cause for anger with him and could not

offer sympathy. When she spoke, her voice was tense and
untrusting. "Where are we going?"

"The future," Tayem said. "Five hundred years from
now. For starters." He turned away from her, removed
his black cape, and hung it neatly in a locker. He was not
wearing the sword and belt pouches she remembered, she
noticed. "Brrr!"

*Home! I'm supposed to be going home. What has gone
wrong?*

"Why?" Somehow she managed not to shriek.

Tayem looked at her stolidly till her eyes dropped from
his. "Didn't they tell you? I'm going to train you to be
an Agent."

For another war? she thought wildly. *Are the Algherans now at war with Kh'taal Minzaer? Or is this some
private plan of Tayem's?*

"No, you won't," she said narrowly.

"Not much choice, kid. The Project's made a mistake
I have to set right, and you're all the help I'm getting. I
need you, Kylene."

"No," she repeated.

He was supposed to take her *home*. The tra'R'sihuc
had promised an Agent would restore her to where she
belonged. The Algherans wanted her to be happy. They
wanted her to go home. He had mentioned none of what
Tayem spoke of.

Tayem was *cheating*. He was betraying the Algherans
and her, all over again.

She wouldn't let him. Somehow she'd find her way
home. With or without the help of Tayem Minstrel. Somehow.

A long moment passed. A hand like a leather gauntlet
moved to cup her chin, lifting it upward till she was facing
the man once more, forcing her to look into his gray eyes
and to notice the jagged scar on his temple and the parch-
ment crease lines on his broad forehead. A finger stroked
her cheek delicately, as though she were made from but-
terfly stuff, then moved along her jaw. Tayem's finger.

"Kylene, I'm sorry." His voice was no louder than a whisper. "Trust me, please. I don't know just how, but everything's going to turn out all right someday. Believe me."

A portion of her hostility died. Tayem could not be trusted. He was doing something wrong, and it would eventually rebound upon him. But he was not conscious of this, she was sure. His own unhappiness was deceiving him, making him react this way.

But she could not say that. The emotion that had poured into her when he touched her could not be argued with.

Nor had she any wish to argue. She was not sure how Tayem had confused her fate with his, but it was clear that he felt they were intertwined. So now the man's despair had broadened to encompass her as well, as though she had become a companion in his personal misfortune, rather than a cause of it.

He *did* blame her for his misery, she sensed dimly. Or he once had. He had no reason for that. But he was radiating sympathy and compassion for her. That was also without reason, but it was not to be turned down.

So she said nothing, and let Tayem push her gently toward the tall block facing the window. "Let's get ready to leave."

The block was one of the Algheran cube chairs, she found, but taller than most, so that when she sank into it, the back stretched above her head. An overhanging rail attached to the armrests kept her arms close to the chair. She struggled for a moment as the soft black plastic collapsed underneath her, leaving her seemingly trapped in an insane combination of cocoon and infant's highchair.

"Don't fight it," Tayem reproved. He bent to fasten a set of seat straps loosely about her ankles, then across the front of the chair. "Move slowly and steadily and you'll have no problems. This is a military aircraft, and that seat is designed to protect you from all sorts of stresses. At the same time, you can control the vehicle while you're wrapped up in it—but until you find out what you're doing, please don't try."

Kylene relaxed and waited while Tayem dropped into his own seat. He fastened straps around himself, she noticed; he had not been applying special restraints to her, and she had been right not to object.

Tayem leaned forward, then waited motionlessly as the plastic cocoon draped itself loosely about him. "Pay attention, and I'll explain some of what I'm doing. If it doesn't make sense, don't worry—you'll get more experience later on."

His fingers danced over the cabinet tops before him. She heard a succession of clicks. The cabinet bases remained in place; their tops slid forward a few hand widths, stopping as they touched to form half a ring-shaped table. Sections of the table took on pastel shades.

There were more clicking sounds. Within a dozen heartbeats a similar platform was arrayed around her. Small squares became visible, covering the surface, seemingly just under translucent coverings of blue and green, red and yellow. Algheran numerals were on some; others bore words she did not recognize, although the letters were familiar.

"Control consoles," Tayem said unnecessarily. "Pressure-sensitive; the buttons don't depress." The red lighting in the cabin darkened until illumination came chiefly from the consoles. Tayem's table seemed to be brighter than hers, she noticed. The temperature was rising to an uncomfortable level, but he seemed unworried, so she chose not to complain.

She heard a low-pitched whine, which quickly subsided. Then an air current moved past her face, too feeble to stir her hair but enough to make her feel cooler. Her nostrils twitched; she realized that the faint musky smell she could not place was coming from Tayem's body. It was not unpleasant; for an instant, she wondered if the man was similarly aware of her own aroma, and what his reaction was.

A column rose out of the floor, stopping just as it reached her left hand. Perhaps the diameter of a man's arm, it was topped by a fist-size sphere resting in a sort of cup. A second column had risen beside Tayem's chair; now his hand moved out to rest on the sphere.

She copied the motion, finding that the ball was fixed in position as if welded to the cup. It was plastic, she suspected, but hard and cool to the touch, seemingly denser than the normal Algheran materials.

Tayem's hands darted over his consoles, fingers pressing here and there to cause images of gauges to appear and disappear on the panels that hung from the cabin roof. "Checking power levels in the batteries," he explained. "Generator output levels. Life support systems. Weapons checks—even though we probably will never need them. Any dial that has a yellow color means the system is functioning as it should. If it is purple, and flashes, we've got serious problems."

A faint hiss sounded. "Speaker patches on the central consoles," he commented. "Those big black squares. Lean back and let the seat wrap around your head, and you'll find patches next to your ears, as well."

"*Tower to aircraft,*" a voice said in an incomprehensible language. "*Do you read me?*"

"English," Tayem said absently. "It's close to Trade Talk—you might recognize some of it."

"*You are cleared for takeoff,*" the voice continued. "*You have a ceiling of thirty feet and visibility is poor.*"

"*Ain't it the truth though,*" Tayem muttered.

"*Go when ready.*" Then the invisible speaker switched to Algheran Speech. "Timithial, Mission 17. The time now is 44,938 by the Long Count, Day 96, fractional seven seven five four two . . . mark."

The voice was comfortable in tone, and friendly. Listening, Kylene realized unhappily that despite his strangeness, Tayem Minstrel had found acceptance among these people, while she remained no more than a captive. His captive, once and again. Rebellion had accomplished nothing.

The contrast was a bleak one, but curiosity allayed the sense of futility. Impatience fought nervousness within her as Tayem's fingers flew over the console, making numbers appear upon the central roof panel. Now he read them back: "Nine three eight. Day nine six plus seven seven five four two. *Roger, I'll be seeing you in five minutes.*"

His hand slipped from the switch he had pressed. For a moment, he stared directly at Kylene, caught up by some emotion she could not recognize. Then he turned away and reached for the switch. *"And tell the old farts I'm going to see them choke on their little joke."*

His right hand slapped at a bank of switches. A row of gauges marched over a panel, blinking violet at first, then shading into a steady yellow. "Power up," he said curtly. The dim, red-glowing ceiling lights winked off. His left hand dropped onto the control knob beside his seat and spun it clockwise. Screens at the right and left sides of the cabin suddenly brightened, showing the interior of the hangar. Additional screens showed the gray concrete floor underneath the shuttle, and the ceiling above. "Watch."

His hand rocked the control knob, and the vehicle bobbed in all directions. "Here we go." From the console, a plastic tongue suddenly lapped out to hang above his knees. His right hand danced over the pressure patches. The ceiling shown in the panels seemed to drop toward them. Then all the panels were black.

"Lights off," Tayem commented. "We've got fifty years to go till a landslide exposes us. No one occupies the station the last part of that time, apparently, so there's no light."

Numbers floated in the air above them, startling Kylene until she realized they were emblazoned on the central roof panel. Tayem explained them. "The brown number at the top shows where we just left. The red one at the bottom is our destination. The middle, blue one, which keeps changing—that's where we actually are. We're speeding up, so in a short while you won't be able to read the last few digits. Five hundred years—we've got just under a day tenth of travel ahead."

She was suddenly conscious of his gaze. Having nothing worthwhile to say, she remained still. Eventually he looked away.

"Always expect I'll crash into someone in this section. But it never does happen." His remark might have been addressed to anyone.

Light burst through the long window, not sunshine but the translucent gray of early dawn. The levcraft was aboveground. Flickers rose past the window, dancing shapes which Kylene saw first as flame, then as sparks; suddenly they formed a shadow bridge of glittering motes that rested upon the horizon.

"Time travelers," Tayem said, noticing her gaze. "'F' a Alghera's up that way." Then he returned to manipulating his controls.

"Two thousand man-heights," he announced shortly, waving his hand over the top of his console. "Take a good look, kid; it's a big, beautiful country, and I bet you've never seen so far in your life."

She didn't want to give Tayem the satisfaction of seeing her obey his suggestion, but her head moved involuntarily. *Green*, she found herself thinking. It was an ordinary landscape. *Tayem must like green.*

"Looks like the morning of creation out there, doesn't it?"

Jade-green cabinets and walls, dark-green flooring, a green and black uniform... *I wonder he didn't paint the outside the same colors.*

The Algherans had placed a green badge upon her forehead, she remembered bitterly. Did Tayem like the color of that as well?

"'With Earth's first clay, they did the last man knead,'" Tayem murmured to himself. "'And there, of the last har-

vest, sow'd the seed. And the first morning of creation
wrote, what the last dawn of reckoning shall read.'" His
hands tapped at the counter before him.

"That's us, kid. The all-powerful They who run things."

Kylene shook her head, warding off his voice. Somehow, she was going to go home. She'd never see Tayem
again. Perhaps she would even manage to forget all about
him—and it would serve him right.

More cheerful now, she bent forward to look at the
forests below. *Pine trees*, she guessed. A small lake, a
river; still no signs of people. This was not a good place
to escape from Tayem. *This is the first time I've been
above the ground since he captured me*, she realized suddenly.

The world was visible through some of the roof panels
as well, she noticed.

"Look at the ones on the sides," Tayem advised. "The
center one is for real—*radio waves*; it's what you'd see
if you didn't have this vehicle around you. It doesn't have
much detail because—" He broke off. "You wouldn't
understand yet. Need to educate you, kid."

Light flared from the central screen. "Super *nova*," he
said cryptically. "Like the Crab." Then the light was gone.

"I can't explain everything," he continued, as if complaining. "Anyhow, those outer screens that look real really
aren't. They're photographs of a sort. Every tenth of a
second or so, our time, the time field cuts out for a micro-
second to let in some normal light and some air. Of course,
we're visible then, too, but not long enough to be noticed,
unless there's some other time traveler in phase with us.
And if there is, odds are, it isn't for long. Rest of the
time, most real light, such as you would get from the sun,
is deflected by the field, so it passes around the outside.
A good thing—it makes us invisible. Also, it keeps us
from being cooked by *gamma rays*."

His hand dropped back to the control knob. "Anyhow,
we've got a view. I'm going to spin the ship now to show
you the territory. We're pointed northwest at the moment,

since that's where we're headed. Forests mostly, going all the way to the *Pacific*. Those hills out there: during the First Era we called them the *Berkshires*. The Algherans call them the Border Range for some reason; they actually are well this side of the border with Loprit, and always have been.

"Facing due south now. More forests. Pine, spruce, hemlock—cold-climate vegetation, even now. Same for the east. Look hard and you'll see that the ground is sloping away from us; in my time there was an ocean over that land and someday there will be again, when more of the ice melts. That's a long time off though, maybe twenty thousand years the other side of the Present.

"North now. See that thick gray line on the horizon? Storm front. Ice is a quarter million man-heights away, and basically static right now. In your day, a bit later, it got down this far year round. For a good long time. And just as high, or higher, than we are now.

"West again. The valley you came from is about three million man-heights in that direction, so you're a ways from a *galleria*. End of the travelogue. Kylene—you *can* speak, can't you?"

Nothing he had said had suggested that she would ever see her home again. "No." Her voice was bitter, sullen.

"Hmmm ... You can hear me all right, even if you can't speak?" Tayem's voice was deadpan.

"Yes." She regretted the admission as soon as she made it, and hunched back into her seat to avoid looking at the man. She was even more annoyed to hear him chuckle. He was supposed to be miserable, she remembered. How dare he forget himself and laugh at her!

"All right," Tayem said finally. "Lean forward slowly in your seat, so you have some freedom to move. Now, stick out your left hand and bring it back till you touch the control knob—that ball on top of the column. Got that?"

Oblige him, she decided. It would be a good idea to learn what she could about operating the vehicle. And she didn't have to speak to him, even if she did take orders from him. She leaned forward.

He continued to give commands. "At the bottom of your seat, just behind your heels, is a rectangular plate. Kick that till you feel it move, and let it return. Got that?"

It took a couple of kicks, since he had not told her how hard to strike the plate. Then it rebounded with a *boink*ing sound. Fortunately, it did not require enough effort to hurt her feet, which had become much too soft while living underground with the Algherans.

Now her consoles seemed brighter than Tayem's. "Your seat is activated," he confirmed.

She was suddenly wary. "What does that mean?"

"You have the comm," Tayem said casually. "You can fly this bird."

He was taking her for granted, and she didn't like that. "I don't want to."

There was silence from the other side of the cabin. When Tayem spoke next, it was obvious that he was picking his words carefully.

"Kylene, this is a Fourth Era military vehicle, designed for combat. At maximum velocity, it will travel two thousand man-heights with every beat of your pulse. With enough battery power, it can travel completely around the world eight times in the course of a day. It's fast. It's capable of going fifty thousand man-heights up. It's built to withstand twelve-gee turns, so you can make it spin on a *dime*. It's—"

"I don't care." And she didn't.

Tayem stared at her. "Why not?" His tone was supposed to be reasonable, she guessed; he actually sounded as if his feelings had been hurt.

"I don't *want* to fly this."

Tayem made fishlike motions with his mouth, then glanced toward the ceiling. "A great truth dawns on me," he commented to the empty air. "Little girls are not the same as little boys."

Kylene repressed a smile. It had been pleasant to see Tayem at a loss.

Of course, he didn't stay that way for long. "Kylene," he said formally, "it would be useful for you to learn to control this vehicle. It is possible to do things with it that other Agents cannot do with theirs, and just maybe we will someday need its abilities. But it handles very delicately, and so far I am the only person in the Project capable of flying it. If you learn how, the Algherans will need you—and they'll be willing to admit it."

She felt shock. She had been hoping to hear Tayem say something that indicated that he would eventually release her. But it was clear now, as it had not been before, that he had no plans to take her home. Somehow he had blanked his instructions from his mind.

Should she tell him? That was her natural impulse, but—

Indecision hit her. However well-meaning he might be, Tayem was not a friend. He was not capable of seeing into her mind to know she told the truth. And even if he did believe her, he might not be willing to cooperate. No, she did not dare inform him in advance of her intentions.

Perhaps this was a mistake. Perhaps Tayem was not the Agent the tra'R'sihuc had referred to; perhaps Tayem was supposed to give her this "training" and then another Agent would take her home.

No! She was not going to cooperate with the Algherans. She was not going to work for them. They owed her her freedom. She had not promised to buy it from them. They were enemies—why did they think she would continue to be their slave?

If only she had more information.

"Take off your 'blind," she ordered suddenly.

"No." That sounded final.

"Why not?" she asked bluntly. "No one else is here but me."

"You're enough," Tayem said wryly. "Forget it, Kylene. I won't let you read my mind."

"You let other Teeps," she pointed out.

Tayem grimaced. "And sometimes I wish I didn't." He sighed. "I have a number of memories which are not especially pretty, and I don't think you should go rummaging through my mind till you're older and more ma—older, anyhow."

"You don't trust me. Why should I trust you?"

He nodded. "Fair question, with no answer. Except that you don't have any choice. You were assigned to work with me, and I know what I'm doing, but you don't. So you have to trust me just because."

That's what you think. She shook her head gravely. "How do I control this?"

Her choice had been made. She would find a way home without Tayem, without any of the Algherans. She would have to learn the secrets of this vehicle. And after that . . .

She wouldn't let her thoughts go far down that path. But if the Algherans believed that no one but themselves would ever gain control of time . . . They were afraid of the people of her time, she had learned. If she brought that knowledge back to her people, the Algherans would have only themselves to blame.

Fortunately, Tayem accepted her capitulation without comment. Perhaps he was satisfied to have the topic changed.

"Be very careful," he cautioned. "This is delicate. So even if you can fly it some today, I'm going to take charge for landings and takeoffs. Now, put your hand back on the control ball and wiggle it slightly. Just a bit. Watch the viewscreens. See the images tilt, and move back and forth? That's because the orientation of the vehicle is tied to the knob."

"Are we moving?" she asked. The screens showed no motion.

"Not yet. We're hovering. Raise the nose again. That's it. Now move us to the left . . . other way . . . hold it. Now we're headed in the right direction. Make sure we aren't tilting. Doing this by eyeball and seat of the pants is good enough, but there are gauges to use if you want, in that panel on the left of your console that lights up whenever you touch the control knob. Here comes the touchy part: The amount of current going to the levmotor depends on how far up the shaft that knob is. Right now we're balanced. Feed more power in, and we go straight up; feed in less, and we sink. To increase the power, spin the knob clockwise with your fingers; to cut it, go the other way. You may feel some resistance—you're properly trimmed when you don't notice it."

The vehicle bobbed erratically, making Tayem shake his head. "No," he explained. "Don't tilt the knob; give it a pure spin. Keep trying." And when Kylene had mastered that, he continued the lesson. "You're rising now. You don't want to. You want to feed that extra power to the thrusters so we can move. Lower the nose a bit, then hold the knob and press straight down, as if you're trying to push it down the shaft. You're still rising, so angle us down a bit more. Press down again."

The green horizon on the viewscreen jerked, then finally settled. "You're getting it," Tayem complimented her. "Very good. Eventually you'll be doing all these motions simultaneously. You can take your hand from the ball now; the cuff will hold it in place—what?"

Kylene had abruptly spun the control knob, cutting off the power to the engines. The horizon vanished as the vehicle's nose lifted. She slapped viciously at the knob, using the thrusters to force the levcraft into a dive. It fell like a meteorite.

45,412 L.C.

CHAPTER TWO

*I*ndividual *trees could be made out on one viewscreen.* How close to the ground were they now? Kylene wondered. Her palms were moist, but she barely noticed. Her breath was shallow and rapid. Excitement poured through her veins.

As if to answer her question, numbers appeared on the rightmost panel. "Twenty-two hundred man-heights," Tayem announced calmly. "Sinking at about three hundred, Kylene. Just in case you change your mind about killing us, get the craft level first. Pull up to kill the thrust, and then spin back to hover."

She wondered absently how he could be so unruffled, then forgot about him. She was hypnotized by the viewscreens. A small creek showed on one, first as a wandering line on a white background, then swelling to become a river surrounded by trees from which green exploded; the river slid underneath the vessel as the leaves darkened and fell away. A clearing appeared, blackened by some long-gone fire, and grew wider; suddenly it was blanketed

by white, then it, too, was under her and the screens were
again filled with bare-limbed trees.

"Six hundred man-heights," Tayem said, as before her
another spring season blossomed.

Time!

She slapped her hand out—and moaned. Her dampened palm had slipped!

The nose of the vehicle was canted downward now,
and they were still falling. Treetops could be seen now in
the window, green, rising, lancing upward.

She was being thrown forward. Her mouth opened to
scream. The seat tightened about her cruelly, pulling her
hand away from the control knob even as her fingers
scrabbled over its plastic surface. Her vision blurred. Then
blackness came.

Something pressed against her cheek. Warm. A finger.

Kylene breathed in cautiously, afraid to open her eyes
for a reason she could not remember. The finger moved
away.

"Tiny little girl." The soft baritone voice was somehow
familiar; the words had no meaning, though affection registered. An air current stirred. She sensed she was alone.

A subdued clatter. Rustling sounds. A footstep. Something breaking, far, far away. She could move if she wished,
but it would be too much trouble. Just as it was too much
trouble to open her eyes.

An acrid odor stung her nostrils, a sharp burning sensation that made her think of knife thrusts. She sneezed.
"Don't do that," she mumbled. "Don't do that."

The stinging sensation went away. She opened her eyes
carefully, first the left and then the right.

Tayem. That was Tayem. She couldn't make out what
was in his hand.

"Don't move quickly," he cautioned.

A question must have appeared in her eyes.

"We didn't crash," he told her. His hands moved out

of her sight. The webbing that bound the seat together slackened, and she could move more freely.

The ground was far below. They had not crashed.

"But I didn't—" she began. Her voice was troubled.

Tayem nodded. "You tried." He smiled wryly. "Told you, didn't I, that I'd take care of takeoff and landing? We'll call that one of each. Now, enough said. Forget it."

Kylene moved timidly. "You're not—" *Will you be mad at me? How are you going to punish me?* "Won't you ask why?"

"Trust," Tayem said somberly. "You wanted to find what the limits were." He turned away from her, his face taut. The tissue papers in his hands were red-streaked with blood. He pushed them awkwardly into a trash slot, then glanced at the calendar display.

Her eyes dropped. "About a half day tenth to go," she heard him say. "We've got some flying left to do. Will you hold down the fort?"

She didn't understand the words. The meaning came from the tone.

She held her breath. Then, without looking at him, she slowly nodded.

"Here we are," Tayem announced. His hands danced over the consoles, switching off power to the levcraft systems. A whirring sound indicated that the access ramp was being lowered. "Home of a sort. 45,412, Long Count. Day 1. Spring. All ashore that's going ashore."

It was late evening by the clock within the vehicle, but the scene on the viewscreens was of midmorning, and the sun's rays brightened the clearing in which Tayem had parked the levcraft. Through the front window she could see golden and scarlet wildflowers on a gentle hillside, and the brown-black roof of a strangely misshapen building that looked as if it had been built from logs. Dark-green pine trees swayed in a passing breeze. Ripples crossed the surface of a beaver-dammed pond. Tayem was standing, seemingly impatient to leave the vehicle.

Kylene's clothing bag was in his hands; she moved to join him.

"Has something happened to your home?" Kylene asked politely.

"To my little barn?" Tayem was amused. "It's fine. This is a modified A-frame, with a gambrel roof. First Era design, very practical for places with lots of snow, so when I got back to Alghera I had one built for me on this spot and brought it back. About fifty years downtime from here, I return it to the same instant of time—there's a forest fire that night which wipes it out. No one notices it missing up at the Present, and I've got it to use here."

He seemed pleased with himself. Kylene murmured appreciatively.

He stopped suddenly. "Uh . . . never been another person here but me. Since—never mind. I, uh, hope you like it."

Then he regained control. "We'll be here a good long time, so make yourself comfortable. C'mon, I'll show you around."

The cabin was not small, though it rested on less ground than the levcraft took up at the foot of the hill. Perhaps it had the length of six men, and the width of four; the peak of the bi-sloped roof was far above the porch that surrounded it on three sides.

The interior of the building was cool. The floor was made of large, flat, gray rocks, fitted together with finger-width cement lines between. The walls were yellow pine planks, sealed under some clear plastic, as were the exposed rafters. The front of the building was open to the ceiling, but farther back a railing stretched across the width of the upper floor. Open shelves stood against the walls; semidarkness prevented her from making out their contents.

"Cabins like these were built in mountain areas," Tayem explained. He touched switches, making ceilings glow at the back of the cabin. "Places where a lot of snow could fall in a winter. Not too far from where you started off, actually—southern *California*. Batteries underground keep it warm, heat the water, and generally make it livable. Or you can pitch some good-sized logs into the fireplace. Outside windows slide up to let in the breeze, if you like that sort of thing. I do, so you'd better."

As he spoke, he pulled back yellow draperies. Except for the frame around the sliding doors, the front of the building was all glass, a squashed-in pentagon four times the height of a man. Sunlight splashed over silvered veins within the glass, making it a mosaic of irregularly shaped crystal. "A nice view," Tayem said ruefully as he followed Kylene's gaze, "but a real lady dog for keeping clean."

The he guessed at her unspoken question. "Mesh in all the windows," he confirmed. "And under the roof and the floor and around the walls. Complete protection against charming people like you. A very expensive little house here—except that I brought back a couple of tons of chicken wire from the First Era."

"Why?"

The redhead shrugged. "Safety first. As far as I know, we're the only people in this spot for two or three hundred years on either side. So we've got privacy. Might want to keep it that way."

More curious about the nature of Tayem's caution than the cause of it, she asked who it was he wanted to avoid.

"No one definite. It's just general policy to keep Teeps from discovering about the Project, even if the Second Compact will make them keep mum. Some kinds of memories we don't want people to have when Chelmmys gets going. So that explains the mesh. Otherwise, now and then I worry that the Project will come up with a history where the Alliance cooks up time travel too and finds out about us. If that happens, I imagine it'll be easy for them to find the Station, harder to track down anyone here."

"Would you hide here?"

Tayem raised an eyebrow, perhaps hearing disdain in her remark. "Fall back, I'd call it. Regroup. Make some kind of base of this. If nothing else, sit around and do some thinking." His shoulders moved up and down. "If you ever need a place to retreat to . . . not having one can be terribly embarrassing, kid."

Kylene bit her lip, remembering his refusal to blame her when she almost crashed his time vehicle.

He waved an arm. "Kitchen at the back of this room, behind the breakfast bar. Beyond it is a bathroom and the master bedroom. The steps over there go up to the loft. There are two rooms up there—you can see into one of them from down here. I've been using both for a study; I'll turn one of them into a bedroom for me. That way you can have the bottom one. Solve the modesty problem for you?"

Her mouth opened. That was a complication she had not thought of, and her unpreparedness again left her embarrassed. What would she have said or done if—but that was just dumb. The entire idea was silly.

It probably wasn't even possible: Tayem wasn't fully human, she had been told. Something had gone seriously wrong with him, and only being under Nicole's cloak had kept him alive this long. As it was, he would die while still a young man, little more than fifty years from now.

No. Even if Normal and Teep were allowed by custom . . . Tayem and—even if she wanted to—the thought was just insane.

Surely he hadn't even thought of it!

Tayem shook his head. "Whatever the *hell* is going through your head now, kid, this is a working relationship, and we'll keep it on that level."

Her face flushed, but she felt relief nonetheless.

A bird sang nearby, a song that Kylene could not recognize. Almost as loud was a low-pitched *whirr*. The second sound was completely unnatural and she wondered at it, uncertain as to whether she should feel alarm. It had caused her to wake, she realized with slight anger. So what was it?

Machine, she decided gravely. *Machine*. That was a

word the Algherans used for a metal or plastic contraption
that sometimes did incomprehensible things and sometimes sat doing nothing that could be seen. Machines did
not have minds, even though they occasionally acted as
if they housed living things.

So, a machine was out there, doing something that
might make sense to another machine or to an Algheran.
She yawned and kicked bed covers aside. Air currents
touched her body. A curtain flapped. She reached upward
to touch the inner window, and felt it move on its hinges.

The machine sound changed, becoming deeper and
noisier. Superimposed on it was a steady *plop-plop-plop*.
Cattle dropping, she thought at first, but the sound was
suspiciously regular and it was lasting too long. She sniffed,
finding pine and grass aromas but no manure odor. Probably it was another machine. She felt irritated; she wished
she could hear the bird again.

Her mind reached out, trying to discover where the
bird had flown—and met blankness. The sensation was
not unlike blindness; for an instant, she almost panicked.
Then she realized she was safely back inside herself.

Metal was all around her, she remembered. This was
like being underground at the Station, where mesh-lined
and metal walls made a cage for the mind. For safety,
Tayem had said.

Far away from here, at a place he called the Present,
the small nation of Alghera was fighting against the rest
of the world. Tayem called the leader of Alghera's enemies
Chelmmys; she recognized that now as one country in
what he called the Alliance. In the dormitory, she had
heard of the Alliance for Mankind; that was probably the
same thing.

Most Teeps favored the Alliance, she had learned.
Tayem had not disputed that—some of his conversation
last night had suggested that he expected Teeps to prefer
the Alliance—but his loyalties were with the Algherans.
He had not explained his reasons to her; she did not
believe he even felt explanations were necessary.

Ironwearer, some of the Teeps had called him. It was a good name, she decided. Inflexible, dogmatic, hidebound, stiff of neck—it had all those connotations, and added the certainty that some thoughts would bounce off him with absolutely no affect.

He had explained the Project instead, the strange war-within-a-war in which a handful of refugees from the capital of Alghera fought and refought the same lost battles in hopes of changing the outcome. A war in time, he told her, as if a trip from year to year was just as conceivable as walking from one place to another. And yet a secret war, to be kept from the knowledge of the Chelmmysians and Algherans outside of the Project. "And you and me." He had smiled. "Privileged characters, us."

Who had kidnapped *him*? she had wondered.

"Did it myself," he said, after she worded the question diplomatically. "Or maybe I hitchhiked into it, on old Herrm ha'Cuhyon's experimental time machine." He did not claim the invention for himself; he said little to confirm the stories that circulated among the Teeps in the Station.

He had opposed saving an Algheran general from assassination, he admitted, he alone of the Algheran Agents. He had been right, the Algherans wrong, and now, while they realized that their original version of history had to be restored, no one but him was willing to make the change, and he'd had to fight a duel to get permission to do it.

"You're the only help I'm going to get, kid," he had said, repeating the words he had used in his flying craft. "I need you, Kylene."

With morning here, it all seemed a bit silly.

She yawned again and stretched, twisting sideways and scissoring her legs over the jumbled bed covers. This was such a big bed. No one in the Station had a bed this size, she was sure; not even the tra'R'sihuc. Perhaps even in the Coastal Tribes no one had had a bed this big and this comfortable.

Tayem's bed, she suddenly recalled. Tayem Minstrel

slept in this bed, or would have if she were not in it. It even smelled faintly of Tayem, and she was taking it away from him. She stretched catlike, still with her eyes closed, and smiled, enjoying the satiny feel of Tayem's bedding against her body, pleased with herself for taking possession of something that belonged to Tayem Minstrel, and knowing that he would have to do without it.

Ironwearer. She giggled, picturing Tayem tightly bound up in metal bars, lying on his soft bed and unable to enjoy it.

Tayem. He was strange. Loyal to Alghera, but not an Algheran. A Normal, but not a real Normal, A young man with the looks of middle age, who would die of old age before he reached a century. An ordinary Agent, but the leaders of the Project spoke to him. Blunt and unperceptive, but at times showing almost Teeplike subtlety.

Perhaps that was why he—no, "liked" was not the word. Tayem reacted to the Teeps in a very strange way. As did they to him.

The Teeps were afraid of him, she realized suddenly. Whether they liked or disliked him was immaterial—he was *different*, and unpredictable. They could pin a nickname on him and pretend to know him, but despite their usual amusement at the doings of Normals, Tayem would always do things that surprised them. So they could not trust him.

Just as they don't trust me, she thought half bleakly, half contemptuously.

Did Tayem trust her? Had the incident in the levcraft proven anything? No, she admitted. Tayem trusted no one. He would smile and tell people he trusted them, and perhaps inside his mind he believed that, but he would hide behind his Teepblind regardless, relying on his own strength and speed and cleverness—his Tayem-ness—to save him from the problems others might cause.

Her eyes opened, to focus on the massive ceiling beams and varnished pine walls of Tayem Minstrel's bedroom. To die so young . . . All his strength and ability could not save Tayem from the frailty of his body. How could he live with that?

Kylene shivered, suddenly understanding the man as clearly as if he stood before her without his 'blind. *It is lonely to be Tayem Minstrel.*

She shook herself deliberately, pulling back from the abyss she had discovered, and rolled to her knees on Tayem's bed, then tossed the hair out of her eyes and pulled back the muslin curtain so she could stare through Tayem's bedroom window.

She saw a hillside made green by short-cropped grass, and a low building at its top backed by tall pine trees. It was morning; the sun was no more than a handsbreadth over the horizon, she estimated. It could not be seen directly, but she could determine its position from the shadows. How early had Tayem risen?

Her mind darted over the interior of the cabin. Yes, she was alone. Tayem must be outside.

Moving quickly now, she tossed the covers over the big bed, smoothed them down to approximate the prissy tidiness that the Algherans took for granted, then moved to retrieve her clothing from the floor. What was the man doing?

She stopped abruptly, the seams of her brown skirt still unsealed, her hair half tangled in her pullover blouse. Oh, Ancients! She did not need to wash, for her skin was free of grime, but the Algherans had insisted on daily baths. Tayem might be just as bad; he might even send her back to take one, even though she would have to get dressed all over again. Alien he might be, but in some ways he was very Algheran-like.

Feeling put-upon once more by all the unreasonable Algherans, she stripped off her clothes and opened the bedroom door.

A small mountain of transparent cartons fell upon her. She was more alarmed than hurt, but it was another unneeded injustice, and she kicked her way through them angrily. Tayem should be more careful!

Clothes, she suddenly realized. Clothes were in the boxes. Here, by the door to *her* bedroom—they had to be for her. How?

Tayem. Tayem had done this. He had left her at one point and gone away in his time shuttle, to return almost instantly with huge stocks of food. He must have made another trip to get clothing. He had said she would need some, but she had not expected him to do anything about it.

Now, would these things fit? Would she like the colors? She tore at the boxes, breaking through the cellophane film to pull out her new clothes, and holding pieces up in front of the tall mirror in the bathroom.

There were mostly dresses and blouses, she discovered, and a complement of underskirts. There were some unusual pants, brass-buttoned, made from a stiff blue canvaslike material, but none of the coveralls commonly worn by Algherans of both sexes. Tayem had done the shopping; she suspected he disliked coveralls. So there was one difference between him and them.

The colors were bright, she noted approvingly. The designs were simple, with vertical or sloping lines and checkerboards on the few garments that were not solid-colored. And she was sure it all would fit: Most Algheran clothing one simply wrapped about oneself, making it hold together by pinching the seams tight; it was seldom attractive, but a few sizes managed to fit everyone.

She found no jewelry, which was disappointing but not surprising. Men wore jewelry in Alghera, and it always had some kind of meaning; it wasn't worn because it looked nice. The Algherans could be very dull.

He had brought her a set of combs with silver inlays, a square mirror on a handle, and red and yellow metal bands for restraining her hair.

Three boxes held shoes and two more had boots in them. She had left her sandals in the time shuttle; perhaps Tayem had used them for measures.

She found a quilted white parka with attached mittens;

a full-length red coat of thin plastic; a blue jacket; three
bulky men's shirts that were obviously too small for Tayem.
Her eyebrows rose, then subsided with the thought that
Tayem obviously had strange notions at times.

One large box held colored undergarments, utilitarian
in appearance, but from experience completely useless
for keeping a body warm. She frowned, and approved her
frown in the mirror. She would dress to look like an Algheran if Tayem insisted, but he would have to learn that
there were some limits. She bit her lower lip, reflecting
on that, then brightened with the realization that Tayem
had merely been pressured by local convention when he
made his purchases. No one but a born Algheran would
share their clothing fetishes.

A man had picked out clothing for her; he had not done
it as well as she would have done, but it could have been
done worse. Maybe someday Tayem would let her select
her own clothing. Maybe she would even select some for
him.

Feeling more cheerful with the world, she carried the
boxes back to the bedroom to dump onto her bed, then
returned to the bathroom. She closed the door so she
could look at the mirror again, and smiled at the nude girl
standing behind it. The freckles on her face and limbs
showed. The green color of her almond eyes could be
seen clearly, as could her cheekbones and the broad V of
her rib cage. How athletic she looked, how clever and
intelligent she must be! Algheran mirrors were so much
better than the ones she had been used to!

Perhaps she could find a way to take this one back to
the Second Era. She considered this, nodding gravely and
breaking into a grin as she watched herself nod. Then she
jumped up and down and swung her arms about, partially
for the pleasure of feeling her muscles move and partially
for the pleasure of watching herself. She was pretty, she
realized happily, swinging her hips back and forth. She
was desirable, and someday she would be beautiful.

Her hand stopped the sideward slide of the glass door

above the bathtub. No one was here to admire her prettiness. No one but Tayem Minstrel. Why should she concern herself? His opinions did not matter.

She frowned. Prettiness was something for everyone to see, wasn't it? So she should not try to not be pretty for Tayem. But an effort to be especially pretty—to be beautiful—was surely not justified for any but a very few people, none of whom Tayem would ever be.

On the other hand, how could one know in advance when to be especially pretty?

This was certainly not such a time, she decided, stepping into the bathtub. Tayem would probably not notice her prettiness, and he would never allow himself to show it even if he did. Still, it might be amusing to practice being especially pretty on Tayem.

She permitted herself a low-pitched giggle.

"Looks about like they did in your time and mine," Tayem had said. "But on a cold day, plastic is a lot easier to bear than *porcelain*." She had no idea of what *porcelain* might be, but she had understood his meaning. Now she wiggled her toes comfortably and agreed that Algheran bathtubs were not unpleasant things in which to sit and stretch out one's legs.

Which of the buttons would turn on the water? For some reason, this was set up differently than those she had encountered at the Station. She stuck a foot out at random.

"Ancients!" she moaned seconds later. Water should be seeping through the sides of the tub, tepid and gently scented. Instead, the ceiling had opened. A torrent of ice water was pouring down upon her—she swallowed some in her surprise.

The downpour stopped as she staggered to her knees, then gave her just enough time to push her drenched hair to the side of her face before it began again. This time the water was hot, agonizingly so, growing hotter with every instant. Just as Kylene felt she could stand no more, the flow turned lukewarm, as it should have been, and soapy.

Slightly mollified by this partial return to normalcy, she used her hands to rub the slippery fluid over her skin. The tub was not filling up, she noticed incuriously. Good, that would save her from the need to experiment with more of the controls. Tayem would have to be told to fix the tub, though; it was not working as it should.

Suddenly, she was once more drenched by buckets of hot water. Then by the cold. When it stopped, she stood in the middle of the tub—wet, bedraggled, her teeth chattering—numbly listening to coin-size drops splattering on the white surface.

Tayem had done this to her, she was certain. He had set the controls so no one but him could use the bathtub safely. He had deliberately put her through this ridiculous experience, and if she said a single word to complain about it, he would laugh at her. She just knew it.

Angry now, she left the tub and faced the nude girl in the dew-clouded mirror, wiping it with her hand to get another look at herself.

She was thin, Kylene admitted unhappily. Skinny.

Her face was too long and too thin, too tanned. Her cheeks were too high. The freckles that absolutely no one else had showed all over her face and up and down her arms and legs and partway down her back. Her *bony* back. The aureoles on her underdeveloped breasts were too small to please anyone, and skin still showed beneath the scanty black hair on her groin. Her chin was narrow and pointed, and her water-matted hair was too straight, and her lips weren't full enough, and they were pale and chapped and no one in this world had eyes that sloped down at the sides like hers and it wasn't fair, it just wasn't fair! Plain, plain, so plain—and where she wasn't plain, she was *ugly*!

Someone rapped on the door. A voice came through. "Kylene! Are you all right? Did you hurt yourself?" Tayem, she recognized. He sounded worried.

"Go away," she sobbed. "Leave me alone."

"Are you all right?" His tone insisted on an answer.

"No!" she moaned. "Yes. Leave me alone!"

"Kylene!"

She ignored him. *Oh, Ancients! Why have you done this to me?*

"Stand back!" She heard a harsh grinding sound. Almost imperceptibly the door bent inwardly at its top and bottom. The grinding continued, then suddenly ceased as something snapped. Broken pieces of the lock mechanism fell tinkling inside the hollow door. Tayem Minstrel stood in the doorway, scowling at her.

He was wearing faded blue trousers, tucked into calf-high tan boots. The boots were old, white-stained over his toes, and water dripped from them onto the bathroom floor. His torso was bare, sun-darkened and streaked by splotches of dark-brown mud. Red-brown hair made a thin mat over his chest and ran down his flattened belly in a broad line that disappeared inside his pants. Ribs could be seen just under his skin. *He looks human enough*, Kylene found herself thinking.

He also looked extremely angry. "What is the matter?" he demanded.

She suddenly remembered. "I'm not pretty!" She began to cry again.

He looked furious—and foolish. He opened his mouth.

"Don't hit me!" Kylene shouted. She had to be shouting something, and those were the words that came. "Leave me alone!"

Tayem's mouth made silly fishlike gulping movements, so that despite her tears Kylene was almost able to laugh at him. A decision formed on his face. Now he wore a dangerous expression, and she lapsed into silence, staring at him.

"I'm not going to hit you." He spoke slowly and distinctly, but his voice rasped. "I *may* decide to give you a spanking, if I decide you deserve it. Start explaining yourself, Kylene." He stepped past her, yanking a towel from the wall dispenser, then soaked an end at the sink and began cleaning the streaks of mud from his body. "I am waiting."

"Your Cimon-taken bathtub doesn't work." She pouted.

"Works fine for me. Go on—but don't use that kind of language."

"It *doesn't* work. It *won't* fill up. The water comes out of the ceiling, and it's *all* the wrong temperatures and it stops and starts and—"

Tayem gave her one of his crooked smiles. He was amused, she could see. Cimon and Nicole take him! He was going to laugh at her. She'd just known he would.

But he managed to control his humor. "Use the buttons on the right after this," he suggested. "I finally got that thing rigged to give a decent shower, and I'd prefer that you not screw it up. It really was doing what it was supposed to, Kylene. Now, what else is wrong?"

"Nothing," she said, knowing that her voice was surly and childish, hating that but not being able to control it.

Tayem stretched to the dispenser for more towels and tossed a pair of them at her. "Get yourself dry, *September Morn*." She couldn't tell if he believed her.

She obeyed awkwardly, keeping her eyes focused on the redhead. What would he do to her?

"Something's wrong," the man said finally. "Better be, anyhow—I'd better not have busted that lock for nothing. Why the tears, kid?"

"The bathtub," she said in a tiny voice.

His head shook sideways. According to the Algherans, that meant agreement, but he did not seem to be agreeing. "You wouldn't cry just because of that." A pensive look crossed his face. "Something else you said—are you unhappy about your looks, Kylene? Do you really think you aren't pretty?" His voice was earnest now, almost worried in tone.

So it was out. "I'm not! You know I'm not!" Her voice broke, and suddenly she was sobbing again. "I'm not. I'm not. I'm ugly!"

Then she was in the air, moving, being carried in Tayem's arms, rubbing her eyes and her tears against his shoulder.

He brought her into the front room and sat down in one of the long chairs, placing himself where he could look through the big glass wall at his silvery vehicle, holding her in his lap so her legs rested on the cool black plastic. He clasped her two wrists in one hand and lifted them to drop over his head, then wrapped his own arms about her, holding her close to him. "Stop your tears, little girl," he ordered calmly. "Don't cry, Kylene."

She tried to obey, sniffling, feeling somehow embarrassed by this attention, but squirming closer to him and remaining still rather than struggling against the unwanted restraint.

Tayem's muscles were firm, she sensed. She was acutely conscious of her too-bony back pressing against the man's unclothed arm, her still-damp ankles touching his thighs. The rough red-gold hair on his chest scratched at her side; his pant legs were pleated stiffly under her, rough-textured and warm. He must have been uncomfortable, but he made no effort to shift her weight, and she kept her eyes shut, feeling grateful and somehow reassured by the nearness of him, by the warmth of his body.

She could smell his faint musk, his sweat. His breath was stirring strands of her hair. Her hands were touching his neck and shoulder. That was his heartbeat that pulsated against her skin, slower than hers, almost audible. She had never before been so aware of touching Tayem, she realized, nor any other man. She wondered why that was so, and why the thought had come to her.

"I am not crying," she said stiffly. Her shoulders squirmed, freeing themselves of the unnecessary towel.

"Good," Tayem agreed. "Are you seeing my mind?"

"You've got your 'blind on. So I can't." She opened her eyes and looked at the side of his head, noticing the infrequent glint of silver mesh that had escaped conceal-

ment under his short hair. She could have nudged it with
her nose. Yes, he had his 'blind on.

Tayem made a humming sound, pulled the towel up
from her hips, and patted it against her shoulders again.
"You aren't like all the other Teeps, remember. You can
see a bit through a 'blind, if you touch someone, you told
me once. So look—do I think you're ugly?"

"No," Kylene said at last. "You don't." The towel
dropped again.

He even enjoyed holding her, she could see with some
surprise. He was trying not to; he was trying to keep the
knowledge from her—and from himself. Why was he doing
such a strange thing?

No matter. Suddenly she felt a need to strike out again,
as if to make up for the hurts that still lay within her. She
made herself tense, and broke free from his embrace. "But
you don't count!" she told him angrily. "You aren't a real
person—you're a *freak*! You're going to die soon—and
what you think doesn't matter!"

Tayem might have been carved from rock. All at once
Kylene felt sick, abruptly realizing what she had said,
feeling ashamed, not daring to see into his mind and discover how deeply she had wounded him.

The hands that had soothed her released their hold,
moving wide so that she sat without support. "My judgment is generally pretty good," Tayem said quietly and
slowly. "So what I think about your looks, other men will
agree with—some of them anyhow—many more than
you need worry about. You won't have to depend just on
my words."

He twisted so that she slid from his lap, and his voice
was gentle. "Go get dressed, Kylene. I should be doing
some work." Then he was striding through the doorway
in the glass wall, whistling shrilly and tunelessly. Kylene
was alone beside the unlaid fireplace, wet hair streaming
down her back as she forlornly held out a single towel.

CHAPTER THREE

She had been ignored when she knocked on the door.
Now Kylene moved sideways along the building, then
with a sandaled foot pushed a rock into place to stand on
while she peered through a dust-veiled window.

Tayem's *shop* was a single room, almost two man-
heights in width and ten times that in length. The walls
were brown, shiny and smooth, identical to the exterior
of the building. The ceiling was the same, large panels
resting on widely spaced wood rafters. The floor seemed
to be tamped earth. Bright tubes mounted on the ceiling
beams cast a harsh white light; she could see no other
windows.

Benches and tall racks of tools lined the far wall, separated by unidentifiable machines. A deep V-sectioned
tank quivered minutely; a metallic rod, which stuck through
one side, seemed to be spinning.

Near this end of the room was another bench, its top
barely knee-high above shiny ground. A vise held a long
tube clamped at one end over a triangle of light wood. A

41

second vise gripped the middle so that the tube extended
beyond the bench, pointed at the far end of the room.
Finger-size cylinders of green, red, and white plastic were
stacked in handful lots like miniature cordwood. Shallow
boxes lay open on the ground, tightly packed with more
of the cylinders. Kylene could make out smaller boxes
on the far side of the bench; black cables reached from
them, then disappeared against the dark earthen floor.

Tayem sat cross-legged before the table. Padding was
fitted over his ears and a writing block rested on his lap.
He wore *jeans* but his chest was bare, gleaming in the
actinic light. He did not notice her.

At intervals, he took one of the small cylinders and
pushed it into the near end of the tube, pulling up a piece
of wood on a hinge to cover the end. This brought the
wood near a very small machine also mounted on the
bench. He pressed a tiny lever at the base of the machine;
a tongue stuck out from it to lick at the side of the wood.

An explosion came then, a short-lived thunderclap heard
clearly even outside the *shop*. From the open end of the
tube smoke billowed, thick and white, then settled. Flame
seemed to spurt from the tube as well; it did not last long
enough for her to be certain.

Tayem merely looked sideways at his little boxes, then
scribbled onto his writing block.

He could be doing this for most of the day, she realized.
It was foolish to wait to be noticed.

The door was unlocked. As she entered, noise hit at
her—clanking and grinding sounds, then a sharp crack
of thunder that made her ears ring loudly. Smoke reached
for the far end of the tube, twisting turbulently, then fading
as it drifted toward the ground. A tendril moved snakelike
past the enclosed end of the tube, settled over Tayem's
chest. He looked up at her. His lips moved soundlessly.

Evidently he recognized her deafness. He held up a
hand as if to ward off speech, then rose and led her to
the door. Outside, he wiped gray-white powder from his
skin with a rag, then removed his ear padding and waited

patiently till she could hear again. "Don't go in there without permission," he said then. "It can be dangerous."

No more than a smithy, she thought. But she had not come to argue.

She looked for words, but could not find them. Perhaps she could get him to speak, she decided; then an opportunity might show. "What are you doing?" she asked finally.

Tayem smiled briefly. Midafternoon sunlight was behind him, showing through pine limbs, brightening sections of the rough earthen wall he had carved from the hillside a ten day ago when building the *shop*. "Nothing very exciting. Turning *smoothbore muskets* into *Kentucky rifles*, basically."

She shook her head. Was he being deliberately obscure?

"I have a device that throws small projectiles very fast. It is used for killing things. It is not very accurate. I am making it better. Okay?"

She had dressed especially to please him, wearing an apple-green blouse above a short, green and black checkered skirt, fastening both garments to fit snugly on her. She had even put on shoes to walk the short distance up the hill. It seemed only fair that he oblige her if she was so willing to oblige him. But instead he was patronizing her.

Her resentment must have shown, for Tayem smiled ruefully. "Sorry, Kylene. We're from different ages, from different backgrounds. It makes it hard to pitch an explanation at the right level. Didn't mean—" His hands spread wide.

That was mollifying. "Is that your—" She looked for a word, trying to carry on a conversation. "Will you kill Mrat with it?"

"Mlart. Voridon Mlaratin tra'Nornst."

"That's what I meant. That man."

"Going to try," he said calmly.

A piece of memory came back to her. "You told me once you wouldn't kill anyone. You had lent something, and—"

Tayem chuckled. "Said I'd quit killing for Lent. Not the same thing. You remember that, huh?"

"Well, why didn't you kill then?"

"Uh..." Tayem seemed to be picking words carefully. "I wasn't willing to kill just for your benefit, when it wasn't necessary. I didn't want to change history. Killing Mlart—that puts history back the way it was before the Algherans changed it."

He frowned. "Different things when a soldier kills a soldier. The *guys* chasing you just wanted to get their horse back.

"Doesn't it bother you that I intend to kill someone, Kylene?"

"Are you going to hurt them also? Like—" She looked for the name. "Someone said Herlmil was like—"

"Herrilmin ha'Hujsuon. I think his little career is over." Tayem closed his mouth firmly.

"You're not going to be like that."

"No," Tayem said. But she already knew that.

"And you've got a reason." That was statement. She did not understand why killing one Algheran soldier in a faraway place would keep many other people, most of them non-Algherans and some of them Teeps, alive in another place. Nor did she believe that the Algherans concerned themselves with strangers, though Tayem insisted that they did, against all evidence.

"Yeah." Mercifully, for once he did not repeat his plague story.

"Then it's all right."

"Tolerant, aren't you?" Tayem pulled back slightly.

Of course. "You have to kill sometimes. Thieves. Poachers. Immoral people. Irreligious people." She snapped her fingers, as the Algherans did, to show lack of concern.

Tayem coughed. "I'm not religious, Kylene."

"Well, you should be." *I should be*, she added guiltily.

"Borct would agree." The man grinned wryly. "So did my *chaplains*."

Then he smiled at her. "But somehow I don't think you came out here to talk about my soul. What's your problem, kid?"

How had he guessed she had a request? Could he be seeing into her mind? No, of course not.

"I'm bored," she complained. "I want something to do."

Tayem pretended to think. "Take up running," he suggested.

"No!" Running was one of his activities. Long before this, Tayem had laid out a narrow trail, paving it with an Algheran machine so he could use it in bad weather. She had walked it once, thinking that it might lead somewhere, but it had only meandered along brooks and hillsides through the woods, leading back to her starting point. Tayem had run past her twice, slapping her on the back the first time, slowing only to laugh and toss back a water-soaked pine cone at her the next.

"Fix supper?" He wore a fraudulent look of helpfulness.

"No!"

"Why not? We both have to eat sometime."

"Because. And I'm not hungry."

"I am." Tayem's face was without expression.

"So fix it yourself!"

"All but two nights, I have," he pointed out. "Ten out of twelve."

"Well, you complained so much—" she snapped.

Tayem held up a hand to hush her. "I am perfectly willing to eat your cooking, Kylene. I'm sure it'll be delicious. If you ever *do* learn to cook."

"I can too cook!"

"You could stand some more practice."

"I don't need practice! You're making that up! And you know it!" She ignored the looks that crossed his face. "I cooked for me when I was on Pilgrimage, and I had a job doing cooking. I even cooked some for you—I remember—and I cooked for Clan gatherings before that and after my mother died I cooked for my father and I did that for three years and he was a lot more choosy than you so there!"

"Picky eater, huh?" Tayem responded cruelly. "I can see why."

Her jaw dropped.

Tayem pressed his advantage. "So that's why he let you go off on your own. I'd been wondering about that— and about why you were wandering so far. No wonder you couldn't find a boyfriend at home! Clan gatherings, huh? They must have learned to watch out for your stuff!" He snorted.

No! He was getting it all wrong! It hadn't been like that at all! And it was *mean* of him to make fun of her!

"I had suitors too. Just like all the rest!" She sniffed unhappily. Well, she *could* have had suitors, if she had wanted them.

"Pimply louts getting twigs in your seams," Tayem said contemptuously. It was a metaphor; her face flushed when she translated it.

"They did *not!*" She was breathing heavily now.

He smirked. "Bet they did."

"No they didn't! I wouldn't have let them anyway but I didn't want them anyhow I didn't need them I didn't need them and *I don't need you!*"

"Yeah," Tayem said sourly. "The tra'R'sihuc told me your little heart belonged to Daddy. And what else, kid? After all, what were you good for if you couldn't cook?"

This couldn't be happening! This couldn't be Tayem Minstrel. He shouldn't act like this, shouldn't treat her this way, shouldn't make up lies about her or about her father. She loved her father. And Tayem was making it seem all wrong.

"Oh, stop sniveling, Kylene!" Tayem shouted.

She couldn't help but sniff. *Father*, she thought unhappily. *I miss you and home and I'm far away and all by myself and I'm being hurt and—*

"No!" she screamed. "No! No! You aren't supposed

to be doing this! You're supposed to take me home, Tayem, you're supposed to take me home, you're supposed to—"

"Forget it, kid!"

"No!" It was a wounded howl more than an actual word. Kylene began to cry in earnest, great gasping sobs that shook her shoulders and left a soreness within her lungs. "Home, you're supposed to take me home, please, Tayem, take me home, you're supposed to, please!" And when the man refused to answer, she sank to her knees and buried her face in her hands. "Please—please—please," she moaned.

Then she felt a sickness in her belly . . . something in her throat that wouldn't go down when she swallowed . . . her jaw aching from the tension she had put on it . . . her vision unclouded but her eyes tightly shut nonetheless . . . the pride that kept tears away from her . . . finding it somehow hard to balance . . .

. . . dropping to her knees not caring about the dust marking her jeans . . . wrapping an arm around the shoulders of the crying girl . . . guilt flowing like fire through her veins . . . *No healing without pain so she must be broken, so I had to force this, but* . . . hating herself . . . knowing she deserved to hate . . .

Tayem Minstrel.

She was in two minds, tasting mucus and the salt of the tears that ran down her face, patting Kylene on the shoulder awkwardly. "There, there," she murmured at herself, and heard herself say. "There, there, now. Things'll be all right."

Would they really? she wondered bitterly, feeling waves of loss and grief roll over her, not knowing whose pain she felt, or whose cynicism. *So easy to manipulate the little barbarian I watched so long. Still wanting to go home, but how could they let her think that? Find out later . . . not while someone hurts . . . while someone needs . . .*

Pity, compassion, concern, empathy, love. Tayem

would never use such words. The thoughts broke off suddenly.

She was in her own mind again, feeling herself on her knees with an arm about Tayem's neck, her cheek resting on his shoulder so she looked away from him past the corner of his *shop* and into the nearby trees. Moisture was on her cheeks and on Tayem's shoulders, but she was not crying anymore. A squirrel scampering down a tree trunk paused, its jaw distended, and looked curiously at her. A jay screamed in the distance.

Her hand moved over Tayem's side, tracing ribs, coming to rest over smooth hairless skin that must be ancient scar tissue. His arms dropped away from her to simply hang by his sides. His eyes were closed, she sensed. He was waiting, shrouded by emotions beyond her comprehension.

"My mother Samtha died when I was six," she began, wanting to explain herself to him, seeking to ease pain they both felt through understanding. She used the Trade tongue, with which he was familiar; she could feel his breath moving through his chest, and the reluctant hammering of his heart.

"She was tall, with wheat-colored hair. That I remember. They say she was very pretty, and that I do not remember. When I see into the minds of those who knew her, I think they do not remember her either, for memories become indistinct with time, and confused with thoughts and memories of memories. I think instead that she was kind and gentle and that in their memories people return that kindness and gentleness.

"My father Edgart loved her. She died in childbirth, long before her time was due. A son was in her. It died when she did and perhaps it was fortunate in that, for I do not know if my father would ever have forgiveness for it. He had to be restrained to keep him from following her into the mists, I learned; I was never told that, and no one would ever speak of it. But I saw it in his mind; he loved her that much.

"She was young—perhaps not even equal to you in age—for I have heard it said that Edgart had a decade for each year of hers. Such marriages were rare among us, and seldom accompanied long by love. But my father loved her.

"It was not his first wife. That one died long before, and he lived by himself. He had no children by her, and I think that is why my mother attempted another, much too soon after my own birth, so Edgart would not go into the mists without proper remembrance.

"She loved him too, I am told. I was not able to see into minds while she was alive, so I cannot swear to it, but so I have been told.

"She was the daughter of a Clan leader on the far side of the valley, and met my father on his travels. Perhaps he was kind to her; perhaps he seemed powerful and she was attracted to that. And when she came of age for her Pilgrimage, she came to Clan Otter and asked Edgart to take her, though she had suitors elsewhere.

"I sometimes wonder if in truth that was her desire, or if it was a duty she had assumed. Not because Edgart was the Recorder of Treaties, for his judgment could not be swayed and it would be unlawful to try. But he was also First-in-Council, and such a pairing might have shaped or made firm an alliance of Clans. No matter—Edgart remembered her as in love with him."

Tayem stirred slightly, seeming to shrink away from her. *Be careful*, she sensed him thinking. *Girls often repeat the lives of their mothers.* The thought was followed by a subdued flash of anger; neither seemed aimed at her, and she chose to continue.

"My mother died," she said simply. "My father did not. He wanted no other woman, and I never sensed even the desire for one in him. He needed someone to cook for him—and I did. He needed someone to clean his house—and I did. He needed someone to patch his clothes—and I did. He needed someone to talk with—and I did.

"It left me with little time for other men, and I grew accustomed to that. So there were no—none of what you said, Tayem. Perhaps in other situations. Perhaps not, for our village was smaller than your Project, in people, and few of those were close to my age or untrothed. And I— I was not often noticed.

"I was young, which is explanation enough. But sometimes I think now I was set apart. For if my mother was perhaps a gift to a powerful man, could I not become the same? Edgart would not have willingly consented to that, I know, but Clan Otter was poor, and he could not be Recorder forever.

"When it came time that I might go on Pilgrimage, he told me I should go far away. He knew I could see into minds, and that no others in the Valley had that ability. And I had had dreams—messages from other Teeps, I understand now, but he thought those were sendings from the mists. They said I could find a—a home, elsewhere, in a place where Edgart chi'Allin of Clan Otter was unknown, were I to leave the Valley region far behind me.

"So my father told me to leave him—and I did. He still wished to follow my mother..."

The ending seemed obvious. She said no more.

The Algherans would have had rituals and words for reply to such recitals. She could sense that Tayem sought appropriate remarks, and when he did not find them she was grateful, for she did not want the alien responses to besmirch her memories.

"I'm sorry," the man said at last, coming to his feet. Then he spoke formally. *"Lord, have mercy, and grant him your salvation. Lord, be with this child."* His hand moved, touching his forehead, chest, and both shoulders. *"Amen."*

He stared at her a moment, his jaws clenched. "Let your father find his peace, Kylene. Whether or not you find a home elsewhere, don't go back there and interfere."

She could not agree, but her eyes dropped. Something

pressed her forehead then, just under the green plaque
the Algherans had put on her. It was a fingertip; Tayem
had kissed it before touching her, she knew.

"You don't have to feel like an orphan, unless you want
to, kid," she heard. "You got R'sihuc back of you. Not
the biggest Sept, and I don't know that any of them were
family as much as your clans, but it's something. You're
automatically doing better than two people out of three,
Kylene. When we get Alghera back, you'll be a rich
woman."

"Don't care," she muttered.

"Yeah. Well, you've got *gun smoke* on one side of your
hair. Go wash it off. I'll be along shortly and fix supper."
It half seemed Edgart's voice.

Supper was not a success, Kylene admitted. She pushed
gravy around her plate with a square of the yellow crum-
bly stuff Tayem called *cornbread*, wondering what was
to be done.

At first she had been able to chat with Tayem about
his cabin and about clothing in the different eras, but there
was little more to be said about those topics. She and
Tayem lacked mutual acquaintances to gossip about, and
neither of them had a gift for small talk. Now he answered
questions for her; he talked of history and Algheran politics.

She had been able to please her father by listening to
discussions of Valley politics. But two years had passed
since that time, so her memories were incomplete now,
and those stories were no longer current. She did not think
Tayem would show interest were she to repeat them to
him. She was not even sure she retained her interest.

Politics bordered on matters that the Algherans did not
permit Teeps to discuss, she realized uneasily. It would
be better not to mention them to Tayem, despite his apparent tolerance, better not to ask questions that could be
misinterpreted. Not that she had any curiosity about
them—the tra'R'sihuc had told her she could go home,

and she would get away from the Algherans and their
stupid squabbles in spite of Tayem, even if she could not
persuade him to help her.

Tayem was thinking private thoughts as well. He had
spoken very little since returning from his *shop*, and stayed
far apart from her most of the evening. Now he sat barely
an armslength from her, staring into his second cup of
coffee, then glancing directly at her and away. Calculation
showed in his eyes; she wondered anew what secrets he
kept under his 'blind.

He moved suddenly, standing to set his cup on the
counter between the kitchen and the front room. Uneaten
food he dumped down the disposal chute over the sink,
along with the outer skins stripped from the plates and
utensils. The clean things he put into the cabinets, then
flashed a damp rag over the countertop and the table.
With the exception of her plate, the after-dinner cleanup
was done.

So fast, Kylene thought. *So impatient.*

She remembered an aunt, an older sister of Edgart,
who had moved with the same jerky efficiency when
season-taken. Wolida, who had served as crop recorder,
had been a tall, raw-boned woman with an angry expression. She had two sons living in nearby villages, a pet
dog, and bad breath, and her time of the year was late
fall, after the harvest, which had probably been convenient and maybe gave her something to look forward to
after the year's work was done. Despite the sons, it was
always Edgart she chose to visit, husband in tow, when
sociability afflicted her, to drink Edgart's beer and complain about the laziness of the town's farmers.

Late in the afternoon, Wolida would always discover
that she had monopolized the conversation. Seeking to
leave, with a certain businesslike embarrassment, she
would apologize for the amount of beer she had con-
sumed. Edgart always reacted by dispatching his brother-
in-law or sometimes Kylene for more beer, then would
enmesh his sister in reminiscences about nearly forgotten

acquaintances and relatives. Genially bored almost beyond pretense, they would keep the conversation going late into the night. Eventually Wolida's yawns kept pace with her husband's blinks and a self-composed Edgart would escort her considerately to her carriage with Uncle Jon tagging behind. Then he would reenter the house with subdued feelings of triumph for having solved once more some puzzle of familial affections.

Kylene had watched this behavior countless times without ever discovering whether her father and aunt had realized that they were repeating a ritual.

Brother and sister, she remembered, sister and brother. How strange it must be to have a life so bound up with another's, not because of marriage or other choice, but simply by an accident of birth. Had Edgart and Wolida truly been fond of each other? What would it be like to have a sister or a brother? And was it better to be older or younger?

She would never really know, she saw. The memories people carried were images like the waves, rather than the complete ocean of experience, so that even their impressions of a whole experience were nothing but brief glimpses.

She let her eyes fall on Tayem Minstrel. *How are you like my Aunt Wolida?* she asked mentally.

"Ninety thousand years of progress," Tayem said blandly, "just to get rid of washing dishes." The idea seemed to amuse him. He took his seat beside her at the table, turning sideways so that his legs could stretch into the kitchen. His cup of *coffee* was once more in his hand; his eyes were focused on the twilight world beyond the kitchen window.

"Storm before morning," he commented. "Thunderheads building up out there. We're in sort of a pocket here, and get hit whenever the wind comes over the ice. Funny, you think of glaciers in terms of ice and snow, but unless you actually live on top of them, what you mostly notice is a lot of summer rain. Very anticlimatic.

"I should tell you a story, Kylene, to match the one you told me."

He was started even before she realized that the subject had changed.

"There was a man once in the Project, not terribly different from you in that he didn't feel all that comfortable with the Algherans. He was an orphan too, for whatever that's worth. But they had taken him into one of the Septs and generally treated him well, so he felt he owed them some loyalty.

"He got mixed up with a woman, a Teep woman, who was part of the Project. Actually, I guess you could say he was in love with her, and she—I don't really know how she felt about him. Doesn't matter. Then, a couple of years ago, she was killed. An accident, maybe. They were sightseeing in a time machine; it stopped functioning while they were over a battlefield, and she was killed. He wound up in a hospital bed.

"And when he got out, he wanted to save her, of course. Everyone with access to a time machine wants to save someone from dying, I suspect. But the Algherans told him they had changed history a tiny little bit while he was laid up, and they wouldn't change it back to let her be rescued.

"Which upset him.

"So he left the Project and ran away back to his own time, to get away from it and everything else.

"But he didn't fit into his home time anymore, either. He couldn't talk to anyone about the things he thought about, because the Algheran Teeps had done things to his mind so he couldn't tell people about time travel, and he didn't have much in common with them anyhow, because by then he was at least partially Algheran in his thinking. Maybe he felt a bit homesick too. And maybe he felt ashamed of himself for giving up.

"So, despite everything, he decided to come back in the hope that somehow he'd figure out a way to change things to save his girl friend. But regardless of his intentions, he'd made enough impact on the world that history had been changed. He got back to a different Project. People had changed; situations had changed.

"In particular, his girl friend had never existed in this world.

"Moral: Going home isn't as rewarding as you may expect."

CHAPTER FOUR

"*What happened then?*" *Kylene asked, her voice* ragged. "What happened after he came back to the Project?"

It wasn't necessary to ask for the name of the girl friend.

"Nothing much," Tayem answered curtly. "He made a stop along the way, at the year 5000, and kidnapped a little girl who otherwise would have died. He brought her back with him. He rejoined the Project and fortunately the Teeps got to him before he spilled his guts to the Normals. Eventually they decided he had not flipped his lid, and they told him that he had changed history somehow, and that the girl friend had never existed. He built himself a cabin out in the *boonies* and had a nice long rest. And when he got over it, the Normals sent him out on another mission. After a couple of years, he came back from that and ran into the same girl. It seems someone had stuffed her full of lies, and how that part of the story ends, I do not know."

"What are you going to do to get Onnul back?"

The redhead sighed, then tapped the tabletop. "Don't know that either. It all depends on what happens when you try to change history, and that depends on how time travel works, and that's more of a mystery than the Project guesses. The only foolproof method would be to go back and undo everything I did in the past."

He stood and pulled shut the curtains at the front of the cabin, isolating the two of them from the night. "Please don't ask me to take you home again, Kylene."

He moved past her and headed for the stairs beyond the kitchen. "If you're still bored, we've still got a good part of the evening ahead. Why don't you clear off the table?"

She obeyed numbly, unable to think of anything to say or do. Only her own plate was left; Tayem had left his empty cup on the fireplace mantel. Mechanically, Kylene peeled the outer skins from both and was placing the clean dishes in the cabinets when the man returned.

"Thanks," he said. "I need the space for this junk." He dropped bulky equipment on the table, then made a second trip to get smaller containers and cables from upstairs. While she watched, he began assembling pieces. The machinery looked familiar.

"All right," he said at last. "Have a seat and I'll show you how this little toy works. It's a book viewer, basically, with interactive controls."

"Why should I?" Kylenee asked suspiciously. She wanted to be by herself, thinking of the implications of Tayem's story, not doing things with his "little toy." He must be aware of that, but he was deliberately being high-handed, manipulating her. So she was in no mood to cooperate.

"You've been bored," Tayem said calmly. "This is something to do."

"You did not set this up just to occupy my time. Not now."

Tayem smiled briefly. "True enough. Have a seat anyhow." He pushed one of the lightweight glass-and-canvas chairs at her. "Here."

Reluctantly Kylene obeyed. "It's an Algheran teaching machine," she announced after a short inspection. "I've seen them before."

Tayem shrugged. "This is more advanced than the one that's back at the Station, but it shouldn't take you long to learn to operate it." He leaned over her and pressed a switch; meaningless words appeared on an illuminated screen.

"These things got talked about in my time, but never really implemented," the redhead commented. He did not explain the remark, but asked instead if she was thirsty. When she said no, he shrugged again. "I'll be around, if you do want anything. You just stay put, and I'll get it for you. You're going to be busy. Ready?"

He took her hesitation for assent, and pressed a switch.

"Good afternoon," a calm female voice announced. Kylene looked around, startled. Tayem gave her another of his brief smiles and pointed to a small red box connected to the reading machine by a pair of wires. The voice was coming from the box.

She had seen those boxes before, she remembered. They were machines used by the Normals to speak to one another when telepaths were not available to relay messages. Presumably Tayem had arranged for a woman to speak to her this evening, and hadn't wanted to interfere with that schedule.

If so, then the appearance of this "toy" had been prearranged. And her boredom, she realized suddenly. Tayem had deliberately left her unemployed with the intent of making her cooperative when he chose. Cimon take him!

In another portion of her mind, she wondered about the woman and her relationship with Tayem. But Tayem was obviously still grieving for his Onnul, so that made no sense.

She shrugged inwardly. No doubt this would be explained eventually. Tayem must have some purpose in mind, so she probably should pay attention to this, meaningless as it was now.

The little box had continued to speak, and she had missed some words. She leaned forward. "... preliminary portion of the admission examinations for the Institute for the Study of Land Reclamation Issues. Testing will be divided into three sessions, each lasting one half day tenth. There will be a brief rest period before each session.

"Admission to the institute depends on many factors, of which this examination is but one. Consequently, there are no passing scores as such; this functions as a predictive medium, so we may determine in advance how successful your career within the institute would probably be, and to highlight your areas of special strength and weakness, to serve as a guide for individualized instruction. Subsequent examinations will measure your aptitude for specialized fields of inquiry and your existing knowledge ..."

"Standard *ess-ay-tee* bullshit," Tayem muttered obscurely. He shook his head and removed a container of beer from the food locker, then levered off the top seal and pitched it into the disposal chute. "Ninety thousand years and civilizations toppling like duckpins and the academics never go out of business. Knew I should have stayed in the racket."

Kylene ignored him. Four balls had flashed onto the screen, the one on the right being much smaller than the others. Following the instructions of the voice from the box, she moved her fingers over a pressure plate to steer a white dot into the second smallest ball, and pushed down on the plate to register her answer. A buzz from beneath the viewscreen cabinet indicated that she had chosen correctly; a numeral flashed at the bottom of the screen, and the picture changed. Now she looked at three flights of stairs.

"Which flight has more steps?" the voice asked. "Indicate it with your light ball and enter the number of steps using the keyboard ..."

"What a kludge." Tayem peered over her shoulder, bringing with him a pleasant aroma of beer and Tayem. "Fifty grand of electronics to replace a couple sheets of paper and pencil, and it's just home movies with sound and punched tape. I wonder why only us First Era types ever made real computers."

She swung an arm, slapping at his midriff. Tayem hated to be ignored, she realized absently, but this was all his idea. This was interesting; he had told her to do it; it was just serving him right if he felt neglected. Besides, perhaps she should still be mad at him.

He moved away, chuckling softly.

The test tape ran out without warning and she was looking at a blank screen. Kylene poked irritably at the keyboard controls, trying to make the equipment work again.

Tayem patted her on the shoulder. "You're through, kid. Getting late, anyhow. But we'll see how you did before sending you off to bed." He shifted her empty water glass to the kitchen counter, then his fingers moved to the back of the book viewer cabinet and pressed concealed toggles. He removed a roll of paper tape that was coiled loosely about a spool inside the machine, and reclosed the cabinet.

"Been a buzzy little girl, haven't you?" he commented, holding the tape up to the light. "Go upstairs, please, and bring down my writing block. It's on my desk in the front room."

When she returned, the book viewer itself had been pushed to the back of the kitchen table, and the remaining equipment was stacked neatly on the floor. Tayem had also moved a small lamp from the living room area and fastened it to the wooden wall, to provide a brightly lit work space.

"Good." Tayem accepted the plastic block from her, then thumbed a recessed knob until dark lines appeared, covering the clear upper surface of the block with thousands of tiny squares. "Graph paper," he said, as if explaining something to her. "*Kay and Ee* would have thrown a fit if they ever saw this gadget."

He didn't seem to expect an answer, so she gave him none, but pulled up one of the chairs. He was not looking at her, so she watched him curiously as he moved a finger along the paper strip. What was he thinking of now?

"Easiest part of teaching," he commented. "Grading. You won't mind if I do without a *tweed* jacket on, will you?" His hand danced over the writing block, filling in blocks to form a half-dozen uneven columns. "We had something like this in my time—intelligence tests, we called them. We didn't look for quite the same thing the Algherans do, but the principle is the same—to find out what your mind is capable of. They made some effort to keep this culture-free; I'm not sure if they really managed that, but they get some credit for trying it without having to have riots to prompt 'em . . . Here you go, Kylene."

It meant nothing to her, and she said so, even when he used his scribe to draw a brown line across the page, and called it the "average."

Tayem gave her one of the infuriating smiles he reserved for occasions when she was forced to admit ignorance. "You're supposed to jump up and down and feel superior," he said jocularly. "Then you go around to everyone else and ask 'How'd ya do? How'd ya do?' Then they have to ask you the same thing and you can tell 'em. So then they go home and tell their folks that teacher gave them a test and that drippy little Waterfall girl got the best grade, just like she always does." He snorted. "You aren't gonna do that, huh? You'd have a terrible time getting by in the First Era, Kylene."

She brushed her hair to the side with a hand and stared at him. How could school pupils compete fairly when they were all different ages? "Why did you speak so fast?" she asked at last. "What has made you mad?"

Something like hurt and puzzlement suddenly showed on Tayem's face. "Nothing. I don't—" He broke off and shook his head. "Guess I'm remembering I didn't have parents to go home to. And there was always some *sonuvabitch* who scored better than me, no matter where I went."

He sighed. "So what are you thinking of, little girl looking so hard at me?"

He could be so transparent at times, even with his Teepblind on, Kylene realized with amazement. The silliest little things could affect him, and the more he tried to hide them, the more visible they became. Didn't he realize that? What a very strange person he was!

So now she smiled at him, deliberately making it a real smile and not the short-lived, one-sided sort he used so often. She stood up next, and hopped up and down, chanting his words back at him. "How'd ya do? How'd ya do? How'd ya do, Tayem?"

Tayem's face froze, and he ceased to breathe. He seemed to be trying to smile also, but without success. Then he managed it, and covered his reddening face with his hands. "I am pretty obviously an idiot," he said ruefully behind his fingers. "I was going to show you my scores, to tell the truth. But I can see I've been beaten out again."

"Tayem!" she protested.

The big man laughed, genuinely for once. "Never mind. I'll recover. Okay, bedtime for you, little girl."

Morning had come again accompanied by noise inside and out. Rain splattered against the window behind the bed—Tayem's bed, she remembered anew with a pleasant shock as she did each morning. Tayem's window. And Tayem's rain too; he had predicted it, just before telling his strange story.

A loud pounding noise came from the front of the cabin. More Tayem, she decided sleepily; she could hear the shrill whistling he called the Colonel Bogie March.

She yawned widely and rolled out of bed—Tayem's bed—and went to take her bath.

This was completely senseless, she told herself as the warm water rose in the tub. With all the bathing the Algherans did, it was surprising they didn't shrink away into nothingness. There was certainly no good reason for her to risk that or to waste a part of her life this way.

But Tayem took a shower each morning, and sometimes one in the evening as well, just as if it were normal for him to conceal his natural scent, even though it was generally barely noticeable. It was natural behavior for him, he had said, not something he had learned from the Algherans. And it would be a good idea for her to acquire the same habit. "Hint. Hint."

She had decided not to argue, but she also wondered momentarily if perhaps wild animals had been more prevalent in the First Era than in her own. Would it do any good to tell him this place was safe and such precautions were not needed? Probably not.

Safe ... She thought about Tayem's story as she lathered. Time travel was not without risk, he had said later. People going into the past had not always returned. He preferred to leave it that way, he had implied, to keep earlier eras isolated from the Algherans.

But there had to be a way home. The Algherans had worked so many other miracles, they would surely find a way to travel far downtime, even without his cooperation. They had told her she was going home, so they must already have known how to do so, and Tayem simply did not know about it. She would go home after Tayem returned her to the Station.

Home. Somehow the prospect wasn't as exciting as it should have been.

The new feeling came from speaking to Tayem, she realized. He had managed to bring back unpleasant memories and not the happy anticipations of her future life there.

Had he done so deliberately? Yes, he had admitted it.

That surprised her. He could not see into her mind; he should not be able to manipulate her thoughts that way.

But he had spied on her—he had admitted that too; he would have found out anything he wanted.

To be watched by Tayem... She shivered deliciously.

But Tayem had been thinking all the while then of his Onnul, and not really about Kylene. Even now...

When she went home, it would not be with Tayem.

The soap filter whirred, removing the scum from the water and breaking into her thoughts. She began to rinse. Tayem was a problem that could not be solved today. She would see what happened next, and treat him accordingly.

The door to the bathroom hung open, its broken latch still unfixed. The room would be chill when she left the tub, but the mirrors would be clear. Good, she liked to look at herself in the mirrors. "Arrested development," Tayem had said once when she mentioned that to him. Obviously she would be *pubescent* for the next four hundred years. "Watched pots and all that, kid."

She hadn't recognized the word, and she didn't think it was from Speech. Was it a good thing?

He had given her one of his lopsided grins. "For pubescent males."

The pounding noise continued.

"Tayem, what are you doing?" she called.

"Building a desk," he called back.

Curious to see his handiwork, she climbed from the tub and set it to drain, then tore towels from the dispenser and draped them over herself after pirouetting to toss off water.

She looked very healthy today, she noticed in the mirror. Her hair was raven dark and shining; all the time at the Algheran's Station, it had seemed dull and dingy. It was one of her best features; she was grateful now that she had not given way to arguments for cutting it short in the Algheran fashion. But it had grown so far below her shoulders that it would soon require trimming. Perhaps Tayem would help with that.

She smiled, remembering her earlier intention of practicing her prettiness on Tayem. She was pretty. And yes,

the hair on her groin was fuller than she had been willing
to admit, and darker. Tayem's words to the contrary, she
was approaching maturity. The day would come—

She froze, remembering how Samtha had died, how
other women had died. Health and strength were not
enough to get a mother through childbirth. And yet, children were adorable and only women could have children.
It was something she could do. Painful, fearful, rewarding—something she could do.

The racket from the front suddenly stopped. *"Damn!"*
Tayem's voice thundered and she could move again, shak-
ily, then almost normally. Then he walked into the bathroom, shaking his left hand. He was wearing low boots,
jeans, and a long-sleeved shirt with a tartan plaid. *He
looks very un-Algheran today*, she noticed with pleasure.
Then she was startled by a new realization. *I'm fond of
him.*

Tayem could be handsome, she suddenly saw. She
wondered if he was aware of it. Proably he wasn't, and
she was sure no one had ever told him. *Not even his
Onnul, I'll bet. She didn't treat him very well.*

"Hit my thumb," he said curtly, and began rummaging
through the little supply bin above the sink he called a
medicine cabinet. "Good morning, Kylene. Where's that
painkiller? Ah, here."

"I'll do it," she said, taking the bottle of spray from
his hand. "But first—" She raised his hand and kissed
the hammer-blackened thumbnail. "There. Samtha used
to do that for me. Does it feel better?"

Tayem snorted. "Yes, little mother. But the painkiller
would help too. Ah, thank you." He shook the hand again.
"I guess we'll find out in a few day tenths whether the
thumb drops off. Want to see your desk?"

She put the painkiller away and closed the cabinet.
Tayem could never close it so it stayed shut. Something
for her? She noticed the implications: Tayem was not only
expecting her to remain with the Algherans, but he was
anticipating a long stay in this cabin.

She was not agreeing to that.

The towels she had draped over her had dropped away when she reached up, leaving her nude. Tayem eyed her with a quizzical expression, one eyebrow raised, then bent to pick up one of the towels. He held it out to her, grasping it at the corner with two fingers. "A desk, not a staircase, kid."

The desk was a solid plank-topped bench with legs, a bit longer than the height of a normal man, about the size of the desk Tayem had upstairs. He had moved one of the low Algheran couches from the wall opposite the fireplace to make space for it, placing the couch before the counter separating the kitchen from the front room. This made the room quite cluttered.

Kylene remembered following Edgart into the house of a woman who had died of extreme old age. Furniture had been stored in all the spare rooms, and sometimes it had been stacked on other furniture, piles of objects both strange and familiar, both utilitarian and bizarre, so high that it had seemed half the town could have been gifted from the collection. There had been a sharp musty smell Edgart identified as mouse urine; there had been spider webs. And spiders.

Tayem was far from that type of senility, but the cabin might not always be equal to his urge for construction. Obviously, something from here would have to be moved soon into one of his storage buildings. Inspecting the desk cursorily, she made her selection. She wondered how she could persuade Tayem to dismantle it.

"Like it?" Tayem asked cheerfully. "It needs to be sanded down, of course, and then a good coat of varnish. But it's not bad-looking, even if it is me saying so. The top is all one piece too—not often you see something like that. Went out this morning to cut it—from the end of next summer, which is why it's good and dry."

The top of the desk was less than hip-high for her, so it would be too close to the ground for him to use. "Thank you. It looks very nice, Tayem," she agreed, and leaned against it, then squirmed herself onto its top. A splinter poked at the inside of her knee. She reached to brush it aside, using that as an excuse to keep moving.

"And it's a dark-colored wood, instead of being yellow or white like everything else in this room," she said, trying to speak in neutral tones. "That's worth noticing." Cimon and Nicole! The desk was not going to budge. Tayem had built too solidly.

Tayem smiled approvingly for an instant, then his brow wrinkled and the smile disappeared. *Anxious*, Kylene diagnosed. *Like a little child, or a puppy, wanting approval. Do the Algherans have dogs? I've never seen one. I should ask Tayem—but what do I say to him first?*

She would have to compromise, she realized with an inward sigh. She could make this cabin look as pleasant as possible, but it would always belong to Tayem. He had undoubtedly worked hard to make this desk, whatever he intended it for.

And it was a gift to her. What was here to please Onnul?

"Make it lighter, Tayem," she said gently. "Paint it. Bleach it. Do something simple so it won't clash with everything else."

He looked confused. "Does it?"

"It does. Don't you see it?"

He shook his head sideways. "Not really. But—if you say so. Uh, those tests—one area you're ahead of me on the scores is art, esthetics, that sort of stuff."

"Does that bother you?" It did, she could see. She tilted her head sideways and shrugged her shoulders, copying his gesture and making the towel fall away from her.

"Uh, I guess I'm ahead on the important parts of that test," Tayem said. "Your towel slipped off again, you know."

She shrugged again, and pointed her feet and hands toward him, stretching. "I'm dry, except for my hair. Will you dry my hair, Tayem?"

Almost imperceptibly he drew away. "Suppose I start

a fire, and you can dry your hair in front of that. Would you like that?"

"The towel will do." She smiled prettily at him and held the cloth out. "You can do such a nice job of drying me. Please?"

"Uh..." Tayem hesitated. When he spoke again, he sounded hurried and angry. "I'm going out for a while, Kylene. Dry your own Cimon-taken hair."

What had provoked him? Surely not the desk. "It's raining," she protested, pointing to the gray sky visible through the front of the cabin. "You'll be drenched."

"That's all right," Tayem said curtly. He pushed through the glass doorway and closed it quickly to keep rain from splashing on the flagstone floor, then shook himself and ran a hand uselessly through his hair as if to comb water out of it. Even before he was off the porch, the rain had darkened his jeans and shirt.

Abandoned, Kylene went to the door and peered through it, not caring that she stood in the puddle of water he had admitted. Tayem walked away from the cabin deliberately, not moving faster in spite of the rain, not looking back, until he reached the silvery levcraft at the base of the hill. Was he going to wait in it for the rain to stop?

He slipped and fell awkwardly onto one knee, and she bit her lip, thinking—hoping—he would return now to the cabin. But he did not. The ramp lowered and he stepped into the vehicle.

The hatch closed. Moments later, the time shuttle vanished. Kylene, staring at the empty place where it had rested, was stunned, unhappy. Lonely.

Perhaps a hundredth of a day passed, perhaps less. The levcraft suddenly became visible again. The hatchway opened, the ramp lowered to the ground, and Tayem Minstrel emerged. He was wearing an outer garment to protect him from the rain, a green and brown dappled cloak that fitted over his head to form a triangular peak, so that he looked rather like a moving tent.

He nodded to her at the doorway, and she moved aside to let him in and to stay out of the rain, only then remembering her nudity. Water dripped on the floor when he entered, pouring from folds in his garment.

"Whew! Forgotten how wet it was," he commented. His words were muffled as he half shrugged, half pulled his way out of the cloak. "Get me a beer, Kylene."

He wore light-brown breeches that buttoned along the left side and a loose pullover in dark brown, filigreed with golden lace on the right shoulder. Fringes of short tassels ran the lengths of his sleeves. His moccasins were gone as well, metamorphosed into narrow black boots with upward-pointing toes. A small pattern of blue and white bars had been painted on his left cheek and on the back of his right hand. His hair was cut differently, close-cropped on the left, long on the right. He smelled of cinnamon.

His attitude seemed different. He wasn't looking at her, and he did not seem as tall. His clothing was rumpled, she suddenly realized, and he was slouching. She looked at him askance, not sure she liked Tayem Minstrel in this guise. "Where did you go?" she asked suspiciously.

"Out." Tayem moved to a closet and hung up his wet cloak. Water still dripped from his clothing. "Get me that beer, will you, kid? I'm a bit hung and need all the help I can get."

She didn't move. "What did you do?"

"Nothing." He seemed amused for some reason. "If I can't have a beer, why don't we eat?"

Kylene shook her head. "You're not the same."

The new Tayem gave her one of the old Tayem's lopsided smiles. "Just a bit older, that's all, kid. But a watch ago—ah! Then I was a great dandy. Nothing special, actually, just your typical, garden-variety war hero home on leave."

His voice changed, becoming more sibilant, softer, slightly hesitant. "A humble Master of Blade in the Swordtroop, Mistress. Presently on convalescent duty whilst this trifling incision in my shoulder heals, and then I shall of course return to the field. Why, I am most appreciative of your kindly interest in my unimportant existence, Mistress. A sword thrust from an unpleasant fellow at the battle of Black Ridge—my attentions were on another individual at the time. A mere flesh wound, Mistress, a trifle to be ignored—perhaps some moderate exercise would be good for it. You wish to inspect it more closely, Mistress? Of course; I would be most honored by your ministrations. Your place or mine?"

Kylene stared at him, aghast. This could not be Tayem Minstrel. "You didn't do anything like that," she protested.

Tayem looked at her at last, then slowly nodded. He walked into the bathroom. She could hear water flowing. He returned shortly, wiping away the patterns on his cheek and hand with a dampened towel.

"Might change things—couldn't run that kind of risk," he said harshly. "Went to a whore. You don't know that word, huh? Someone you pay for sex. A slut—not like you pure little Project Teeps. Too high class to be called that, and too expensive, but—that's where I was." His voice turned cynical, bitter. "Just your typical, garden-variety war hero home on leave."

"But why, Tayem?" Kylene again was suddenly conscious of her nakedness. Nervously she fastened her towel around her waist.

"*Horny*," Tayem said curtly. "Why not? Do you want to eat?"

"But—but—" Kylene started. Something important was happening, she sensed, and she had to understand what was going on. She had to understand Tayem for some reason. But she couldn't.

She tried again. "Paying a—that's not for—they're for—"

"Old men, perverts, Blanklings, and those without Septs." Tayem supplied the words. "Not for a nice young idealistic Ironwearer of Sept Dicovys. Is that what you want to tell me?"

"Yes. No. I mean—someone you didn't care for, Tayem? In my time—and people in the Project think—"

"Careful, kid," Tayem growled. "You'll turn into an Algheran." He sank onto the couch he had moved hours—days?—before. "Go get dressed."

She had to try once more. "What about Onnul?"

That was a mistake, she knew immediately. His eyes closed. "I don't owe faithfulness to her. Or you," he said at last, tiredly. "Or to any other woman. Go get dressed, Kylene."

She settled for a lemon-yellow wrap that could be put on quickly, afraid to leave him alone. But when she returned, he was seated in the same position, still in his unfamiliar damp clothing, staring at the empty fireplace.

"Are you hungry?" she asked hesitantly.

"Just coffee," he said dully. "I seem to have lost my appetite. You aren't supposed to be taking this seriously, you know."

She bit her lip at that, and went off to ladle coffee grounds into the bowl of Tayem's coffeepot, guessing at the level because she had never done this before. "I am not shocked," she said carefully. Brown coffee grains had spilled onto the white counter; she pushed them into the sink with the side of her hand and ran water into it so he would not notice the wastage.

"That's nice." Tayem's voice was sarcastic. "Who cares, anyhow?"

Kylene worried her lip again. One of the buttons on the stove controlled the heating element under the coffeepot, but she was not sure which it was. Why did the Algherans put so much machinery between them and their food?

Water, she remembered. She had to put water in the coffeepot.

She ran water into the spout of the pot until it became heavy, then sat it back on the stove. Which button to press? Inspiration struck, and she pressed all the buttons. "You seem to care," she said neutrally.

"No, I don't," Tayem said disconsolately. "I know—good, high-class Algherans don't go to whores in this world. Good Algherans aren't interested in sex lives of any sort. Or good Chelmmysians. Or good Teeps, on either side. Screw 'em."

All the heating pads were glowing now. Kylene picked a button at random and poked to turn it off. She didn't like this conversation, she decided. But it was too late to back out of it. She grimaced, and poked at another button. "I'm sure you're wrong, Tayem. Or there'd be no people left."

"*Touché*," Tayem answered. "Point taken. Still, there were a lot more of us during the First Era than you'll find around these days. I suspect we were more interested than you people."

Kylene finally found the button controlling the pad under the coffeepot and turned off the others. "We. You. Why use those words, Tayem?"

"Why not?" He moved to the fireplace and sat on the hearth while he lifted kindling from the scuttle. Splintered bark and punk went under the grate; he began to lay a fire, in ironic counterpoint to his words. "I can wear iron for Dicovys, but never find a hearthmate in it. You know that. You have some kind of chance in this world and I don't."

She could hear the water boiling inside the coffeepot. It was doing the internal geysering Tayem called perking. Kylene opened cabinets, looking for one of his special cups. Would a regular mug do? "I don't know," she said over her shoulder. "Have you looked for one?"

His Onnul, she recalled sickly. Of course he had.

Tayem swirled ashes with his fingers. "Freak, remember? You called me that your first day here."

Kylene closed her eyes and froze, remembering, smelling the acrid odor of coffee, and trying to keep her voice steady. "I'm sorry, Tayem."

"No matter," Tayem said heavily. "You were right enough. Perhaps if the Algherans took wedding vows as lightly as people in my time—but they don't, and I can't ask someone to spend most of her life as a widow. So good luck, girl. You've things to look forward to, and some ways I envy you."

She poured coffee into a mug, slowly to avoid spilling it, and carried it out to him. "Thank you." There was nothing else to say.

"Ah, forget it. I'm just being maudlin." He turned away to strike iron on flint, blew at the punk till sparks led to flame, and slipped it under the kindling. Then he picked up his coffee, sipped at it, and made a face. He smiled wryly, reminding her of the way he had been before. "Kylene, this is probably the worst coffee I've met up with in all my life. But it is—much appreciated. Peace?"

She had to guess at an answer. "Peace," she echoed, and he nodded.

CHAPTER FIVE

"*Tolp—has—six—grandchildren,*" *Kylene read from* the viewscreen, her finger tracing down the sentence column. "*Their—average age is—one hundred fifty. If—they are—equally spaced—and—the oldest—owns—twice—the years—the younger—owns—a question demanding answer is—the age—*"

One of those problems again. Kylene scratched on a writing block without bothering to read further, then keyed a "100" on the control console. The machine made a blaring sound at her; she reread the question and substituted "200." Happier now, the machine buzzed softly and presented her with a new problem. If Tolp had a contract to deliver a thousand man-weights of apples at—

Nothing, she thought rebelliously. "His fat grandchildren ate them all and got bellyache." She flipped the machine off. She had done enough of this for one day; the afternoon was half gone and Tayem couldn't make her study any more.

Except that he could. She had found that out. If he

wasn't satisfied with her progress, he would ignore her, refusing to speak and making her fix her own meals until she gave in. In the end, he always won.

He had painted the desk though.

She picked a speck of lint from her dress, then leaned forward on the yellow enameled surface, resting her weight on her forearms and staring malignly at the pile of books and reels Tayem had given her. Arithmetic, history, introductory science . . . "Just a starter," he had said. Had he been serious?

Probably, she admitted. Tayem wouldn't make a joke without letting an audience know when to appreciate it. She sighed, then looked outside through the front of the cabin. The day was unreasonably warm for summer, without clouds to keep the sun at bay. The door and windows were open in case a breeze should visit, and a forest smell had permeated the air. "*April* showers bring *May* pine needles," Tayem had said.

He had spent the morning upstairs doing what he called studying—mostly scribbling onto his writing block and mumbling to himself—before leaving the cabin. A plopping sound came now from the distance, which meant that he was up to something else Tayem-ish.

She curled her toes and moved about to stretch, enjoying the satiny feeling of her clothing and amusing herself by throwing her weight against the slow-reacting material of her cube chair, outwitting its responses. What was she going to do about Tayem? What did she really want from him?

She couldn't answer that. She didn't want to be here in his cabin, she knew. She didn't want to be studying. She didn't want to take orders from him, or to be part of his Project, of his Alghera.

She jammed a bare foot under her thigh and rocked back and forth. What did she want?

To go home? But when she said that anymore, Tayem answered that she had been leaving her home when he kidnapped her and that she had not planned to return to it.

She had changed her mind, she had told him. She was willing to live very quietly in her home village, doing nothing that might have consequences, and that way she would have a life that was agreeable to her while he could bring back his Onnul. It had sounded very convincing and there were even moments when she thought she might do what she had told him.

He had laughed uncharitably.

Tayem could be aggravating. She didn't want to go home anyhow.

What about her City of Silence? she had wondered. The city of telepaths she had been seeking when Tayem had kidnapped her. Would it be possible to visit it, at least? Just to see it?

It was a daydream, Tayem had said curtly. A real city would have been famous from coast to coast in her world. "Someday, sure," he had admitted. "But in your time— a mountain town, Kylene. Fifty or sixty people at most, fewer Teeps than you'd find back at the Station, living in much worse conditions. Dirt roads, monotonous diet, diseases, no real commerce. You'd make a fine peasant's wife, all right. Sharing a hearth with some lout because he was the right age and no one else for miles around would take someone without assets like you. Mud on your hands each day, and a sore back from working in the fields, and clothing to be patched each night, and a couple of kids tugging at your knees—you'd really love it! Particularly after a couple of centuries."

"It wouldn't be like that," she had protested. It would be, he had repeated harshly, amplifying his description with a grimness she had not been able to drive from her mind. Tayem had hurt her; he had taken something important away from her, and she sensed that he had done so deliberately.

Just once had he relented. She had spoken of building things, of creating with others objects and institutions that one could not create alone, of watching the growth of something more valuable than oneself that one had nurtured. Clan Otter could never offer that to her; her city had, even if she never could have seen it become more than the squalid village Tayem had described.

"'And we will build us a shining city on a hill, as a beacon,'" Tayem had said. "'Let the word go forth... we will bear any burden, meet any price.' Idealism's just rhetoric, kid. It takes a full belly and a lot of self-indulgence to be idealistic, and reality always catches up with you."

He sighed. "I've seen it happen. And something else— pretty words like yours get used to justify all sorts of nastiness, by all kinds of people, some of whom even believe they're doing the right things.

"But you're young, and you want to be a true believer, don't you? And I'm being an old fart ruining your day with a lecture. Sorry about that, but I guess old fart-iness has its privileges too.

"Look, kid. You can't go back and build that city. Even if you could, it didn't last—it's been dead and buried for thousands of years, and it just wasn't the wonder you had in mind. So look around—you've got a long life ahead of you, with all sorts of opportunity. Maybe something as big and important as you'd like will come along here someday."

He was not telling her that Alghera represented such a goal, she had realized only later. If Alghera was not his ideal, then what was he fighting for?

When she asked that the next day, Tayem had laughed. "Mental privacy and equal time in the bathroom," he told her. "And I'm losing on both fronts." She had not been able to get him to say more.

Only once, she decided, had she caught a glimpse of his motivation in kidnapping her. One morning after he had finished his studying, she had spoken to him of going home, ignoring the signs that he was in a bad temper. Tayem had exploded.

Her world was a dump, he had snarled. A cesspool.

A broken-up corpse of something decent, filled with two-bit counties calling themselves countries and Cimon-taken *Indian* tribes with stupid pretensions, who couldn't imagine, let alone remember, something better than what they already had. An insect-ridden, scummy, degenerate, dangerous place that wasn't going to be improved a Cimon-taken incestuous bit till the Cimon-taken glaciers had flattened it. He was sick and tired of hearing about it and he most incestuously well didn't need to have it smeared into his hair anymore. She was well rid of that Cimon-taken hole, and by Nicole's *tits*! she should thank the Lady for dropping her cloak over her little Cimon-taken ass.

Eventually, Kylene deciphered this as meaning that Tayem actually saw some prospect of getting her home safely. But at the time, she had been devastated by the completely unheralded revelation that Tayem did not like or approve of her world—his shouting, while novel, had been infinitely less upsetting.

His final bitter remark, made just before he threw his writing block onto the floor and stamped out of the cabin, was still unexplained. Who were *America*? Why should Tayem feel shame for what they had become?

Tayem. Stuck with Tayem, she thought grimly. Tayem and Alghera. What was she to do? Make the most of it, accept the situation, the words in her mind ran. But that was to accept defeat, and she had not done so.

Wait. There was no other alternative. Some solution or some strategy would present itself eventually.

And in the meantime? There was Tayem to deal with, she decided.

It was only fair. Tayem made her do things that were dull. So she would continue making him do things also. Manipulating him was fun. When it worked. Sometimes it would backfire on her. Not wearing clothes, for example; Tayem would pretend not to notice that for a few days, then he would be irritable for another day, and try to hide his irritation. It could be very amusing.

But if she were nude too long, he would stomp out of

the cabin and go away in his time shuttle, and when he returned an instant later, nothing she did had any effect on him. She had learned not to do that.

Sex. Tayem went off to have sex. She unclipped the scribe from a writing block and tapped it gently against her teeth.

Sex was pleasurable, she knew, an exciting mixture of unreason and risk. She looked forward to it someday. But she was being patient about it, and Tayem wasn't. He was totally abnormal. If a male could be season-taken, then Tayem was in such a state.

She'd asked him about that once, when he was feeling unhappy for some Tayem-ish reason.

He had snorted. "I guess you could say both sexes in my era got season-taken. We got that way once a year, just like you people."

So he would come out of this mood eventually. "How long does your period last?" she had asked curiously.

He had raised both eyebrows before answering. "Three hundred sixty-five days. Plus a few hours. Any more questions?"

"No!" If he wasn't going to give her polite answers, she wasn't going to waste her time asking him questions.

Her resolve had lasted less than ten days. Tayem had gone away again, and returned in an unusually contrite mood. It had seemed a good opportunity to reason with him. She had not been successful.

"Find someone to love," she had told him. "Have sex with her, if you must."

"Did once. We didn't."

That was a reference to his Onnul, she understood. But that had been years ago. "Fine someone else, Tayem. You're an Ironwearer and—"

"Found a whore. That's all I'll find. Shut up, Kylene."

But she hadn't.

"What in hell do you know?" he had finally snarled. "You aren't me, and you aren't in my head. By the Lady, Kylene! You're a sixteen-year-old kid with sixteen-year-old kid notions, and you don't know what you're talking about. I'll bet you're still a virgin, so stop bugging me!"

She wasn't married; of course she was a virgin. She had told him that. But she was also a Teep, she had reminded him. He had sputtered, then refused to speak for another day. She had not been able to talk to him about sex since then.

She shook her head, feeling hair brush over her shoulders. Perhaps it should be cut short in the Algheran fashion. But Tayem had once said that he liked her hair when it was long; she was letting it grow to please him.

She needed new clothing also. The Algheran garments were flimsy and easily torn. They were, she admitted guiltily, far more comfortable than any clothes she had known in the Second Era, but they lacked the ruggedness necessary for life in the middle of a wilderness. Only the blue denim jeans Tayem had provided seemed able to hold up, and according to him they were not worn in Alghera.

Fortunately, he had not asked her to mend any of the clothing, so she was spared that chore, as he had spared her from most chores. Sooner or later he would make another trip uptime and return with replacements, he had said. She should make a list of what she wanted. He had also said he would not take her with him.

Too much risk, he claimed. Too much was strange, because of what the Algherans had done to history. She could fly the levcraft around Tayem's clearing under his supervision and watch the seasons race by for a couple of years, but long trips he would take alone.

She sighed. Tayem. Always Tayem.

"Problem?" The voice was Tayem's. "Why aren't you studying?"

The redhead was standing in the doorway, the mid-morning sun behind his back turning the ends of his shaggy hair to gold. He was wearing his work clothing, mud-splattered jeans and canvas shoes, without a shirt. His torso was bare, tanned brown, and sunburn had left white peeling skin on his arms. He smiled as she looked at him, and for a moment she thought of him as a very tall little boy.

"I was thinking about you," she admitted.

He quirked an eyebrow. "Doubt you're old enough." He moved into the dark-shaded kitchen and took a container of beer from the food locker.

"I'm getting old enough."

"And I'm such a heartbreaker," he said solemnly. "I know. It must be terrible for you, Kylene."

"I don't want you," she said bluntly.

"Course not." His tone had changed; she could not see his expression. "You need another telepath. One of these days you'll meet some nice fellow from Nyjuc or R'sihuc, and there'll be wedding bells, or smashing stones, or whatever the Algherans use. Sure."

"Yes. What will you do?"

"Die of a broken heart." He used his mock-solemn voice again, and leaned backward while clapping his hands to his breast. "I'm going, Kylene. I'm going!"

"Be serious, Tayem."

"You mean I'm not? Has all my passion gone for nought? Oh, Kylene, you are so cruel!" Tayem put his beer on the kitchen counter and toyed with it awhile. "Go on with the Project, I guess. Only game in town, after all."

"But when it's over? What about the rest of your life?"

Tayem snorted. "Rate things are going, that's not apt to be a problem."

She stared at him, but his face was still in the darkness. "Why? Don't you expect the Project to succeed?"

"Hard to say." He took a long swallow, then moved to drop the beer container down the disposal chute. "Not moving all that fast, after all. But—only game in town."

"That's not enough, Tayem."

Tayem shrugged. "You'll make out all right, kid."

Kylene gnawed her lower lip. It was not herself she was concerned about, and she watched unhappily while the man took another container of beer from the food locker.

"I want to finish up the *corral* this afternoon. Come out and watch if you'd like a break. Company is welcome."

Tayem's latest construction project was on a neighboring hillside, a hundred man-heights from the cabin but hidden from it by an arm of the surrounding forest. He had laid out a path through the trees, and Kylene stopped for a moment to enjoy the shade. Through a gap in the trees she could see the pond beyond the time shuttle; the waters were still, and she wondered idly whether the beavers were within their lodge, hiding from the sun.

On the other side of her, the chittering of squirrels could be heard from farther inside the woods. Her mind reached out.

Greedy, thoughtless little animals, she decided quickly. Squirrels seemed so curious and cheerful; it was always a disappointment to discover that they were interested only in food. Even in summer, when food was plentiful.

It *was* summer, she realized. Real summer now, in the sense that Clan Otter had used—and Tayem Minstrel too—not just the overlong Algheran season that partially coincided with it. Two year tenths had passed since Tayem had taken her from the Station. A year of her life had been spent with him and his Algherans. Her Pilgrimage had begun more than two years before and she was no closer to the end of it than she had been when leaving the Valley and Edgart.

Such a strange Pilgrimage it had become, and so unnecessary. Surely, if she had stayed with Edgart, an acceptable suitor would have arrived eventually on his own Pilgrimage. The pride and curiosity that had drawn her across the continent in search of others like her could have been forgotten, couldn't they, outgrown, submerged in child-raising and the peaceful contents of family life?

"What do you think?" she heard Tayem ask. He waved an arm at his handiwork. "Not bad for one day, is it?"

It looks like a fence around a grass yard, she thought.

But there was no point in saying something that obvious, so she merely nodded approvingly to satisfy him. It did seem more interesting than most of Tayem's projects. For some reason, it looked familiar to her.

The fence was made of transparent piping, taken from a bulky roll in one of Tayem's sheds. Under tension it was quite firm, and oozing mud was being pumped into the hollow posts and rails from a machine at the top of the hill, where the *corral* ended. The fence was about as high as her forehead, she estimated, almost even with the base of Tayem's neck. Inside the fence, on the far side of the structure, was a small, low-lying earth-walled shed; presumably Tayem had built that today also.

As she watched, he lifted a small rod from the ground and pointed it at the base of a post.

"Push stick set for glazing," he explained, then touched the rod to the black-filled plastic and stroked along its length. The post withered and shrank as he moved the rod, the encased mud turning color to red. A shrill whistling sounded; a white plume rose from the top of the post.

"And begorrah, Mick," Tayem said. *"For sure without that monster there'd be a thousand of us down there with our cigarette lighters."*

He smiled, noticing her blank look. "It doesn't translate." He had not reached the top of the post, but he moved away and stooped to apply the rod to a bottom rail. "Let the steam vent. Go too far and you get hot mud raining down. Uncomfortable."

"What goes into the storage shed?" she asked.

Tayem moved his push stick along another rail top. *"Stable,"* he said. "I'll be getting some horses."

Horses? No wonder the structure had seemed familiar. A horse yard!

But she had seen so few animals in the last year. "I didn't know they still existed," she admitted. "Do the Algherans ride them?"

Tayem nodded. "Some. These won't be much different

from the horses you knew. Healthier, perhaps, since I'll
be getting them from near the Present. Bigger, brighter,
and sturdier than First Era types, I suspect. I don't know
if it's just selective breeding or if someone tinkered with
their genes also."

"Also?"

He nodded again. "People got different, remember?
They changed—so someone changed 'em."

Humor him. People had always been as they were now.
The tra'R'sihuc had stressed that to her, shortly after
Tayem brought her to the Project, when the Sept Master
was still taking an interest in her instruction. All available
evidence showed that Man's present form was the one he
had always known.

Tayem's abnormality was well known, if not often discussed, and she had asked about it. Was it possible for
many people to be like him, as he claimed?

The answer had been no. A rare disease sometimes
caused a person to be born with an incomplete set of
chromosomes—little things in the centers of the cells of
the body. Tayem was extremely unusual in that he lacked
six of these. He was almost certainly unique in that this
had not impaired his appearance or his intelligence. But
the abnormality showed up in his reduced life span, his
susceptibility to diseases other persons did not catch, and
his limited tolerance for temperature variations. The
Algherans had been able to correct some of these flaws
with surgery; they could not cure all of them.

No, Tayem ha'Dicovys-once-ha'Ruppir was a freak.
This must have been the case even among his own people.
Perhaps they had shielded him from the truth as a kindness. Otherwise, his insistence that numerous other people—utterly fantastic numbers of people—had shared his
abnormality was understandable as a psychological defense
mechanism, but not to be believed.

Was he insane then?

A name had flashed from the tra'R'sihuc's mind. *Nicul-
ponoc Onnul Nyjuc.* It had meant nothing to her at the

time. Then his mind screen had gone up, and she had not been able to penetrate it. "No," he had told her, using Speech rather than communicating directly. Tayem was extremely irrational at times, and did stupid things, but he was not insane—not because of a delusion about genetics, anyhow.

Could anything be done for him?

She must have repeated that aloud, for Tayem answered. "Probably not, kid. There's a lot of stuff in the Plates, but..."

The archives the Algherans had found, she remembered vaguely. The records left by some previous civilization. Why did he mention them now?

Tayem waved his rod for an answer. "There's information in the Plates that can lead to manipulating genetics. The Janhular used that in their war against the Alliance, to create plagues. But they wasted a lot of people that way, so it's pretty dangerous stuff. Which is why—" He shrugged, smiling tightly.

Nothing could be done, the Sept Master had said. It was senseless to raise false hopes, and the tra'Dicovys was deserving of some censure for deluding his Septling.

"No one has such knowledge in the Project," she said neutrally.

Tayem's hand tightened around an untreated fence rail. "True. The information was hidden in the Plates. Somehow, when we changed history by saving Mlart, we changed other things so people learned to read the hidden stuff. After we change things back...we may have to check to make sure the hidden stuff stays secret after this."

"And if you don't change things back?"

"Then we'll have to adapt to a very different world." His head shook. "Nuclear wars. Most of the Teeps dead. Probably other disasters. Don't even think of that, Kylene."

She puzzled over that. "Must it be so bad?"

"Yes." He turned away from her.

She bit her lip, thinking. Could he learn some of the information held in the current future, just enough to teach the Algherans how to modify his body?

The redhead shrugged when she asked. "No such thing as a little dangerous knowledge, kid. Don't worry about it."

That line led nowhere. "Go back then," she suggested gently.

He misunderstood. "1970? I'd be an alien, all over again."

That was more evidence of his delusion, she realized soberly. Going back to the First Era would force him to recognize his abnormality, so he would never return.

"Fourth Era," she made herself say. "Third Era. Go to where the Plates were prepared and the knowledge is known. You must be able to return—you've done it before. Go there for help."

He shook his head sideways. "And risk killing the Fifth Era? The Algherans took me in, and that'd be a poor way to repay them."

"You'll grow old and die working for them," she protested. "You might as well be a slave."

"Men grow old. They die. Free or slave—all of them." Tayem shrugged, looking away from her again. "I should get back to this fence."

It was evening when Tayem came back to the cabin. A full moon was rising, two handbreadths over the horizon, and scattered stars were diamond points in the purpling sky. Kylene stood on the porch, her eyes closed, letting the pine-scented evening air brush past her. A distant splashing came from the pond; the beavers had returned.

Tayem came from the same direction, running, slowing to a walk as he neared the porch. His clothing was grass-stained; he breathed heavily and was sweat-soaked.

"Evening," he gasped before she could respond. Then he was past her and into the house. Discarded clothing cascaded against the wall opposite the bathroom door; she heard water splatter. Tayem was taking one of his showers.

Bread was heating inside the stove. Kylene stopped to smell the odor of rye and yeast, and to check the levels in the meat canisters. Then, satisfied that no peril or problem awaited, she absently copied the man's shrug and returned to the porch.

Tayem joined her shortly. He was wearing one of his green and black uniforms, as he had in her first memories of him. Red Bear, she found herself thinking. Clan Bear for him. She wondered if she'd had that thought before.

She had known him only a year, she remembered again. What a strange person to find in the middle of her Pilgrimage. How her children would wonder when she spoke of him! Her grandchildren. Great-grandchildren, long after Tayem had entered the mists. They would believe she told them fables; she hoped they would listen with the same pleasure she felt at bedtime under her mock gravity when Tayem told her of Cinderella and Little Red Riding Hood.

Once he had seemed so large and frightening, so sure and fearsome. Now he was only Tayem, a big, ungainly man awkwardly toweling his tangled hair beside her.

She smiled at him. "Sit down, Tayem. I'll dry your hair."

The redhead murmured a protest, which she ignored. She tugged the towel from his hand and pulled down on his shoulders till he was sitting on the edge of the porch.

Water had run down his neck. She dabbed at this with the towel, then used both her hands to dry his hair, pressing down till her fingers sensed the silver mesh resting on his scalp. The Teepblind—there could be no need of it in the wilderness; would he ever trust her enough to remove it? But she knew better than to ask.

"There," she said at last. She had no comb handy, so she used her fingers to rake his disheveled hair into place. "You're all taken care of now."

Perhaps he smiled. She wanted to think so. "Thanks," he said. "What would I do without you, Kylene?"

"Fend for yourself. Or die of a broken heart—as you promised."

"Or both? Careful, little girl, it'd be easy for me to get dependent on you. And—no future in that."

"No future," she agreed. "You need someone, Tayem."

He snorted. "As a keeper, you mean? No, I don't. I'm self-sufficient."

She hesitated, unsure as to whether she should continue. "Isn't that what you want?" she inquired finally, lightly.

Tayem paused before speaking. "Careful, Kylene," he said evenly. "Or you'll grow up to be a telepath."

There was nothing to say to that, and she let the silence continue.

"Finished with the corral," he said at last. "Then I figured I should run for a while. I'm getting out of shape."

"When will you get horses?"

"I'm holding my horses," he said dryly. "We don't need them yet, and looking after livestock is not my idea of fun."

She had watched him spend endless periods of time in uncomfortable positions working on the levcraft, emerging from underneath it covered with dirt and ill temper. Were horses so much worse? she wondered.

He snorted again. "Cimon, yes. Horses aren't natural. Machines are. All animals are unnatural, when you get down to it."

She stifled a smile. "Including human animals?"

"Especially them!"

She didn't argue with him. "I have a question. Horses still exist; what else does? Are there still dogs and cats?"

Tayem chuckled. "You begin to sound like another old-timer. Yes, there are still dogs around, and cats. Maybe not the same types you were used to, but you'd recognize them as dogs and cats. No space for them around the Project, which is why you haven't seen them, but people

still like to have pets. Dogs and cats have filled that role
pretty well, so there's never been any reason for them to
die out. Relieved?"

She had been more curious than concerned. "What else
is the same?"

The man shrugged. "I haven't made a survey, so I can't
say. Remember there have been some ice ages, since my
time and yours. Most of the sizable animals got pushed
south and haven't wandered back yet, or died off. Funny—
the other day I was wondering myself about rhinoceroses
and giraffes and lions and elephants. Those were sort of
exotic in my time, and I don't have any handle on whether
they survived."

She recognized none of the names.

"Come inside, then. I'll dig up some pictures."

"Welcome to my humble abode," he said shortly after.
"Sit on the bed, and I'll get the book."

Kylene obeyed, resting cross-legged on the narrow,
wall-mounted pallet. This bed was no better than what he
had been used to at the Project, she realized. She had
been occupying his real bed for more than one of the
Algheran seasons. He must be tired of that. But he had
not complained; she would not volunteer to trade rooms
with him. She looked about curiously.

The upper portion of the cabin incorporated two small
rooms, or rather one larger room split into halves by a
partition. Both were lined with red-colored wood panels.
The furniture was made of darker hardwood. The ceilings
had a broad inverted V slope, reaching close to the floor
along one side, so that there was headroom only near the
open space that served as a corridor. The staircase was
on the other side of the one true interior wall, which was
lined on this side by long rows of wooden shelving. This
room held Tayem's bed, a mirror, and chests for clothing.
A small window was at the head of the steps, directly
above the one in her room.

The farther room lacked an end wall, its place being

taken by a low balustrade, from which one could lean out and peer down at the main living area. Tayem called this section of the cabin "space for company." Lacking the need for guest space, he had installed a small desk, with one of the spindly canvas chairs and a plastic trash bucket to complete his office. A window had been cut through the redwood wall in this room; when Tayem was especially silent, Kylene had often glanced up from her own studies to see him peering through that, unmoving, contemplating she knew not what in the surrounding forest.

"Here we are," Tayem said, handing her a cloth-covered package, one of the hundreds of similar objects on his shelves. Kylene fumbled with the wrapper, looking for an opening, till he took it away again. "Here."

His thumb moved, splitting open the package from one side. Separate pages could be seen, as on a writing block with used but undiscarded pages. Printed lines lay before her, lying horizontally on the page. Tayem muttered irritably and riffled through the sheets of paper.

"There. That's a *rhino*."

"What?" she asked blankly.

"The picture," Tayem said impatiently. "The animal in it."

She shook her head. She could see no animal.

"Where is the picture?" she asked finally. The lines on this page were not the same as elsewhere, she could see, being sparser and longer and not arrayed in even, straight lines like others, but there was no image of an animal. Nor could she make out what Tayem referred to as shrubbery or a river. She told him so, with some asperity.

Tayem blew breath through his mouth and stared at her. "It's a sketch," he said. "A drawing. Not a viewscreen image. Does that make it clearer?"

It did not.

He sighed. "Afraid of that. I guess I have to teach you how to look at pictures too. That must be an acquired skill. All right." He folded up the package and put it back on its shelf, then moved into the next room to return with one much larger and more colorfully covered.

"Coffee-table book," he muttered. "Hello, little coffee table."

He sat beside her on the pallet and turned pages. "You are about to get a history of western *art*. First Era western *art*." His finger jabbed at the slick colored paper. "It starts with this bison—a type of cow. This is a *painting*, actually very large, made on a cave wall in the Mother continent a very long time before you or I was born, long before there was anything to point to and call 'the First Era.'"

She shook her head. She still did not understand him. But it was uncomfortable to be leaning over the book; she scooted sideways until she almost touched the man. Interestingly, the material on the pages stayed the same when she did that, rather than shifting, and no light source was needed to give the images being.

"Close your eyes," Tayem ordered. "Now open them, just a crack, so you can still see your eyelashes. Notice how blurred the world looks, as if you're looking through water? But you can still make things out and recognize them if you look hard, can't you? So—open 'em now. Look at this painting as being like that."

You smell nice, she thought. But it would be a mistake to say that. She nodded instead, pretending to pay attention.

His finger moved, pointing out details. "Here's the back of the animal; here's its tail. This is its head, tucked down, and its horns down here. These are its feet, raised up to the body as if it were jumping, or curled up dead. This black splotch is its back knee, this one on top is the hair along its backbone. The body is red—probably close to the color of the original bison. Squint again, focusing just on the animal. Ignore the background; or think of it as a dirt field on which the animal is lying. Do you see it now?"

There was something on the page he thought she should

notice; she understood that. "Maybe." But her voice lacked conviction.

Tayem glanced skyward and changed his approach. "Do you understand what I mean by art? Or painting?"

Happily she could answer that. "No."

The man sighed. "Everything with you is infinite regression, kid."

"I'm sorry," she said, puzzled by the words but responding to his tone.

"Ah, well . . . Don't be. Not your fault. Anyhow, art is concerned with making things that are nice to look at, or hear, or whatever."

She still did not understand.

"It's like decoration." He stood, causing her to feel faint disappointment, and turned about, seeming somehow indecisive. "Nothing here," he muttered. "Look— your buildings back at your home. Did they have carvings on them, to make them look prettier?"

It took effort to recall. "Some of them." Honesty surfaced. "I think."

Tayem grimaced sympathetically. "That's decoration. Now—imagine you had the carvings by themselves, not on the buildings."

"But carvings aren't supposed—" She stopped and gnawed at her lip. Sometimes boards were carved before they were placed into position. Was that a memory, or just a response to his question? She couldn't decide. But she could imagine what he had asked for. "All right."

"Would they be pretty by themselves?"

She remembered her village, with its drab buildings and muddy streets, the hungry dogs fighting for food scraps, an injured man limping before a storehouse, fatigue-worn elder women slumped on benches in their lodge. Nothing seemed pretty about it now. "Perhaps," she said slowly.

"That's art," he said simply. "Something designed to be pretty by itself, rather than to make something else pretty. Something solid, like the carvings, is called *sculp-*

ture. Something flat, like the pictures in the book, is painting. Or perhaps a *print*. Does that make sense?"

When she nodded, he returned to the pallet, turning sideways to pick up the book again. Kylene used the opportunity to move closer.

Fortunately, he did not notice. "Most art is a representation of something that already exists, like the images on a viewscreen. It's an abstraction—like this bison. You can't keep a real bison around to show people, but you can show them something that has the same outlines, the same color. It doesn't have a smell, or make noises, or any more of that good stuff, but a painting is better than nothing. Particularly since people use their eyes much more than their other senses. You follow me?"

Explaining things excited Tayem, she noticed, as if he were doing work he found enjoyable. His pleasant, musky odor became much more noticeable. She edged slightly closer. "But shouldn't a cow be bigger?"

Tayem sighed. "This is a small copy of a cow. Let's go on." Kylene struggled to repress a giggle, while his fingers scooped into the book's edge, pulled over a mass of bound paper. "This will do. What do you see?"

Outlines and color. "A horse," she guessed. "The front of a horse."

The man nodded. "Tell me about the horse."

She bit her lip, concentrating. "It's colored white." Tayem made a noncommittal sound. "It's rearing. And—and—it's surprised."

Tayem raised an eyebrow. "Why is that?"

He had not disagreed. That gave her the courage to continue. "It just seems that way," she explained seriously. "Its eye—that's why. The eye is too big. And it seems to be looking this way."

"Out of the page," Tayem agreed. "What else do you see?"

This was getting easier. "A man. A man or a woman—I can't tell."

Tayem grimaced. His voice was wry. "That's Napoleon

Bonaparte, crossing the Alps. You can assume he was a man."

"Oh. He has on a funny black and yellow hat. He has a long red cape wrapped around him. He's looking out of the page also. And his legs are brown—why is that?"

"Pants," Tayem corrected. "Notice the seam, where the fabric is hemmed together. The red-brown part under that is a boot. See the sword hilt? And the saddle? Okay— you're getting the hang of it."

He glanced at a wall clock. "Six and fractional five? No wonder I'm starving! Look at the book if you want; I'm going to fix supper."

CHAPTER SIX

"**S**oup's on," Tayem shouted.

She would go down in a moment, Kylene decided. Such funny pointed hats! People with raccoon masks and bright striped clothing, dancing. It was colorful, but what did it mean?

"Kylene. Supper." Tayem had come up the stairs.

"Just a moment, Tayem," she said plaintively.

"You've had several," he answered dryly. "Why don't you bring the book down with you?"

"Could I, please?" She looked up at him expectantly, holding the book to her chest.

Tayem gave her one of his lopsided smiles. "I can see I'm eating by myself tonight. Bring it down, kid. No—" He stopped as if a thought had struck him, and moved into the next room, returning with a marking tool. "Give that to me a bit."

Had he changed his mind? Kylene bit her lip but obeyed, watching unhappily while Tayem scrawled across the first page. Her heart lifted as he returned the book. He had even kept her place with a finger.

"A coffee-table book for Kylene Waterfall, even if she isn't one," he muttered hurriedly. "Given by Timothy Allan Harper."

He was at the head of the stairs before she could react. "For me?"

His hand waved. "Ah, I never did find time to read it." He seemed annoyed.

So strange, Kylene thought as he trotted down the steps. She closed the book—her book—carefully. It was filled with pictures; it would make no difference where she reopened it. And she was hungry.

Halfway to the stairs she stopped abruptly. The colored thing on the wall between two sections of shelving—that was a picture also. She had not noticed its details before. It was too large to come from her book; had Tayem removed it from another? A white and black thing with a dark sky behind. What could it be?

"Not a painting," Tayem told her after supper. "A *photograph*. A viewscreen image that never changes, to give a very accurate picture of something that really is, or was."

"But what is it?" she persisted. "It isn't very pretty. Why look at it if it is so ugly?"

Tayem exhaled loudly. "It reminds me of something," he said at last. "Something we did during the First Era and that you people never did. There's a man inside that white suit. His name was Buzz Aldrin, and he was standing on the moon."

She misheard the last word. "Where is that?" she asked.

"The moon," Tayem repeated. Exasperation sounded in his voice. "You know, the one up in the sky?"

He was being strange again. Was he being season-taken again? Kylene stared at him, and wondered how to calm the man.

"Here, put the book down. Come with me." Tayem

tugged her to the front of the cabin, pushing a switch that turned off the cabin lights. As they stepped onto the porch Kylene was blind in the comparative darkness; then her pupils adjusted to the light and she could see shapes once more.

Like one of the uncolored pictures, she recognized with pleasure. Form only, without color. She had skipped over those pages in the book, unable to understand them. Now that she had gained this insight, they made more sense. When Tayem released her, she would look at them again.

"That moon," Tayem said proudly, his chin pointed high. "Ours."

Once before he had made her look at the moon at night, through the bulky, eyesight-magnifying machines he called binoculars. She knew it was more than a friendly light in the sky; she knew it was not perfectly round or evenly lit, and that it would appear rough and pitted when it swelled to apple size in her vision.

"What of it?" she asked.

"I told you. We put a man on it—a dozen men."

"So?" It was a place in the sky, he had explained to her. The Algherans had machines that took people into the sky. It had seemed magical at first, but she had adjusted to that. Why was it so important to know that his people could do the same thing?

Her bewilderment must have shown. "Don't you understand what an accomplishment it was?"

Hurt tinged his voice, making her unwilling to speak. She pursed her lips and shook her head sideways, repeating the gesture he used to mean no.

Tayem made the same motion. "Well, it was. But if you aren't impressed, you aren't impressed. Let's go back in."

A fire would be comforting, she sensed. It would serve to distract him. She asked if they could have one.

"Sure." He smiled ruefully at her.

A spark popped. Kylene looked up from the pages of her book at the sound and stared toward the fire, watching Tayem kneel at the hearth to poke at the flames. The fire crackled; she could feel its warmth from where she lay.

She pushed the book aside, rolling over on the small rug and arching back her neck to continue watching the man. Now she had put Tayem upside down, she reflected. She could turn him sideways. In a sense, she was controlling him. The thought was pleasant.

Scraping sounds. Tayem was pushing ashes into the trap. His back was shadowed and black; the red and yellow flames darkened the front of his green tunic as well. He concentrated on his sweeping, ignoring her.

She rolled over again. She had had a bizarre thought. "Tayem."

He murmured at her. So he was listening.

"You spoke of leaving the earth. Are there—could there be—other people who did that? Or who don't live here?"

To her relief, he did not laugh. "Sure," he told her. "The tiMantha lu Duois, if they existed, probably were from off-world."

She tried to remember. Funny sharp faces, fur-covered, somehow connected with Cimon and Nicole in the strange Algheran religion—she could recall nothing else. "I didn't know they were real," she admitted.

The redhead laid his fire-blackened stick in the ashes and turned toward her. "The tiMantha lu Duois who are gone now were our brothers in the stars. They came to earth in vessels powered by unseen fires to make new homes among us. Honor the tiMantha lu Duois. Never let the friends of man be forgotten."

His voice was singsong, and she realized that he was reciting from memory.

"Liturgy," he explained. "Pagan, but it gets pounded into you eventually by repetition. Anyhow, if the stories make any sense, you have to assume the tiMantha lu Duois were *extraterrestrials*—from off the earth. Since they made just the one trip, they probably came from outside this solar system, and since they stayed, their ship must have needed repairs it never got. There probably never were a lot of them, so as time passed on, they went with it. Long, long ago—although not as far back as you and I came from."

Was he leaving something out? "Why should they be remembered?"

"How did they end up as minor deities? Don't you know the story? They won the First Eternal War for the Normals."

But that meant little to her also. She shook her head again.

Tayem was startled. "Good thing you told me. You have to learn that story till you're letter perfect at it. Everyone knows it. It's—" He smiled ironically. "It's bred into people."

"Not into me."

He repeated the smile. "Oh, I know. But this is mostly stuff that's recorded on the Plates. It's history, or at least treated that way, and some parts of it I'm willing to believe. Listen, and I'll summarize. Come here." He took his fire-charred stick from the hearth, drew the tip across the floor, making a black streak across the width of a flag-stone, then marked it with his fingertip.

"We'll use my numbers," he commented. "Most of them are guesses, but the dates other people suggest are worse guesses. So . . . This end is the Present, at roughly 92,000. Way back here, at call it Minus 50,000, is where my part of the human race got its start."

Human history was a record of mankind's inability to control climate and a recessive gene. Viewed in sufficient perspective, all other considerations could be seen as trivial.

Climate first—Man's forebears had existed before the Pleistocene, but all his subsequent existence was encompassed within its two-and-a-half million years. This was a cool epoch, on the average; it was one of several periods when the planet had ice ages.

The vast continental glaciers did more than scour the land; forcing him to flee from one environment to another, and to adapt or perish, they created Man. Fifty thousand years before Harper's birth, *Homo sapiens* appeared, shouldering aside his brother *Homo neanderthalensis*. When the ice receded forty thousand years later, man in his modern form lived everywhere on Earth but its poles. But a migratory, hunting lifestyle was not practical everywhere for him, or perhaps climatic change had opened a new evolutionary niche; men began to farm, to domesticate animals, to invent cities, to multiply.

When Tim Harper vanished from 1970, the world held four billion people.

Three thousand years later, it held ten million. These people had life spans three centuries longer than the men of 1970. And one in a hundred was a telepath.

"No one knows why," Tayem told Kylene. "So much time has gone by, it's just taken for granted. Some people see into minds; they may live a bit longer than those who don't; they may have larger families. The trait is recessive, so telepaths prefer to marry telepaths and give their abilities to their children, but now and then nontelepaths have mind-reading children."

"What happens then?" Kylene asked when he hesitated.

"It's seen as a terrible embarrassment, even in Chelmmys. Old notions die hard, and genetics is a fairly new science—easier for most people to assume someone's sins are being punished. The ability shows up in early adolescence, when the kid has a lot of his social attitudes already determined, and the parents have all of theirs, so it can be a bit rough. The kid gets tossed out of his birth Sept with as little publicity as possible, and everyone tries to pretend little Johnny was never in Dicovys or whatever, but was always an orphan in R'sihuc or Nyjuc. Fortunately, it's rare."

Telepathy might have been a chance mutation, but Tayem would not believe it. The First Era geneticists had spoken of reengineering the species someday—why not assume they had done so? Suppose by A.D. 4000 it had become obvious that the world was headed for another ice age? A snow-girded planet could not house billions of people. But if the population were halved, to allow maintenance of the same living standards, then halved again, and again...

A longer life traded against lower fertility: that was his guess.

Perhaps it had happened too slowly, for Kylene's world of A.D. 5000 had been a barbarian one. No records of a global civilization remained; even the cities had vanished. The First Era was over in Kylene's day; the Second had not yet been born.

"Fifty-two chromosomes," Tayem mused. "A brute-force technique, I bet, but it worked."

Forty-six, she remembered. She nodded, but did not speak.

If the information in the chromosomes were changed, eventually different people would appear, raising different children. Long life could be such a difference. So could telepathy.

"Too Cimon-taken clever to be chance," he explained. "Most spontaneous mutations are bad, and the people who get them drop dead. Particularly if the change is a major one. But telepathy might have been deliberately engineered to spread."

A recessive trait, he said again. That meant telepaths could be born anywhere, in any family. It did not appear until adolescence. "And teenagers are big enough to get by on their own, if need be. Also, sort of a bonus, it lets you develop a personality of your own, so you can be individual people, rather than some kind of human ant."

Telepaths had a longer life span—"Barely noticeable, until you look at the statistics"—and a slightly higher rate of fertility. Given enough time, only "dumb luck or stupidity" would keep them from taking over the world.

"Did we ever try?" Kylene asked. He seemed to be expecting such a question from her.

Tayem nodded. "Oh, yeah! You sure did. Made it too."

The Skyborne. Kylene had heard the phrase, had known others to refer to her with that title. An unfriendly epithet, she had thought.

"No one knows where the name came from," Tayem admitted. "It's used in the oldest of the Chronicles, mostly, and it seems to have been old even then. It's definitely one that has stuck in people's heads."

The Skyborne were the citizens, or perhaps the aristocrats, of Kh'taal Minzaer. They were telepaths. And Kh'taal Minzaer had ruled the world.

"They probably started small," Tayem said. "Even with their advantages it would have taken a long while for their population to grow till they had enough people for a small city. Probably the population went up mostly because of people like you, who simply wanted to live with other telepaths. And maybe they didn't even set out to build an empire."

Merchants, politicians, or useful slaves—it would have made no difference to the outcome. Telepaths had an advantage in dealing with nontelepaths, they shared a common community, and their numbers increased steadily. By A.D. 10,000, people from Kylene's "City of Silence" dominated human existence. Power turned to rule.

"Perhaps it was a good thing," Tayem admitted. "Winters were already rough in your time, and they got a lot worse. All across the north of this and the Mother continents, the winters went on without stopping for maybe twenty thousand years. Things didn't really collapse, though, and the population kept going up till it hit the fifty million mark—right where it is now. Maybe the Skyborne were responsible for holding things together."

But precisely what role they had filled, no one knew. They ruled; history had recorded little more.

"Somewhere in the middle of this—15,000 for want of a better date—the Skyborne screwed up. Maybe they put taxes too high. Maybe they acted too high-handed. And someone revolted. His name was Cimon."

His wife's name was Nicole.

"They lost," Tayem said simply. "The books say there wasn't a real battle—just a massacre. And Cimon and Nicole were executed by the Skyborne." He stopped abruptly.

Kylene bit her lip. "Go on," she urged.

"Uh, it's a sad story, so I'll let the details ride. It's all written down in the Chronicles, and you'll get to it someday. People used to think that marked the start of the Long Count calendar, but it was later, actually. Anyhow, that started a real war."

The First Eternal War lasted twelve thousand years.

"A reasonably long time," Tayem said dryly. "Even by the standards for wars in my time."

Fighting would not have been continuous, he explained. "Mostly, I suspect, it was a batch of little revolts, which all got squashed quickly enough. A town might refuse to pay taxes for a while; Kh'taal Minzaer would send in troops; a garrison would stick around till the taxes were paid. A low-key guerrilla war. Population was too small to allow for big armies to be formed. And that was an ice age—I doubt the social surplus was there to support many fighting men. Advanced technology was probably lacking; reading between the lines, I get the impression civilization got near to toppling a couple times, probably just because of climate problems. I suspect the Skyborne spread themselves too thin—they couldn't breed soldiers fast enough to chink up all the gaps, but they probably kept trying anyhow."

The war had been waged indecisively for millennia. Then the ice began to retreat. Suddenly the Normals found new lands to move into; the Skyborne found themselves with more territory to police. The tide of history flowed away from the telepaths.

"They got desperate," Tayem summarized. "Bigger weapons, more powerful. Harsher reprisals, heavier taxes. More revolts, so things got worse, and more revolts because of the methods used to quash revolts."

It was perhaps A.D. 25,000 when the tiMantha lu Duois arrived.

"We don't know much about them either. They aren't mentioned in the Chronicles, as far as I can tell, but references pop up here and there in some of the other Plates.

"Anyhow, they decided to stay on Earth, for some reason, and they sided with the Normals. A few years later the Eternal War was over."

Tayem stood and left the room for the kitchen. "It is customary to credit the tiMantha lu Duois for that." Light showed over the counter; Tayem had opened a food locker. He returned with tall glasses in each hand and gave one to Kylene. "Sip this. And I want you to bed early tonight."

The glass was two-thirds filled with ice cubes, covered by a clear fluid with a musty odor and an almost familiar taste, sharp and raw, which made tears come to her eyes. "Your beer has gone bad, Tayem."

"*Scotch*," he corrected. "A fair approximation. Choke it down, kid."

A medicine, she guessed. Its purpose was unfamiliar, but the man seemed to think she required it. He had moved to sit near the fire, and was drinking it himself, a morose expression on his face. Perhaps he would explain this shortly. She swallowed the fluid then, slowly, nearly gagging, and carefully set the glass aside as Tayem watched impassively. Her throat felt seared; something firelike radiated heat within her stomach. The medicine? "Is there a reason for this?"

"It kills time." His face twitched with a short-lived smile. "I can see I don't need a lock on the liquor cabinet. Just as well."

"The war," she reminded him. "You were talking about the war."

"Yeah." But he hesitated before speaking. "Your city—Kh'taal Minzaer apparently held three to four hundred thousand people at the end of the war. When they surrendered."

She nodded politely. "Yes?"

"There was a *pogrom*, Kylene," he said gently.

The word meant nothing to her. She watched blankly while the man tossed off the final half of his Scotch and toyed aimlessly with the empty glass.

"Stories again," he said reflectively. "Twenty or thirty thousand survivors, when the tiMantha lu Duois stopped things." He stood and picked up both glasses, took them to the kitchen for cleaning in the morning. "God only knows what they thought of their human allies by then. Maybe it affected the wording—they're supposed to have written the treaty everyone had to agree to."

Her head had swollen a small amount, and it would be best to move it carefully, Kylene realized. Tayem was hinting at something, but typically he was being overly subtle. It would be embarrassing to admit that she had not understood; she would keep her silence until his remarks made sense.

His voice was singsong; he was quoting. "'To end eternal war, it is agreed by the telepaths and normal men that never again shall telepaths establish a separate state and exercise their dominion over men. This Compact shall be preserved by the thoughts and actions of both human races and witnessed by the tiMantha lu Duois. The penalty for violation, in thought or action, shall be death.'"

The Teeps at the Station had repeated the same remarks, Kylene recalled. She nodded gravely, closing her eyes momentarily to help them focus.

Tayem sat by the fireplace again, and looked at her with a show of concern. "Get used to the idea. Learn that quote, if you haven't already. Remember that everyone means it."

He was lecturing her, she realized. She preferred him to be subtle. "Yes, Tayem. What happened next?"

The big redhead made a humming sound. "No matter—we did not all live happily ever after."

Men guessed at the existence of a First Era, called the rule of Kh'taal Minzaer the Second Era, and declared that they had entered a Third Era.

Two thousand years later, that civilization had collapsed.

"The ice came back," Tayem said. "Squabbling over resources started all over, or so the stories suggest. The telepaths didn't help."

"Why not? Did they break your unbreakable Compact? And what did you Normals do about it this time? Ask someone else for help?" Her voice probably sounded insolent, but Kylene didn't care. She wasn't surprised to hear that nontelepaths ran things incompetently—certainly not with the Algherans as examples—and she wasn't going to pretend otherwise to protect Tayem's feelings.

Tayem raised an eyebrow. "No. The Teeps obeyed the Compact. They spread over the world, and settled in, and tried to be good local citizens. But they had this little gift, remember, which no one else was willing to forget. So they found themselves working for Normal governments, and each state tried to get more and more of them, to figure out advantages over their neighbors. So the Teeps became very important people again. They took to pulling strings behind the scenes. And eventually it led to more wars. The worse the weather got, the more intense the fighting got. People—and countries—took bigger and bigger risks. And the whole Cimon-taken house of cards fell down."

He shrugged, his feelings apparently unharmed. "So much for the Third Era. After that came a long dull period. The tiMantha lu Duois died off somewhere in the middle of it, but that's all anyone recalls."

He used his stick to etch another line on the floor.

"Around 60,000 things started up again. Telepaths were involved once more. They decided to build themselves another city, and got a jump on it before anyone realized what they were up to—after all, conditions were pretty barbaric just about everywhere. The climate was on their side this time; another ice age had gotten going."

Good. "Did we take over the world again?" Kylene asked.

"You did not," Tayem said decisively. "When the Normals did find out about it, they were not pleased. In fact, they started another war. The Plates stop around here, but it seems the Normals won on their own hook."

"Oh." *Disappointing.*

"Oh," Tayem echoed ironically. "We believe the Normals won, anyhow. And since one of their war aims was getting the Teeps to agree to the second Compact, it's generally believed that it was accepted. But there isn't any hard evidence, just more myths that can be twisted to fit that theory. That's what Onnul told me anyway. There certainly was one *hell* of a war—I can testify to that—but I didn't stick around long enough to find out when it started or stopped, or even who was in it. Anyhow—"

The response to the war and the weather brought technology, spurring industrialization, which made possible population increases, and an increased demand for resources, which led to additional warfare.

"A spiral," Tayem commented, wagging his hand to illustrate. "Things went up and up and up. Soon everyone was civilized again so they decided they were living in a Fourth Era and that they were fighting a Second Eternal War. This lasted for three or four thousand years.

"Or more. Some of the sets of Plates indicate one number, others another. Maybe the war ended about that time, maybe it lasted much longer, but we don't know. Finally the telepaths lost, though—people remembered Kh'taal Minzaer too well not to cooperate this time, and that

included Teeps who figured separatism was a bad idea.
So it was probably a short war, as eternal things go."

A war, Kylene thought. Tayem had mentioned a war,
and even though she had been staring directly at him, she
had lost track of what he was saying when he mentioned
that dead woman. She grimaced and made herself speak.
"How did it end?"

"Peaceably, it appears from the myths. Probably a
negotiated settlement proclaimed as a great victory. And
another Compact." Tayem had not noticed her confusion,
but closed his eyes shortly and quoted. "'To end the Second Eternal War, the Great Compact is reaffirmed by the
Teeps and the Normals. It is also agreed by the Teeps and
the Normals that never again shall Teeps employ their
abilities in the service of national states and thus exercise
their dominion over men. This Compact shall be preserved by the thoughts and actions of both human races
and witnessed by the spirit of the tiMantha lu Duois. The
penalty for violation, in thought or action, shall be death.'"

He snorted. "Aimed more at what happened in the
Third Era than the fourth. No matter—you have to mem-
orize it too. Then, judging by the myths, the Normals all
decided the telepaths had been dealt with and that there'd
be no more problems. But the ice kept coming on, and
they kept squabbling among themselves, and after a short
while the whole kit-and-kaboodle fell down again. So much
for the Fourth Era."

His finger moved, smearing another ash mark near
the end of the original line. "Dark ages again, including
where we are now. Somewhere on the other side of this
line people got back into the city-building business, and
we can call that the Fifth Era. Make that 90,000 or so,
and make the Present be 92,000. And right in the middle
is Hemmendur."

"I've heard of him!" Kylene said incautiously. "He
founded the Alliance. And he said—he said—'the Teeps
are entitled to a role in human affairs.'"

"Very good, little girl," Tayem said sarcastically. "Did you learn that speech in the Teep dormitory?"

She had displeased him, she realized. She nodded gravely, then shook her head the other way when he asked her to recite the rest of it.

"So I will," he said somberly. "'We have observed that neither Compact prohibits the employment of the Teeps, in whole or in part, in any role whatsoever, by a single all-encompassing world state. I suggest to you that such a state must ultimately arise. By its nature, it will be everlasting and unopposable. I suggest as well that, given that inevitability, we attempt ourselves to give birth to that state and shape its growth. If our intentions are worthy, our actions honorable, and our ambitions steadfast, we shall be successful, for we shall gain strong allies. Not the least of these will be the Teeps, who are entitled to a role in human affairs, and for whom I propose a most sacred responsibility—which is to ensure that men exercise no dominion over men...'"

It sounded familiar. Kylene hesitated, then asked, "Is that wrong?"

"Yes." Flatly. "I don't care how good his intentions were. He set out to build a totalitarian state, he succeeded, and it took over the world. My era saw a whole batch of would-be world empires, and they stunk! Every single one of them."

Kylene closed her eyes, trying to concentrate against growing nausea. "Is Chelmmys so bad?"

"Not yet."

It still sounded like such a good idea. "They've got the Teeps." That was half a statement, half a question.

"That means they've got a secret police," Tayem said sourly. "That's all it boils down to. Power corrupts, Kylene, and absolute power corrupts absolutely—a First Era saying, but it'll never go out of date."

She was feeling tired, so she let her head slump downward and closed her eyes. "You just want to argue," she mumbled. "You don't care what I say."

"I don't care if you're wrong," she heard him say.

She did not want to argue, she decided. It was not worth the effort and Tayem would not be convinced in any event. He was happy with opinions he already had. *Never talk to the Normals about their politics*, she remembered. That was said constantly in the kennel; arguing with Tayem had given her some of the cynical wisdom of the Algheran Teeps.

But it was more than cynicism, she realized now. It was an echo of the Second Compact. *The penalty for violation . . . shall be death*. Would Tayem kill her if she were to violate a Compact, or if he thought she had?

Yes. He means well. He doesn't worship every little thing the Algherans do, and he tries to make the Algherans bend some. But I can't see into his mind, and I don't dare push. And I can't take the risk of breaking the Compacts just part of the time, lest unfriendly Normals find out about it.

Was she a slave, to be casually killed if she said the wrong thing?

Yes. A slave, or a prisoner. And Tayem Minstrel was her jailer, as earlier he had been her captor. Now he was trying to make her obedient.

She would not let that happen!

"A penny for your thoughts," Tayem said, breaking the silence.

She was tired. That was affecting her coordination, but she got to her feet on a second try and stared at him insolently, leaving one eye closed. "I'm not allowed to have any," she snapped.

"That's just silly," he started to say, but she ignored him. She was sleepy and he was keeping her awake; she slammed the door of her bedroom behind her, then fell facedown on the bed and yawned deeply. Her stomach was rolling, she noticed. She would breathe heavily to let it settle, then get undressed for bed.

"Kylene, what's the matter?" he called at her. "Please?"

He knocked on the door frame. "What's the matter? Kylene?"

Why wouldn't he let her get her sleep? "Go away!" she shouted finally. "Freak! Leave me alone! Go away with your Onnul and die!"

After a long while, she heard his footsteps going away. He had said not another word.

She did not sleep well that night.

Part 2: Landscapes—Chiaroscuro

Kylene Waterfall, 45,413 L.C.

CHAPTER SEVEN

A knock on her doorway, rousing her from half sleep. Then a voice said, "Rise and shine, kid. It's morning." Tayem's voice.

Kylene shook her head and rolled onto her stomach to force herself into wakefulness. A heating duct pushed warm air across her bare back as bedclothes fell to the side. She groped without success for blankets, then squirmed onto her knees to look out the back window. It was a dreary morning, she decided, and would probably lead to a dreary day. Beads of water on the glass showed that rain had fallen most of the night; gray skies and mists indicated that drizzle continued. Even the grass seemed gray-tinted, and a patch of bare soil near the cabin gleamed slickly. *Spring.*

"Kylene!" Tayem again.

"I'm awake," she called back. "Just a moment." Tayem had let her oversleep, she realized, even though she had chores to do. She did not want to go outside in this weather.

For an instant she toyed with the idea of being ill; maybe Tayem would feed the horses then.

But it was too late to try that. Besides, he would only make her swallow pills and tell her she'd feel better soon; *flu-and-colds* were a First Era luxury she wasn't allowed to have. She'd tried it before.

He would probably also remind her that getting the horses before they were needed was her "bright idea," not his own, and that she had willingly agreed to look after them.

She sighed. It wasn't possible to win arguments with Tayem.

If cleverness would not work, perhaps he would be nice for the sake of being nice. Which meant she should be polite to him, so that the idea would suggest itself. "I'm coming," she called out politely.

Tayem could not see into her mind. He sounded satisfied. "Breakfast is on the table. See you there."

So one of us is happy. She shook her head, then kicked aside the bed covers, letting them fall all the way to the floor without attempting to straighten them. Tayem would not approve, so she would have to make the bed before breakfast. And she would wear a green dress to please him. But first, she had to take a totally unnecessary bath.

"Good morning, sleepyhead," Tayem said from the side of the kitchen. He seemed extremely pleased with himself.

Kylene eyed him suspiciously. It was unusual for Tayem to be inside at this time of day, even in bad weather, and it was doubly unusual to find him barefoot, with a white cloth around the top of his jeans. But here he was, plaid-shirted, leaning against the food locker and stirring the contents of a large yellow bowl held in the crook of his arm. A red squirrel perched on the window ledge, its nose against the glass, sufficiently bemused by the sight to ignore its water-bedraggled coat. For an instant, she felt sympathy.

She closed her eyes, reaching out. Then she snorted. The squirrel was female, well shielded from the blustering wind, comfortably fed, blandly confident that the big clumsy animals inside this strange tree would offer her more food. *Squirrels!*

Breakfast *was* on the table, she noticed. Cold juice, a steaming slab of sweetbread coated with Tayem's *marmalade*—he must have placed it in the oven while she was in the bathtub. He was being considerate.

The table held no meal waiting for him but a half-filled coffee cup rested on the counter between the kitchen and the front room. Evidently he had eaten already, but dressed as he was, he was not planning to go outside soon. She sighed inwardly.

She noticed something else. "You're using Speech," she said irritably. "I thought we had to use that other language."

The other language was, according to Tayem, called Lopritian, and for most of the past season he had allowed conversation only in that tongue rather than the one used by the Algherans, reinforcing her training by refusing to speak to her and making her fix her own meals when she reverted to Speech, or when he was dissatisfied with her progress.

The big redhead ladled the contents of the bowl into a broad rectangular pan and slipped that into the oven. The mixture was a gray-brown substance, she saw, fluid-seeming as river-bottom ooze. Was he experimenting again?

A horse's neigh sounded faintly through the open front door, causing her to grab angrily at the sweetbread. She would have to hurry. Her brow wrinkled at the thought and she rubbed her palm across her forehead.

The green plaque was still gone. And that was Tayem's doing also.

"Holiday," Tayem said finally, as if the single word solved all problems. "I decided I owed myself a *birthday*."

He smiled at the squirrel on the window ledge and tapped the glass to make it sit up. "How's your head?"

Another strange word. But if he could use Speech for this conversation, she could also. "All right," she admitted. "I don't have a headache this morning. I can go back to studying—but don't I need to feed the horses first?" That was a hint; she waited for his reaction.

Surprisingly, it worked. "Holiday," Tayem repeated with a shrug. "No work unless you want to. Anyhow, I already took care of the chores."

She rubbed her forehead again. No work? No study? She was pleased by that, just as she was pleased to be rid of the plaque, but she had spent most of a ten-day period recovering from what Tayem had labeled "minor surgery." He had given in to her unspoken request too easily; memory made her suspicious of his gifts, and she frowned once more.

The redhead gave her a lopsided grin. "No operation today, honest."

Not for the first time, Kylene wondered if he was secretly a Teep. But no, she could see his Teepblind under his shaggy hair; if his mind could not be seen into, he could not be seeing into hers.

"You're planning something," she said warily. "I can tell it."

Tayem poured powders into a small container. One of them was sugar. She noticed that with interest and watched expectantly as he added water. Perhaps he would let her lick the liner when he was through.

"Not much of a discovery," he chided. He put the container into the food locker, leaning against the counter, and grinned at her. "I'm always planning *something*."

"Yes," she said dourly. Her sweetbread was gone now. She drew her finger over the rectangular plate and scooped up drops of *marmalade*. Such a nice tart sweetness. Tayem had said this jar was his last and that he would not be replacing it. She hoped he would change his mind. "More?"

"More what?"

Tayem was at his games again. "More sweetbread? Please."

"You'll get fat." That was another of his games.

"No, I won't. I'm hungry."

"Well . . . all right." Tayem was already moving, sliding long strips of sweetbread into a food processor. He had cut extra portions already, she realized. "Long as you're a groaning little girl."

He raised the window, knocking the squirrel off the ledge, and tossed a scrap of sweetbread after it, then peered out at the ground. "Surrounded by greedy little beasties today." He seemed pleased. "Mind if I join you? I could stand a piece of *toast* myself."

"I'm surrounded by huge greedy beasties," Kylene told him.

"Huh?"

"Sit down, Tayem."

"I was going to anyway."

"I was going to anyway," she said simultaneously. She knew when this line was coming.

"Careful, Kylene—"

"—or you'll grow up to be a telepath."

"Caught you that time," Tayem said with satisfaction. "Didn't finish it." He poked a spoon into the *marmalade* jar, then frowned as the utensil tapped against the bottom. "We are entering barbarism," he muttered. "Here, hold out your *toast*."

The last scoop from the jar fell onto her sweetbread. "Don't you want it?" she made herself ask. *Say you don't*, she urged silently.

Tayem shrugged. "Yours." He picked up the white jar and contemplated it momentarily. *"Ladies of Spain—Laddies o' Scotland—we salute thee."* His singing almost sounded musical. Fortunately it soon ended.

The jar shot across the room, hit the lid on the disposal chute, and vanished from sight with a clatter. "Two points," the man said obscurely. "So much for the last *Saville* orange."

Kylene licked *marmalade* from her upper lip. "You still have the red spread," she reminded him.

"That's true. I should have gotten you hooked on strawberry jam instead of the good stuff. But I guess—"

Kylene slapped hands against her chest, mimicking Tayem's already exaggerated gestures, raising her head toward the ceiling exactly as he did. "Some things are just not meant to be," she echoed lugubriously.

"Careful, Kylene," he said calmly. "You'll grow up to be a telepath."

"It's too late. I already did."

"Hmmmm." He nodded. "Still some growing to do. But you're getting there."

Slapping her chest as Tayem had done had not produced the same sound—of course she was getting there. "I've had such a good teacher," she said blandly. "At *periods*, anyhow."

He had not expected her use of a First Era word, and when he understood her, he reddened. "You'll have real problems growing any more if I strangle you," he growled. "That was a *damn fool* stunt to play."

He had spanked her for it. "But it was very funny, Tayem."

He stayed red. "Not for me."

She reached out, stroked the back of his hand, conscious of the red-gold hairs bending under her fingers and the minute occasional freckles so much less noticeable than her own. "Poor humorless Tayem."

The hand moved away. "It was not that funny."

"Are you still mad at me?" she asked. "Are you going to leave me alone again?"

"Don't tempt me. Not till after breakfast, anyhow. Child." The last word was clearly an afterthought, intended to provoke.

"But I can't be a child," she said innocently. "Why else would I—"

"Kylene!"

"—have needed you to show me how to put in—"

"Cimon take it!"

"—those funny little paper plugs to stop the bleeding?" She finished with a chortled rush of words. "Oh, thank you, Tayem!"

Tayem glared at her. "It was *not* funny. It was the middle of winter and the weather was lousy, and I had to go two thousand years uptime for something you already had a stock of, and on top of it, you decided to play that stupid Cimon-taken prank!" He stood abruptly and stalked back into the kitchen, not looking at her.

Kylene giggled. "You were *so* serious! And *so* worried, and *so* helpful!"

"Well, I was worried," the big man said sourly, his back turned. "A first time . . ." He kept his face away from her, staring at the top of the food processing unit as if expecting it to attack him.

"And you were *so* silly-looking when I asked you to help put it in!" Remembering, she collapsed into giggles again. "Thank you, Tayem!"

"It wasn't funny," Tayem insisted doggedly.

But it had been. And next year he would be just as silly, she was sure. She kept on giggling, then broke into laughter as the squirrel returned expectantly to the windowsill and stared adoringly at the man.

Tayem marched past her, deliberately and uselessly pounding the flagstone floor with his bare feet. The front door slammed.

So funny! And so touchy. She stopped laughing then, wheezing.

He *had* left her by herself. "Cimon and Nicole," she muttered. She sighed and remained seated.

And he had left her alone the ten-day before the bleeding began, fleeing uptime when she confessed that curiosity about sex was becoming an obsession that made study impossible. He had understood before she had that she was season-taken.

He had left her alone. At the time, it had been impossible to forgive.

The front door moved again. Tayem had returned.

He wore a green and black uniform now; his hair was neatly cropped.

"Good morning, Kylene," he said pleasantly. "Still so amused?" He stepped past the table into the kitchen and opened the oven door. "This should be done by now." One hand slapped at control buttons; the other used a fabric pad to pull out the rectangular pan. He flicked a finger at the window, dismissing the squirrel.

"How long were you gone this time?" she asked tonelessly.

"Not much. A year tenth, two." Tayem pushed things inside the food locker with his forearm, making room for the pan. "Getting lazy," he commented absently. Then he was past her, on his way up the stairs.

When he returned he was wearing jeans again, with a brown shirt and low-cut shoes. A writing block was in his hand.

"Sit here," she said. She was still at the table, but she had skimmed the outer skins from the plates and put the clean dishes back in their cabinets and wiped the table. "Do you want coffee?"

"No, make it stretch," Tayem said absently. He sat at the table and manipulated knobs on the writing block, then began marking symbols on the narrow lines with a scribe, ignoring her eyes. "Finish eating, while I get *organized*."

A First Era word, she guessed. She wondered offhandedly if there was an Algheran word for the concept that he simply did not know, or if he was forced to use his native language for First Era activities that were meaningless in other cultures. Probably the latter; Tayem was fluent in several important Fifth Era tongues.

"You're killing yourself," she said, trying to keep her voice level.

"Hmmm?" Tayem looked up. "What was that?"

"You heard me."

The big man shrugged. "I'm still breathing. Must not be doing a very good job of it."

"'A year tenth, two,'" she quoted back at him. "You're doing a fine job of it, Tayem."

He looked at her steadily, politely, unspeaking.

"How old are you, Tayem? Now?"

A smile flickered. "Old enough not to play word games with little girls."

"Be serious!"

Tayem frowned at her, then shrugged again. "Thirty-four years old. Two tenths. Give or take five or six days. That's reasonably exact." His eyes dropped back to his writing block. He had not asked why she wondered about his age.

She would explain anyhow. "How old were you when—"

Tayem sighed loudly. "I am two years and six-tenths older than when we left the Project. Satisfied?"

"I am a year and one-tenth older," she said earnestly.

Tayem glanced rapidly at her, then back to his writing. *"Bully for you."*

"Tayem!"

"What is it, Kylene?" He sounded impatient.

"You're ignoring me."

He gave her a sardonic smile. "No, I'm not. Just trying to."

"Well, don't. Listen to me."

He shook his head. "I can see where this lecture is going, and I won't listen to it. Now, whether you believe it or not, I got some useful work done while I was gone. I followed Mlart's last campaign, so I know exactly where he was and when, and that's one job out of the way. Now I'm figuring out what's needed for another job, and I don't want interruptions."

"But, Tayem—"

"Don't argue, Kylene. It'll be a nice day yet—go out for a walk and work off some of your cabin fever."

She stared at him hopelessly and tried to take the words

in her mind and push them into his. It did not work, as
it never worked, but somehow she could never manage
to speak the words that needed to be spoken. So she left
the cabin soundlessly and stumbled along the damp pathway toward the horses and the words went with her.

*I wanted to hug him and tell him I appreciated him
and he got mad before I could do it and went away and
when he came back we were strangers again...with
strands of hair turned gray and lines etched over his forehead...little by little, he makes himself older and older
and closer to that too-early death as if he wants nothing
else and he knows what he is doing to himself and he
does it anyhow...Tayem!*

Then she was through the section of woods and nearing
the corral—Tayem's corral, where they had argued once
before. What had they argued about? Death and dying,
she remembered as she leaned against the rock-hard fencing. All her arguments with Tayem made her think of that.
It wasn't *fair* for him to age so rapidly and to die so young;
it wasn't fair to—to anyone else. But it would happen
regardless, and he was making it worse.

Poor doomed Tayem.

She wanted to cry for him, but the tears would not
come. She was left with an ache in her chest that did not
go away even when she ceased to hug herself against the
railing.

Tayem's gold-brown gelding and her roan mare came
to her then and nuzzled her outstretched hands, looking
for another bite of oats or a cube of sugar. There was
nothing for them to find, so they stared at her with their
heads turned sideways as if embarrassed, then ambled to
the far end of the corral and left her all alone.

As Tayem was all alone.

What would have happened if he had remained in the
cabin while she was season-taken?

She was still by the corral a day tenth later when he
came to tell her to pack for a trip that would begin that
afternoon.

The rain returned, a fine cold drizzle that filled the air like fog, but Tayem did not change his plans. They were beyond sight of the cabin and deep into the forest even before the invisible sun could reach its maximum height.

There was no trail to follow, but the trees were tall there and spaced far apart. The ground was firm enough under its cover of red-brown pine needles to give adequate footing to the horses, and Tayem led the way without hesitation. At intervals they passed brambles and fallen tree trunks, blackened by rain and decay. Otherwise, they seemed to have the forest to themselves.

Noisy, Kylene observed. The heavy breathing of the horses, the sodden pine needles crunching under their hooves, the creaking leather saddles—no matter how quiet Tayem and she might be, the horses were enough to scare away other animals.

"Why so suddenly?" she asked finally. She had been expecting an explanation for some time, but Tayem had been short-spoken and she wondered if he sought to punish her for her earlier conduct. Already the morning was beginning to seem distant, far away and long ago.

She was not comfortable. Tayem had had saddles built to his specifications somewhere in the future, using one he had brought from the First Era and kept at the cabin as a model. These were extremely heavy, raised at front and back so her movement was restricted, and with thick padding for the horse but little for the rider. When she bent forward a protruding handle jabbed at her stomach; it seemed appropriate that Tayem had termed it a "horn."

Bending forward was not easy; Tayem had given her a broad leather belt to wear over her clothing. It was to keep her insides from jostling around, he had explained. Its concealed pockets held vials of useful drugs and medicines; what seemed decorative bosses were actually a radio transceiver and a device that pointed to the time shuttle.

He had also insisted that while riding she be corseted

into a *brassiere*; his deadpanned excuse was that it would keep her "outsides" from jostling around. The *brassiere* was a cloth undergarment that pinched in some places, tickled embarrassingly in others, and promised to rub her sides and shoulder tops raw; it did not stop her breasts from bouncing.

The other attire he had provided was also primitive: thick gray cloth impregnated with wax, layered to make the patterns of weaving at right angles. It was stiff and heavy, overwarm—and already she could tell it would not protect her clothing for long from the rain or the water dripping from the tree limbs under which they rode. The bulky garments were oppressive, claustrophobia-inducing; if the rain were not so cold, she would have copied Tayem and ridden with her hood down. *Normally he notices cold when no one else does. Doesn't he feel this?*

Beside her, perched high on his gelding, Tayem shrugged. He too was covered in gray, but a broadsword in a plain scabbard dangled from his belt and slapped erratically at his leather-clad leg. A canvas-shrouded longbow and quiver of arrows were strapped to the left of his saddle. "Did some thinking while I was gone." His voice was even; heard through her cowl it sounded distant, and pitched lower than normal, though the rain should have sharpened his tones.

That was not a satisfactory answer. She said as much, tartly.

"We'll be gone awhile. Going to get wet sometime, no matter when we left," he said equably. "Be reasonable, Kylene."

"How long is awhile?" she asked carefully.

"Five, six year tenths. Maybe seven." He seemed unconcerned.

"*Seven* year tenths?"

Tayem shrugged again, not looking at her. "We're taking a field trip. Don't worry. It's a place I've already been; it's perfectly safe."

"Where?" she made herself ask.

"Alghera," Tayem said. "Algherans, anyhow—fifteen centuries before they settled down enough to build that city of theirs."

Her stomach tensed. She had no wish to encounter Algherans, and she was certainly not eager to spend most of a year doing that. "But the ship," she protested. "What about the ship?"

He misunderstood her. "It'll be all right. It's moving on automatic, breaking in and out of run-time on a random schedule. Besides that, no one but you and me has the fingerprints to get through the door lock. And finally, just in case, I yanked some fuses so it can't be flown and stored them in the cabin."

She stared at him with open dismay.

He gave her a wry smile and answered one of her questions. "Go back to the cabin if something happens. Directions for getting into the ship and fixing it and for flying it back to the Project are on a writing block I left on your bed. They're in Lopritian, so they shouldn't make sense to anyone but you—try and not forget your lessons."

He had not read her mind, she realized, or even guessed at her thoughts. He still wore his Teepblind. He was simply being Tayem, prepared as ever. She continued to stare at him, looking at the raindrops that beaded his red-brown hair, noticing how prominent the scar on his left temple had become in semidarkness, watching the trickle of water that moved along his jaw and dropped unheeded onto his thigh. Suddenly she shivered, and the movement of her knees made the roan break step and toss its head.

Tayem put out a hand, patting the mare on the neck till it calmed. "What are you thinking, little girl who looks at me so hard?" he asked with amusement. He moved his hand from the mare to his hairline and swept water away. "I don't seem to be sprouting antlers, do I?"

"You're another Tayem now, aren't you?" She almost whispered that.

The big man smiled briefly. "I suppose so," he said kindly.

"The cabin?" And that was a whisper.

He smiled again. "I was Tim Harper there as well. Never doubt it, Kylene."

Her eyes closed. "Are there more of you?" she made herself ask.

Tayem chuckled. "Only one of me. If I seem so different to you, it's because you are finding different things to look at. You can keep lecturing me on my failings—if it makes you feel happier."

She bit at her lip. "I'd like to believe that."

For an instant, he was the cabin-Tayem again. "So would I."

He smiled ironically, slaying the cabin-Tayem. "We're wasting time."

"But—why not fly there? We don't have to ride."

"Afraid to be on your own?" he asked quietly.

She was, she knew suddenly. Even though unused for that, Tayem's levcraft had been a lifeline all the past year, connecting them with the Project. That was not an environment she had liked, but she had been familiar with it, and so it was more attractive than the unknown world now around her.

Tayem—the new Tayem—saw her hesitation. "Occupational hazard," he commented. "Agents have real problems doing stuff on their own. But you have to do the job that way. You have to learn to rely on yourself. And have to keep relearning."

"But it'll take so *long*!"

Tayem nodded. "Yes. But you need to get a bit older before we finish the mission. And I think you'd be better off around the Project if you're grown up a bit." He drew his reins high and moved to go ahead of her on the trail.

"Tayem!" She put out a hand, grabbing at his gray-jacketed arm to stop him. "How much older?"

"Maybe another year." He looked at her dispassionately, then smiled. "Depends on how long it takes to carry out the real mission, and on how many unscheduled stops we have."

"And when we get back to the Project?" she asked urgently. She had seldom thought about returning to the Project or Tayem's mission; until now, she had never thought of becoming significantly older. "What did you mean by 'grown up'"

"Just that," he said.

"But—" This could not be right! First him—and now her. Becoming *old*. She stared at him in horror. "When do I get to have my own life?"

"Sorry." Tayem's expression was stern, rather than regretful. He pulled at his reins again. "This *is* life. Let's get moving."

They pitched camp in the late afternoon. Rain was not threatening, but Tayem had brought tarpaulins along and while Kylene carried water from a small icy brook to the grazing horses, he sliced at pine branches with a hand axe to make pegs, then put down dropcloths as flooring within the two small tents he had erected.

When he was done, Kylene promptly made a beeline for the nearer tent. She emerged with the *brassiere* in her hands and went to examine its straps carefully in a small patch of sunlight. Somewhat to her surprise, she failed to find bloodstains.

Meanwhile, Tayem arranged tree boughs within the tents. "I'd use air mattresses, if I had my *druthers*," he said obscurely. "But it would be anachronistic. 'When in Chelmmys, dance Chelmmysian style,' after all. At least we don't have to put up with *mosquitoes* anymore."

He seemed normal enough, Kylene decided. Perhaps he had been correct in telling her there was only one mind within him. But—and her suspicions rose again—what did he hide from her by never removing his Teepblind?

Tayem eyed her speculatively, as if seeing into her mind, then sat in the entrance of the farther tent and poked through his saddlebags for a collection of spring-and-wire contraptions.

"Going trapping," he said to her. "You might clear a patch and get the material for a fire while I'm gone."

He was leaving her alone, she realized uncertainly. She was not sure she was pleased with that either. Then she frowned at herself; she did not have to depend on him; she had made her own way in the wilderness long before she had met Tayem Minstrel.

It was not clear whether Tayem—this Tayem—understood her. "I've left a set of throwing knives on your bedding," he told her.

She closed her eyes and moved her hands, imagining the knives were in her grasp. Tayem watched stolidly, waiting for her to answer.

"I'm out of practice," she admitted.

He shrugged. "The fire can wait if you want to throw for a while. If something too big to handle comes up, use the sword on my bedroll, or take for the trees. Or both. Or holler—I won't be far off."

She bit her lip. "Can I keep the sword?"

He looked at her quizzically. "When I'm back? Sure what it is you're trying to defend against?"

She shook her head. "No."

"I don't bite," he said gently.

She did not answer.

"Give the sword back when I ask for it," he said. He put the traps in the crook of his arm and vanished noiselessly into the woods.

"Brings back old memories," Tayem remarked that evening. Supper had come from cans in his baggage; their dessert was part of the sweet-tasting pastry he had been preparing at breakfast. He sat cross-legged in the entrance to his tent and waved a cake-filled hand at the crackling fire. "You, me, ten thousand pissed-off *Sierra Clubbers*."

A book rested in his lap, a small, thick volume with a red-brown cover and very thin pages. He had brought three of these with him; they were called *Norton anthologies*, Kylene remembered. Tayem had once pointed them out to her in the cabin and described them as a monument to First Era civilization.

Now she licked icing from her fingers, trying once more to decide if she liked the taste of *chocolate*. She did not understand Tayem's reference, but he seemed pleased by the thought, and she said as much.

She was in her own tent, facing the redhead. If each reached out, their fingertips might have touched. But neither of them would make that effort, she realized. Tayem had joked earlier that being removed from the vicinity of the time machine would cause him more strain than it would her; she had no wish to test that. His sword lay beside her, its edge red-lit by the fire; neither mentioned it.

Tayem beamed at her and ran a finger across a page of his book. *"A Book of Verses underneath the Bough, a Jug of Wine, a Loaf of Bread—and Thou beside me singing in the Wilderness—Oh, Wilderness were Paradise enow!"*

She let the unfamiliar words sweep past her, recognizing that she was being teased, and ignoring it. "How far did we get today?"

"Eight thousand man-heights," Tayem answered. "Roughly. Not bad for the time we put in. Figure on the same for tomorrow, then twenty thousand per day after that, with one day in five off for rest. The horses need it, even if we don't."

The horses were silent now, staked out on the other side of the dying fire. Perhaps they were sleeping, but she was not ready yet to do the same. She stared at the fire, then wiped her fingers dry on her blanket, wondering whether she should keep the conversation going and how, and remembered that she did not share Tayem's memories.

"What did we speak of, when we met first?" The words

came forth by themselves, for she had not intended to reveal her curiosity.

"Many things," Tayem said. "Nothing that would surprise you. Your travels, your family, your hopes for the future. Boyfriends you had had, and what you were looking forward to." He smiled at some private memory, his teeth gleaming momentarily in the firelight. "Mostly we argued, and I always lost—told you, nothing surprising. And once you called me an old man."

She almost remembered. "An Ancient," she guessed. "A wizard from the past—from the First Era. I might have called you that."

He chuckled. "Perhaps that was it. I thought you were teasing."

She tried to remember, and failed. "Would I have done that?"

"Sure. You called me other things, so why not that?"

It had happened long ago and she could not remember. But surely she would have been too afraid to risk his displeasure. "Did I anger you?" she asked. *Even before I knew you would be harmless to me?*

Tayem laughed. "You called me a 'guardian demon' once. That was more amusing than upsetting."

The fire crackled noisily, distracting her. When she looked back at him, Tayem's face seemed to float over the ground, a flame-lit mask above his dark shrouded torso. He seemed serene and ageless, as if he were indeed the magician she had once named him, and she was not able to say the words that rested within her lips.

"What was I like?" she forced out at last. "How did I seem to you?"

Tayem smiled. "You have to be very young, you know, to ask what sort of person you were when younger. You were very much as you are now, as I recall. Smaller and younger; rather more short-tempered generally—usually you weren't very well fed, which may have something to do with that. You were very tomboyish, and very determined, and you certainly were not going to let unimportant people like me keep you from doing just what you wanted."

"And what did I want?"

The man sighed. "Girl stuff. A husband. A bunch of kids. People around who understood you and whom you felt comfortable with. You didn't really want adventure and excitement. You didn't want any part of what I was offering."

She looked into herself. "I still don't, Tayem."

"I know, kid." He shook his head unhappily. "Long day tomorrow. Let's get some shut-eye."

Curled in her blankets, Kylene listened to Tayem's distant breathing during the night and knew that her guardian demon only feigned sleep.

CHAPTER EIGHT

In the morning they ate the last of Tayem's cake for breakfast and continued riding to the south. Midday found them at the banks of a narrow river that Tayem called a tributary of the Ice Daughter. They traveled east, following its course through rolling grasslands.

She had been pent up for two years, first by the Algherans in their Station and then in the vicinity of Tayem's cabin. At its beginning, Kylene enjoyed the journey, seeing new landscapes each morning and taking a released prisoner's pleasure from the sheer sensation of movement.

But after a few days, the pleasure palled. River, forest, grassy hillsides—even as it changed around her the scenery resumed the guise of locations she had already seen. Soon, what had been petty annoyances became major ones: the chafing *brassiere*, the monotonous diet, the dull routine of making and striking camp, the never-ending isolation.

As an added irritation her mount became balky, refusing to follow her commands. Tayem blamed her for that, saying it was her fault for mistreating the animal and accusing her of sawing the roan's mouth with the bit while giving contradictory signals with her knees. He made her walk as punishment, so she led the roan by its reins for several days, till Tayem said its gums had healed and bribed it with sugar to let her ride under his supervision.

She was simply out of practice at riding, she knew. But it did no good to protest, so she put up with his instruction till her style satisfied him, though she did not follow his inane suggestion about naming the animal. Finally the horse obeyed her once more.

Normally, Tayem was not so attentive. During the days, he rode alternately before her and after, lost in his own private thoughts, letting the river be their guide and trusting her abilities to warn of approaching game. In the evenings he practiced archery inexpertly before preparing supper, and smoked any game he had snared. And at night he sat before the fire, desultorily scrawling over his writing block or engrossed in a volume of First Era prose. He ignored her as Edgart never had and seemed perfectly content.

This could not continue, Kylene sensed. Something must happen soon or she would explode. But it would serve no good purpose to throw a tantrum and make Tayem angry with her, even though this tedium was all his fault.

Tayem. Very well, then. He had insisted on this journey, so making it be interesting was properly his responsibility. She would poke him into it.

Almost without planning, after refueling the fire early one evening she found herself behind him. An untouched mug of coffee rested beside him; his fingers danced over the surface of his writing block, inscribing fan-shaped symbols. His lips had been moving soundlessly, she had noticed, and his head bobbed gently, in time with the movements of his hand, as if he were in some private conversation. Earlier he had risen from time to time to stir the stew pot containing the evening meal, but he ignored that now and he showed no awareness of her presence, although she had changed from her trail clothing into a clean blouse and a loosely styled plaid skirt he liked.

Several ten-day periods had gone by, and Tayem's red-brown hair was shaggy once more. Her fingers were at the nape of his neck, lightly stroking absently at the golden fuzz that had regrown there, thicker than would be normal on any other man, but somehow not objectionable. The full moon was climbing into the darkening sky, she noticed absently, a reddish coin shape only partially visible behind beeches shedding their white bark. The smoke from the fire was almost vertical, so there would be no rain tonight. A short distance away the horses stood, muzzles touching companionably.

She sniffed, her eyes closed. On the trail, it was impossible to bathe with Algheran-style regularity. Tayem's musky aroma should have been masked now by sweat and wood-smoke, but if anything it had become more noticeable, still as much an identifying characteristic as his green and black uniforms. The odor was pleasant; for an instant, she wondered uncertainly if her own smell was objectionable to him.

Tayem shook his head away from her fingers. "What are you up to, little reader over my shoulder?"

"I'm bored," she complained. "I want something to do."

She sensed amusement passing through him. Evidently he had rejected a possible response. "Dinner's still cooking . . . Do some drawing," he suggested at last. "You haven't done that recently."

"No!" Sketching was a pastime she had taken up during the winter, as an outgrowth of her lessons in *geometry*. For a while it had been entertaining, but Tayem had ruined it as a pleasure when he decided to encourage her. By that he had meant studying textbooks on art and practicing daily. Soon she had hated the sight of blank paper, and almost felt relief when Tayem abandoned that enthusiasm and set her to learning Lopritian and more *algebra*.

If he realized that, the man did not show it. He held

out his writing block instead. "Here. I'm not getting any-where. You might as well have the thing as me—I've got a spare."

She accepted with ill grace. "What were you doing?"

"Thinking deep thoughts about the Whichness of the What," he said sardonically. "Nah—I'm still trying to figure out how time travel works. Not the mechanics of moving the machine, but what happens when you try to change things and go back."

Did it matter? she wondered. He had a time machine. It worked; why should he ask questions about it?

"Not going to make a *physicist* of you, are we, Kylene?" he answered to her question. He chuckled briefly, then stood abruptly and went into his tent. He returned and handed her a small book. "Explain this without *physics*."

What was she to explain? Kylene put down the writing block and opened the book at random. It was a copy of a manuscript written by hand. All the pages were much the same: *algebra*-like equations with symbols she did not recognize, a few paragraphs of incomprehensible text, and perhaps a sketch of a fan or a circle inside a box in a corner. The title page read *The Wit and Wisdom of Harper Timithial ha'Cuhyon*. At its top was a name she recognized as belonging to the tra'Ruijac. The book had been printed in Alghera in City Year 702. It was very thin.

Nothing about it seemed significant. She shook her head and gave it back to Tayem. "What was I supposed to see?"

"A dog that doesn't bark," he said cryptically. "Do you know how I came to Alghera?"

A time machine? She waited, realized the question was rhetorical.

"Go back and ask the people in the Project." Tayem slapped the book on his thigh, then dropped it carefully on the writing block. "They'll tell you that in City Year 657, there was an enormous explosion at the institute, which killed a faculty member named Herrm ha'Cuhyon. To make up for it, when they checked the rubble, they found a busted-up time machine and a busted-up time traveler."

"You."

"Sort of." Tayem showed no pleasure in her deduction. "A guy, let's say. The Algherans took the guy in and kept him around the institute as sort of a curiosity piece. They never fixed the time machine, never took too seriously any of the stories the guy told them about his homeland. And finally, about 705 or so, he died of old age."

There had to be more. Kylene frowned to make him continue.

"He was a junior faculty member at the end. He gave a couple of classes on First Era science, which were taken by Sict ha'Ruijac and Borct and a couple other people you might have met at the Station. And so, when the Final War got going and the same people were looking for bright ideas to hold off defeat, they remembered their old, dead teacher. They dug up what was left of the time machine and figured out how to get it running and they set up the Project."

"And they rescued you!"

"Sort of." Tayem smiled cynically. "They didn't want the Chelmmies to get thinking about time travel, so they waited for the guy to show up, and grabbed him while he was still groggy and took him back to the Station before anyone in Alghera knew of him. Tolp ha'Ruijac was in charge of that little operation; he thinks it's where we first met."

"Wasn't it?" Kylene frowned again, wondering why Tayem had chosen to tell her this story.

"Let me tell you how I came to Alghera."

"But—"

He ignored the interruption. "I started off traveling with Herrm ha'Cuhyon's time machine, all right, but I was on foot most of the time. I walked along the City wall and got inside the City and suddenly the time machine stopped. A squad of soldiers showed up and arrested me and that evening they turned me over to Borct ha'Dicovys, who had never met me before. But it was City Year 892, the Final War was obviously going against the Algherans, and Borct was looking for any weapon he could find. So he and Sict figured out how to duplicate the time machine— and Tolp and I and a few other people went out to change some history.

"And that's how I saw the Project begin, Kylene."

He bent to pick up some sticks and fed the fire.

"You figure out how all that happened, and maybe I'll figure out a way to get you home."

A way home. Kylene thought about that while they ate, until Tayem teased her for her silence.

"Your story," she said then. "How do you explain it?"

Tayem snorted. "Go off and get a First Era physics or math degree and we'll exchange wild guesses." He sighed, then stood abruptly and walked into the woods. A muffled snapping sound came from that direction. Soon he returned holding a small pine branch. "Have a seat, girl. Might as well have you as ignorant as me."

More schooling, she recognized unhappily. *He said he had been a faculty member*. She should not have given Tayem the excuse for this. But it was too late to avoid a lecture; she seated herself before the fire on his blanket, leaving room for him and the branch.

"Might as well start you off with *phase space*," he commented cheerfully. "I really ought to explain *atoms* and *electrons* and *baryons* and all that good stuff to you first, but the Algherans don't hold with it and I don't want to confuse you too much. The important thing is that the entire universe is made of things. You and me, for example. And we're made up of hair and bone and skin, and each of those can be divided and so forth. Eventually, keep doing that, we get down to very tiny particles. In principle, I can give each of them a set of numbers to define their position and velocities—just like in your arithmetic problems, but on a bigger scale. Each of them has a position in space defined by three arbitrary coordinates; each has a velocity, and thus a momentum, which can be defined in three more coordinates. They also have *spin* and *angular momentum* and various other interesting things—but that's not important.

"What matters is that if I do this for all the different particles, that tells me everything I need to describe the entire universe."

He chuckled at her expression. "Take my word for it. *Statistical mechanics* is a theory that works very well in some situations, so I'm just extending it a bit. I'm entitled to do that, as long as I don't have sixteen different Algherans leaning over me screaming '*superstition.*' Nobody here but us consenting adults, after all."

He chuckled again. "Hand me back the writing block, please."

"*Indian giver*," Kylene muttered as she obeyed, using one of the First Era phrases she had learned from him. He paid no attention.

"Now. Say the universe is made of N particles—"

"—where N is a large but finite number," Kylene chorused sourly. Tayem had a peculiar fondness for those words.

"—where N is a large but finite number," Tayem agreed. "Very good, Kylene! Then the universe at any instant can be described by a vector of, say, ten times N components, or a point in a space of dimension ten times N." He sketched a rough square onto the writing block with his finger scribe, then tapped it to produce a dot and tore the sheet off for her. "Something like this, using two dimensions rather than ten times N. Because of uncertainty, we can't pin things down too closely, so instead of a true point, we ought to be using a little box, but phase space is so big, a point is just as realistic. Understand that?"

She nodded. Disagreement would only prolong this.

"Here." He tapped the writing block, producing a copy of the sheet he had given her, and touched it with his scribe to draw a wavy line. "Yesterday here. Tomorrow there."

It was only a line in a paper box. Kylene nodded again and pushed flat bread through her broth.

Tayem grinned infuriatingly. "The question I know you have now is: Is that line continuous? And the answer is no. Uncertainty again; the line will look continuous from a distance—that's one method of defining 'causality' in prequantum terms—but when you get close, you'll see that the points making up the line are splattered all over phase space. However, the points seem to form a continuous line at the macroscopic level, and the more particles there are, the more the points stick close to that line. Which explains why First Era physicists let *laymen* like you go on believing in causality."

"Thank you, Tayem," Kylene said solemnly.

The man smiled smugly. "You're welcome, little *non-leman*. Let's go on, since I've been giving you the simple picture of things. Look at the universe-line from the standpoint of someone trapped on it. Yesterday, today, next year . . . And whatever happens seems to be perfectly logical—from your viewpoint, you see what looks like causality.

"Other hand, different things could happen that are also perfectly logical. Or at least allowable by *quatum mechanics*—by physical laws. So this line is just one of a lot of lines that are possible. So I can draw a kind of fan. And I use a large number of universe-lines. Zillions. Large, but finite; I'm going to use uncertainty to argue that if I can't tell a couple of points on different lines apart, they must be the same point—if it looks that way to the universe, it *is* that way. You see what that means?"

"No."

"We aren't going to make you a physicist, are we, Kylene? It explains why the Project finds it hard to change history."

"If you say so." Kylene licked her fingers and reached for Tayem's plate. He still had an untouched squirrel leg.

"Yeah, you're losing lines. It means two intersecting points are really the same point."

"If you say so," Kylene stretched a little farther.

"Like *fermions*. The universe is mostly *fermions*, after all." Tayem mumbled to himself and absently held his plate toward her. "Don't know that it means anything, though."

Kylene said nothing. Her mouth was full.

"Anyhow." Tayem picked up the tree branch. "Viewed from some sort of perspective then, things look like this. I start at the base, go up one side of the fork, out on one of the twigs, and along one of these needles—that's a universe-line. Lots of universe-lines; the wood is a way of showing where they're bunched together—where the lines are dense in phase space."

He turned, tossing the branch onto the fire. "Different theories now. The simplest is that the universe is described by just one line, and nothing we can do will change that. That is dissatisfying on philosophical grounds. Another drawback—it happens to be wrong.

"Second theory. Only one universe-line is real, but we can change which way it goes when we time travelers interfere with history. Drawback to this, you can potentially create paradoxes—you could go back in time, for example, to murder your grandparents, which ought to make it impossible for you to ever be born to go back in time, and so on. Murdering your grandparents is usually illegal; violating causality while you're at it is completely immoral."

A joke, she guessed. Kylene wiped her fingers clean and yawned.

Pine needles crackled in the flames. Tayem smiled whimsically. "Of course, with small enough grandparents, causality *could* be violated that way, but . . . Anyhow, we don't find it that easy to change things, and the universe seems to reject paradoxes, so it has to be more complicated than this theory allows.

"Third theory. *All* the possible universe-lines are real, but they aren't connected. So all the possible versions of history are going on right now, all the time, and always will be. Travel in time and change things, and what you are doing is changing some of the universe-lines. Maybe you can do enough of this that the distribution of lines in phase space changes enough to be noticeable—something like bending that branch. It's not phrased the same way, but this is basically the theory the Project uses.

"Theory four. Everett's 'many-world interpretation' of *quantum mechanics*. All the possible universe-lines are real and connected. Possible futures evolve stochastically, at random but in accord with probability and physical laws. The things time travelers do also involve stochastic processes, necessarily, so they may or may not work."

He shrugged. "It explains some things. Travel forward in time and a copy of you goes to all the possible futures you can reach. The more realistically you do things, the more apt you are to succeed."

He shook his head, then stood. "It's a theory. If I think up more, I'll let you know. Make any sense, Kylene?"

She blinked, realizing that the pleasant sound of his voice had stopped and that her sleepiness would have to be dispelled.

The man smiled without rancor. "You're a fair audience, anyhow. Let's clean up the mess."

Coals popped, embers glowing redly under dying flames. As she watched over it, Tayem glided into view between tree trunks, then moved soundlessly across the clearing. A small shovel was in his hands. "Buried the trash," he told her. "But I think the only varmints here is us'n."

She agreed, then scooted forward on her blanket to sit with her arms around her knees while Tayem stretched out behind her, his head resting on his hands. Fireflies twinkled over nearby grass; imperceptibly the purpling sky had turned to black, a curtain pricked by tiny pins that were stars. The full moon was high above the horizon, silvery, smaller than it had been when red-tinted. "Peaceful," he murmured at last. "Brings back some old memories."

"What other kind do you have?" she teased, and he chuckled.

"None." Then, when she reached to scratch her back, he said, "Here, let me."

She obeyed, squirming backward to lean against him, hunching from side to side to unkink her muscles, enjoying the sensation as he touched her, taking pleasure in the warmth and nearness of his body, contrasting it with the cool tickle of grass under her calves. "You smell nice, Tayem."

"I just smell period, kid. Don't distract me while I'm doing delicate work." His hands rubbed her itch firmly, then moved beyond it, the thumbs pressing hard into her shoulders and spine, pushing into her muscles a comfortable pain, subsiding into tingles as he decreased the force. His fingers gently caressed her through her blouse again, kneading the flesh over her shoulders and along her sides, making her shiver deliciously as they traced across the small of her back.

"You should probably stop," she said finally, reluctantly.

"Do you want me to stop?" His voice was calm, under control.

"No," she admitted tinily. "But you should."

Tayem chuckled again, briefly, humorlessly. "I suppose." His hands moved away from her and she could breathe again, as he lay down at her side. "*Old* memories." Then he moved a hand to her left ankle, stroked it lightly with one finger. His face was without expression.

Distract him, she thought frantically. But with what, when everything she could think of was so ordinary or, suddenly, so charged with emotion?

The moon, she remembered. To Tayem, the moon was not ordinary.

So she looked outward at its face as if she had only

now noticed it. "Tayem, why did your First Era people want to go to the moon?"

Tayem sighed, releasing her touch-chilled ankle. "It was there."

When she remained silent, he sat up and continued, "Look around, and you find that people spread out all over the one world, as if they have some natural instinct that makes them explore and keep going over the next hill. There were a lot of us, and we'd pretty well covered the globe, so keeping on going out into space seemed inevitable. And the people in my country—" His hand waved in the air. "Right here. This ground, from ocean to ocean. All the people that lived here and were ancestors of me, and you, and the Algherans—they once had that instinct deeper than most."

He was expressing a judgment, she sensed when he stopped, and she looked within herself, half hoping, half afraid, for the emotion he had tried to evoke—and could not find it. "Does it matter?" she wondered aloud, knowing that it did, staring away from him toward the dying fire.

"I suspect your Ancients had that instinct pretty deep," he said gently. "Is there an answer in that for you?"

She did not speak, feeling somehow diminished, and lost. *Different species. Aliens.* She shivered.

"Don't let it bother you." A hand rested on her shoulder, shaking her minutely. "Some of us First Era types had *wanderlust*. But not all. We used to argue about it."

Curiosity returned with redemption. "Not everyone agreed?"

Tayem sighed. "Probably most people felt like you."

She could smile again. "Then was your instinct truly so natural?"

Even without looking, she knew that Tayem was grimacing. "*Touché*, little girl. But that picture on my wall that you asked about once. When it was taken, a lot of people—me, for instance—figured that was just the start of something big. Someday we'd have cities on the moon, and colonies on Mars and Venus, and eventually people would travel to the stars."

It didn't happen, she read in his voice. "Why not?"

"I really don't know. People lost interest, for some reason. Perhaps they had other problems, or they took it for granted, or they thought it would all happen automatically, without any work. I don't know. I got back to there, a few years on, and the program was just dying. And no one really cared, or seemed to think it ought to be any different. Some pretty pictures from Mars, and that was all anyone wanted." Bewilderment sounded in his voice, then resignation.

"That made you unhappy."

"Yeah. Silly of me. But—how do I say this?—for a while, there was something awe-inspiring about space exploration. Grand, heroic—noble. Then it all fizzled out."

And what was she to say to that? "Put some wood on the fire, Tayem."

"Sure." Perhaps he had been wanting something to do.

While he was gone, she moved back on the blanket, to give him the position nearer to the fire. The rough wool scratched at her knees, even as she scratched it, moodily widening a char-edged hole that a spark had made in the plaid skirt. When the big man returned, she looked up at him somberly.

"Awe-inspiring, and grand, and noble—do things have to be that way for you, Tayem?"

He seemed surprised. "Sure. I mean—how else should things be?"

He actually is serious. "Sit down, Tayem." And when he had done that she turned sideways. "Lean back and put your head in my lap."

"Why?" he asked warily.

"Just because. I thought it would be nice."

"Kylene." His voice had a warning note.

"Tayem. Lean back. That's it." *Such a heavy head*, she mused. *So very warm, as if he is almost feverish, and the skin is taut and so close to the bones.* A scar showed

on his left temple, long and jagged. It was the pink-white
color of his skin elsewhere, too old to be a memento of
his duel with Herrilmin, and she wondered absently where
he had earned it and if it would vanish if she kissed it.

She smiled then at his upturned face and traced the
lines across his forehead with a finger. Would they never
be erased? *Keep smiling. He cannot see into minds.* "Good
little boy!" she crooned.

The big man scowled at her. "Are you having fun?"

"Yes. Aren't you?"

"You don't expect me to answer that, do you?"

She smiled. "Too late, Tayem. I grew up to be—"

"—a telepath. I should have seen that coming. All
right, kid."

With the man relaxed and willing to listen to her, she
picked her words carefully. "Are you happy?"

Tayem moved his head restlessly, postponing an answer.
"Comfortable, some way." *I shouldn't be*, his expression
told her.

"Is this 'grand, heroic, and noble'?"

"It could soon be uplifting." Tayem grimaced and started
to rise.

She grabbed at his hair and pulled his head easily back
into place. "All that grandeur, and awe, and nobility—it
can get in the way of living, Tayem. People are not built
to grand standards. Because they appreciate and approve
of something does not mean they feel forced to work for
it themselves—they are willing to leave that to others, to
people who want it more than they do."

"Perhaps they should though," Tayem answered with
equal gentleness. His arm moved awkwardly, fitted naturally and safely around her waist. "There was a word in
my time—I can't find it now. The best I can do in Speech
is 'Acting for more than one Sept'—which isn't the same
thing at all. *Idealism*, we called it. Trying to meet high
standards, having important goals—are those things so
bad?"

"Goals. Standards. Being noble. Those things are too

big for real people, Tayem. No one can measure up to them constantly."

"Oh, sure." His head lifted impatiently from her lap, as if he were explaining some basic misunderstanding to her. "I know. *Ideals* are what you strive for, knowing you never get all the way there, just closer. They are guidelines; they show us *how* we ought to act, not just what sort of conduct we can get away with."

"But failing makes people unhappy. Can't you see what that means, Tayem? People cannot live up to impossible standards. So they don't even try to. They try to be decent normally without all that thought, without worrying, without wondering."

"You're the Teep," Tayem said sourly, and the hard comfortable arm dropped away from her. "Maybe I shouldn't argue. But it strikes me as more likely that they tell themselves they really are measuring up to those standards all the time, even if they aren't. They don't have the nerve to admit to themselves they don't always act for the best."

"You are being cynical," she chided.

"Uh—" Tayem swallowed. "Yeah."

Kylene moved slightly, using the excuse to look away and permit herself a half smile. *Darling Tayem.* "You assume all people spend as much time thinking of such matters as you—and you're wrong."

"Should I be?"

He sounded wounded. "Let them be, Tayem," she suggested gently. "Most people are happy. Don't condemn them for not trying as hard as you." She touched the lines on his forehead lightly, let the fingers moved along his cheeks and jaw. It took an effort to stop there, to draw back before her hand moved to his chest and beyond. She shuddered silently, hoping the man would not notice it, would not feel her fingers tremble on his cheek.

He drew in breath. "Here I am getting into arguments with a little girl and keeping her up way past her bedtime—guess I'm not a whole lot better." That was half reflective, half amused.

A little girl? I know more of people than you, dear giant. "Are you?" she asked. "Do you make errors, even with your worrying and thinking?"

"Yes." His voice was flat. His eyes had closed.

Poor Tayem. "So are you really better than other people?"

"I don't claim that." The neck against her thigh was tense.

"But you think it," she told him. "Even if you don't admit that to yourself, you do. And who is more to blame for making an error? Someone who simply acts? Or someone who thinks about his actions and motives continually—and still makes errors?"

"That can't be answered." She heard pain in his voice.

She made herself continue. "All that thought, and all that worry, Tayem, and you still make mistakes and do things you regret."

"So what!"

"So act naturally, more often than you do. Don't think so much about everything you do, or want, all the time."

Tayem's eyes opened. Suddenly his tenseness had gone. He reached up to stroke her chin gently with calloused fingers. "Got to, Kylene," he said softly, in control of himself once more. "It is bedtime, you know."

She stared down at him. Poor self-damned Tayem, always forcing himself to act, who never let up on himself, never stopped tormenting himself. What sins had he committed that he could not forgive? How cruel to be so close to tears and so far from them when only your own conscience accuses. If only it were possible to hug him against her and make the evil memories vanish, to dispel his pains with a kiss.

"I guess I am sleepy," she said, and yawned deeply.

"Sure enough. Good night, kid." He was on his feet and gone without questioning her lie. She breathed heavily, watched him without moving.

Had all the Ancients been like him? she wondered alone, late at night. Then it was not surprising that people did not choose to remember the First Era. Or had Tayem been unique even in his own time?

Snuggling into her blankets, she realized that she might never know. But the one world was filled with strangers; why should it matter if she never solved Tayem's private mysteries?

Before she could answer that question, she was asleep.

CHAPTER NINE

*T*ayem *stopped beside the road. Waiting, he took his* reins in one hand and dismounted to check the gelding's hooves.

Black clothing against a yellow background, Kylene thought critically. *Bad. He makes a target of himself.* She rode toward Tayem, keeping her mount on the short grass, skirting bushes and stepping over blood-red flowers.

It was late afternoon. The sky was clear of clouds. The sun was dropping toward pine tops on the far side of the road, and she and Tayem had not eaten lunch. Was he planning a meal in such an exposed location? It made no sense to halt for the day this early.

She stopped by Tayem, relaxing the reins to let her roan shake its head and brush its muzzle against the gelding. Tayem slapped the horses' necks to get the animals' attention, then moved between them, shouldering the roan aside to continue his examination, not looking at her.

"Getting into familiar territory again," he said in a soft voice. "The camp should be over this next hill. Those jokers still following us?" His fingers plucked at a perfectly clean hoof.

She had no need to search. "To the right," she said in an equally low voice. "Ten, fifteen man-heights behind. Five of them." Tayem managed to look that way while inspecting the mouth of his horse; she kept her gaze on the gray-surfaced pavement that led through the trees ahead of them and around the hill. He would see no more than she did.

"Uh-huh." Tayem remounted, tossed a piece of gravel to his left, and patted his horse's neck. "Good boy, Trigger," he crooned. "Any idea what they're up to?"

She shook her head regretfully. "No. The language is not Speech. Soon, when I am more familiar with it . . . but not yet. Sorry, Tayem."

"Asking for miracles, I know. Never mind." The redhead shrugged. "Easy enough to guess. I think we switch to Lopritian now," he continued in that language. "Halfway up the next hill should be more sentries."

She closed her eyes momentarily, then nodded. "I think you should just take off the Teepblind and not worry about them overhearing us."

He ignored her. "They'll pin us till we can be surrounded. Try and act surprised when the ones in back come running after us, but not too surprised. I don't want a fight yet."

Something has broken, she sensed from a strange mind. But what? She pushed out mentally, trying again to fit unfamiliar thought patterns into her vocabulary. *I have broken something.*

Probably a twig, she thought in one mind, simultaneously trying to make sense of the sensations in another. *Call it a twig.*

Then: *She is motionless, arms extended to preserve her awkward balance, waiting to see if the intruders have heard her. But they remain by the roadside, speaking casually, unaware that warriors have them under scrutiny. She smiles, pleased with her stealth and cunning, amused*

*at their innocence, then relaxes her rigid pose and signals
the men behind her to approach. One traveler is a woman,
raven-haired and fair-skinned.*

Kylene's mind returned to her. How much of that was
true thought? How much imagination? She was sure of
the presence of the watchers. A feeling of purpose, of
anticipation—or were those her own emotions? "Try and
act surprised," she muttered sarcastically.

The fighting came after captivity, she discovered. She
could not read thoughts here with clarity yet, but she
could sense bloodthirst and anticipation in the men who
shoved them into the small canvas-covered wagon.

Tayem had expected it. "I'd as lief sing for my supper,"
he commented wryly when they were alone. "Don't they
strike you as being culture lovers?" He kicked straw aside
and sat on the floor to inspect the contents of their saddlebags.

"I'm sure that would be devastating," she agreed. "But
they must have been warned against you. Perhaps they
are culture lovers?"

He grinned ironically, mirroring the expression she had
forced her own face to show. There was another telepath
nearby, she had discovered. For an instant, someone's
mind had pressed against hers as she and Tayem rode into
the camp. Surprise had made her raise her mind shield,
and when she lowered it, the other's mind could not be
detected. But she was not alone here.

Tayem would wish to know. But the other Teep was
not a time traveler, she had grasped. There was no risk
in waiting to inform him and he seemed absorbed in himself right now, patting his uniform and toying with its
ornaments as if plagued by vanity. Perhaps the knowledge
would be of more use to her than to him.

A canvas flap at the front of the wagon was pulled
aside, and a thick voice rumbled out what was unmistak-
ably an order.

Tayem translated: "Come and be judged, strangers."

Three men awaited them on the ground. Their swords were sheathed. Kylene probed quickly but could read no more than watchfulness in their minds, so she ignored them to look around her surroundings.

This was not the camp Tayem had intended to visit; their captors had bypassed that one, leading them north for most of the day to another. This was a larger community with an air of permanence despite being a wagon train. Tayem had laughed at that innocent description when they were brought into the camp, pointing to the trash heaps on the outskirts. Garbage and dead animals and unbathed people—that was where the air of permanence came from.

"More settled people north of here a ways," he had explained. "Still barbarians, but they have genuine towns. These nomads will conquer them in six or seven centuries—outbreed them and assimilate them, actually—and get a bit smarter about sanitation then."

It was dusk now, not yet twilight, though a crescent moon was already mounted to the darkening sky. A narrow, rutted, dirt path ran through weeds and short grass along a corridor formed by two lines of canvas-topped wagons. A dog barked in the distance, and was yapped at in return. Perhaps the sound came from the direction of the middens. She had no time to decide before another command was uttered. Tayem took her elbow and made her follow the man leading them down the corridor.

The camp was rectangular, given that shape by several hundred wagons loosely arranged in a dozen rows. The wagons were painted in rainbow colors, but travel wear and dust had reduced their festive air; age-grayed wood showed at corners and where ropes had abraded the paint. Their wheels were more than man high; cupboards and canvas-shrouded packages were fastened along the sides.

A space had been created in the center, roughly twenty man-heights in width and twice as long, poorly lighted by torches mounted on tall poles. A hand's count of long-horned cattle roamed free, squat but broad-shouldered, chewing desultorily at clumps of tall grass. Much of the ground was simply bare dirt, littered here and there by disk-shaped cattle droppings, which Tayem managed to avoid without apparent notice.

She saw no horses. Perhaps they were stockaded outside the camp. For a moment she wondered what had happened to Tayem's Trigger and her roan mare. Were they being well treated? Would they see them again?

The thought made her lower her mind shield. But no one attempted to communicate with her. The unknown Teep was not willing to be discovered, she decided, or was not going to be helpful. But she had Tayem to rely on; the other's silence was only cause for minor annoyance.

Food was being prepared at one side of the cleared space. Cauldrons steamed temptingly, their contents being ladled out into waiting bowls by a group of elderly women. The pieces of conversation Kylene overheard were low-voiced and unintelligible, but good-natured in tone. Now and again she heard laughter. A troop of children played a game with ropes woven between the spokes of the man-high wheels of a wagon at the side of the clearing. A woman came near them to seize the ear of a very young girl and lead her away protesting.

The children were nude, Kylene noticed, or wore only loincloths. The elderly were plainly dressed as well, in long tunics that fell over bare legs or cloth breeches, and walked unshod. The manufacture of clothing was time-consuming and thus expensive in primitive societies, Tayem had explained once, forgetting her own background in the course of his lecture. Perhaps he had had this tribe in mind.

Most of the adult males were better-dressed. Breeches with rawhide lashings, leather or cloth upper garments, normally sleeveless, short boots—these men could have walked unchallenged in her era. The colors daubed on the clothing might indicate rank or simply be decoration; Tayem had not explained that.

The women were drab, with featureless expressions and high-pitched singsong voices. Many were missing front teeth. Standard attire for them included a short-sleeved tunic with cord lashing across the front and a rope or thong midriff belt. Under this they wore loose-fitting breeches. Those who were not barefoot had soft leather boots similar in pattern to those of the men.

The breeches were made from canvas, she noticed, as were most of the cloth garments she saw. Probably they were lined with softer material inside. Her mind reached out, searching, until she confirmed her guess and supplemented that by finding that the liner material was not made by the nomads but was acquired through trade. None of these women were familiar with *brassieres*, she also discovered; she would bring that to Tayem's attention soon.

Men were drinking in turns from a wooden bucket, while the fat-covered carcass of some large animal rotated on a spit behind them. Glowing coals in the firepit beneath hissed as grease fell upon them. Rabbit, Kylene guessed, noticing the bulky hind legs. She was unhappily aware of her own hunger.

If Tayem was thirsty or hungry, he did not show it. Left to himself, she suspected, he would have taken the lead position and ignored the armed men at his back. Now he matched his pace to her own, keeping his left hand on her upper arm. The grip was not to prevent her from breaking free; she decided its purpose was to demonstrate to onlookers that he bore responsibility for her.

His thoughts were hidden behind the Teepblind, but she sensed from his touch that he was unworried, and that eased her nervousness. It was also a comfort to see that he towered over the other men by half a head or more; familiarity had made her forgetful of his great size. She could admire him now for that stature, for the contrast between his neat green and black attire and the drab homespun garments of their guards. *He acts as if he owns the one world*, she thought, and unthinkingly she drew nearer to the man.

They passed between wagons again, until they were outside the encampment. A large stream could be seen, and a few trees, but darkness was descending; only the space around a small elevated fire nearby was not gray and black.

A conversation halted. Perhaps a dozen men waited silently, seated on blankets around the fire. The open hearth was circular, about the height of her waist, and rested on stone walls. *An altar*, she guessed. Embroidered hangings dangled limply from wooden tripods twice the height of a man. The images she could not make out in the semidarkness no doubt would show funny animals in bondage and other religious emblems. *A shrine*. Were its flames consecrated now to Cimon or to Nicole?

"The Muster," Tayem commented quietly. But she had not needed his identification. She had already probed minds, seeing in them evidence of authority and responsibility. Though drably dressed, the men on the blankets were not priests but the heads of Septs.

The man gnawing a bone before the fire bore golden insignia on his chest, pendants hanging from a thin metallic necklace. He was no older than the other men, no broader, no taller, but the vest of white fur he wore singled him out, as did the thoughts of the others. This must be the chief, the man whom a future age would call the Warder.

As she decided that, the Warder threw the bone into the fire and wiped his fingers over his vest. He said something in a gravel-voiced monotone and nodded amiably at the man leading them, who nodded back and stepped aside to join the two guards behind them. Kylene heard subdued clattering sounds. Her nervousness returned, making her draw nearer to Tayem, but she followed his example and did not look behind.

Her mind reached out instead; light and sound were a kaleidoscope within her. The images froze; the noise stilled;

then she saw with two sets of eyes, heard with two sets of ears.

With her own eyes closed, she looked at a tall black-garbed man with red-brown hair and a scarred forehead. Her eyes moved to the slight raven-haired woman beside him, then beyond to three grim men with unsheathed swords. The guards were properly dressed, she noted absently. The unusual clothing, too tight, too sleek-looking, too thin, belonged to the prisoners.

Tayem spoke first. The words were slow-paced, and she guessed thankfully that this was for her benefit, even as she registered surprise that the unknown man knew the language of the People. "Where is your hospitality? You make us stand in your presence, Warder, and we have not been fed."

"You are strangers." That much of the Warder's response Kylene could decipher from within his mind. The words that followed were too rapid for understanding, but seemed to be a complaint. A frown crossed Tayem's face finally; the expression was repeated on the faces of several of the Masters, making the Warder sense that he was not making a good impression. He stopped abruptly.

The woman stared about uncomprehendingly through almond-shaped green eyes, then shook her head and leaned against the big man, her eyes closed now for some reason. The Warder wondered idly what thoughts passed through her mind, and waited for a response from her companion. The strangers posed a problem, but they were no threat to the People; it was a private worry that clawed at his concentration.

"The People have always been friendly to strangers, as I recall," the redhead said. He smiled reminiscently. "Very friendly."

"Not now," the Warder said.

The redhead's shoulders jerked abruptly, but he appeared not to notice it. "Just as well," he said, and although he toyed nervously with his sleeves, his voice was calm. "Wouldn't be much of a trade, anyhow. The woman's got some sort of *jungle rot* so no one sensible is going to touch her—and to be honest, even when she's season-taken she's no fun in bed. Completely frigid."

Perhaps she guessed she had been mentioned. The woman jerked away from the man abruptly. Undecipherable emotions crossed her face, though she kept a decorous silence. The redhead ignored this and looked upward, toward the cloud-shrouded moon and beyond. The Warder waited.

"I suppose we could claim innocent passage," the man said finally. He made it sound like a helpful suggestion.

The People were extending their territory, claiming the valuable grazing lands to the north as rapidly as population permitted expansion into the Cold Barrens. It would be risky to encounter other tribes with the same intent before the warrior Septs were fully prepared. Information about the People could not be permitted to other people. "No," the Warder said firmly.

Oh, Gods, guard me. Powers of Heaven, guide me. The man would die. The woman—he had no need of additional women. She had an exotic appearance, not totally unattractive, and the high breasts of the very young; despite the problems the man gave warning of, one of the Septs would take her in if he did nothing. Perhaps his second son would have her. Or she could be a gift to a political ally. Or an offering to clinch a treaty—that might be the best use for her.

The woman stared at him unhappily, and again the Warder wondered what matters she had found to think about. But the shieldmen were ready for his signal; he raised a hand.

The tall man's shoulders twitched slowly once more, but fear was still absent from his voice. "My hearthmate and I have been named by the People."

Kylene returned to her own mind, feeling shock. That terrible insult from Tayem—to be followed so quickly by this? It was logical to pose as hearthsharers, but—

Later. Her mind returned to the Warder.

The Warder frowned, echoing the look on the woman's face. Names were kept secret from outsiders. If the strangers had true names, then they must be of the People. But they were unknown, and thus could not be of the People. How did they claim to have names?

An answer came to him: The man must be lying. Very well, let him lie. He could rise to the Gods on his own responsibility then, and at Judgment Day the Warder would not be required to answer for that. Unless, perhaps—no, that race of wizards was surely dead now. This was only a man.

"Name yourself then," the Warder made himself say. He forced a smile.

The man looked away and put an arm around the shoulder of the woman beside him. "Waterfall Kylene," he said. "Dicovys." He smiled, and ice formed around the heart of the Warder. The stranger's right arm snapped outward, the wrist turning as metal gleamed in the fire light. "Harper. Timothy Allan. Tra'Dicovys." A handle was in his fist, hammered iron fastened to a golden ball with embedded spikes—the mace of a Sept Master.

"You claim to be the Master of Dicovys." The Warder's voice was wooden. Nothing good could come of this. "That Sept has a Master."

"An Acting Master." The black-garbed man spoke flatly.

The Warder exhaled slowly. "A Master. I set the irregularity right many years ago. The other Masters agreed."

For a long moment there was silence, and Kylene could hear voices from the center of the camp. The members of the council waited, unmoving, filled with ignorant anticipations, unaware that their memories pinwheeled through her mind.

The Warder had spoken the truth, but before Tayem could be told, he had broken the silence himself, with a laugh. "Very well, Warder. Since I must, I challenge for Dicovys."

A sigh passed over the council, as if all the old men had chosen that instant to begin breathing.

"The Master of Dicovys is not present," The Warder said. But when Tayem only smiled narrowly, he forced himself to continue. "I will appoint a champion for him. My personal champion. Tonight, within this day tenth."

The decision was made. The fate of the strangers was in the keeping of the Gods now, and not his responsibility. He could look them in the face unflinchingly, and regard them as individuals. The tall somber man in black, this adventurer claiming to be the vanished tra'Dicovys, the woman, little more than a girl, for some reason now strangely familiar...

"May the Goddess's cloak cover you both," he told them. "Masters, we are adjourned for a duel. The Gods guard us all; the Heavenly Powers guide us."

Now his mind was free to return to private worries.

"The Gods guard us, Heavenly Powers guide us."

She had never seen a duel before, and they had taken Tayem away from her. As the final words of the Warder's invocation sounded, Kylene stared unhappily at the torch-lit space before her, not certain of what she should be doing or even thinking. Light and sound were a kaleidoscope within her mind; then the images froze and her consciousness moved from one council member to another. But the Sept Masters carried the same confusions as she, tempered only by varying degrees of anticipation. Duels were not usual occurrences.

Her apprehension was not reduced by the setting. The fighting space was simply spaded over earth, slippery and rough, just across the stream from the site of the Muster, and poorly lit by torches haphazardly shoved into the dirt.

Her feet were wet. The noise of the brook and the chirping of insects drowned out sounds from the encampment. Facing in the proper direction, Kylene could imagine herself alone in the middle of the steppes and she did so, deliberately accepting a feeling of isolation in order to avoid the men about her.

A clanging sound recalled her to the present. *Tayem.*

Tayem was facing his opponent, a heavily built man of indefinite age who had nodded gravely when introduced to the big redhead. "Do your duty, Herrn," Tayem had told him. "To the third blood?"

Contempt had showed in the faces of several Sept Masters hearing that remark, but the Champion had waved his head and the Warder had agreed to that acceptance, his feigned reluctance covering relief only Kylene could detect.

Tayem had been given a sword. A "saber," he had named it, a narrow-bladed weapon with a sharp edge and a leather-wrapped handle within a basket hilt that was smaller and very different from the broadsword that had been taken from him.

"What material is this?" their captors had asked.

"Iron. A form of iron," Tayem had replied.

"Then we will guard it for you," they had told him. Perhaps that had been true.

Both fighters had stripped to loincloths. Paradoxically, this seemed to increase their bulk, even as it made them more difficult to see. Though Tayem had acquired a tan during the past year, he was much the lighter-colored, she noticed; the flames that showed only the outline of the other man made his skin seem red and burnished. Kylene was reminded of the aborigines Tayem sometimes spoke of, the people who had roamed this land during the early First Era.

Human beings, she thought now. Tayem's Indians had been human beings, with human thoughts and desires. They had been alive just as Tayem and she—and the council members around her—were alive today.

Today. Or ninety thousand years ago. And ninety thousand years from now surely other human beings would look back and wonder as she did that all persons had an equal share of existence. "No man is an island, entire of itself," Tayem had read to her one night. "Every man is a piece of the continent, a part of the main ... Any man's death diminishes me, because I am involved in mankind;

and therefore never send to know for whom the bell tolls; it tolls for thee."

All of humanity linked together so that no action stood in isolation . . . She could not accept the sentiment, but in Tayem's voice words from a man dead when the First Era was young had echoed in the forest, still freighted with meaning for the Fifth Era world that would be. For the first time, Kylene sensed history as Tayem must have viewed it.

Tayem and his opponent were motionless, standing on the balls of their feet, their outstretched swords pointing toward each other. Tayem had crouched slightly; his back and legs were invisible, but red and black flickered over his bare giant's arms, and red flashed from his weapon.

Tayem. Remembering his voice, Kylene suddenly felt as if the passage of time had been suspended, as if this frozen instant were to last for all eternity, and that all who would ever live were somehow present to witness it. Then she shivered, and the sensation passed.

The two men circled, shuffling counterclockwise. Tayem's back was to her, little more than a man-height away. She could hear him breathing heavily. One foot dragged the earth.

Another memory returned to her: Tayem kneeling in the snow, casually denying ability with a sword. Her heart froze. Had he foolishly provoked this fight, as he had provoked the duel in the Station, relying on endurance and Nicole's cloak to save him? *Tayem!*

How badly would he be hurt this time?

A flash of light—a *thumppf*! Herrn leaped toward Tayem, his blade swinging.

Tayem was not there. He had somehow moved a pace to one side and nearer to the Champion. He fell sideways, one leg bent before him, one stretched far behind—

Then he was upright, his sword swinging loosely in his hand. His left arm was in the air, limp-wristed. His breath rasped, heavy but regular. Kylene could smell his sweat, acrid now rather than musky.

But the single loud gasp she had heard was from Herrn.

She whirled toward the Warder, her fingers pointing accusingly. "Say it!"

Without his word, the count was not official, and it was too dark to see clearly. It was not his place to make such judgments. But the Sept Masters were staring at him. He had to speak. "First blood," the Warder admitted reluctantly, hoping this would prove incorrect.

Hammer sounds began then.

A fight, Kylene realized. *This is what the people call a sword fight.*

Not the slow circling and sudden movement she had seen at first, but this frenzy of sweeping blows, of dancing feet—the more than smithy's din, the stink of sweat, the heavy chests, the grimaces and rope-corded necks of men who locked blades together and strove to force each other back, their panting grasps for breath, the clatter, clatter, clatter of metal against metal—this was a sword fight.

She tried to concentrate, to halt the dancing images in her mind and over her vision to the men around her. But it could not be done. Tayem's mind was concealed from her by his Teepblind; all the others were now too alien, too excited to yield intelligible images. She must watch without understanding.

The fight was not equal, she saw at last. It was Tayem who danced the most, who leaped this way and that; it was Tayem whose blade flickered most frantically in the torchlight; it was Tayem's sweat she smelled most clearly.

But it was Herrn who remained near one spot, who turned stiffly and reluctantly, whose sword moved in greater arcs; it was he who bore a stolid blank expression, he who had crimson streaks along the leg he pivoted on, he who was forced back when both men strained chest to chest.

Tayem is not stronger, Kylene had time to realize. Yes, he might be stronger than other men. But his secret was his speed. Tayem was impossibly fast.

The clattering noise hastened. Herrn was attempting

to down Tayem by main force, trying to smash the Agent's lighter weapon out of his grasp. Tayem was accepting the risk, not making a true attack of his own but stepping into the blows, stopping them with the base of his blade to stay close to the older man, to force Herrn to step away from him, to make him use that wounded leg.

They were chest to chest again, leaning toward each other, their swords pressed together in a cross above them. Tayem slowly pushed his blade down, overcoming the other man's resistance. In return, Herrn reached out equally slowly with his free hand toward Tayem's chest, as if seeking to rest against a tree. Tayem's face showed a wide grimace—a smile?

Then the hand jerked upward, the palm smashing at Tayem's chin, the fingers scrabbling at Tayem's eyes.

Tayem half stepped, half fell sideways. His face could be seen in the torchlight for an instant. His mouth was open, his eyes closed.

But Herrn was off balance, and Tayem had convulsively shoved outward with his saber as he fell, forcing the other's blade away from him. As the other man teetered uncertainly, Tayem's legs skidded beneath him. He hit the ground full length on his side. Kylene heard the impact.

She did not have time to scream. As her mouth opened, Tayem jackknifed, pivoting upon his hip to sweep his arms and knees around Herrn's legs, tripping him. Then the redhead was over the Champion, one arm around his neck, the other brutally clubbing Herrn's head with the basket of the saber, shouting at the other man even after the sword had rolled from his limp fingers.

Then she could scream.

Somehow Tayem heard her. Suddenly, a man's arms were around her, pulling her tightly against a bare chest made slimy by sweat. Hot moist air pulsed against the top of her head—breath. The man said nothing, but she knew who it must be and became silent, then twisted her head to one side. When she opened her eyes, they focused

on a giant's fist, barely a handsbreadth distant, clenching
a sweat-darkened sword hilt. Mud streaked her front.

"All right," she gasped finally. "I can stand."

"Stay close, kid." Tayem stepped before her, his sword
half pointing toward the Warder. "Do you want me to give
him a few more cuts?" he growled.

"No," the Warder said. His eyes closed, then opened
slowly to focus unblinkingly on the man. "It is not necessary—tra'Dicovys. He is yours."

Tayem nodded abruptly in his alien fashion. "Very well."
Then he stepped back into the fighting square, where the
defeated Champion was struggling to rise. Tears were
streaming down the man's face.

"Stop blubbering," Tayem snapped. "Act like a hero,
prick."

Herrn gaped at him foolishly. The tears stopped.

"If I say you're still a warrior, you are," Tayem said
angrily. "You're done here. So go pack up your family,
get your asses over to my village, and tell that Acting
Master that I'm going to show up eventually and ask for
an accounting. If I don't like what he's been doing, he'll
shake hands with the Gods before I hear his name twice—
you tell him that."

He turned back to the Warder. "I want a tub and twelve
buckets of hot water. And feed us. In whatever order you
choose."

This is appalling, Kylene thought. *A Sept Master should
be given more than this. The wagon isn't even very clean.*

All manner of obnoxious, mindless, disgusting things
surely crawled under or on this filthy carpet, and she
would have been looking right at them, were the lighting
any good.

It was not, naturally. The red glow from the distant
campfire, pairs of tallow candles flickering in clay baskets
at the corners of the wagon . . . What could one do at nighttime with such useless lights, she wondered, except see

just enough to extinguish other lights? She snorted irritably. *Someone should be here to complain to*.

Tayem must have guessed her thoughts. "We'll get something else tomorrow. It'll do for tonight."

It was still night. It was not even late, Kylene realized; the moon was still ascending, and she could see on it the white face Tayem had described peeking past the folded cloth at the end of the wagon.

Dirty. Ill lit. And unguarded. Her own people would not have been so inhospitable. Tayem had had to fight a man for this?

Tayem kicked at a low platform near the front of the wagon, then knelt to run a hand through straw. "The bedding is reasonably fresh. Clean sheets. That's enough for me."

That was another cause for annoyance. "That's a very small bed."

"Space for two, if neither kicks. Willing to sign a non-aggression pact? I'll try not to snore."

He isn't apt to try very hard, she thought tartly. She had learned that on the trail. But she had little choice.

It would be an uncomfortable night. She was *not* going to enjoy it.

Tayem walked past her, his head stooped but still brushing against the canvas roof, and pulled loose the strap holding the flap at the back. That made the back portion of the wagon darker, but some light still penetrated the loose fabric, and he had done something to make the candles brighter. She could make out his silhouette as he pulled open his shirt front.

"Kylene? What are you thinking about?"

She grimaced sourly, then copied his up-and-down shoulder motion. "I was thinking I was certain to dream about you tonight."

Tayem chuckled. "Go ahead. I don't mind."

"*I* do."

Tayem chuckled again. His silhouette made boot-pulling motions.

He was very pleased with himself, Kylene recognized. He was feeling smug and cheerful, and he was radiating that obnoxious air of superiority he put on before her whenever he felt he had done something beyond her strength or comprehension.

What was the Algheran word for that? Oh, yes. *Masculinity.* It was a psychological disorder, one of the Teeps had explained to her. Young males were very susceptible to it. How very strange that someone from the First Era, not even completely human, could be affected by a Fifth Era disease.

Tayem padded past on bare feet to blow out candles, then pulled down the bed covers. "Let's hit the sack, kid. Tomorrow will be a busy day."

At least he wiped his feet off before getting in bed. Kylene hesitated a moment more, then began unsealing her sleeve. "Don't get ideas," she warned.

Tayem laughed, but there was an edge to his voice. "Little girl, I am tired. I am black and blue. I am sleepy. I do not have ideas, of any kind at all. I am doing my best just to keep my eyelids up—let alone other pieces of anatomy. There's another sheet here. Wrap yourself in that if you want."

Kylene bit her lip. It would be very pleasant to have a warm body against her during the cold night. But Tayem was nude, as she would be. "Tayem?"

"Hmm-mm."

"Can we put the sheet between us? To guard against embarrassment?"

Tayem half snorted, half coughed. "You're built very strangely, Kylene, if you're worried about my bare ass."

"Tayem!" She could tell from his voice that he'd made some kind of joke. "Be serious!"

"Oh, I am, I am." He obviously was not.

"Stop being masculine."

That hushed him for a short while. "Broad humor, Kylene?" he asked at last, sarcastically. "Do what you want, kid. Good night." His arm reached out to close the cover of the nearer candle box. The tiny hiss from the dying light could be heard quite clearly.

He *did* sound tired, Kylene realized guiltily. But she was only being sensible, and had no reason for apologizing. Wordlessly, she stripped off her clothing, hanging it on hooks sewn into the canvas, and walked to the bed platform. The carpet was every bit as gritty as she had thought it would be.

She rubbed her feet against her calves to clean them and got under the bedding with Tayem, then pushed at the grasses under the ground cover to arrange them for comfortable sleeping. Fortunately Tayem was at the far right of the bed, with his back to her; she did not touch him often and he did not move though she could tell from his breathing that he was still awake.

The extra sheet Tayem had spoken of was on the floor at her side of the bed platform. When she was satisfied with her mattress building, she unfolded it partially and draped it over her side and front before pulling up the covers. In the morning Tayem would be understanding again and agree that she was just being sensible. Content at last, she reached out to extinguish the last candle and wriggled comfortably in the darkness.

"Tayem?"

"Hmmmm?"

"Good night."

"Good night, Kylene."

"Tayem?"

"Hmmm."

"Can I have more of the blanket?"

Tayem sighed. "You really have most of it already."

"Oh. Good night."

"Good night, Kylene," he said distinctly.

"Tayem?"

"Hmm."

"I'm *cold*."

"Hm-mm."

"Can you get closer?"

Tayem produced tea-kettle sounds. "Lift your head," he said then. "Okay."

She lowered her neck onto Tayem's arm, and settled back comfortably. Tayem made a very nice, warm, firm pillow. "Hmmmm."

"Kylene."

"Hmmm?"

"I'll want the arm back in the morning."

"Hmm." Something had amused him, she sensed. She would figure out what it was in the morning. Tonight— Tayem had a very enjoyable smell tonight. His normal musky odor had combined with that from the newly pulled grass to make a spicy aroma that seemed to permeate the space around the bed like the warmth of his body. Exercise was good for him. She nodded her head on Tayem's arm and put out a hand to pat his side, then rubbed his chest hair to transfer some of his aroma to her. He was very close to her.

"Tayem?"

"Hmmm."

"Don't get too close."

A long pause. "Yes, Kylene. Good night, Kylene." He spoke patiently.

"Good night, Tayem. Tayem?"

"Yes, Kylene?" he asked, not so patiently.

"Someone is trying to get in the wagon."

"Yes, Kylene. *Huh?*"

"Someone is trying to get in the wagon. Hear the scratching in back? Look."

"Oh, *shit! Damnitalltahell!*" This First Era religious ritual often preceded Tayem's actions, and she had already sensed that the shape at the back was not hostile. Kylene's momentary unrest began to ease.

Tayem tossed back the covers with his free hand. "Let me up, Kylene."

"You're awake!" a husky feminine voice said. Canvas rustled at the back of the wagon. A head poked through the flaps.

"More or less," Tayem agreed. He propped his sword against the side of the wagon and went to extend his hand. "You need something?"

"Would I be intruding?" There was an eager tone to the voice.

Kylene began to feel alarm. She sat up abruptly, but instinctively fell back to avoid notice and pulled the bed covering to her face, while her mind reached out. Light and darkness whirled about her, then even through tightly closed eyes she gazed at the silhouette of a man.

The tra'Dicovys. That had been his voice. And this was his body before her, so tall and finely shaped, even as she had remembered it. She stared at him hungrily in the semidarkness, hardly able to breathe.

"No problem," he was saying. A hand reached toward her, touched her, and she was scrambling over the back gate, careless of her dignity as a young girl, not noticing the splinters that tore at her clothing.

He was nude, she noticed absently, but her eyes rested on his face, eager to see his expression. What must he think of her? "I—I wanted to see you," she explained. Speaking would keep his eyes focused on her.

The man held his arms wide. "So you're seeing me," he said, and she could not miss the irony of his voice. "Let me get some light." He turned away and went to the back of the wagon, taking large but nearly noiseless strides. "Go back to sleep, Kylene."

That remark had not been addressed to her. So she *had* heard a voice before the man rose to meet her, and he was not alone. She was too late. Disappointment gathered at the back of her throat, even while scraping sounds proved that the man was striking flint and steel.

Then he was moving toward her, a lighted candle held in one hand, the flame shielded by the other. Red and black flickered over his flat belly and across his chest.

"So you wanted to see me," he repeated, and lit candles casually at either side of the wagon until the interior colors could be seen. "What about? What's your name, by the way?"

"I'm from Dicovys." That came as a rush. "Chardis-cil—"

"Tayem! She's season-taken! Can't you see that?" The voice was feminine—high-pitched, with irritation obvious.

"Pipe down, kid," the redhead said firmly. "Go to sleep."

His name was called out again. He ignored it, to her surprise, and gestured at the carpet, then sat down cross-legged, facing her rather than the angry woman lying on the bedframe. "So. One of my people." His eyes focused on her unblinkingly, moving from her face to her carefully maintained leather dress, then to her bare arms and calves. "Chardiscil? What's the rest of it?"

He was the Sept Master of Dicovys, she made herself remember, conscious of the thin pale arm on the bed cover, the narrow face glaring at her, the dark hair so different from her own ash brown. A woman of the Sept was already in his bed. Nothing could come of this, but he was actually looking at her and speaking to her.

She could not look at him. "Terocu. Chardiscil Terocu Dicovys."

There. It was out. She had given him her name. Perhaps he would remember it; the Goddess's cloak might cover her someday. Surely the Lady would not object to her dreams!

She waited for a response, motionless, while a corner of her mind noticed the tapestries over the lacquered side-boards and the bright paint on the bedframe and interior trimming. The carpet pile was so thick the underlying boards in the wagon bed could not be felt. Such wealth! Her breath quickened.

"Terocu," the tall man said slowly. His baritone voice changed it into the name of a stranger. "Terocu. That's a very pretty name."

Oh, she might hope! Terocu raised her head slowly to face the Sept Master. For an instant, memory struck at her and Jeridul ha'Dicovys stood again on the brown summer grass outside the wagon calling out her name. The memory died, as Jerd himself had more than a quarter century ago, and she was once more by herself, simply Terocu Dicovys, weakened and terror-filled, resting on her knees in the wagon of another and facing a man she did not know, fearful that he would laugh at her, at the pitiful finery she had worn on her wedding day.

The strange man smiled at her, a quirk of his expression showing frown lines etched across his forehead. Age was cutting back his hairline, she noticed. Strands of gray could be seen amid the red-gold and an old scar was visible on his left temple. The Master of Dicovys was no longer a young man, not now the almost boyish figure who had led the Sept briefly during her own youth. The years had touched him also.

Maturity had not made him less attractive, she realized with innocent surprise, but merely changed the manner in which he was handsome. Long ago, when she had never dreamed of being so close to him, he had attracted her attention; now his presence was overwhelming. Unaware of her motion, she leaned toward him, preoccupied by the warmth and sudden tenderness in her lap, dimly conscious of the dampness that bathed her.

"And you're a pretty woman," he said. "So what brings you here?"

She could not decipher the emotions in his voice nor continue to face him. Her eyes closed. She spoke gaspingly. "I—I wanted—I have no one else."

There was silence. Then he spoke. "So you're lonely. Frightened a bit too, I suspect."

"Yes," she whispered. She could hear her heart pound.

"Season-taken." The voice was calm, not asking a question.

"Yes." It was necessary to say more, to break the hush. "I—sometimes young warriors—when I—never—"

"I understand. Biology and many more women than men in this camp. It happens. Does this bother you?"

Fingers touched her right forearm, stroking gently over

skin turned suddenly to goose flesh. Terocu shivered but the stroking continued.

It was only a hand, she told herself. She made her eyes open, so she could watch its movements. Only a hand.

It was such a large hand. The hair on its back gleamed like gold in the candlelight, contrasting sharply with the dark-brown hair on her arm. It was a strong hand, she sensed, attached to a heavily muscled arm, yet unused to toil, for the callouses were few and strangely placed. Her own hands were more work-hardened than this; for an instant the thought covered her with shame.

"Does this bother you?" the man asked again. His voice was even, low-pitched. Terocu forced her gaze to move along his arm and up to his face. His eyes focused upon hers. They were gray, she noticed, metal-colored, and the red-brown brows above them were crooked and thick. His face was curiously without expression, as if it belonged to the body of another man far distant from here. The gentle stroking continued, freezingly, hypnotically, turning her ragged breath to panting.

The pressure seemed carried through her body, so her thighs tensed and eased in rhythm with the sensation in her arms. Soft waves of pleasure undulated through her, rolling through tissues made pillow-plump and moist, weak and unresisting. Her body was no longer hers to control, but a pliable abject instrument played upon by another.

With that realization came fear.

Shaking violently, Terocu broke free from the spell and grabbed the Sept Master's forearm with both her own hands, and looked at him with despair. "Please," she whimpered.

"Tayem!" The protest from the background she scarcely noticed.

Neither did the man. He leaned forward, rising onto his knees to stroke her arms with his free hand. Terocu could not move away from it, did not want to move away from it. Unable to control her voice, she made mewing sounds.

"Isn't this what you want?" the man asked softly. His voice was kind, she noticed dimly, but his face was still expressionless. His hand moved lower, stroked between her knees.

Yes, she wanted to say. *Yes. But I am Terocu Dicovys and no more than that. I was curious, yes. I hoped—but I did not anticipate this. For I am not noticed. I have seen the seasons' cycle two doubled hands of hands and I know that I am neither wanted nor desirable, for I only work in the fields.*

Her legs separated without volition. The hand patted her inner thighs and kneaded the yielding flesh softly.

Once . . . but I have already seen my man go to Cimon's flame and raised two sons to maturity, and I have no one who wants me now—only the young men who take me contemptuously before battle or when need causes me to beg.

This can not be happening. This is my Sept Master, and not one of the warriors. Cruelty is buried in his face and his body is hard and he is about to use me, brutally, as would any other man. But I am here . . . begging. Yes. Yes. Please. Use me. Fill me. Crush me. Be cruel. Only make me feel again. Yes . . .

The big man's eyes were still focused on her, narrowed now in concentration. He was not releasing her. Her eyes closed, and she surrendered to sensation. Her heart was beating rapidly, lightly. Her breathing was ragged, and she could hear air moving between her lips. Blindly, she clawed back the tight fabric of the dress, widening the space between her legs to lower herself on the warm insistent hand. Sudden perspiration cooled her limbs, made them clammy. An arm moved about her shoulders, pulling her tight against another body. Feather touches moved along her neck, and she drew her head back to expose it to the Sept Master's kisses.

A strain at the back of her neck—that was from a tug at the drawstrings that fastened her tunic. She pulled her shoulders back, to draw the soft leather taut across her breasts and ease the task, and moaned as the binding eased and the interior lining slid caressingly over her erect nipples.

"Yes," she gasped. "Yes!"

Then everything stopped.

"Are you sure?" a voice asked from an enormous distance. It was filled with sadness.

Terocu was frozen, nearly screaming in her frustrated need and disbelief. To be abandoned now . . . *Oh, Lady!* Tears would follow soon; she fought for self-control before she slowly opened her eyes, awaiting other torment.

The pain-filled face of the Sept Master made quiet fall on her. "I shouldn't be doing this," he whispered, and his head turned from side to side. "I've no right."

"You are Master of Dicovys," she said simply.

The big man smiled bleakly. "That does not make me master of Terocu. Not if she does not truly want me."

She understood suddenly and tears beaded her eyes. Oh, Lady! Oh, that he would feel this way!

Now she was conscious of herself as a half-nude woman lying on a carpet intertwined with the mixed softness and hardness of a nude man. She was again in the normal body of Terocu Dicovys and for a short time all desire was gone.

Tenderness remained. She lifted a hand to his cheek, no longer fearing he would object to its work-roughened touch, and traced her fingers down the side of his face. "My lord . . . I know. I have been lonely also."

The man's face distorted. For an instant she expected tears. Then his mouth bent in an unfamiliar curve, and it was as if her heart moved upward in her chest. "Sept Masters never admit to feelings," he told her mock-sternly, and chuckled softly. "Do you think for tonight you could call me Timt?"

She nodded. "Timt. Timt. Yes."

"Very good, my little Terocu." Timt smiled happily at her, then glanced down his front. "Uh . . . gotta rebuild a bit before going any further," he said apologetically.

For now, he belonged to her. *Lady, I know this is not my doing, and that all that happens is Your gift. Oh, You have been so kind tonight.*

Disbelief still remained in her. She must touch him, hold him. She put her arms around the man's neck, pulling him down beside her. Yes, he was here, still here. "I'm in no hurry now, Timt. Dear. Timt. We've all the night."

The man made a purring sound and rested his head for a moment on her exposed breasts. Lightly—the hair strands pressed no harder than a mass of autumn grass and she tugged at his shoulders to make his weight fall upon the soft tissue. An arm reached around her back; another stroked along her side. Oh, to be feeling such touches again!

Something damp and slick glided across her right nipple—a tongue, she realized suddenly. No one had done *that* to her for many years. She exhaled loudly, and moaned as Timt moved a finger lightly across her left nipple. Tenseness rose in her, waiting a signal to pour into her breasts; she could sense stiffness returning to her nipples.

The hands moved lower on her body. The lips followed, strewing soft kisses like flower petals across her stomach and below. Terocu raised her hips and squirmed as her dress slipped toward her feet.

Tayem was laughing.

Kylene lay on a straw-littered floor, blanket-swaddled, snuffling miserably to herself, her face contorted to hold tears back in silence, flinching at each chuckle. How could he be so cruel? What excuse could he have for behaving so crudely?

That season-taken peasant, she thought bitterly. *That's all that he cares about now. She had no right. No right.* Hatred flowed through her suddenly, then ballooned to make her body iron hard. A tic distorted her cheeks and mouth. But she remained motionless, afraid to draw attention to herself.

Almost as quickly, anger turned to despair. *I should*

have stopped him, she thought unhappily. *But I didn't know he would be as bad as her. I didn't know he was going to do this. I let him become an animal.*

Unable to interfere, Kylene had pretended sleep rather than acknowledge Tayem's lovemaking. Finally noticing that, he had broken off coupling with the Algheran woman to call out her name. She had not answered, and he had grunted with satisfaction, then casually dumped her on the carpet beside the bedframe. Now Terocu was in Kylene's place, nude, stinking of sweat and other secretions, making mindless animal noises, while Tayem lay laughing between her legs. He had not even taken the time to extinguish the lights.

Within armslength, Kylene watched disbelievingly.

Through half-closed eyes she glimpsed the big man's back. He was resting on his side now. Shoulder motions showed a giant's arm extending toward the foot trapped between his knees. "This tiny piglet went a-trading," he was saying. "This tiny piglet stayed in camp. This tiny piglet ate stewed beef, and this tiny piglet got none." Rustling sounds must have been a startled Terocu. Then the woman giggled drunkenly.

Tayem chortled. "So now you know what toes are for. Bad poetry and good hostages."

The woman's voice was lazy. "What do you have for *me* to ransom?"

Snake slithering sounds followed. A board under the bedframe creaked as dingy tan-brown hair shook about the man's body. A grubby-nailed hand waved over Kylene's slitted eyes, wrapped about Tayem's hips. Smacking noises. "What is this, Timt?" Sucking.

Tayem exhalted loudly and tossed back his head. "Just my Peter," he gasped. "The little boy—ahh!—that lives with me. Ooh! Be careful now. I can't replace the family jewels."

He exhaled again, a long drawn-out sigh. At last he flopped backward, vanishing from Kylene's sight. Sounds indicated that he pulled the Algheran woman toward him.

"Little Peter had grown up again. Let's see whether you can hold him for ransom with more success than you did the first time."

Terocu chuckled in unison. "At least I'll keep him longer, Timt."

"Kidnapper!"

Kylene heard bodies moving across the sheets, murmurs. A subdued slapping sound began, liquidlike, rhythmical, punctuated by heavy breathing.

It stopped suddenly. "Cimon-taken foot," Tayem muttered. "Cramp, Terocu. Sorry. There." Straw shifted under his weight, till Kylene could see his head and part of his back again, awkward-seeming, as if his weight rested on his elbows. "Comfortable? Let's go."

The rhythmical slapping sounded again, softer and more slowly this time. Kylene watched with horrified fascination as Tayem's back and buttocks tilted up and down in time with it. Imperceptibly, the tempo increased. Terocu moaned.

She would *not* enter Terocu's mind, Kylene vowed. She would not let herself be trapped with season-taken insanity. She would never lose control of herself this way, not for anyone.

Despite that, sensations pressed hypnotically at Kylene. Her breathing began to keep pace with Tayem's. His weight thrusting against Terocu might be pressing down upon her own thighs, forcing her legs apart as if his lunges pounded deep into her own melting body. She was tense, unmoving, but she did not notice. Her eyes were open now, focused on Tayem, while a pleasurable excitement began to mount within her.

Tayem did not see her glances. He began to move more rapidly, till he was frantically slamming his groin against the woman writhing beneath him. Strain showed on his face. Kylene saw beads of sweat dripping down one cheek, and his body glistened damply in the candlelight. He groaned softly, saying something undecipherable. His pace began to slacken. His head drooped and his body sank out of sight. Unendurably firm flesh softened, dwindled within a sloppy yielding portal. The slapping sounds were gone. There was a big smacking kiss to be heard, followed by a suddenly calm "I'm dead, woman."

Kylene paid little attention. A light sheen of perspiration covered her entire body now. A fire burned in her groin, painful but not to be stopped. Her forearms were held tightly against her abdomen, muscles in them aching but not to be needed. Her fingers were almost touching, pressing hard into her flesh with tiny strokes. Tension made her body into an archer's bow, pulled into an arc, tighter and tighter. She was rising into the sky, an arrow that waited for release. Higher. Higher. Faster. Harder.

Oh! She was thrown heavenward as if by catapult. Into stars!

Stars! For an instant she floated among them, then the flashes of light were gone. She could feel the contractions now, as if ecstasy had become solid to undulate within her body. Tension flowed out of her suddenly, numbing her limbs and leaving her limp and exhausted. Kylene moaned breathlessly, threw back a portion of the blankets. Again—she could do this again.

"Are you all right, kid?" A face looked down at her. It was very large, topped by red-brown hair, and ruddy. Tayem. It took a short while to give the face a name; just for that moment her unconcerned ignorance was amusing to her.

Consciousness returned suddenly. Portions of her body were sore, raw-textured. A tacky liquid was on her hands and in the hair upon her groin. Her legs were parted, sweat-dampened, exposed. Flesh clamped her fingers.

She had not received sensations from Terocu's body, she realized sickly, but from her own. She stared up at Tayem, horror making her face into a mask, and rubbed her fingers uselessly against her belly, trying to clean them, while comprehension flowed into his expression. Amazement.

"No!" she cried. "No, Tayem!" She twisted aside, to

avoid his outstretched hand. "Nothing is right!" Then she was struggling to be free of the blanket wrapped about her, ridding herself of its grasp, and stumbling across the floor of the wagon. "Everything is wrong!"

"Kylene, come back!"

But she ignored Tayem's voice as she half climbed, half fell over the bulwark, she ignored Tayem's presence as she bloodied a knee on the footstep at the back of the wagon and scrambled to the ground, she ignored Tayem's shocked face as the canvas flap dropped to conceal the interior of the wagon. She tried not to remember Tayem as she rushed into the night.

Pain came to her at last, when a bare foot landed too near a rock and she stubbed her toe. Other feelings came through then: cold blades of grass tickling featherlike at her thighs, thistles prickling against her soles, and soil pressure-stuck beneath her feet; sore muscles and drying tears, perspiration, cool air against her body. The wagon camp could no longer be seen. She heard a distant lowing sound that must have come from the cattle herd.

She was nude, she remembered abjectly, standing stock still. She could not face wilderness without clothing. She would have to go back.

Back. She could not face that yet, and she had no more heart to run. She sank to her knees, shaking with cold and exhaustion. *Tayem.*

She retched suddenly, first with dry heaves, then spewing vomit onto the ground, choking, feeling pain sear her nose, splattering hot stinking droplets onto her toes and into dangling strands of hair, till there was nothing left of the Algheran camp to expel.

And now she was ugly and unkempt outwardly as well, she realized. No one wanted her; no one cared what happened to her. No one in her homeland, no one in the Project, not even other Teeps, no one in this or any other era. Her father, her City, the Algherans, now even

Tayem—they had all left her alone, abandoned and betrayed.

Tayem. Tayem had not followed her.

Tayem, Tayem, Tayem. She threw herself sideways, falling face downward onto the slime-smeared grass, cradling her head in her arms, sobbing without end.

CHAPTER TEN

*M*orning came eventually, in the form of a hand shaking her shoulder.

"Rise and shine, kid," Tayem said. There was a pause that must have been a yawn. "Cimon, these folks get up early. I'd forgotten about that."

Softness underneath her, not boards. Straw, she knew somehow. She was lying in bed. A bedframe. Blankets were wrapped about her. She murmured and pulled them closer to her chin. She really was awake, and she would open her eyes in a while.

Then she remembered.

She threw the clammy stinking blankets away from her and rolled off the smelly bedframe as quickly as she could.

"Good morning," Tayem said. "Campaigning to be a *centerfold*?"

The tone of his voice defined the unfamiliar word. Kylene colored and snatched at the discarded bed clothing for protection. "Get out!"

"Sure. I'll wait outside." Tayem took his banning philosophically.

She dressed awkwardly, looking toward the exit rather than at her clothing, postponing the moment when she would have to face Tayem again. But she could not stall indefinitely; eventually she pushed a belt through the loops of a pair of jeans and examined the seams of her blouse for the last time. She *had* returned, she remembered. Life must go on.

When she joined Tayem, she saw that he was dressed in green and black clothing like that he had worn the day before. The sword was not on his waist, but he had strapped the golden mace to his belt with a leather thong. Otherwise, he seemed unchanged. Kylene looked at him warily.

Tayem did not mention the previous night. "Let's get breakfast."

Breakfast was more of an early lunch, she discovered. The camp invalids and the elderly were served at this time of day. Life in the Project had removed her familiarity with the aged; without knowing why, she was grateful when Tayem placed a tankard and utensils in her hands and led her past the small fields the women tended, over the creek, and away from the wagons.

Deep in the tall grass, the man stomped around to create a small clearing, then sat cross-legged, his own tankard and a dripping platter of meat before him. "Eat up," he urged. "Beat the ants to it."

Kylene knelt uneasily, half expecting to find the threatened ants. But Tayem had been joking. Assured of that, she haggled still-hot meat away from a charred thigh bone with her teeth and turned awkwardly to look back toward the camp. She was not eager to speak with Tayem.

The green stockade about her blocked her view of the wagons, though voices and other sounds could be heard. When she lowered her mind shield, she learned that a hunting party was returning. One of the giant rabbits had been killed and was being pulled into camp on a travois.

There was only the babble of Normal minds, and no message from another Teep. Had she been mistaken?

No, she decided finally. Someone had touched her mind. If that person did not wish to be discovered, she could be patient. The mystery would surely be solved in the future. She raised her mind shield again and turned her attention back to her surroundings.

The leafy top of a stunted tree, for some reason not yet converted to firewood by the Algherans, rose over the grass in the opposite direction. The sky was clear, she noticed automatically, and a light breeze came from the south; the weather would be good that day.

Tayem followed her gaze and nodded as if seeing her thoughts, then carefully stacked gnawed bones and scraps of fat along the rim of the platter. "So this is history, undercooked and greasy," he said in Lopritian, while wiping his hands in the grass. "How does it look?"

At least he was not asking when she had come back to the wagon. Memories from the early morning flashed before her, showing her again the predawn mist over rolling prairies, the gray and black shapes that became a wagon camp as she approached, cattle moving lazily in the distance and curious dogs nuzzling her bare legs with cold snouts after she bathed in the stream . . . the bodies intertwined in sleep on the bedframe. She froze inwardly for a moment, then resolution returned.

Meat muffled her voice, so she made finger-snap motions. What was history supposed to look like?

"More than this," Tayem answered when she got the question out. "Little tribes wandering around, illiteracy, no ambition, no progress—not even a notion of progress. I sometimes think there is a curse on humans, to keep us from getting too high."

"What would you prefer?"

"Doing stuff!" Tayem exclaimed. "Building cities. Putting men on the moon. Living underwater. Trying to live a thousand years. Turning everyone into Teeps. Whatever. Something with purpose. Trying to make dreams come true!" He shook his head and looked past her, as if arguing with the wind. "Not staying in the same Cimon-taken ruts."

Kylene reached toward the platter to conceal a frown. "Men have built cities before," she said neutrally.

"Once, twice, three times and four," Tayem quoted sourly. "And one more try uptime. But they never last. A couple of thousand years, and civilization always collapses—to this." He waved a hand contemptuously. "Ninety thousand years since my time, and probably eighty looked exactly like this."

He was in a mood for a quarrel, she realized, and he had done nothing lately to justify victory in one. "You were not complaining about this life last night," she said tartly.

"I don't know what you mean." The words came too quickly and too loudly to Tayem's lips. His eyes moved past her.

"Yes, you do! That woman—"

"For crying out loud, Kylene! She was lonely and unhappy. What else was I supposed to do? What kind of argument is that anyhow?"

A good one. But Tayem could not see the thought. Kylene breathed deeply, her eyes closed, concentrating on feeling the expansion of her chest to restore calm.

"Lonely and unhappy," she repeated. "Are all these people—all *your* people, Sept Master—lonely and unhappy? With *you* to lead them?"

"Careful, Kylene. I don't need sarcasm," Tayem said warningly.

"Then answer the question."

"I'm not a Teep. How would I know?" Exasperation sounded in his voice, but it had a forced tone. His face took on a preoccupied look.

She smiled at him, rather than answering his words. Tayem had lost the argument, she knew. His expression showed he realized it also, and that was reward enough.

Naturally, he would not admit it openly. "I don't buy

it, Kylene," he said finally. He had become calmer within heartbeats, she noticed. That ability of Tayem's always surprised her. She waited expectantly.

"Yes," he continued carefully. "There are happy people here. And yes, there are unhappy people in civilization. I'll grant that much of your argument." His voice turned sour. "I trust that makes *you* happy."

"Tayem!"

"All right! A low blow—I apologize. The point is, being happy isn't all that matters."

"What else is there?"

"Doing stuff," he explained once more as if it were self-evident. "Accomplishing things, rather than just staying alive. Cimon and Nicole! Any animal can eat and sleep and be happy; people have the ability to do more than that. Thinking and building and creating—and even being very emotional, Kylene—those are human traits too, and if you abdicate all of that you make yourself less than human. It's a betrayal."

Forty-six chromosomes, she remembered suddenly. Who was he to say who was human? But the gibe was too cruel to use.

"Different things make different people happy, Tayem," she said instead, speaking as if to a small child. "Maybe 'doing stuff' makes you happy and people like you. Maybe being less than what you call human makes other people happy. But everyone tries for happiness."

The big man grimaced. "Maybe."

"Let's talk about something else," Kylene said wearily, unhappily.

Tayem made his shoulder motion. "Sure." He stood then, the bone-laden platter in his hand. "Guess this area doesn't really need policing. Why do women always want to talk about happiness, anyhow?" His voice was cheerful.

He was eager to be traveling again, she soon found. "Figure you get time for play," he explained at the camp border. "I have to see him again this afternoon but I've already talked to the Warder about leaving you here, while I go to Dicovys. You'll have the wagon to stay in."

She had not anticipated being separated from him. "For how long?"

"A ten-day period. Maybe two," he said casually. "Depends on what sort of mess things are in. I'll get back for you eventually."

Ten days. Maybe twenty. Without her. Kylene looked around wildly, but no one was close enough to overhear. "You're taking that woman!"

Tayem raised an eyebrow. "Terocu? Not likely. She'd just be in the way—and the Project can't use her either if you're wondering. Why? Feeling jealous?" Kylene could not interpret the look on his face.

"But—" Kylene gnawed at her lip, then decided that the unpleasantness must be faced. "You and she were— you can't just leave her! What if she is pregnant, Tayem? Carrying your child? Didn't you even think about that?"

Tayem snorted. "Not enough chromosomes, remember? And it's hard enough for the average guy to get some woman in this era pregnant. For me—the Lady's cloak isn't big enough."

She wondered if she had heard bitterness. But a question still waited to be answered. "Why can't I go with you?"

The man looked toward the camp and smiled harshly. "I could use a Teep, kid. You'd be a help. But this Warder has some kind of bug on his brain. I don't know exactly what, but I think I'll have to leave you as a hostage."

In the end, Tayem's plans had to be postponed. "Should have expected it," he told Kylene after leaving the Warder's wagon. "I built up a reputation once, and now I have to keep it going. *Heap big medicine man, me!*" But he seemed more pleased than upset, despite his talk of wasting the day.

He worked through the day, and late into night. When

Tayem closed his impromptu surgery, faces could be seen only by torchlight.

"Those people weren't just from this village, were they?" Kylene asked when they were alone in their wagon.

"Probably not. Several Septs in riding distance." Tayem undressed at the back of the wagon. He seemed uninterested, as if aware that she knew the answer to her own question. Pus and blood had crusted on the sleeves of his shirt. Now he reopened the rear flap and leaned through the canvas opening with the garment. A muffled voice came back to her, punctuated by slaps at the wood. "That dead woman. Carrying a corpse. Across country. In your arms. Like that. Some ride that must. Have been. For her hearthsharer."

Kylene frowned. "Does that still bother you?"

Tayem's head reappeared. "Didn't *bother* me. Wasted my time." He looked at her unblinkingly, daring her to challenge him.

A woman had died in childbirth, leaving a boy baby and a mate who had despairingly sought a miracle. Tayem had given them neither sympathy nor miracle, but she remembered the expressions that had lain upon his face. "Time," she repeated. "You could change what happened."

Tayem shook his head sideways. "I won't alter history. Putting a broken leg into splints or cleaning a wound so it heals properly is one thing; keeping alive someone who actually died is another."

Then why bring this up? "Even a mother?"

"Particularly a mother." His voice was flat, and Kylene suddenly remembered that he had been an orphan all his life. She said nothing but straightened bed sheets while Tayem moved about the wagon.

A basin of hot water rested on a stand near the rear. Kylene had dabbed at her face to please him; when she denied any further need for it, he sponged water along his arms and face, then dropped the shirt in to soak. "Wonder if I can get this cleaned properly tomorrow."

He did not continue undressing, but tugged a padded tunic over his head and swiped uselessly at his ruffled hair. "I'm going out to look at stars. Do you want to come?"

Kylene nodded her head in the negative. Stargazing connected with calendars she could understand, but Tayem did not read dates from the skies. He simply enjoyed looking at random patterns. He might as well do that by himself.

When he was gone, she moved the bucket containing his shirt to the side of the cabin and stared at it pensively. After breakfast she would walk about the camp to see where the washing was done, then clean Tayem's shirt. *Acting like a hearthsharer*, she thought self-consciously. For a man who would never be one and would always seem a stranger.

But Tayem had fought for her, and he was asking nothing she had not given to her father; she felt no resentment. Still, the self-consciousness remained.

And uncertainty. She had to give thought to dealing with Tayem.

But it was too late. She had no direction to steer her thoughts, nor cause to give them passage tonight. She pinched out lights, then turned back the bed.

The wagon was comfortable now, she decided, squirming as she pulled the bedclothes to her chin. She would enjoy the warmth and feel of the bedding and not give thought to Tayem. He would not be thinking of her, after all; to pay attention to him would be a form of defeat.

Their clothing and equipment had been stowed along the walls, and the carpet had been shaken out during the day. This still seemed untidy when compared to Tayem's cabin, but it was sufficiently neat that she did not worry about his reaction to it. Life could be pleasantly domestic now—she wondered uneasily if the improvement had been brought about by the Warder's order or at the initiative of someone else.

She was still speculating when she heard Tayem's voice.

He spoke to someone whom she could not hear and his own words were unclear, but she sensed from his tone that the conversation had lasted some while.

Curiosity and habit won out. Light and darkness whirled, sound danced toward her and retreated; then she was in the mind of another.

Terocu. Kylene froze at the identification, then waited, uncertain as to the reactions she should be feeling.

Time passed. Kylene was dimly aware of a scrabbling sound at the back of the wagon. Consciousness returned with attention. Her head turned that way, her awareness limited now to the inside of the wagon.

Tayem's head came through the canvas flap, followed by his shoulders, as he mounted the back step, then a leg and the rest of him. He stared at her and walked heavily toward the bedframe. When he looked down, she saw no expression on his face.

"Just talked to Terocu," he said curtly. "She was planning to stay tonight. I sent her away."

Kylene took a breath, suddenly conscious of the rise and fall of her breasts. "I know," she said quietly.

Tayem grimaced. "I guess you would. Well—she's not here. Does that make you happy now?" Anger vied with exhaustion in his voice.

She had already searched for an answer. "I don't know."

"It was supposed to." His anger was clear now.

Kylene faced it calmly. "I know. Come to bed, Tayem." Her arm swept over the vacant side of the bedframe. "You need your sleep."

"I was trying to make you happy, Kylene," he said sourly.

Kylene focused her eyes on Tayem's face, without speaking, until he blinked and turned away. While she watched, he moved along the side of the wagon, desultorily picking at loose strands in the canvas. He made no effort to undress or to extinguish the remaining lights.

Finally he stood at the end of the wagon again, toying with the entrance flap, refusing to look at her.

"So you're unhappy now, and Terocu is unhappy. Is that what you are thinking?" Kylene asked.

"That does not need an answer," Tayem growled. And when Kylene remained silent, he said, "I ought to go get her." But his voice was plaintive. He seemed strangely shrunken, Kylene noticed. Smaller, withdrawn from the world. *This morning, he claimed she meant nothing to him.*

But remembering aloud would be cruel. "Let her go, Tayem."

"Why? I want her, after all. And—Cimon!"

"She wants you too. She's lonely. Yes," Kylene agreed. "But let her go. You can't keep her. You know that."

"Just one more night."

"It wouldn't be the same, Tayem. She has memories of you now. She'll be happy with those."

"She *said* she would. But—" He raised a palm to show doubt.

He still was not facing her and Kylene permitted herself to smile fondly. "Really she will, Tayem. Believe me."

"But why?" Hurt and confusion sounded in his voice, and showed on his face when he turned. At this moment he was very like a small boy, she sensed.

But he could not be given small-boy answers. "Because you have no future together. Terocu is not your equal, Tayem," she said gently.

"Kylene!" Shock showed on his face; genuine anger was in his voice.

She had expected that and stood her ground. "Terocu is not your equal, Tayem," she repeated. "She does not want to be. She is content as she is."

"But—" Tayem started grimly, then tapered off.

"Do you want her as a hearthsharer, Tayem?"

"I don't know what you mean." The big man spoke sullenly.

Kylene suppressed a smile. "Yes, you do. Tayem, be

honest! An illiterate barbarian herdsman, knowing nothing about your real life, who wants little more from her existence than what she already has, who can only meet your lusts five days of the year—is that what you want at your side? For the rest of your life?"

"No." Torture might have been used to extract that answer.

"Then why are you arguing with me?"

Tayem was silent, but his expression said he was unfairly treated.

My own very small boy, Kylene thought warmly. "You can't do everything you want for everyone, Tayem. It isn't possible—even for Cimon and Nicole, and no one expects it of you."

"They do." Tayem was suddenly adult, without sign of complaint.

Kylene found herself wondering what chord she had struck. But it was not important. Once more she patted the other side of the bed. "You need sleep, Tayem. You're showing it by the way you walk, and talk, and by the way you argue. Come to bed. It's the best thing you can do, and Terocu would agree with me." Then she added lightly, "Onnul would agree with me."

Tayem said nothing, but his eyes closed. He was motionless.

Even without mind-seeing, Kylene felt his pain. "I'm sorry, Tayem."

Her head shook, postponing further speech. She had thought Terocu a replacement for Onnul in Tayem's mind, not understanding until now the depths of the emotion he had given the lost woman. *It's been so many years*, she thought with dismay. *She's gone, Tayem. Accept that. Learn to forget. Bury her, Tayem.* But those words could not be said.

"Do it for me," she said finally. That was half a prayer.

"All right." Tayem's voice could barely be heard. But he began to remove his clothing, and when he had hung his garments on the wall hooks, he moved about the wagon to snuff the candles.

He came to bed in the darkness and slipped under the covers without a word, nude, but with his back to her.

She hesitated, then touched his shoulder. "Tayem. Look at me."

"Hmmmm?"

"Turn over. Don't argue. Just do it."

He growled inarticulately, but obeyed. She was able to slide her arm under his massive shoulder before he tried to speak again. "Ky—"

"Move down," she interrupted. "That's it."

Tayem squirmed for a moment. "My feet are off the platform."

She was touching him and could sense from his emotions that the complaint was baseless. "It's all right, Tayem. Turn over some more."

The man grumbled to himself, but obeyed as she had expected. Now Kylene could wrap both arms about his warm body. Soft flesh rested against her thigh; for an instant she thought it a fold in the covers, before sensing the coarse hair on the man's groin. Then she dismissed the unimportant novelty from her mind. "There," she cooed soothingly. "Go to sleep, Tayem."

Hot breath cascaded over the upper portion of her chest. "Kylene!"

"Go to sleep, Tayem." Her cheek rubbed against the top of his head, and she squeezed him quickly, her forearms tugging downward at his shoulder blades. "I want to hold you this way tonight."

"I—"

"Yes, Tayem. You don't like this. Put up with it."

"Oh, Cimon! This is—"

"Very embarrassing for an Ironwearer, and just what you need."

That brought silence. "It's only for tonight, Tayem," she promised, and suddenly knew that promise to be dishonesty.

"Why?"

"I don't know why," she said truthfully. "I want to, that's all."

"This is awkward." It was more comment than complaint, and she was not surprised when Tayem moved his own arms around her waist. For an instant she was squeezed deliberately against him, then the grip relaxed and outsized hands patted her buttocks softly.

Tayem said no more. Kylene closed her eyes and rubbed her cheeks against his hair, enjoying the feel of the hard and the soft portions of his body against hers, luxuriating in the warm breath dancing across her breasts. And perhaps the cords of his neck were less taut now; perhaps the flesh upon his upper back had softened.

Eventually he slept and she was able to retrieve her numbed arms and drape them about him more comfortably. *He needed to be treated this way*, she confided to the darkness, contrasting Tayem's peaceful breath to the subdued creaking of the wagon. *But he never would trust Terocu so.*

Terocu. In truth, Kylene knew if the nomad woman had ever desired Tayem himself, she did no longer. Terocu had no wish to unsettle her existence; she wished to possess the unchanging memory of a love rather than risk the uncertainty of an affair. And she was Algheran; she might find something enjoyable in the bittersweet memory of her loss, in the admiration given by others for the constancy of her pain.

Kylene's head shook minutely. Tayem was not the man he pretended to be; Terocu's emotions would never make sense to him. She was grateful for that—she did not want him to become an Algheran.

Being in Tayem's arms had become unexpectedly pleasant. She was still wondering what that might mean when she also fell asleep.

* * *

"Evennle is inside," the Warder told Kylene. "She—the tra'Dicovys is here. He tells me your presence is necessary." His hand waved uselessly.

Kylene pulled herself to the back step of the wagon and tugged the canvas flap aside to peer within. The interior was dingy and ill lit, she noticed quickly. It was cluttered with half-filled sacks and wooden boxes; rug-wrapped bales were lashed to the walls and the air was beclouded with the musty smell of unwashed linen and unbathed bodies. Her nose wrinkled.

Typical barbarian litter, typical barbarian stink.

Now that she had an excuse, she looked down at the Warder with additional disdain. His language was still too unfamiliar for seeing clearly into his mind but that was not required to establish his character. A sluggard, she had decided. Stupid. Weak. It was appropriate that this contemptible man lived in squalor. "Go away first."

The Warder colored but obeyed. Kylene watched impassively as his form shrank and was lost in the depths of the camp.

Let him be displeased, she thought. *His mind shows he needs us.* This day had begun badly, with sleep-disturbing nightmares at dawn. Now she was thirsty and her head ached; she thought well of nothing in the one world.

"Good morning, Kylene. Feeling better?" Tayem was near the back of the wagon, bent over a small bedframe. Silvery instruments were in his hands; in the darkness, she could not decipher his motions.

His voice was also unrevealing, to her disappointment. Barely a day tenth before, she remembered, he had awoken at her panicked cries, holding her patiently till the now-forgotten dream images faded and dawn reddened the horizon. That was pleasant to recall; even then, she had regretted the need for sleep that took her away from him.

But when camp sounds carried her again into wakefulness at midmorning, she was alone and the bedding where he had lain was cool. He had made an early start for his village, she had thought at first. But while dressing she saw that his bloodstained shirt remained soaking in the bucket and that his saddlebags had not left the wagon. He must still have been in the camp even if no one she questioned knew where to find him.

So she had not been surprised when a messenger accosted her before the midday meal and led her to the Warder. Now she pulled herself into the wagon and moved through the jumble toward Tayem. What was he doing?

"Testing reflexes," the redhead responded when asked. "Waiting for you." He stepped backward and stretched his back. "She's out now."

She? Kylene stepped past lengths of curved wood. On the bedframe she saw an adolescent girl swaddled tightly in bedclothes so that only her face could be seen. Straw had been spilled from the wooden box to litter the wagon's plank floor, and graying chaff lay sprinkled on the coarsely woven blanket. A pungent odor, both sweet and sharp, filled Kylene's nostrils; though familiar, she could not place it, and made herself ignore it.

The lighting improved suddenly. Tayem had pulled aside the flaps at the rear of the wagon and fastened them to admit the sunlight. Kylene bent over, seeing a chubby face, round and red-complexioned, with snub nose and tiny ears buried under blond hair. *A pig's face,* Kylene thought. *But healthy-looking.* She wondered at Tayem's presence here.

"Evennle," Tayem commented from behind her. "The Warder's daughter. But I imagine you've met."

Kylene nodded a "no" automatically. The child's face awoke no memories. She said that, murmuring, then closed her eyes in the silence that ensued and let her consciousness reach toward the young girl.

"Easy." Tayem reached to steady her.

"She's mind-shielded. How?"

"At the moment she is," Tayem agreed. "Lucky for her. Evennle's been telling some interesting stories." His hand moved, patting significantly at the belt compartments in which he carried chemicals. "She's a very sick little Teep. You should have told me."

As if to emphasize that, Evennle made burbling sounds. Drool slid down her cheek. Tayem dabbled at it with a corner of the bedding. "Too much drug for the weight," he muttered. "Always takes out facial tension." He turned back to Kylene. "Do you have anything to say for yourself?" he demanded sternly.

He was angry, Kylene realized suddenly. Because the child was ill?

No, she decided. Discovering a telepath among the People had upset him. She could have told him one was present, and she had not. Guilt pushed at her, but she shoved the emotion away, then nodded slowly to mollify him. "What was I supposed to do, Tayem?"

The big redhead gestured uselessly before speaking. "Tell me about Evennle. That seems simple enough, doesn't it?" His fist plunged down, forcing the homespun blankets deeply into the straw. "Cimon and Nicole, Kylene! What's the point of having you here if you aren't going to do any mind-seeing? I could have brought along any of a dozen different Agents if all I wanted were an idiot."

I did not choose to be here, Kylene told herself deliberately. *And I will remember these words.* "Sorry," she said aloud.

Tayem grunted. Evidently more contrition was necessary.

"Yes," she admitted quickly. "I sensed that someone saw into my mind. But the feeling only lasted an instant and it only happened a few times. I thought I might be wrong—I didn't find any hidden Teeps here; I didn't even find people who knew much of Teeps. And I looked, Tayem, I looked. I didn't know about Evennle! No one did! No one! If I had had anything important to tell you, I would. But if I just imagined things—was I supposed to tell you about them too?"

Tayem frowned and spoke words she did not understand. "Yes," he said then. "Better safe than sorry, Kylene.

I do *not* want to wake up some morning in a Chelmmysian prison camp, just because you worried more about holding on to your dignity than giving me information I needed."

Why must I be so trustworthy? she thought briefly, then lowered her gaze to advertise penitence. "I am sorry, Tayem." Perhaps that would satisfy him.

"All right." Tayem shook his head, a puzzled expression on his face. "Now, tell me about becoming a Teep. How long does it take, from start to finish?"

Kylene snapped her fingers. "It is a part of puberty. Several year tenths. Why?"

"Cimon! We don't have that time." His head shook again, then his eyes moved from the child on the bedframe to her. "*You* did it by yourself. How did you keep from becoming insane?"

"Why should I?"

Tayem's jaw worked but words did not emerge. He turned instead to grip a shoulder of the sleeping girl, pressing down as if to hold her in place, then rocked her back and forth. "Wake up, Evennle," he muttered, "Wake up. And Kylene—if she throws a fit again, tell me what happens this time, please?"

Outwardly, the girl awoke. Her eyes opened and appeared to focus on the man and woman watching her. She said nothing, although her tongue could be seen moving over her teeth. Her limbs were motionless, as if paralyzed, but Tayem knelt anyhow to hold her firmly in one position. She gave no sign of noticing this. Inwardly . . .

"Enough!" Kylene cried after a brief while. "Stop it, Tayem."

Tayem moved onto the bedframe, an arm keeping Evennle pressed to his side while he moved the other hand to his belt, then back to rub fingers across the child's throat. Evennle was tense, iron rigid for a moment, then stiffness departed from her. "Not normal?" he asked as she sagged against him.

"No," Kylene said. "No. No!" she repeated through

distorted lips. "I still hear her. Her mind is still awake, Tayem. Stop it!"

Tayem grimaced, but her expression must have convinced him, for his hand darted to the base of Evennle's throat. Kylene closed her eyes while ocean waves sounded in her ears, the roared whispers of surf drowning out the babble of human voices—then Evennle was unconscious, her mind stilled.

Kylene exhaled raggedly and moved to sit heavily on the bedframe, not caring that her hips brushed against Tayem on one side and against Evennle's limp fingers on the other. The odor she had noticed earlier was intensified; this close to it, she recognized urine. She slumped forward, breathing harshly.

"Bad?" Tayem was sitting straight again.

"Yes. I was not expecting it."

"Do you know what's wrong with her?" he asked quietly.

Kylene nodded a negative. "Her mind-seeing is real. She is a true Teep—but with no more control than she has now over her body. Her shield must rise or fall irregularly, unaffected by her will."

Tayem grunted. "So? What did that do to you?"

"She is young," Kylene explained. "Her—her internal being, image—her knowledge of the true self—"

"*Soul?* That which rises to Cimon?"

Kylene accepted the word. "Her *soul* is weak. Behind her mind shield, she has control of her awareness. But within stronger minds—those of adults, for example—she has only a memory of her identity. She sees as they see, hears as they hear, tries to act as they act ... and if she remembers her true existence and attempts to return, she may transfer to yet another mind.

"She does this frequently. It is a usual thing for her to be in other minds. And that further weakens her *soul*, making it even more normal for her to enter other minds. Soon she may forget her own body entirely, except on the occasions when her mind shield should rise and keep her mind pent up..."

"She's turning into a vegetable."

Kylene considered the imagery. "Yes."

Tayem stood, and moved to the side of the wagon to poke fingers into the canvas. "Her spells are becoming more common, I'm told, and lasting longer. She has uncontrollable tantrums and hurts herself without realizing it. It fits your description. So—does this happen often?"

"No."

"What can be done?"

Kylene snapped her fingers. "Nothing. She lacks control of the workings of her mind. She cannot learn them. It is as if you wished to raise your arms and had been born without muscles to move them. She will never improve."

Tayem jabbed at canvas before facing her. "Never's a harsh word. Must be something."

Kylene snapped fingers again. "Take her to the Project?"

The man shook his head. "She wouldn't fit it. Even if they decided to take her. No, she's better off with people who know her already."

Kylene used the pause that followed to look once more at the unconscious girl beside her. *Still a pig face*, she decided critically. *And she stinks of urine*. But Evennle was also a live human being: a concrete reality difficult to connect with the abstract discussion she and Tayem were having. Alive—and going insane. "Make her a wise-woman?"

Tayem smiled. "Not in this culture. Besides, is she wise?"

That could not be answered. Kylene merely waited until Tayem spoke again. "Is there a way to teach her to be a nontelepath?"

She had answered that once, she thought. "No, Tayem. Slay her."

Tayem was shocked. "Are you serious? She's a *child*, Kylene!"

"You mentioned tantrums," she said reasonably. "A message between minds can carry more than words and pictures, Tayem. In the end it simply turns into electrical stimulation of the brain, remember. Most Teeps would resist such things without notice, but Evennle . . . If she controls her own body now, that probably will not last. Ultimately, she will die in an accident. Kill her now and be merciful."

"No. Absolutely not."

She had no more suggestions. Kylene waited while Tayem drew fingertips absently along the canvas, then stared at them. "What if she got her mind shield now?" he wondered aloud. "Or something like it she could control, and turn on and off. Would she grow up all right?"

Kylene thought about it. "Probably," she said at last. "Yes."

Tayem sighed, then turned to face her in silence. His face was shadowed, so she could not decipher his expression, but Kylene did not like the sound of his voice. Nor was she pleased when he spoke next. "Do you think you could make it back to the Project by yourself?"

"I could." She made the admission reluctantly. "Where would you be? With Terocu?"

Tayem shook his head. "With you. Unless that becomes too much trouble."

Tayem held a square-edged tablet in his palm. It was barely visible in the semi-gloom of the wagon, but Kylene recognized it as one of the drugs he stocked in his oversized belts. "A come-along," he had once called it. "It separates short-term from long-term memory, so you don't remember afterward what happened while you were drugged, and you can't recall then any more than the last few heartbeats. We use it normally to keep prisoners tractable."

The antidote was in the time shuttle. At the cabin.

Kylene looked on unhappily. She knew Tayem worried about having his mind seen into by time-traveling Chelmmysian Teeps. He had discussed it in the past, but she had not thought his fears so strong as to force him down this path. Her attempts to argue with him had been fruitless.

He was not ready yet, she could tell. She had time left, and she moved to peek through a slit in the back flap of the wagon. The sun was well past the midpoint of its arc, but the low clouds in the sky were still white, rather than pink-tinged. It was a good sign, she decided. She wanted away from the Algherans and this showed that the cloak of their Nicole hovered above her.

The Warder stood outside, looking blankly in her direction. His face displayed hopeful interest, rather than anxiety. "Tell him it'll be black magic," Tayem had suggested. "For all he knows, it will be. And it should make him easier to handle afterward." But that was not language to use on a priest, she had sensed; when she located the man, she spoke of contemplation and prayers to heavenly powers. Perhaps he prayed himself now.

The Warder's companion was restless. A pudgy man of medium height, with a sour expression, in need of several baths—this was the Warder's son, Evennle's half brother, Kylene had discovered. His feet shuffled back and forth in the dirt. His shoulders moved constantly, and his rabbit-skin vest rippled along his back as if alive and devouring him with great reluctance.

Her gaze returned to the inside of the wagon, then moved to Evennle. The child was sitting patiently on the edge of the bedframe, her eyes on Tayem. Had they found something to talk about? By coincidence, the girl's mind shield was operating now; she could have held a private conversation with the man, while Kylene located the Warder. She was not usually this quiet, her father's mind showed. But it did not matter.

"*Geronimo,*" Tayem said suddenly.

Kylene was startled, as was Evennle. For an instant

their eyes met, then both turned away, feeling embarrassment. Meanwhile, the man swallowed the pill, grimacing at the taste, and stripped the Teepblind upward
through his hair and pushed it over Evennle's head.

The blond girl had taken her coaching well; she shook
her hair in place so it fitted through the silver mesh, and
if she winced while the vampire needles pierced her skin,
Kylene did not notice. But Kylene was not watching
Evennle. *Tayem*, she thought. *For once his mind isn't
protected from me.*

But Tayem's thoughts were already inchoate. She could
glimpse no more than mumbled integers, coupled with a
strong self-prescription to count to some number. Tayem
had already forgotten what that number was.

Finally he lost his chain of thought. Uncaring, he
glanced aimlessly around the wagon, until his gaze returned
to her. "Kylene!" he said loudly. "Hi, Kylene." A child's
smile settled upon his face.

For an instant, Kylene let herself enjoy his obvious
pleasure. "Hello, Tayem," she answered automatically.
Then she switched to Lopritian, hoping he would respond
in the same language. "What do we do now?"

"Why? Is something the matter?" His brow furrowed
intently, then became smooth as he smiled idiotically. "Can
I help? What do you want me to do?"

Kylene knew sudden frustration. She ignored Evennle
and kicked the man on his shin. "Get us home, Tayem."

The redhead's broad face contorted, childlike still but
unhappy. "Ouch! You hurt me, Kylene. Why did you do
that?"

You've done things to deserve it, she thought angrily.
*Starting with two nights ago. Even if you don't remember
it now.*

The emotion stayed in her voice when she turned to
Evennle, watching agog from the back of the wagon. "Get
out of here," she snapped. "Your father is waiting. I'll
talk to you later."

Wordlessly the girl obeyed, dropping the canvas flap

behind her and leaving the two time travelers in semi-darkness. Kylene grabbed Tayem's wrist, pulled on it, then pulled again.

"Hello, Kylene." Tayem beamed happily at her once more. Then indecision showed on his face. "You wanted something? Didn't you want something? What was it, Kylene?"

Get us home, she thought at him. *Back to the cabin.* But that was useless; Tayem no longer remembered his cabin. He might have spent his life in the People's wagon train. She closed her eyes, feeling near despair, only now realizing the magnitude of the task Tayem had placed on her shoulders. *Tayem!*

A giant's hand pawed at her shoulder. "Kylene? What's the matter?" Tayem's voice, sounding very young and scared.

Mindless. She forced a smile to reassure him, took his arm in her hands, and rubbed her cheek against it. "Nothing, Tayem," she made herself say. "Everything is fine."

He moved closer and awkwardly draped his other arm over her shoulder. "Oh, that's good, Kylene." He began patting her, stroking his hand heavily along her back as if she were some well-loved pet as he poked at her hair with his chin. "What do we do now, Kylene?"

She shook her head and broke free from his embrace. "We have to get away from here," she told him. "We have to leave now, Tayem."

"Yes, Kylene," he said trustingly.

She felt terribly alone.

CHAPTER ELEVEN

*T*he Warder placed obstacles in her way. "They can't be spared," he insisted to her. "Our scouts need them."

"Three horses," Kylene repeated grimly. "All mares. And the ones we came here on. Plus the supplies I asked for. You owe them to us."

She felt as if she were walking a tightrope, with Tayem strapped to her back. But she must press the man. She and Tayem would need remounts. To win a race with winter, with Tayem handicapped as he was now, she could allow no rest days on their return to the cabin.

The Warder's wagon was being cleaned once more, so she was with him in his son's quarters. A day tenth had passed, and through the back of the wagon, she could see that the blue sky was darkening. The once-white clouds were pink-tinged. She and the Warder faced each other, sitting on low benches mounted to the wagon walls. Tayem lay on the floor near her feet, curled on his side, staring with fascination at the patterns his fingers were making in the dust on the carpet. Otherwise they were alone.

"Nothing was said about this," the Warder protested. "The Master of Dicovys healed before without demanding a price."

This is the price for healing the Master of Dicovys, she thought angrily. *Shall I tell the People how you reward him for saving your daughter's mind?*

But it would be useless to say that, and perhaps dangerous. The Warder still spoke of gratitude, but his mind showed that already he had come to accept Evennle's cure. A child's illness stemmed from the father's seed, it was said, so her sickness had been kept secret, lest it hold embarrassment for foes to use against him. Now he wished to forget it.

He was well satisfied by Tayem's mindlessness. That removed both a threat to his authority and a witness to his past distress. And it meant that someone would have to be appointed to the again-vacant Mastership of Dicovys, someone who would appreciate the favor.

He was not eager to give attention to a debt holder, and Kylene did not want to encourage such thoughts as he might develop. He was not being helpful, but he did not intend harm—yet.

The tightrope feeling returned. They had to get away from the camp, and she needed the Warder's assistance. How could she persuade him? Her eyes moved, looking for clues, with no success.

"Well," the Warder said testily. "Do you have anything to say, child?"

Kylene froze. Tayem might call her that kind of name, but he meant no harm to her, and he would use it as a label rather than an insult. She would not take condescension from this lout.

"Child? I'll show you a child," she said hollowly. The Warder stared blankly while she turned her face toward the side of the wagon. The movement was not necessary; she simply had no desire to look at the man.

Light and sound kaleidoscoped within her mind; colors

sparkled and pinwheeled. She saw through two sets of eyes, listened through two sets of ears . . .

She was hungry. The strange man had been frightening, but he had not harmed her, and his gift was safely tucked into her interior blouse—she remembered again the instructions he had given her, the feel of the band tightening around her temples, the prick of the needles. He had lectured her about other things too; she must remember them without forgetting.

But she was hungry. She would think of them later. Now she was the Warder's daughter again, and not yet the tribal wisewoman. The man tending the fire under the roasting rabbit could surely be wheedled into slicing off just a small bite for her to eat . . .

But her father wanted to see her. She could just run back . . .

Evennle was too inexperienced to recognize a telepathic message, and insinuating the command to return was easy. It was even proper, Kylene thought austerely, remembering the discipline of the Project. The child was spoiled and much too fat already, and could afford to miss a snack. If Tayem had to throw his mind away, surely he could have found a better cause. *Tayem!*

At her feet, Tayem Minstrel carefully pressed his palms into the carpet, making handprints in the dust. He chuckled happily to himself and wiped gray streaks into his red hair while the Warder looked on smirking and Kylene closed her eyes to keep her tears pent and together they awaited the return of the Warder's daughter.

"Daddy?" It was Evennle, at last. "Someone said you wanted me?"

Kylene turned. "I did."

Evennle pouted, her little pig face reddening. "I have nothing to say to you." She seemed extraordinarily pleased by the realization.

Kylene snapped her fingers loudly, so both the Warder and the girl stared at her. "I don't really care what you think, Evennle. You cannot hide from me," she said calmly.

This step on the tightrope she made with sureness, treading in the pathways of the tra'R'sihuc. Color and sound spun about her. The one earth whirled, then she was reaching out.

Reaching. Holding. Twisting. All with her mind.

Evennle screamed, then slumped to the floor in silence.

"Three more horses," Kylene said woodenly. "Fully packed."

Evennle screamed again.

The Warder looked at her with horror.

"And Evennle," Kylene added. "Just till dawn. You understand my reasoning?"

The Warder nodded dully.

"Stop here," Kylene said tersely. Evennle pretended surprise, which Kylene ignored. Darkness had long been upon the world, but the exhaustion now in her body prophesied dawn. She yawned silently and wriggled fatigue-battered shoulders, then let the horizon feel the weight of her gaze.

A depression lay ahead and the trees were pulled back from it. A stream was more likely than a path, she decided. Call it a thousand man-heights distant; they would reach it before dawn arrived.

Her eyes moved again, surveying the world with wary approval, naming in her mind colors black-garbed by night. Up above, a bronzed quarter moon lurked among the gray clouds creeping across a gunmetaled sky. On the ground, blossoms at the road's edge cupped scarlet and ivory petals together to pray for dew, and darkness hung like ebon tapestries within the depths of the waiting forests.

Alien, she thought. *Like some picture from Tayem's art book.* For a heartbeat, she gave thought to painting the scene, selecting pigments in her mind. Then a horse snorted and her attention returned. She and Tayem had been on this road only days before, she realized; the site should be familiar. But it was not. Too many memories intruded to restore that recognition.

Leather made creaking sounds. The reins of Tayem's gelding were fastened to her saddle horn. She stroked at them reflexively, pulling the palomino nearer till it nudged muzzles with her own mare.

Tayem nodded eagerly and rocked back and forth alarmingly, but kept his seat. His sword hilt poked over his left shoulder, barely visible. Moonlight showed no tiredness upon his face and his cape hung loose behind him, so probably he still was warm and comfortable. When she smiled to show him relief, he beamed at her and the one world with delight. Mercifully, he remained quiet.

Her jaw clenched as she looked behind her to the north. Evennle was close, buckskin-clad and stiff-postured on a brown pinto. The silver of Tayem's Teepblind showed upon her hair as a cap. The child was much too small to be astride that particular horse; she had little skill as a rider, and Kylene wondered if she had foolishly chosen an animal dwarfing her for its speed or whether the Warder had selected it as appropriate for his daughter.

Evennle had not paraded resentment, nor attempted to escape. *Probably thinks this is adventure*, Kylene thought cynically. But that did not matter. The child had been obedient and had not annoyed her with chatter. They were far removed from the camp. She had used none of the throwing knives fastened along her side. She would have asked for nothing else.

Now light and darkness spun in kaleidoscope patterns; sound was jumbled around her. Evennle could not be detected, and the firefly images of Tayem's mind had to be screened out, but after that, Kylene still saw through two sets of eyes, heard through two sets of ears, thought within two minds.

Her hand moved, pointing. "Your father lied as usual. The man he sent to spy on us is on that hilltop." *Just one. The Project people would thank their Lady.*

Tayem's Project. And Tayem's people, who would never understand the risks he bore for them, never appreciate his efforts adequately. For an instant, she hated them.

Evennle shook her head, not arguing, then turned her mount back to face the north. "You want me to make him take me home. All right." But she paused to rub awkwardly at her head. "Is the man going to recover?"

The question was completely unexpected. Kylene stared at the smaller girl for long moments before she understood and an answer came to her mouth. "I believe so." Her hand reached out blindly, somehow finding Tayem's fingers. "He told me what I should do." But the tightrope feeling returned.

Evennle nodded again, her gaze darting from Kylene's face to Tayem and back. A note of concern sounded in her voice. "Will you succeed?"

"Of course." It was difficult to maintain a show of disdain now; Kylene found herself reluctant to end the conversation. "Evennle, what did Tayem—the tra' Dicovys—talk about when you were alone with him?"

"Mind-seeing." Evennle turned away, scanning the dark horizon. "He said the Gods had given me a great gift, but that there would be a price to pay if it became known, because some people would be jealous and others would hate what they did not understand. I should keep it secret, practice often, and use it so I could give good advice to my father and the People, rather than for nothing but my personal gain." Her voice was flat, monotone, and insolent.

Well-intentioned platitudes, Kylene thought. *Oh, Tayem!* But she made herself speak neutrally. "The tra'Dicovys takes such matters seriously. He will be displeased if you disappoint him."

Evennle snapped her fingers. Her heels swung sharply, digging into the flanks of her pinto. Then she was gone.

Kylene watched her departure with envy. Evennle was a dirty, ignorant barbarian and would never rise above that level, but her attitude was that of one who would always find, or be given, simple answers to all life's riddles. While Kylene—but she did not have the time to fill baskets with moonbeams.

"Stay," she said aloud, half to Tayem and half to the horses. She stepped down from her mare. The roadbed surface, her fingers told her, was smooth-grained, hard but dusty. It was not kind to animal hooves, and it was impossible not to leave spoor on it. *Might as well turn off the road now.*

That decision came easily. If they stayed in control of themselves, they could hope to outdistance any trackers the Warder sent behind them.

If the Lady's cloak did not provide enough coverage, perhaps the horses would. She thought for a moment, ordering the future, then her fingers moved toward buckles. "Tayem, get down. I want you to shift the saddles."

The depression held a nearly dry creekbed. She did not venture into that, but followed the edge of the bank with the forest to her right. The pace was slow till the sun arose, and even then she kept to a walk. She gave the horses rest only by dismounting along with Tayem, and leading the procession along the bank. When she thought about it, she led the horses down to water.

She was being cruel, she recognized, but the feeling of balance on a tightrope returned whenever she thought of the Warder. And she thought of him frequently, for he was not to be trusted and she had a great distance to go.

Peril kept her awake. But there was no way for her to explain the circumstances to Tayem. Throughout the morning he remained cheerful, speaking seldom but staring at his surroundings with the innocence of the newborn. But as the sun rose to its apex, the length of his silences increased and frown lines creased his forehead. Fortunately, he was also hungry, and she hit upon the expedient of feeding him slowly.

In early afternoon they reached a place where the banks of the creek drew together and dropped toward the water, so that the trees closed overhead and blocked off the sun. Soon there was no path at all, only a strip of uneven ground between the creek and the trees. Golden-brown pine needles lay everywhere, and the footsteps of the horses made rustling sounds that kept pace with their breathing. Tayem reacted to the dim light with late-evening grumpiness, but fortunately he did not insist on sleep.

Since the ground was covered and possible dangers to the horses could not be seen, Kylene dismounted and led the way on foot. This was slow, but she realized after her initial dismay that the forest would delay pursuers as much as it did her and Tayem. In the meantime, the exercise kept her awake.

But finally exhaustion rode upon her so heavily that she lost track of all but her own movement. A misstep jarred her back to wakefulness.

She stopped walking. The horses were still on their line, she noticed dully. She had not lost a horse. But Tayem was not with her. Tayem. She would be with Tayem.

Where would he be?

Mind-seeing failed to locate him, since she was too tired for the necessary concentration. Kylene slapped herself to increase consciousness, then knelt to examine the ground. The leaves and fallen pine needles before her had not been disturbed, so he had not passed her. He had to be behind her. If she went back, she would find him. All five horses were with her, and he was tired, so he could not have gone far. She could find him.

She nodded groggily at the profundity of her thoughts, then gathered the reins together and tethered the horses to a trio of young silver beeches. Then she trudged back along the trail the horses had left, shuffling deliberately to make it more visible. Tayem could not be too far behind.

She found him at last in the streambed, standing on gravel and small rocks just beyond a small overhang. He was peering intently at a large boulder, taller than himself, which the shallow waters skirted. The rock was granite, rust-tinged, far from unique in this area. The slanting rays of the afternoon sun that penetrated the forest canopy showed a belt-high wet area. The creek gurgled with the sounds of happy infants.

"Tayem!" she called down. "What are you waiting for?" Worry festered within her. They had not made the distance she had hoped for; the instruments in her belt showed her that, and that the pathway along the creek no longer pointed toward the cabin.

Now Tayem was acting foolishly, and she did not know how much longer her pleas would control him. "Come on, Tayem! Climb out!"

The big man turned and smiled idiotically. "Kylene! Hi, Kylene."

"Fasten your pants, Tayem," she said wearily. He had looked after himself so well until now. Would this ritual be needed each day? For how many days?

He nodded, pleased with the idea. "What do we do now, Kylene?"

Scream for a while, she thought. *How could you do this to yourself, Tayem?* "Come on, Tayem. Fasten your pants. Climb out. Please, Tayem?"

"All right, Kylene." But he did not move to obey, and she scrambled down the embankment, prepared if necessary to lead him just as she did the horses.

The irritating man. The gravel was loose under her moccasins—she might trip here and get a sprain. And she had risked scratching her hands and had put stains of gray-brown clay on the knees of her breeches coming down into the stream bed. Why couldn't he appreciate how hard she worked for him?

He was responsible for her unhappiness, she realized. He deserved some punishment for that, so before he could react she kicked him in the shins, then pushed at his side and shoulder to make him face the boulder for the few heartbeats required for forgetfulness.

Then he smiled again, "Hi, Kylene! How are you?"

In a mood to kick you properly, she thought. But her anger lapsed suddenly. The man was not responsible for himself. "Button your fly, Tayem. Fasten your pants." And, while he clumsily obeyed her directions, she wondered, "Did you expect this to happen to you, Tayem?

Did you know you would turn into a stupid toddler, and that I'd have to be your nursemaid?"

Tayem shook his head eagerly. "Uh-huh. I know *everything*, Kylene. I think of everything, don't I?" He grinned toothily. "Hi, Kylene!"

She kicked him again.

The next day was easier, though no shorter. A light rain fell during the night, and drizzle continued into early morning. Kylene filled water bags, then prodded her sleepy animals away from the stream and deep into the forest, trusting the weather and her turn to the north to slow down pursuers and ruin any signs of their passage.

Tayem was grumpy and childishly vocal. The horses were merely bedraggled. Kylene took the lead and endured, confident that if only her responsibilities had permitted it she could have felt misery equal to theirs.

The spirits of all improved when the rain stopped and she allowed them time for a cold breakfast. Not that oats or salted rabbit and barley steeped in water were adequate meals, but the rest was overdue. It felt good to do nothing, Kylene acknowledged, to stretch her legs out straight rather than spread them into a rider's posture, to breathe and move without the claustrophobia caused by bulky outer garments, even to sit on stiff coarse canvas rather than balance on a swaying pony.

But a pleasure realized should not be continued. She resaddled the horses with Tayem's help and resumed the journey.

The ground was almost level here, the forest seemingly endless, so she stayed in front, to direct her cavalcade to the north and west. There were obstacles such as fallen trees to circumvent, and once they rode south and west most of a day before finding a place to ford a swollen river, so it was not possible to move along a straight line toward Tayem's cabin.

But the instruments in her belt reassured her. Whatever the Warder might do, they were moving toward safety.

The sensation of walking a tightrope did not fade from
Kylene's mind, but her apprehensions did. She could be
satisfied with her actions now; that was almost enjoyment.

Half the third day she gave to rest. The horses needed
it, and perhaps the people did as well. Tayem had not
complained, but discomfort showed clearly enough on his
face. An examination showed that he was in need of attention, since his clothing was damp and chafing, so after
the horses were fed and groomed, she rubbed an antiseptic
creme into the raw areas of his body, then re-dressed him
in cleaner garments before they continued. Fortunately,
he retained the habits needed to stay on a horse without
collecting stiff muscles and injuries; she did not have to
supervise his riding.

The redhead kept other memories, she discovered, perhaps all of them, although he could no longer direct his
awareness among them. While he slept, the chemical in
his brain partially released its control; he dreamed then
and sometimes she recognized scenes within his mind.
Other images might have been fantasies or echoes of his
First Era existence. For a time they were of interest, but
she had no power to differentiate among them to com-
prehend them, and her interest vanished.

The trip was not without its pleasures, she realized
contentedly. Without the requirement to gather food each
day, she was free to admire sunsets and scenery. The
horses were content to accept her lead, and people had
not appeared to contest her progress.

Even Tayem was less aggravating than she had once
feared. He had been toilet trained as a child, and his
grooming habits gradually resurrected themselves. Beyond
that, his physical strength was of value in erecting camp-
sites and collecting firewood, and if his infantile prattle
was ignored, he was not otherwise a demanding companion. He was docile most of the time, could obey simple
instructions, and tried to be helpful. In many ways, losing
his mind had improved him greatly.

A pity I can't leave him in this state, she thought from time to time, half seriously. *He'd be a useful ornament for any house.*

Another ten days brought them out of pine forest, to high hills and coarse steppe grass, broad-leafed and close-cropped. The ground was rough, boulder-strewn, matted here and there by clumps of tiny yellow flowers. Lichens grew on exposed rocks. Tayem had called this "tundra," the earth begrudgingly turned back to the world by the retreating glaciers. Permafrost would be just under her feet.

Tayem's "America" had been near this part of the world, she remembered. They could very well have been passing even now over towns and houses buried a hundred millennia. Or perhaps they were in his "Canada," the northern province of a Chelmmysian-like alliance he had called the United States. The recognition was an intellectual one; it was impossible to accept that anyone had deliberately chosen to live in so desolate a location.

Life of any sort was still rare here. Except for insects, she saw few animals, none of them large, and little color. Even the skies were gray and overcast.

But the horizon promised change. Already to the north were the blue-gray silhouettes that Tayem had named the White Mountains. Bypassed, these subsided into nothingness over the next few days, but they were the precursors of mountains appearing to the southwest. Seeking to use these as guides, she inevitably steered toward them, coming at last to a gravel-bedded river of icy water.

The river was easily crossed but broad, and afterward she decided to move parallel to it, thinking to follow it west across the continental plain. But it bent south within a day, leading them through scraggly stands of blue-green spruce, then once more into pine forest. The ground was rising. Within half a ten-day period, she had brought her party deep into the Adirondacks.

They were lost, she realized eventually. Tayem had

taken a route that kept them south of this region, but she
could not remember the landmarks he had followed nor
understand his maps. The instruments in her belt showed
them no closer to his time shuttle, and winter would not
stay at bay indefinitely.

The big man dreamed that night of Onnul Nyjuc; Kylene
paid in lost sleep to witness his nightmares, and reached
no useful memories. In the morning, unwilling to retreat,
she abandoned the river and led her party due west, feeling more determination than cheer.

These mountains were long and narrow, braided
together like loose-wrapped bundles of gnarled sticks. They
were mostly sandstone, not hard to climb, and low enough
that they did not bear snow all year or make a person
gasp for breath, but temperatures showed their rise in
elevation. Even at the crests, they were forest-covered,
so she never obtained a clear view of her surroundings.

The rivers were her real obstacles. Between the mountains were broad U-shaped valleys, and rivers ran in each
of these. They were young, narrow and straight but not
deep, dwarfed by the gentle valleys. Cold and clear and
without life, they were fed by the meltwaters of the
retreating ice cap. Usually Kylene could find no convenient ford, so she and Tayem had to walk the high gully
banks until they found paths for the horses. Then it was
possible to wade or swim across. Fortunately, the early-
summer floods were past, and the water did not flow
rapidly, so this was seldom difficult.

Twice they had to cross large rivers, reaching an opposite bank with bodies and spirits both cold-soaked by
glacial waters. She made camp at once when that happened, laying great fires to dry their possessions and
improve their tempers. Everything soon reeked of burning
pine resin, but with time the odor dissipated—or she
became inured to it. Tayem developed a respiratory ail-
ment, which was worrisome. She treated him with the all-
purpose tablets he called *placebos*, guessing at the proper

dosage, and he was essentially recovered when they emerged from the mountain belt.

It was late summer then, more than a year tenth since she and Tayem had left the People. Before them, far into the blue-hazed distance, lay more hills, the glacier-shaped rolling grasslands known as the Eastern Downs.

And beyond them? A line of great lakes ran north to south beyond the terminal moraine, Tayem had said. A parallel strand was in the distant west, giving together the semblance from afar of a pearl necklace around a neck that was the continental plain.

Tayem had been born in this region, he had told her, but she did not think it held his country. Perhaps he thought to protect his homeland from time travelers, for he seldom spoke of it. "Alghera, your valley, everything in between," he told her once. "From sea to shining sea." He was never more specific about its location.

In the Present, this was—or would be—the northern section of Loprit, and the mountains they had crossed marked the border with Alghera. But fame had been given this territory long ago, three hundred centuries or more, when legends formed around a colony of local Teeps. They had not stayed, soon leaving for the warmer and more fertile valleys of the southern continent, according to Tayem, but the history of the Fourth Era had begun at this point.

It had probably looked no different then than now.

"The morning of creation," Kylene said self-consciously, quoting the words Tayem had several times applied to this empty world, understanding at last his irony. The morning of creation . . . the last dawn of reckoning. The beginning and end of history were bound together with cords unseen upon the face of the earth.

The doings of a thousand generations would leave no trace upon this aged world. In the end, the history men repeated to themselves was without significance except to themselves, mummery that other men willingly forgot. And the world was false as well, for all its colored guise

of youth and freshness. How deluded the Algherans were
in self-dramatizing their great war with the Chelmmysians!

Tayem had watched the rise and fall of eras as through
the uncaring viewpoint of the world. What lessons had it
taught him?

But the man was rocking himself gently on his saddle,
smiling with glee, his eyes focused on a jay. He could not
answer her questions now.

Watching him, Kylene pulled back self-consciously from
some mental brink. Mindless Tayem might be, but his
face showed pain when he was unhappy and delight when
given pleasure. His life was significant to him, even now,
and when mentally complete he had not found it necessary
to live as though the doings of men were meaningless.
Was she not equally justified in taking the events of this
life seriously?

Of course. She closed her eyes, and forced herself to
sense the odors of thistles and milkweed on the afternoon
breeze, then jammed her knees into her horse, increasing
the pace.

On the whole, their progress was smooth. Kylene
allowed few long stops, but rotated loads to give rest days
to the horses. She preferred to begin travel early, so she
did not take the time to trap. Instead they lived on the
dried meat and grain the horses carried, supplemented by
fish or such small game as her knives would reach.

They came to no villages, met no passing travelers. In
part, Kylene understood, that was because she had taken
them along a path far from comfortable terrain. But it was
also true, as Tayem had sometimes stated, that human
beings were very rare in this world. She could not believe
the fantastic numbers of people he claimed had existed
in his era, but that this world had room for more than the
ten million persons who now lived was indisputable.

She had never felt more isolated from all humanity than
during this portion of her travel with Tayem. The trip bore

no resemblance to the journey she had made in her Pilgrimage across the western portion of the continent, lonely as she had been. When she searched her memory for parallels, she found none.

What she remembered now were only fragments of memories, she admitted reluctantly. Mere anecdotes, as if even within herself the Second Era had perished. Imperceptibly, the world of her birth had become one she knew of but no longer truly belonged to.

You can't go home again. She began to understand the lesson Tayem had tried to explain.

This new Tayem gave her few problems. His mindlessness meant that all but the simplest of chores fell to her, but he remained docile, and his transparent joy when he beheld her almost made up for the aggravations. Fortunately, he retained his languages, so she could continue to speak with him. Left to himself, he babbled quietly in a Second Era trail dialect she could almost understand. So they had something in common, unshared with the Algherans, and the discovery was pleasant.

The big man had always enjoyed the appearance of evening. Kylene had always thought that silly, but now she was establishing camp early enough that together they could watch the sun slip into the Earth. She wanted to make his life normal, she explained to herself, inwardly amused at the tractability she was outwardly displaying. Fortunately, Tayem would never remember this; when his memory returned to normal she would behave as she had in the past.

There were other things Tayem would never remember.

Kylene eventually grew tired of the short remarks he continually addressed to her and the childlike behavior he displayed. He was exactly like an oversized baby doll, she decided in a pique, and at last she revenged herself by dressing him in pieces of her clothing, so that he rode with little more than her smallest skirt fluttering about his hairy thighs.

"This hurts, Kylene," he had protested weakly when she pulled tight the straps on the *brassiere*. She had nodded deliberately, knowing he would translate that as a sign of sympathy, and told him gently that it was supposed to be felt. It would protect him from unspecified perils and make him much more attractive, and she knew he wanted that. She had smiled sweetly.

Tayem had been convinced for a few heartbeats, but then his faulty memory destroyed his understanding. "This hurts, Kylene," he repeated.

After a few days she relented, but she treasured the guilty memories.

Normally, responsibility still lay heavily upon her, but she had learned that routine matters did not justify her worries. Consequently, her own pleasure in the journey increased while Tayem's decreased.

His inability to remember concealed the tedium from him, but the diet and inconveniences of travel combined to wear him down. And without his mind to direct it, his body was losing coordination and muscle tone. His hairline changed, retreating on both sides of his forehead. Gray strands became common among the red-brown and the open sun burned his skin, leaving it coarsened even after the red was gone. Crow's feet tracked the outside of his eyes.

Kylene sometimes sensed that a person entirely new was slowly emerging from his shell, a man gawkier and leaner and weaker, subject to aches and twinges of pain that Tayem would never have known. Tayem was growing old, she realized with genuine shock. In the middle of his short life, he was undergoing a transformation that only the very elderly should know. Now she understood why he insisted doggedly on his aging despite the clear evidence of her senses. Poor Tayem!

She kept him at her side while they were riding, and pity waned as his new appearance became familiar to her. This was the pattern of his natural life, after all. His deterioration was not continuing rapidly, and she had seen many people displaying greater evidence of age.

But someday Tayem's mind would be returned to his body and he would wish to rebuild it, she knew. He would feel she had not done an adequate job of protecting him if that task were necessary. Slowly the notion formed that she might substitute her mind for the one that was missing.

One evening she decided to make Tayem perform calisthenics. The task was simple enough; once launched into an exercise, the man would continue until she intervened or fatigued muscles stopped him. It took time, for she was not knowledgeable about his body and was unwilling to risk, through ignorance, injuring the man or causing him great pain, but some progress was visible within a pair of ten-day periods. Tayem's muscles became larger again, his flesh more solid and more youthfully distributed. He was becoming lean and rangy under her ministrations rather than the man-bear she had known in the past, but this was enough; Tayem would not be ashamed of his body's condition when his mind returned to it.

Tayem also filled his clothing better. Shamed by his state of neglect, Kylene used an afternoon to trim his hair to a more fashionable length and to yank out such gray as could be grasped. Unless one looked him closely in the eyes, he was almost handsome then.

For a time, Kylene played at making Tayem presentable, as earlier she had played at making him ridiculous. All this attention made Tayem healthier and more cheerful, as if he were responding to the good treatment he could not remember. He seemed younger, more Tayem-like, and even desirable.

Nonetheless, there was something absurd about him, she reflected critically one evening while Tayem bathed himself in a creek, awkwardly splashing himself and the thirsty horses. He was far more difficult to sketch than a woman would be. Physically, all those clearly visible bones and tendons, so hard and angular, were not easily reproduced in two dimensions. And the main ornament of a man was grotesque when seriously considered, ridiculously outsized for either of its functions and much too vulnerable to possible injury, a preposterous but mesmerizing appendage that invariably fascinated despite its unesthetic appearance.

Mentally he was male as well, an absolutist by nature, fond of violence and simple black-and-white understanding. Men spent too much time with other men. They learned bad habits from one another, and they would never be civilized.

Even he, for all his frequent virtues, was obsessed with rigid standards and goals he refused to compromise, from tidiness to pleasing the Algherans, and she had seen no signs of reform in all the time she had spent with him. And now, this one lengthy occasion where he had placed the reins of his life within her hands, by some fluke of Tayem-ish irony, was a period he would never remember, never learn from.

He had probably realized that all along. He had probably thought it very funny.

In a sensible world, men would be kept in small cages, and let out only when there was need of their peculiar talents or for entertainment.

In the end, Kylene took Tayem's appearance as an example and resumed her knife-throwing practice.

She also found herself wondering how she would react if she became season-taken. She was not eating well enough for that to be a risk, nor was she absorbing water; unless travel upset her metabolism, her sexual functions should continue dormant for several year tenths. But she wondered anyhow.

Tayem's apparent regeneration stirred turmoil within her, for she realized the temporary nature of what she was accomplishing. Ultimately, no one would prevent Tayem's body—and perhaps his mind—from deteriorating due to its age. It was no consolation that Tayem had understood this.

Was there a way to save Tayem from an early death? Would the techniques be found to rebuild his treacherous body and give him a normal life span or the children for which he secretly yearned?

Despite her intentions, speculations metamorphosed into fantasies, daydreams in which a thankful Algheran state rewarded Tayem with a normal existence. Thousands cheered in her imagination, and in the front row—

Reason always brought her back to sense at that point, or troubled her dreams with deserved guilt.

There would be no cure for Tayem's illness.

She was also troubled by the analogies she began constructing. Tayem wanted her to become an Algheran, she knew. He had ambitions for her that had never been specified, perhaps because she had not welcomed such thoughts.

She had not desired to live in this era, and she had no goals to be achieved in this world. She had never thought of herself as having ambitions. She had been very young and very ignorant.

Now she felt discontent and some guilt. She was not willing to be passive. She wanted to do some things better than all other people, and she did not know which. She had no clear-cut goals, but latent ambition was growing upon her, just as did the firm bulges on Tayem's arms. Muscles were not innately part of one, but were acquired only through repeated exertion and willpower. What might she accomplish if she mastered those traits?

Fuel the fire where the coals are brightest. Her eyes scanned the horizon. Gray low-scudding clouds and the sun two hands above the western hills—this would be a good time to make camp. Perhaps the light would remain long enough for her to do some sketches.

When she was done, a face was looking at her: a man's head, narrow, V-shaped at the chin, with thinning hair and the suggestion of crows feet. The mouth was shut firmly, dimpled on one side. The eyes were partially closed, as if weighted down by lack of sleep or the heavy eyelids. The brows were prominent, thin, sharply turned down at the corners, and the lashes were long. The nose was dented on the bridge and twisted slightly to the right. Hair covered the tops of the ears. A single straight line ran vertically on the right cheek; subdued frown markings appeared on the forehead.

Was it accurate?

Kylene frowned to match the portrait, then held it at arm's length to gain perspective. Yes and no, she decided. The face revealed a wariness she could not remember and had not intended, but it was an expression that fitted well, a look it might have borne in private moments never seen by a small girl.

Flame crackled minutely. Her eyes moved beyond the sketch pad to the campsite and inventoried her world.

This was grassland. Short tasseled grasses grew in all directions, the monotony broken at intervals by low hills Tayem had named *drumlins* and occasional birch or willow trees, so stunted as to seem like bushes. Closer examination showed low hairy plants topped by whorls of red and yellow flowers, taller plants with clusters of violet tubular flowers, rhododendronlike shrubs with limp purplish flowers, white-colored violets, patches of tall thin plants with many-barbed round heads, matted plants with short needlelike leaves and dark purple berries, round yellow flowers capped by large dark purple buttons, tall spindly plants with small pealike white blossoms, clover, and dandelions.

At the base of this hill was a stream that widened to form a small pond. Around it could be found cattails, plants with slender paired willowlike leaves and clusters of purplish flowers, violet-tinged mint. Earlier she had seen a pair of brown-coated foxes. Her mind sensed other animals—mice, marmots, perhaps small rabbits—that refused to venture near the humans. She heard frogs croaking, and suspected that crayfish might be in the water. High above, nearing the southern horizon, birds flew in a trio of V-formations.

Shadows were lengthening rapidly now, for the sun was barely a handsbreadth above the edge of the earth, but the air was warm. The fire she had built while Tayem chopped grass about them was for cooking rather than heat. Mostly grass, with a few twigs from nearby shrubs, it generated billows of black smoke and an aromatic odor as it burnt.

The sword he had used was in his tent, resting on a blanket roll. Her own tent had also been erected and was ready for occupancy, except for the blanket she had laid outside to sit on while she drew.

Tayem was farther down the slope, staring at the horses as they cropped grass with enviable intensity. He had turned the same gaze on her in late afternoon, distracting her while she concentrated on filling in the portrait's eyebrows, and she had shooed him away. Now, watching him stealing toward the palomino gelding, caution reawoke in her.

He acted as if he did not hear her call, intent on some private purpose, or on no purpose. The gelding watched his approach warily, stepping away from Tayem's imagined ambush at first, then accepting it. Tayem chortled as the horse stared at him, laughed happily as it butted his chest with its muzzle, and reached to stroke it. The palomino twitched an eye at this, and met the outstretched hand with its teeth.

Kylene rose with alarm but realized quickly that the grip was not harming Tayem. The animal dimly sensed the man's disability, she saw. It did not understand, and she could not be sure if the emotion it felt could be classified as affection or a hunger for sugar, but it would not deliberately cause the man pain.

A baby-sitter, she recognized gratefully. She could tend without concern to the broth that simmered on the fire, and slice the strips of jerky into smaller pieces to simplify feeding her baby. Then—

"Tayem! Timithial ha'Ruppir! Stop that!"

"Yes, Kylene." But he continued to tug happily on the ropes that bound the horses to the stakes she had pounded into the ground.

She called again, and this time gained his attention.

"*Jack and Jill went up the hill*," he recited, drawing near to her. "*To fetch a pail of water. Jack fell down. And broke his crown. And Jill came tumbling after.*"

He was quoting poetry again, she judged from the rhythm. Cimon and Tayem alone knew what it meant, or what had provoked it, but the echo of the old Tayem was uncanny. He said the lines twice, in a deep resonant voice, then burbled to himself, waiting.

Kylene abandoned speculation and waved a practical finger at him. "Don't untie the horsies, little Tayem," she scolded. "If you let them free, they may run off, and if that happens—Kylene spank you, Tayem."

She stopped at that point, feeling exceptionally silly, but he nodded wisely. His brow wrinkled with concentration. "Yes, Kylene. No, Kylene." He did not seem certain of either response, and his face trembled with thoughts beyond his understanding. "Kylene?"

"What is it, Tayem?" She waited, curious, but knowing it made little sense to ask. Tayem's limited attention span did not allow him to formulate a request, and she was not surprised when he turned away.

"Oh, pretty, Kylene," he exclaimed. "What is it?" He had discovered her sketch pad.

"My father," she said carefully. "Do you like it?"

"Uh-huh." He shrugged. "Pretty." Then he lapsed into silence and blinked rapidly. "Kylene, are you my mommy?"

She shoved him back toward the horses.

* * *

Tayem dismissed, she could return to her blanket to watch the sunset, to stare again at the portrait she had made, to feel accomplishment mixed with dissatisfaction.

The work was done, she knew. The first of her works that was not simply an exercise or a means of killing time. Her first piece of *art*.

The creation was not perfect, but whatever additional finishing touches she might add would not improve it, only change it in minor ways. It was a compromise between execution and intent, more skilled in some fashion than she had a right to expect, amateurish in other ways she recognized but could not well define. Greater skill and experience might have made the portrait a better one, but she suspected she would always sense flaws in a completed work.

Was it any good? she wondered. Would Tayem approve when he regained his mind?

Art was the way the race evolved, Tayem had once told her. Art provided ideals, the insights of Gods, glimpses of the possibilities open to men. It showed the boundaries of human existence.

Hidden under the too-sweeping words, she had seen envy, a sadness Tayem felt about talents and experiences he could never encompass.

He was wrong, she understood now. The process of creation was not some mystical transmogrification of an artist's exalted perceptions. It was imagination added to work, technique, persistence—honest toil, without a trace of magic to ease the labor.

And why had she believed as he did for so long?

She had not felt equal to Tayem's goals, she admitted now, and had feared to disappoint him. She had been unwilling to go down a path where he would not follow and could not lead her. She had not thought that what she might accomplish would ever be noteworthy. She had been lazy and she had feared and she had been wrong.

She could be an artist. Her art might not be liked by everyone, it might not even be liked by Tayem, but that did not matter. It might not fill the empty spaces of experience that Tayem saw, and that was unimportant also. She could do what she could do, and that was sufficient.

Tayem's exalted notions of creativity were his problem, not hers. Competence, honesty, genuine effort: those were all that could be asked of an artist, not that she save the world. She must be committed. She must work. That was all. If Tayem could not understand that, the defect was in his own lack of talent—or in his own refusal to develop a talent, his own fear of treading a path he did not understand or his avoidance of situations that he could not easily master.

And if her choices pulled him apart from her, that would simply have to be.

She could feel sorry for him.

Soon, three year tenths had passed. Tree leaves had turned to gold and red behind her, and the days were noticeably shorter. The Algherans called this season Low Winter; High Winter would arrive with the snow.

Kylene and Tayem were deep within the Inland Moors, the broad crescent of water-saturated grassland that rimmed this portion of the inhabitable world. On one side of them, no more than a step down, narrow braided streams meandered through gravel and bare earth, sprawling collectively across the floor of a shallow river valley. On the other side was the low terrace-line of hills that marked the extent of early-summer flooding. Just to the south, barely visible, were the Barrier Forests. Within them, the cabin was concealed.

The North, so Tayem had said, held tundra, then ice. Unending ice.

She shivered involuntarily, then touched her fingers to the rope binding the man's horse to her saddle. It was still taut. But she looked back, regardless, to ensure his presence, before she returned to her deliberations.

A line to Tayem's shuttle would go south and slightly east of her present course, and eventually she would have to strike across country. Much depended on the weather, Kylene realized. Another ten dry days could see them safely arrived at the cabin. But rain must come at some point, and the Lady's cloak was not without limit. Rain would swell the lakes and marshes and make the ground too water-sodden for easy travel. She might regret this decision. But for now she had no direction bearings to take, no hills to traverse—they were making better progress on the path that nature had laid out than on one of her own determination. This was convenient.

Evidently that reasoning was not unique.

At midmorning the next day, she led her party onto the gravel of the streambed for watering and rest. While the horses gulped their fill, and Tayem knelt to inspect his reflection in a small pool, she looked back along their course to measure progress.

Tayem was in need of another haircut, she noticed absently. The stones and brown earth under her feet continued past him as far as a man might throw, coming to rest apparently at the low white spit of land topped by two trees. The trees were larches, *tamaracks* according to Tayem. Their branches were bare now, their needles mostly fallen into the sun-glittered water. Beyond them at a distance was a spruce tree, dark-olive green, with a bottom limb half broken away, pointing downward at the earth. Approaching it was a man on horseback.

The rider moved at a lope, dwarfed by distance but near enough that she could distinguish his dark-clad legs from the sides of his horse and the way his head ducked needlessly as he rode under the spruce limb. A second, riderless horse was at his rear.

"Tayem!" She jerked at the reins in her hands, forcing the horses to turn their attention to her, shouting to make the man look up with surprise. "Get up!"

Even then her consciousness was dividing, light and sound spinning about her as she reached out. She would damn herself for inattention later on, but at the moment what mattered was that the Earth was—

One. She could not reach into the rider's mind.

Teepblind.

Time traveler.

Tayem! Her mouth was dry. *From where? On what side?*

It was too late to run. This would be no accident. The man would have seen her and Tayem, and would follow them wherever she might lead. They were exposed now and there were no convenient obstacles in which to become lost.

Better here than next to the cabin. "Mount up, Tayem."

"Kylene?" He was plaintive, his pleasure interrupted.

She was already rising into her saddle. "Let's get to dry ground, Tayem. To await our friend."

"You!" the man shouted when near. "Ha'Ruppir! I followed you!" He did not sound pleased.

So he was an Algheran. Kylene relaxed the death grip she had maintained on the reins in her hands. Blond and tall, though not as tall as Tayem, perhaps the man was someone she had seen at the Project. His face had a familiar cast.

But his cheeks were drawn in and flushed, and his hair was long and ragged. His eyes jerked about, as did his head, not resting long on anything they beheld. His tan and white clothing was frayed along the sleeves, torn at the side to reveal grime-darkened skin. Only his black vest and wide leather belt retained a solid appearance. The two horses with him, brown and chestnut, bore the same vagabond look.

Hungry, Kylene realized. His journey must have been harsher than what she and Tayem had known. She put knees to her horse, moving closer, even while she wondered—but she could hear his story later. Now he was an ally who needed succor. "We've food—" she began.

"The Teep bitch!" Rage distorted the blond man's face. He moved frantically, as he scrambled with both hands at the scabbard on his belt, to turn his horse to the side.

"This is all your fault!" A horse squealed then. Kylene watched metal flower before her.

"Tayem!" That was instinct. So were the actions that followed.

Kylene yanked at the reins in both her hands, restraining her horse even as she tugged at the harnesses of the other animals. Her horse stopped, but Tayem's gelding was catapulted past her, moving straight toward the angry man. Tayem's face seemed to float before her, young and childishly surprised.

Tayem! The palomino froze, stiff-legged, before it collided with the other man's horse, but the shock seemed transmitted to the blond Algheran regardless. His hand stopped its rise instantly, the long sword stretched across his chest quivering with tension. Emotions Kylene could not decipher made facial muscles dance. Then his arm was moving again, reaching back as fast as it would move. His head rose in triumph. His teeth showed. He screamed without words.

Kylene fell forward, nearly losing her balance while yanking at the reins of Tayem's horse, trying to pull him away from danger.

She did not succeed. The sword fell, whistling, hitting where she could not see, and rose once more, steel jerking spasmodically as droplets of red spurted from it. Tayem toppled sideways, his mouth open, his seat lost. His horse whinnied and reared, hiding the man from her while it twisted in her direction. Panic showed clearly in its eyes.

The sword fell again. She heard no sound, but beads of blood suddenly dotted the neck and throat of the animal. They merged to form a line, first thin and straight, then contorted as the animal pranced about, quivering. Individual drops drifted toward the ground, each distinct and clear-edged as coins. She could have counted them.

Tayem was on the ground, moving with a lethargic lack of grace. His face was calm, expressionless. He flopped sideways as a hoof stamped on his belly, then he made swimming motions. His side was red. His mouth was closed.

She would have all the time she required to redeem the situation, Kylene understood. She had erred and there were things to be done now, without thought or preparation, but she was performing them already. She could be calm, and aware of her calmness.

Her legs and back were rigid, locked tightly to keep her horse unmoving, even while she balanced with one arm and patted at her side with the other. Her actions were very simple: She removed knives from their pockets and launched them openhandedly in the air. That was all.

Once. Twice. Three times. Four . . .

When her pockets were empty, she dismounted. The Earth rocked unsteadily beneath her feet, but she concentrated, thinking of the soreness of her ribs, and did not lose her equilibrium.

Tayem was on the ground, curled so that he lay on his side, unmoving, blood rilling from underneath him. His gelding nudged at his feet, snuffling loudly. Its fright was gone now, though it was also bleeding. Kylene stepped past them both, her attention focused on the blond man. He was not moving either, but she could not relax until she saw his face.

Perhaps the Algheran had sought water to revive himself, she thought dispassionately as she stood over him. His face had seemed so pallid when he stepped down from his horse. He had spun about dizzily, then marionette-walked to the edge of the stream, where he had knelt and carefully folded his body to rest a cheek upon the water.

Now his hands gripped loosely at weeds and he sprawled over the edge of the bank, lying limp as a child. His blond temple pressed stones colored by slime. He had fouled himself, stain and stink both obvious now. His eyes and mouth were open in astonishment. Water covered most of his face. The knife slice across his jugular vein could be seen very clearly in the water, though it no longer bled.

Something about the way he lay stirred memories. Without reason, Kylene remembered Cyomit's squeals of hatred and visions of a duel.

"You earned this," she muttered. "Go into the mists—"

She stopped abruptly. She owed this body nothing.

It was a body now, not a man. Realizing that, she stepped past it and into the water to hold its head, then pried with her fingers at the glint of metal above the ears. She pulled outward with both hands, until a piece of metal mesh was in her grip. It was flexible, clothlike, with a plastic ring around its edges—a Teepblind.

She put that in a pocket, leaving a knife in the ground to make room, then returned to Tayem. Several horses had gathered around him, seemingly standing to keep the man away from her view, pressing their muzzles together as if conferring about him. They recognized him, she assumed, and stayed near because of that familiarity. She gathered reins thankfully, lashing them together and fastening them to a nearby shrub to keep the horses believing they were still under control. Perhaps the other horses would return as well.

Tayem was semiconscious. "It hurts, Kylene," he told her weakly. "I feel sick. Make it stop hurting?" His face was ashen. Sweat was on his forehead.

She bent to kiss his forehead. "It will be all right, Tayem."

His hands groped for her. "Kylene? Kylene? I'm sorry, Kylene. I won't do this again. Kylene? Please, Kylene?"

Tears could come later. She put her hand in his. "It will be all right," she repeated. "Trust me, Tayem."

He passed out as she wrapped his wounds. Tears did not come to her then, though she wished them. She felt hollowed-out instead, empty. Her mind and her fingers showed internal injuries; Tayem's belly was bruised and bloody and a gash from the whip sword had exposed bone along his ribs. He might well die of those wounds before she returned him to the cabin.

Cimon take the Algherans! The blond man's sword was on the ground nearby; she grabbed it up and threw it with all her might into the river, then returned once more to Tayem, her temper slightly appeased.

A trickle of consciousness had returned to him. She frowned as she looked into the sky. She saw no sign of High Winter, but she knew this weather would not last. Tayem had to be moved, regardless of his injury.

Poles and canvas. She could use one of the tents, she decided. The two of them could sleep together in the other one. They would have done that anyhow if the snows made it necessary. *Might as well begin.*

"Tayem, dear, I'm going to hurt you," she admitted. "I'm going to lash you into a litter and carry you between the horses."

He nodded feebly. "All right, Kylene. I love you, Kylene."

She stopped for a moment. "Thank you, Tayem." Then she reached into his mind to pull at connections that would make the man pass out, trying to direct his unconsciousness. A memory of pain—that was what she was after. An agony Tayem had once gone through, that he could repeat safely in his memory while escaping awareness of present tortures.

She found such a memory. She pushed his mind into it, as she had intended, then looked in it herself from curiosity.

And was submerged.

Part 3: Interiors—Pentimento

Tim Harper, July 20, 1976

CHAPTER TWELVE

*The television screen showed a desert landscape, rock-*strewn dirt pink-red under a light-blue sky. Mars.

"Viking Project Engineer James Martin spoke with President Ford," a male voice was saying. The image dissolved to show two men holding telephones. "—like to get right to work on Vikings Three, Four, Five, and Six," the crew-cut man on the right said.

His jaw tight, Harper leaned forward and shut the set off. It did not matter what the President answered, he knew. Six months from now another man would be in the White House and no more would be heard about space exploration.

"Peanut brains," he said sourly. An empty coffee cup rattled on its china saucer as he dropped back into his armchair. He stretched out expensively clad legs and stared beyond stockinged feet at the white carpet. Throwing the future away—like they had done with 'Nam. And no one cared. Like 'Nam.

Spaceflight died during the twentieth century.

And that's just what everyone wants. We're in an era of limits, he thought scornfully. The human race was being condemned to eternal poverty because its leaders found it politically expedient to agree with the feebleminded. Had these people no perspective? Could they not see that leaders who did not strive for greatness had brought them to shame? That giving rule to those who echoed their mediocrity would destroy their country?

No. None of them had that perspective. And he could not give it to them. The country had changed, he admitted. The war ... Watergate ... the oil crisis and the economy ... Now people saw only the costs of honor and only the rewards from self-interest, hedonism, and apathy.

"Sex and drugs and rock 'n' roll," he said wistfully as he moved toward the kitchen. The search for private pleasure was understandable, but it was just such shortsighted behavior that had set the one world up for unending war between Teep and Normal. *Damn the fools!* He poured coffee into the cup again, stirred cream into it absently, and went back to the living room.

Surely all was not lost. Perhaps space exploration could be reborn in future eras. He could hope that. It ought to be done right, once. But now—

Now nothing, he told himself. Today's L.A. Times lay on the black-covered couch; he tossed sections of paper aside till he came to the TV listings. He'd watch a movie now. Or Johnny Carson.

Cimon! The paper slipped from his hand. He moved back to the heavy chair, rested his cup on the arm, and glared sourly at the white stuccoed walls, angry at himself and the world. *I want out of here.*

But perhaps he was being rash. He finished his coffee thoughtfully. There was a solution for boredom, after all. It worked in every era. He padded into the next room and stretched out on the waterbed, turning on the lamp with one hand and scooping up a white telephone and a black address book from the teak nightstand with the

other. He turned over on his back and smiled ironically
at the ceiling. *Some compensation to being here.*

But with the first number half dialed, he stopped. Having a girl come by, or taking one out for dinner and a drink
was no solution. At best it would be an interesting dis-
traction. More likely it would be additional cause for frustration, for there was no one in this era with whom he
could speak openly, and telling lies about his personal
history left him filled with contempt.

He did not really desire a First Era woman at this
moment, he admitted. He was stalling, evading the issue,
and being no better than those he criticized. "Yeah." Then
he said with resignation, "Tired of this."

No more. The redhead rolled over the bed, making the
mattress undulate, and reached to open the closet. *At least
for this, I don't pretend to have shaved.*

Moccasins, keys, wallet, class ring, cufflinks and Rolex,
and gray Harris tweed jacket with Irish linen handkerchief
neatly arranged in the pocket. One of the wide leather
belts on his dresser replaced the belt on his slacks; the
other he folded to stick in a coat pocket. He paused for
a final look around the bedroom, and shook his head at
the stranger in the dresser mirror. "You had your chance,"
he muttered at an unhearing world.

In the living room he pressed the call button for the
doorman. "This is Tim Harper. Will you bring my car up,
please."

"Yes, sir. Right up, Mr. Harper." The Spanish-accented
voice was new to him, Harper noticed, but the man
sounded eager to please. *My reputation for tipping is
spreading.* He grimaced, noticing the direction of his
thoughts. Servility was infectious, a disease that contam-
inated poor and rich equally.

But—*When in Chelmmys, dance Chelmmysian-style.*
He had not made Los Angeles what it was. He grimaced
again, hit the light switch, and left the apartment without
locking the door.

* * *

Down Highland, west on Sunset past the restaurants, then through Beverly Hills with more speed, and into Bel Air, gunning the turbo-charged Carrera as he came out of the winding turns, letting the leather-covered steering wheel slide through his fingers, listening to the guttural roar of the engine, swooping like a gull through the hills at the top of the UCLA campus, swerving to avoid a student riding a lightless bicycle, slowing to take the loop that put him on the San Diego Freeway headed south...

He enjoyed being out at night. The temperature was cooler, more suited to his Algheran-jiggered metabolism. And traffic was lighter, even at the traditional jam-point below the intersection of the 405 with the Santa Monica Freeway, so he could drive more rapidly. Beyond that, there was some kind of freedom in being abroad now, unobserved and unanswerable to others for his actions. *Autonomy*, he decided. It was not simply that the darkness made it possible to ignore the numbers of people around him.

Slauson Avenue. Fantastic numbers—seven million people in the Los Angeles metropolitan area, two hundred million across the country, four billion around the world. What Algheran would believe such numbers?

Jefferson Boulevard. And yet he had readjusted without trouble. One did not live in isolation in a world with only fifty million people. The cities of that world were smaller and farther apart than here. But one's circle of acquaintances did not become smaller; friends were no harder to find. An Algheran could learn to live in this world—if she chose to.

Centinela and Sepulveda. "For four hundred years, fellow?" He grunted to himself. "This era doesn't have four hundred years left to it. And—" *Have to get her back here first*.

La Tijera. "Aye, there's the rub."

Florence and Manchester. "Hell. See what develops." Then, without thought, he recalled words in a future language. *"N'ha forentimal Dicova taunn."*

I am an Ironwearer of Sept Dicovys.

Century Boulevard. Christ almighty, how long had it been since he said *that*? He shook his head, wondering, then became practical, downshifting to make the engine whine, and drifted across lanes. "Gonna miss this car."

Imperial Highway. Down the off ramp, then a right turn. He wanted a meal, he decided suddenly, a double cheeseburger, french fries . . . He smiled as the traffic light changed to green. *Last junk food for ninety thousand years.*

"That'll be three eighty-two."

Harper fumbled through his pant pockets looking for coins, then froze as he noticed the boredom on the girl's thin face. *Hamburger tastes, hamburger habits,* he jeered at himself. *You are not a poor man, Ironwearer. You need not act like one, nor accept insolence like one.*

He handed over a ten-dollar bill. "Keep the change."

The girl busied herself at the cash register, then slid money into a pocket of her soiled apron. "Be a few minutes." She looked at him with no expression.

Not a victory, Harper thought ruefully. Then his self-consciousness vanished. It was not necessary to dominate this situation. *Relax.*

He used the time to glance around the interior. Trays on the tables, discarded newspapers, cigarette butts in ashtrays—the place was more disorganized than dirty, he decided. *Not many customers. Close to closing time and they'll soon be pitching us out.*

There was still money in his wallet. It would soon be useless.

He hesitated, waiting for his tray, then dropped napkins onto the plastic and moved toward a corner booth. "Buy you anything?" he asked the woman seated there.

"What'd you like, big boy?" The woman's voice did not sound curious. It was low, tired rather than soft, with no trace of the Southern accent he had expected. The smile was a match for it, short-lived and shallow, without eye contact. But the woman had turned her attention away from the window. A thin sandalwood hand brought a cigarette to full lips; black eyebrows arched toward straight-combed dark hair as she inspected him. Cords stood out on her neck.

"I'm not a cop," Harper said.

"Didn't think you were." she lied obviously, nervously sliding a tiny purse up and down one bare thigh. A bruise showed on one hip, purple, half hidden under white hot-pants. Something red and fluffy was banded around her chest and her midriff was bare. Medium tall, Harper estimated. Too skinny. He waited impassively till she moved a hand jerkily over the table, dropping ashes from her cigarette. "Sit."

Now what? Harper sat down opposite her. He poked a straw into his shake, then bent over it to cover confusion. *Plastic. Cold but flavorless.*

"What'd you want?" the woman asked.

"I don't know," Harper said honestly. "Company, maybe." He squirted mustard, then held a cheeseburger up, looking past strands of lettuce to her red-wrapped chest, to the hatchet chin cupped inside a narrow brown hand. Not a beauty, but her skin was blemish-free, and she was not overusing cosmetics. Looked at from the right angle she might even be cute. Good hands, no skin sagging under the mascara-rimmed eyes. Twenty-five, at a guess, with a voice ten years older. "Buy you a meal, you want it."

"That ain't enough." The voice was toneless.

Harper's cheeseburger vanished in six bites. "Not trying to buy anything, am I?" He wiped grease from his fingers, then pulled a bill from his wallet and laid it down. "A present. You look hungry."

The woman touched it, rubbing the corners as if she expected that to erase the zeroes. "A cee? You high on something, mister."

Onnul. Harper smiled briefly. "I'm leaving town. Gotta spend it somehow."

"Don't go 'way." She left her purse on the table. Her hips rocked more than was necessary as she moved toward the counter. Harper continued to smile.

"My name's Milly," she told him when she returned.

Perhaps it was true. Harper swallowed undercooked french fries. "I'm Tim."

Milly leaned forward. A hand under the table massaged his knee. "Hi, Tim. Where you from, mister?"

N'ha forentimal Dicova taunn. "Boston, sort of. Sit up, woman. Now—that's me. Where you come from? Midwest?"

"Illinois, downstate. A year ago. I thought by now I'd sound—"

Harper grunted. "No one's a native here. Eat your food, Milly."

"You want to go back to my apartment, Tim? It's near here." Milly took a bite of hamburger, swallowed hard, then again. "Could have us a real good time."

She must have looked into the wallet. "I'm sure we could."

A foot rested between his thighs. Harper looked down at golden toenails and brown-pink skin inside thin hose. The calf pressing his knee was unexpectedly firm, he noticed absently. The woman's face was tilted back, her eyes closed. Meanwhile, toes wiggled. *Definitely must have looked into the wallet.*

"Or you're in a hurry," she said dreamily. "We could get—"

"Just eat, Milly." *N'ha forentimal Dicova taunn.* "I haven't figured out what to do about you." He pushed her foot with a thumb. "Have your tootsies back."

"Oh." The woman put her hamburger down, then swallowed. "Uh—you want, there's a Boy's on Hawthorne—that's twenty-four hours. You could get some steaks for us and, you know, go back. I mean—you want a real meal? I can fix a salad." Now she looked directly at him, half defiantly, her jaws taut.

Harper hid his expression behind a hand. "Best offer

I've heard yet. But supposing I'd pop for steaks and drinks, but nothing more. What then?"

Milly looked out the window. The midnight sidewalk was deserted and few Angelinos drove slowly enough to notice a thinly clad black woman on an unlighted street corner. "Whatever you want'd be just fine, mister. Whatever." The cold outside wind was blowing in her voice.

"No main man?" Harper asked gently.

"They's none of your business!" Milly looked at him again, her face angry. "Shee-it! Not so's you count. He's gone tonight, near every night. I see him weekends, then he's got others." She stopped, breathed deeply. "That's the way it is with him. So I ain't got anyone else. Tonight. Uh—how about it?"

N'ha forentimal Dicova tunn. Onnul. Harper ran a napkin over his face, pushed his tray to one side. "Get away from him, Milly."

"Hey—I can't do that," she protested.

"Oh? Why not?"

"My man, you know? That's what I've got? That's what I've got. 'Sides, I'm doing all right, you know?"

That's what I've got. "I know." Harper stood to pull his wallet out once more and laid bank notes on the table. "Go back to Illinois, Milly. Or get together with a girl friend for those steaks. Think of me, if you want."

The woman folded the bills into tiny rectangles and pushed them separately into her purse before speaking. "When you coming back, Tim? Maybe we could get together for a good time?" The voice was tremulous but clear, each word separately produced. She stayed in her seat. Her face was tilted up, but the eyes looked past his shoulders and would not focus on his face.

"Not likely ever," Harper said. "Good-bye—"

"No. Take this." Milly had a ball-point pen in her hand and was scrawling a number on the bottom of a napkin. "Here! You come back, you call me."

A phone number, Harper saw. He nodded once and

put the napkin in his shirt pocket. "Sure." Then he was able to leave gracefully.

The key poked smoothly into the ignition lock and twisted sideways. *Damn fool*, Harper thought. Not bad-looking. Why had he turned that down?

The motor cranked but he had no answer. Life could be strange.

Then he was rolling, into the street, hands yanking headlight switches and tonguing in the seat belt and mus-cling around the steering wheel and palming back the gear shift lever while his feet danced over pedals—the tech-nique was completely different from riding a levcycle, but the sensations were similar. *I'm going to miss this car*.

But when he switched the ignition off minutes later he left the keys inside and walked away without a backward glance.

"NEW ERA FORWARDERS," the small sign over the lintel read. "Long-distance haulage, fast and dependable. T. Harper, District Manager."

An anonymous name, as Harper had chosen it to be. The building was equally anonymous: the two stories of concrete and corrugated metal butted to a small brick office looked like just another airport area warehouse. Harper had chosen it for that.

The graying man at the desk behind the counter, drink-ing black coffee from a Thermos bottle cap, had been chosen by a guard agency. As Harper entered, the guard pushed a newspaper into the lee of the counter.

"How's the night, Fred?" Harper asked as the door closed.

"Pretty good, Mr. Harper." The man threw his shoul-ders back, the olive uniform jacket opening to display a dark tie and a starched brown shirt. One hand rested casually on a holstered revolver. "Came on at midnight. One round made. Nothing to report." The swivel chair squeaked as he dropped back into it. His hand shoved a visored cap to one side, then moved back to the coffee. "Lieutenant Jensen was by earlier and initialed the log."

Harper grunted as he moved around the counter. He never could remember Fred's last name. "Let's see the bills."

His nonexistent employees did not need bottled water service, he decided shortly. He did not need an independent estimate of weekly cleaning costs. The sewer lines were not backed up and also needed nothing. The quarterly tax check would be handled by his accountant. And he would not be attending a seminar on real estate trusts.

That left an invoice. Coffee—one hundred cases of Yuban, eight three-pound cans per case. The driver's signature was there, and the guard's. $5,760, and net in 30 days. Harper winced. That was little better than the supermarket price. But the delivery had been made. He scrawled his own name with a ball-point pen resting on the countertop, then dropped the green and white flimsies into a tray. The accountant could take care of this also.

He glanced at his watch. 12:55. *Getting to that time.* "I'll look around," he muttered. Without waiting for an answer, he slid open the big metal door to the warehouse area, then let it shut behind him. As he walked, his thumbs slipped casually underneath his belt buckle.

A concrete floor, poorly lit by yellow bulbs in the tall ceiling. Two wooden skids under waist-high stacks of cardboard boxes. A corrugated metal door that took up the back wall. A red-painted fire exit. A forklift with a dented front hood, tethered by black cables to a battery recharger. Metal girders, creamy white only months before, but already brown-webbed by dust . . .

12:57. Harper grimaced as he looked around. No one would be surprised when New Era Forwarders closed. But enough would be left in his accounts to pay his creditors. No one would miss him as a customer, or search for him as a debtor.

12:58. He was under the center light, oriented by scratches carefully drawn into the discolored concrete.

On his belt, an index finger inconspicuously pushed a metal stud. He nodded, keeping part of his attention focused on the doorway to the office. *Some things were not meant for Fred to know.*

12:59. The lighting was instantly bright, blue-tinged, actinic. A silver-white wall was at his side, metal polished till images were mirrored on its surface.

Big, Harper thought instantly. *So Cimon-taken big.* He always thought that.

The aircraft had the form of a wing section, a flat-bottomed teardrop sixty feet in length, with half that width. The height at the front was twice that of a tall man but tapered gradually toward the back, then dropped to a hand-thick trailing edge. The vehicle hovered a yard above the concrete floor and radiated uncomfortable amounts of heat. After fingering the underside of his belt buckle, Harper stepped back several yards until his shoulders met an invisible barrier.

Inspection from here revealed the imperfections in the mirrorlike surface. Gaps that were expansion joints showed between the metal plates. Barely visible channels and protuberances were boundary-layer suction and blowing devices, which controlled the air flow over the moving vehicle. Clusters of small holes were at the front and flat-walled sides.

The vehicle was new, a levcraft built as a Fourth Era troop transporter near the climax of the Second Eternal War. Harper had taken it from a military factory, leaving behind his stolen Algheran time shuttle, only hours before weapons wielded by a Teep suicide force caused the factory and its mechanical and human defenders to disintegrate.

In this era and this city, Harper had explained it as a prop for a forthcoming movie, an elaborate set in need of reconstruction. Whether the welders and electricians who had rebuilt it for him had believed that story, he did not know. They had kept their mouths shut; the levcraft hovered and flew and traveled in time; he had been satisfied with that.

A tongue-shaped crack appeared in the silver wall, then tilted downward like a drawbridge, hinging about its bottom. It extended as it lowered, but did not quite reach the floor. An airlock opening was behind it.

At the top of the ramp, Harper looked back at the office door. It was open now, an entrance to a floodlighted stage. Fred was at the portal, holding the sliding door half open with one shoulder. Perhaps he spoke, but Harper could hear nothing. The guard's motions were jerky, animated, too fast—a mime cast as a puppet on a blue-lit proscenium.

Making his rounds, Harper remembered. He watched impassively as the metal curtain closed and Fred marched at double-time across the concrete, a bulky Detex clock held firmly in place below an elbow. The guard rattled the padlocks on the cargo gate, then rushed to the fire exit and out. At no time had he paid attention to Harper or to the levcraft.

That act was over. Harper entered the airlock.

His first stop was in the larger of the two small bedrooms in the waist of the vehicle, where he changed to jeans and a gray sweatshirt.

A door next to this led to the machine shop, which doubled as a corridor to the cargo area. This normally ran the width of the craft, but Harper had installed wooden barricades as temporary partitions. Wall plates had been fastened back to create an opening. Perhaps in the Fourth Era the boom and tackle here had placed paratroopers in the air; now he used it to pull the cargo skids to the side of the vehicle.

Throwing the boxes of coffee through the entrance was a straightforward job. Finding a place for them after that was more complex. In the end, most of them went under counters in the machine shop; the rest he wedged between bales of chicken wire and the crates that held the Nautilus machines.

He showered after that, Algheran fashion, a scrubbing with chemical soap followed by a cold brief dousing. That removed the sweat from him, as donning the work clothing had removed the First Era from him. He had no cause now to wear the costumes of this age, and after drying himself in a stream of warm air, he dressed quickly in a green uniform with black and silver piping.

Then he could find no excuse for stalling, and returned to the cabin area. He was left with only one uncompleted task.

Every warship should have a name at commissioning.

Scent O'Claws. Harper stood on the ramp and inspected the metal plaque in his hands. The characters engraved in the plate were even and cleanly cut, he noted with pleasure, the bright red Roman letters and Algheran syllabics perfectly distinct against the white enamel. The sketch below, showing malevolent reindeer hitched to an M60-A1 tank, was understandable. The company making the sign had fulfilled his intentions, and he had no reason but ceremony to delay.

"'When a man hath no freedom to fight for at home, Let him combat for that of his neighbors,'" he quoted self-consciously.

So much for ceremony. He peeled off the plastic backing, throwing it onto the floor as a mystery for Fred to solve, then stuck the metal plate to the right of the airlock. Next he sprayed an Algheran chemical over it, to form a transparent bond that would keep the plaque on the metal forever.

He was going back, he realized now. Whatever private doubts and causes for hesitation he might have harbored had peeled away like the backing on the name plate.

Onnul. There would be a way to save her. Knowing that, everything within him became settled. He closed his eyes, imagining her before him, reaching his arms toward her, holding her . . . and a measure of peace came upon him.

Now to leave. No—it was four A.M. by his watch,

which meant five-thirty outside. It would still be dark. He had time for one more look at Los Angeles. Moving quickly, he returned to the bedroom for his weapons.

Scent O'Claws. He smiled grimly at the name plate as he walked from the vehicle, then at the open space that remained when he reached the fire exit.

The work earlier had overheated him, and the predawn air was unexpectedly warm. The lamprey connection on his neck sensed his body temperature and caused his short black cape to billow loosely behind him as he walked across the lot.

Airport noises were all about him. He began to relax.

Directly ahead, a Sabena DC-8 taxied down an access strip to takeoff. Identifiable by silhouette as much as size, a 747 awash in fuselage lights swooped toward the runways. A constellation of stars was behind it: other aircraft in the landing pattern.

Engines shrilled as the DC-8 revved up for takeoff. There was a romantic air yet to aviation in this century, Harper thought. Time travel had increased his objectivity, he decided, but had not made him blasé; he leaned against the chain-link fence to watch with genuine enjoyment.

Before long a flashlight beam drifted along the fence, then focused unmovingly on his head. Harper turned with resignation.

"Mr. Harper!"

Timithallin ha'Dicovys-once-Harper. "Yes, Fred?"

"You've changed your clothes."

Very astute, Fred. "Yes. I put on a uniform."

"I guess so!"

The flashlight beam dropped, and Harper closed his eyes tight to speed readjustment to the darkness. An engine roar moved past his back. That would be the DC-8, he realized. A minute from now it would be over the Pacific, looping back toward the coastline and climbing toward thirty-five thousand feet. But he would still be on the ground, stuck there by a curious security guard.

Never mind. The confrontation between eras might be amusing.

"Looks pretty fancy," the guard said. "You must be going to a costume party, aren't you?"

"No. Just going to visit some people."

"Oh. I'll bet you surprise them all right, don't you?"

Only by the things I intend to do. "They should recognize me. And the uniform—it's field dress for an officer of the Forest Guard."

"Oh." Fred sounded disappointed. "Another company? I never heard of it."

Harper felt grim humor. *Wonderful thing, honesty*, he thought. *He won't believe a word I tell him, so I can tell him the absolute truth.*

"The Forest Guard is part of the army of a small country that is going to exist in about ninety thousand years," he explained gravely. "It's an elite unit, halfway between the Marine Corps and the Green Berets. Very small. First troops into battle, always fighting outnumbered, never retreat and never surrender. That sort of thing. We buy time for everyone else."

"We," Fred repeated. "So that's what you are, huh?" The flashlight beam moved across Harper's chest again.

"Douse the glim," Harper ordered. He tapped a belt stud. Vampire needles pricked at his legs; life-mimicking devices sucked oxygen and heat from his arteries and excreted their wastes into nearby veins. Provided with energy, embedded light sources made his uniform radiate an emerald-hued glow.

Too much of this was fatiguing; his jugular vein pulsed as the lamprey sucked at it, then the black cape wrapped around him to preserve his body heat. Harper tugged it open to reveal the triangular patch on one shoulder.

"Master of Swordsmen," he said. "'Infantry Major' is a good equivalent. I got the rank by action of our—call it 'Senate'—but I seldom use it."

An aircraft passed behind amid hurricane sounds. *Full*

throttle and thrust reversers, Harper had time to think.
High load or he overshot.

Fred waited for the noise to diminish. "That's a pretty
fancy costume, Mr. Harper. Bet it cost a lot, didn't it?"
And when he got no answer, he asked, "What's the stuff
on your collars?"

The redhead frowned and put a hand to his belt, killing
the green uniform lights. "They're miniature swords. They
signify a sort of title—Ironwearer. As a rule, it's not polite
to mention that."

"How come?"

"Just because." But Harper's irritation turned into pity.
Lonely and bored, guy. Go easy on him. "Old tradition."

"Sounds almost like you meant it." Fred's voice
betrayed surprise.

How about that! Harper thought sourly.

But he kept his rekindled annoyance from his voice.
"There was a period like the Dark Ages, but going on for
thousands of years," he explained. "Metal was very
expensive, especially iron and steel. So a man with steel
armor was someone special; rich to begin with, and he
would charge plenty for his services. He could become
immensely wealthy, and he probably hired a lot of retain-
ers who also fought with him."

"Like a knight," the guard suggested. He turned his
flashlight on and moved the beam along the pavement
between them.

Harper shook his head. "Much less common. 'Baron'
or even 'Duke' perhaps. Something of the sort. 'Ironwearer' isn't exactly a title.

"After a while, some Ironwearers became famous. People made up stories about them. Other Ironwearers tried
to emulate them. So eventually an Ironwearer became
someone leading a special type of life. He fought like a
Medal of Honor winner, he had good manners, and he
had *noblesse oblige*—feed the poor, defend the weak,
look after the sick, and so on.

"There never are very many. And since pride goes

before a fall, you do not remind an Ironwearer of his status. You don't want him to lose whatever—call it 'grace'—it is that makes him what he is."

"You're one," Fred said cynically.

At the moment. But when I get back . . . Harper made himself nod and exchange First Era smiles with the guard.

"Well, it's your costume, isn't it?" Fred conceded. "So what do you do to become one of these here Ironwearers?"

Harper gave out another smile. "Tell people you are," he said simply. *"N'ha forentimal Dicova taunn.* Just like that. That's all there is to it."

"Aw, come on! There's gotta be more than *that.* Why isn't everybody one?"

"If you fail—" Harper tapped his palm against tiny swords. "—they take these away. You can't screw up and hide it. Everyone else will know, believe me, and they never forget. Everyone on the one world."

"Oh." The guard changed the subject. "What kind of weapons would you wear?"

"I'm wearing them now," Harper said softly.

The flashlight beam darted across his midriff. "I guess you are, aren't you? What are they supposed to be, anyhow?"

"Short sword, combat knife, garrote, shocker, 'Cease." The big man's hands moved suddenly, and a silver gleam appeared in the air. "Sword. Pretty much like a saber. Made from something like glass, with metal inside to make it visible. Officer gets one."

The gleam dipped and was gone. A hand patted at Harper's side. "Knife. Nothing special about it, or the strangler's cord."

The other hand turned to show a dark flat triangular object. "A gun, call it. Projects a high-voltage electrical field that plays hob with nerves and brain cells. About a mile range. The uniform can be hardened to keep out bullets, so we don't use them."

"You mentioned something else?" Fred's curiosity was

still visible; Harper could not decide if the voice was more subdued.

"My 'Cease." He bent to slap leather. "Bone handle at the top of my left boot. I don't pull it, except for suicide or sending a friend up to Cimon. If it's used, they bury it with you. Just die, it gets passed to someone else."

"Got an answer for everything, don't you?" Fred's voice was not admiring.

"I spent a long time thinking them up," Harper said dryly. He looked at his wristwatch and suppressed a yawn. Almost six now. The ship would be synchronized shortly. He had time to drop the letters with final instructions for the lawyers into the outgoing mailbox, but no more. *Going to be a lot of broken-hearted stockbrokers tomorrow.*

"Ought to be clearing off," he muttered for Fred's benefit. "Oh—one thing more. When do you get off, Fred? Eight? Okay." He pulled a strip of paper from his pocket. "You call this number. If you get an answer, tell her I thought about it and said 'Good-bye.'"

CHAPTER THIRTEEN

The longest journey inevitably began with anticlimax, Harper reflected. But that was the byproduct of caution, and a pilot should not go searching for unanticipated excitement.

"Especially in the dark." The dim lighting had been switched off, to force concentration. The green walls were lost in blackness, and he seemed to float within his tall chair so that only his feet made contact with his environment.

His left hand moved unerringly to the fist-size sphere on the pillar beside him. The ball was hard, cool to the touch, resistant to motion. His right hand drifted over the consoles arrayed about him, making their tops glow with a pastel tint. Blue and pink and yellow dyed his palm with cold flame and his gestures cast shadows bobbing across the ceiling.

His fingers seemed to press randomly at the keyboards, but his attention was focused on the stylized gauges imaged on panels hanging from the ceiling. Orange and amber as they flickered into existence; yellow as they departed and were replaced. *No purple—no problems yet.*

Numbers were blazoned above him: Long Count dates. Now he was at negative 44108.248.0143 in brown and blue and the last decimals could not be read; he was aimed at redness and 44937.129.000000. No changes to make there.

Well, it looks exact. But getting back to the 1970s was a helluva job, with a lot of backing and filling. I just hope the clocks are calibrated for forward travel. Negative 44108.248.0142.

Generator power levels ... Current values ... Electron shunts ... Magnetic fluxes ... Those were Fourth Era machines, he remembered. Not much different from what the Algherans used, but more rugged.

Battery status readings ... Six of them. That was Fifth Era technology, copied in this age; he had wondered how they would hold up, but they seemed to be doing well enough.

"Ah." Switch images were canary yellow above him. "Cannon to the left of me, cannon to the right of me, will volley and thunder. Electronically." The switches vanished, to be replaced by new gauges. "Complete with laser pointing and range finding." That was First Era science; the Fifth knew nothing of quantum electronics.

And First Era sentiment. He was also carrying back a crate of ammo, and a pair of blackmarket Uzis hung in a locker. He wasn't planning on explaining those to the Algherans either.

Other life-support systems. "Yup. I'm breathing, all right."

The radio speakers hissed and he rotated controls until directional antennas picked up a garbled noise. Speech. Marine frequency, he noticed. The Algherans transmitted AM with a ten-kilohertz bandwidth using dual sideband and suppressed carrier. He could live with that, but their radios were low in sensitivity, and he was doing well to get something recognizable as a voice.

His right hand slapped at banks of pressure-sensitive

switches. His left spun the sphere counterclockwise around
the control shaft. The gauge images vanished and were
replaced by camera views of the warehouse. The levcraft
bobbed and rotated to point northward, while pumps
*whirr*ed to move ballast water about. Harper's hand pulled
down, forcing the control knob into the cuff on the shaft.
Then he stood and touched one last switch without ceremony.

Now there was a gloomy cast to the surrounding world,
as if evening crept over the green-painted walls and girders about him. The central number on the date board
was negative 44107 and a fraction. *A million to one*, he
thought. *Twelve days to a second*. Negative 44106 . . . A.D.
1978.

The walls were moving, he sensed. They were hard to
see behind the wooden crates and plastic-shrouded boxes
that sloshed back and forth through the warehouse like
water in a shoe box, but the vehicle was climbing slowly.
1978 out there, going on 1979 . . . Someone else had leased
the building and would soon be tearing it down for rede-
velopment. His hand moved, the thumb pushing the control knob to increase the rate of climb.

Blue-gray showed on one viewscreen, then on several.
He was through the demolished roof. For an instant girders and wrecker-battered walls were before him, then
they dropped below eye level. Pipes and dusty rubble,
planks and a pile of gravel could be made out clearly on
the black pitch, then the detail was obscured by distance
and twilight. 1980, Harper noticed.

A gigantic metal rail was lying on the road before him.
Two rails. They were everywhere, quicksilver mounds
gleaming on each line of every street he could see. Cars,
of course.

The Algherans had modified the time machine he had
brought them, reducing the rate at which it traveled through
time but allowing the world to be viewed while it operated.
Roughly every fifteen minutes outside the field—a mil-
lisecond from his viewpoint—he left run-time for a micro-

second. That collected enough light for him to see his surroundings but did not give time to focus on mobile objects, so street traffic came to him as superimposed images.

On one dark viewscreen, a blue rainbow shape slowly moved up and down. That was as it should have been. Harper kept his vehicle rising and nodded familiarly at the radio sun.

The Los Angeles skyline seemed unchanged at first, but a closer look showed buildings rising on Century Boulevard. Hotels, perhaps. The Rockwell plant to the east and south shrank suddenly. Construction went on in Marina del Rey.

The mountains were in the same places. Harper set the controls to maintain his relative altitude, then watched the viewscreens only to steer as he flew north along the path he had followed south hours—years—before.

He was beyond Mulholland Drive and almost through the pass to the San Fernando Valley when a blast wave nudged his vehicle. The hills about him turned black suddenly and distorted, melting down to bare rock in places, as if the Earth were the face of a long-rotting corpse. The rail lines of automobiles vanished, though a few wrecked vehicles could be seen along the sides of the road.

Harper's face was impassive. The country had turned itself into something he no longer recognized. He could find no loyalty to it in his heart; he owed it no obligations.

His eyes stayed dry while all the green below him faded to a constant brown. Let the trees die. Let the unseen vandals of passing time tear apart abandoned homes and break the brittle pavement to weed-laced gravel. The physical desert that returned to mid-twenty-first-century America was overdue.

He turned *Scent O'Claws* east-northeast and continued to climb.

His elevation was three thousand man-heights, his speed sufficient to keep airborne without use of the bottom thrusters. Harper considered sleeping, then touched the switch that darkened the viewscreens, causing them to go flat against the ceiling, and restored the darkroom lighting to the cabin, making all he saw red and black. Control consoles retreated beneath the instrument panels. He stayed seated, his eyes closed. His head shook briefly. *Onnul*.

His head shook again. His face contorted slowly, like a wax mask held near flame. "I'll get to you somehow," he whispered. Then he slumped forward until his elbows were on his knees. He exhaled loudly, painfully. "Promise. Owe you that."

He spoke to himself in mumbles after that, spacing out the unintelligible words with long sighing breaths. "No way around it," he said finally. "Got to change the Project. Go back before Borct approved that operation. Ask him to put it off for a day tenth. Or disrupt things somehow. That creates a window. Go through that, and I can get to her. Got to be . . ."

But then what? Pain twisted his face into a mask. "Nothing!" *She didn't have to say it; she must have meant what she said. She doesn't want me. It's over. Oh God, Onnul!*

At length he leaned haggardly upon the instrument panel, bending to press his sweat-beaded forehead against the cool plastic. He rested motionlessly, bathing without thought in defeat until all feeling had been washed from him.

"I'll go on," he muttered. "I'll take it . . . Besides, things aren't over yet." He blew out breath, then shook his head and snorted. His eyes moved to the control displays. "Thirty-five hundred 'heights. Hmmm . . . Bedtime, chum."

Cold. Dark. Complete silence.

On an unfamiliar padded surface the length of a bed but narrower, he lay on his back, nude. Air currents touched his face lightly. He smelled nothing. His hands moved stealthily, seeking weapons, but became trapped in thin bed coverings. His left elbow banged into a rigid wall—

Not in 'Nam. Harper sat up quickly, noticing now the thin red lines that framed a doorway. *Time shuttle.* "Lights." A patch of ceiling responded, bringing a sickly green-yellow glow into the cramped room.

Pea soup moon, the man thought absently. He arched his back and stretched on the bunk. *Feel better this morning. I hit bottom last night, for sure.* Then, as his feet were falling to the carpeted floor, he said experimentally, "Onnul."

He said it diffidently, blank-faced, like a child pressing a diseased tooth to see whether dormant pain could be awoken. Yes, pain was still there. He stood and shoved the bed up, folding it into a wall recess. "Don't press it, guy. Get dressed."

Underwear was in a wall bin, cotton briefs from the First Era rather than the fibrous long johns favored by the Algherans. The air temperature was about sixty degrees, he estimated. That was not quite comfortable, but he should be reacclimated to it within a few weeks. "More or less."

A Teepblind was not necessary in isolation, nor was a shower, and the Algherans had made shaving impossible for him. He put a finger into his class ring, pulled on dark-green trousers and fleece-lined boots and sealed exterior flaps on his uniform, then returned to the front cabin.

It was approximately A.D. 3700, according to his translation of the bright numbers on the hanging calendar. A broad blue band, seemingly black in the dim red lighting, moved rhythmically up and down on one viewscreen. Now and then forms other than the arc traced by the sun appeared on that screen, radio waves caused by artificial or natural sources, but none showed now, and from his memories he expected to see none for thousands of years.

Barely started, he told himself. *Slow. I wish I knew enough about the time drive to make big modifications and speed this up. Theory is fine, but—*

He yawned, reminded of sleep by the dim lighting. "But—breakfast."

A galley was hidden behind sliding doors opposite the airlock: percolator and microwave oven resting on shelves over a small sink, next to an outsize refrigerator-freezer. Ultimately, this would all be replaced with Algheran food processing equipment, Harper had decided. Until then, he could picnic.

He filled a Styrofoam cup with steaming water from a wall tap and shook in coffee crystals, then pulled a thin box from the freezer. A hearty appetite went with cold temperatures, he told himself as he stripped cellophane away and pushed the contents onto a tray. The microwave controls were already correctly set. He simply had to push a button.

The buttons he pushed in the pilot's chair caused the ceiling viewscreens to swing downward on hinges. Skies daubed by clouds appeared on them as if shuttered windows had been thrown open. Unnecessary now, the red lights in the ceiling winked off. Harper set his coffee aside. "What we got out there?"

Mountains. Harper looked at a gauge and mentally converted the reading into miles. He was not at the Rockies yet. *Great Basin area. Nevada. Utah.*

"More forest than desert," he noted. "Pretty." His left hand slammed at the control sphere. The world beneath began to slide backward.

From this altitude, the America of A.D. 3700 was copper-sulphate blue and olive green, baby-bottom pink and swan-feather white. Mountains stood out in all directions, arrayed in ragged rows like files of conscript soldiers. Trees covered them, pine and aspens. Between the ranges, grassland ran where once brown and white alkali plains had lain. Small rivers threaded through valleys, gold- and silver-surfaced when the sun's rays touched them. *Probably just mud.*

Fifth Era geology was basically geography, descriptive, fixated on the changes wrought by ice and weather. First

Era geology had changed radically while he was gone, using radioactive dating, studies of rock magnetism, and elaborate oceanographic surveying techniques to give birth to theories of plate tectonics. When Harper looked down now, he did so carefully, using his new knowledge and understanding that he would be the last man in history to view the Earth as a single all-connected whole.

Long before, during the age of dinosaurs, this territory had been the bottom of a shallow sea. Sediments collected on it, becoming limestone and chalklike dolomite, which rested in great flat beds. Time passed. Continental drift carried North America slowly westward, an inch or two each year, on a raft of crustal material. Twenty-five million years before, this North American plate had collided with the plate underlying California and the Pacific basin. The juncture eventually was called the San Andreas fault.

Then an irregular line of cliffs was before him, running north and south almost as far as his eyes could see, dark and light banded limestone rising abruptly from the ground like the prow of a ship.

Soon he was over a canyon, one long wall stretching past him to the west, the face of another looming on the left. Shrubs grew upon the talus; from far above he could even see yellow and purple flowers blooming. But for over two thousand feet above this bare rock showed, nearly vertical, the broken skeleton of Earth emerging as a compound fracture, too steep to carry a skin of soil.

He passed over a narrow pine-topped summit, then was above another sheer-walled canyon. A patch of white rested in a crevice. This grew, then was concealed as whiteness fell all along the mountain, then was exposed again and shrinking. Snow. It never completely vanished, Harper noted. How cold was it down there?

On this side of the range, trees grew: white firs as the gorge widened, then junipers, and a stand of aspen beside a gravel-laden stream, now green-leaved, now yellow. The slope became gentle then. The trees were not close enough for him to call them a forest, but together they obscured both the bare ground and the great rounded slope of the alluvial fan that must have rested at the base of the canyon.

A buzzer sounded. Harper returned to the galley and removed his pizza from the oven. *Nothing like a balanced three thousand—calorie meal for breakfast.*

Inevitably he became bored. A year passed outside the vehicle for each half minute of his time, but it would take almost a month for him to return to the Project. It would have required only five or six days if the Algherans had been able to copy exactly the mechanism he had brought them, and being able to watch scenery was no recompense for the delay.

"Nothing's happening," Harper complained aloud. "No one's home."

No houses, no cities—no sign of man except untraveled roadways. *Where did everyone go?* Was it a catastrophe that nearly destroyed the human race, reducing the billions of his native age to the scant millions of later eras?

"Cold perhaps." Harper glanced at his viewscreens but was unable to find what he sought. At three thousand man-heights, he had a viewing range of hundreds of miles, not thousands, and could not see deep into the north. No doubt the continental glaciers were already growing atop the Canadian shield; it certainly looked as if snow lingered longer each year as time passed. But that was not proof that all the race had migrated to the tropics.

"That's a way off, chum," he reminded himself. "Still First Era down there, as far as anyone knows." Millennia would pass before ice captured this land year round. Only when men rebuilt their fallen civilization would the Second Era be truly begun.

Utah was behind him now, as well as the great lake that had spread over the northern part of the state. Colorado was beneath him and ahead, and beyond the endless walls of the Rockies, haze concealed the Great Plains.

Somewhere within this region, if ambiguous hints in the Plates were more than legend, telepaths would gather and give birth to the city-state that ruled the Second Era world and earned men's hatred until the end of time: Kh'taal Minzaer.

Somewhere. *Lot of land down there*, Harper reflected. *It's a big country, pal.*

He shook his head. "Just used to be."

From sea to shining sea. The United States had been an empire, he understood now. A huge expanse of land, populated by diverse people, a republic with justice and one law for all, created by conquest but secured by the peace and commerce within its borders—the culmination of all Alexander and the Caesars had striven for had been achieved in his homeland. Nothing the Fifth Era built would be its equal; no other nation would come so gloriously close to fulfilling its own high ideals.

It was both amusing and sad to reflect that the war being fought at the Present had begun as a squabble between New England and New York.

No—it was not amusing.

Was that still one nation beneath him? *Probably not*, he reasoned. *Vacant land has to mean frontier—which likely means a political vacuum between states.*

What's it like out there? he wondered suddenly. All the First Era seemed his homeland somehow, for of all the hundreds of billions of human beings who might ever after dwell on this one Earth, he alone would know this age as more than a name. No Algheran would ever possess a world as he did now, and even as he took leave of it, Harper felt a desire to touch this era one last time.

"The year 5000," he said slowly. *December 31, at midnight.* "Then."

"'Leave this damned art, This magic that will charm thy soul to hell, And quite bereave thee of salvation. Though thou has now offended like a man, Do not per-

severe in it like a devil. Yet, yet, thou has an amiable
soul, If sin by custom grow not into nature...'"

A chime sounded, and Harper was no more in medieval
Wittenberg. He pushed a bookmark into place, then laid
the volume on an instrument console as his eyes moved
to the calendar displays. Negative 41084.084.75.

Very negative, he thought. *Five thousand A.D. looks
chilly, even for New Year's. Lots of space for the wind to
blow out there.*

He was deep in the Rockies now, resting on a flat strip
of ground just beneath the crest of a mountain. It had
taken a while to locate a site where the levcraft could be
landed, and even here the rear of the vehicle overhung a
steep drop. The viewscreens showed him landscapes that
went mostly up and down and were covered now by night
and snow. He was above the treeline, although a few
shrubs could be seen in the middle distance. The dominant
image was rock and outsized boulders. *Might as well get
out.*

Cold. Dark. Those were his first impressions and his
last of A.D. 5000. The cold was damp, almost bearable; it
chilled rather than numbed the body. Harper's ebon cape
wrapped about him even as the time shuttle vanished,
wind lashing the garment erratically around his legs and
dangling scabbard.

Half an hour of this. Unprotected by the levcraft, he
turned to face into the wind, shook out his cloak, then
twisted his head to secure a transparent coif to the neck
of his jacket liner. Despite this, his lips soon felt puffy,
novocained, as his mouth was from breathing the thin
cold air. The outside of his face seemed to be shrinking.

*What's the coefficient of thermal expansion for human
flesh?* Then he noticed the night sky.

Mechanically, he stroked his cuffs to fasten invisible
gloves to his sleeves. His footsteps broke the thin crust,
dragging a knee-deep wake of powdery snow behind him.
Harper's attention was focused on the Milky Way. Six
months in Los Angeles had diminished his memories. Now

he was in clear air and the lights of a hundred billion suns were spilled across the heavens for him once more.

"'When I behold the heavens then I repent,'" he quoted from his reading. "'And curse thee, wicked Mephistophilis, Because thou hast deprived me of those joys.'

"'Twas thine own seeking, Faustus, thank thyself. But thinkst thou heaven is such a glorious thing? I tell thee, Faustus, it is not half so fair As thou or any man that breathes on earth.'

"'How prov'st thou that?'

"'Twas made for man; then he's more excellent.'"

Harper laughed scornfully. He was near the edge of the dropoff here. He stopped to hitch his broadsword to one side, then brushed snow away and sat on a large granite boulder. "'If heaven was made for man, 'twas made for me. I will renounce this magic and repent.'"

But first, he would catch his breath. The Algherans kept air pressure in their vehicles close to sea-level values, and he had done the same in *Scent O'Claws*. That left him ill prepared for exposure to high altitudes, and Harper regretted the habits that caused him to go about uselessly armed and armored.

He grimaced, remembering the crude two-handed sword he had carried on his first travels through time. That was still in his possession, back in his quarters in the Station. *Ought to sell it*, he told himself practically. *Much as it snows everyone, that blade is useless to me, even if I learn some real sword fighting.*

But the sword was a link with his past, as was the molded-beaver ring on his finger. He was not about to dispose of either.

He shook his head resolutely, then turned his attention to the view. Very faintly, distant mountaintops could be seen from there, gray shapes heaped upon an expanse of darkness that began almost at his feet. *Eternity is just a step away in all directions*, he thought with grim amusement, then looked skyward.

There were limits to his vision. More than a decade

had passed since Harper had last traced out First Era constellations. The individual stars he sought now could no more be found than individual grains of sand; the patterns he hoped to recognize were veiled behind or tangled in the celestial curtain that was a galaxy and that blocked him from a view of infinity.

If he could examine it closely, that lacy white-gold tapestry would be made entirely of tiny dots, and each individual dot a star. Billions of stars, millions of planets, each with eldritch, uncharted, alien, yearned-for wonders...
"'Thou are damned,'" he quoted in a strained voice. "Damned. God cannot pity thee."

He stood at last. He had wandered far from the time shuttle, he recognized now. Hundreds of feet. He ought to be returning to it. The New Year must be here. He had seen a new millennium enter, and there was no more reason to linger.

Snow fell away from his pants without clinging as he swiped at it, then scrunched like pillows beneath his boots. Harper rocked indecisively, then went to the edge of the drop and looked over. This was not exactly a cliff, he found. The mountainside fell steeply at this point, but it was not vertical. He could see a bush not far below, seemingly tilted as if partially uprooted.

"Brrr," he said theatrically, then turned away and scuffed the snow.

His foot hit something that yielded. A branch perhaps. He pushed at it, then hooked his toe under the obstruction and tipped it back so an end emerged from the snow. A branch.

No—a bone. Harper knelt to examine it, then picked it up.

Quite a large bone. This wasn't from a rabbit.

Nor was it very old. Gristle and scraps of flesh were still attached to one end, like a discarded drumstick, and frozen drops of blood. His fingertips brushed roughnesses—scrape marks. From teeth.

Wolves, he guessed. Or other large predator. Gnawing

bones was something done by a carnivore, and this one had come from a fresh kill rather than an old corpse. Probably not too long ago. He let the bone fall, then slapped at his waist. Yes, his neuroshocker was in place. And his sword.

He laughed. "You really don't have to stick around, fellow."

But the bone was lodged firmly in his memory, and Harper's thoughts turned to it even as he knocked snow from his boots onto the airlock floor and hung his weapons on the wall. *Nothing like horns or antlers. Awful high up and awful cold for any reasonably sized animal.* He frowned, then returned to the cabin area. *Killed enough time,* he thought as he settled into the pilot's seat. *I've got a long way to go.*

But with his hand poised over the switches that would put him back into run-time, Harper hesitated. Alghera was indeed a long way from this moment and he would never be returning. He could satisfy his curiosity now, while it was convenient, or never. "Damned painful, unindulged curiosity." He exhaled loudly, an unhappy expression on his face. Abstract curiosity was not the problem. Something about that bone was familiar. *But what?*

No matter. He was resetting the control calendars already and would soon be able to answer his questions.

Snow filled the viewscreen. Half a second for a dwindling sunset that was really a sunrise, then blackness for a few heartbeats, then snow again, gray at first but quickly a gleaming white. He could make out a drift on one side of that distant boulder, but whether it became larger or smaller with time he could not decide.

No reason to expect this to be easy, Harper reminded himself. *It's no big deal, guy. You can knock off whenever you want.*

He shrugged. *Give it to the start of winter. It's not far off.*

And it was not. Soon afterward only gray showed in

the viewscreens between two spells of blackness. That had been a monster of a storm, Harper recognized when the outside world could be seen once more. Moving backward, the snow had become much thinner on this previous day. Even the ground looked different.

Stop. Here.

Harper slapped at consoles, then reset controls without haste or wasted motion. A hundred to one, that was reasonable. He leaned forward, as if to thrust at time through the walls of the levcraft.

Snow came again, covering the viewscreens with gray, like dirty rain. It was evening, for the light was dimmer. Harper drummed fingers on the sides of his chair, feeling the black plastic deform and vibrate about him, damning the uncontrolled curiosity that made him waste time on such nonsense.

Self-awareness landed on him along with the frustration. Harper crooked a grin at his instruments. *Calm down, guy. Give it a few minutes, and you can be on your way.*

Perhaps the darkness had been rising already. Certainly while he debated that with himself, the heavens did begin to brighten. A brief sunrise brought him into a world of blue skies and white landscapes.

The sun was also white, painful to observe after it cleared the horizon and the low wisps of morning clouds. It threw shadows toward him, elongated caricatures of the hillocks and rocks hidden beneath the snow. As he watched, the shadows became shorter. They turned slowly in the direction of the mountain crest, timidly, shrinking until they vanished from view.

Noon. More clouds appeared shortly, piling up suddenly like whipped cream squirted from a can onto a layer cake of empty air. *Thunderheads*, Harper thought. *Going to snow. That two-day storm.*

A blur appeared just below the horizon, a flickering, as if from a badly focused movie film. But the phenomenon was localized, not over the full screen: It began at a dip in the mountain crest in the middistance, then came to the edge of the dropoff and ran parallel to that for a brief while. It stopped as suddenly as it began, a few hundred feet from him, on the far side of the boulder he had sat upon—would sit upon—on New Year's Eve.

A man. Harper snarled blasphemies at gods in three languages.

He was already in motion, slapping at his waist as he rose from the command chair to verify that he was wearing his control belt, then moving across the cabin almost at a run. *God, what a way to die!*

He yanked weapons from the airlock walls and slipped his feet into boots as the exit ramp descended. Even before it had reached the ground, he had jumped from its end into the snow. *That poor sap.*

The snow was too deep for him to run in, but his feet pulled him over the ground regardless, each long stride skimming the ice-gleaming crust before plunging toe down into powder. "Get back!" he shouted as he ran. "Come this way!"

The words were useless, he knew. No one in this world would understand him. He was only trying to catch the dark-coated stranger's attention, to get him off his knees and moving away from the gray and brown forms racing toward him—away from the wolves.

But the words were lost in the howling.

It was too late to use the neuroshocker. Harper screamed wordlessly as he leaped past the cowering man.

The wolves were checked suddenly, then split ranks. Several continued toward the kneeling man, but the rest of the pack wheeled, then came running at Harper, yapping eagerly like dogs released from a kennel to greet a well-loved master. *Or dinner*, Harper took time to note. *Those babies are Saint Bernard–size.*

Fur was fluffed around the faces of the wolves, and their eyes were narrowed, giving them a fat and Oriental appearance. *Hard to believe this is how dogs started out.* Harper screamed again, spinning wildly on his left foot as he yanked the dark-bladed saber from its scabbard.

Here—there—in between. He placed positions in his conscious mind while there was still opportunity to think, then pointed himself to dash back to the traveler.

But the wolves gave him no chance. He was in their midst now. For a moment they hesitated, as he did, uncertain as to whether they should attack. Then one was rushing at him, then toward his side as if ignoring him, its long tongue slavering along its muzzle. It snarled and leaped as it came abreast of him, bending in the air to snap at his throat.

Harper stepped back and turned as the animal jumped. He pulled his sword across his body, swinging it upright in his fist, pushing it upward and out as hard as he could.

The blow was awkward and against a moving target. Nor had he reckoned with the weight of the ceramic blade. Shock traveled along his arm, then the limb twisted as the wolf fell against the hilt, levering the forearm down, raising his elbow, making it snap to one side. Tendons in his shoulder stretched like suspension bridge cables, but mercifully did not tear.

For the moment, Harper felt the impact but did not notice pain. His wrist had not rotated. His fist buried itself in fur, then was vise-squeezed against the sword pommel as his knuckles were rammed by bone. *Ribs*, he thought carefully. *Never slugged an animal before.*

Perhaps he had knocked the wind out of it, but the animal was not dead. Its jaws fastened onto his upper arm even as it fell back to the ground. Harper threw himself to the left to win back the limb, ignoring the teeth that ripped cloth and raked his elbow. Claws scratched at the suddenly rigid cloth over his belly, but did not penetrate. The corner of his eyes caught red flesh showing through gray and black fur, a narrow strip back of the wolf's shoulder, bleeding, which brought to mind an image of London broil.

Meanwhile, the force on his arm was ballast—he pivoted on his left leg as his sword returned, bringing the right foot around in a kick.

Fur and muscle gave, and perhaps more. Another wolf
threw its head back, then howled in protest, and lunged
toward him on three legs.

Damn sword's too light, balance's poor, Harper
thought, even as the saber descended. He pushed it straight
at the ground, trying to make the velocity of the weapon
do the work of mass. Fluid was thrown along his arm; a
scarlet snake twisted in his palm as his wrist snapped.

There! The sword struck just above the hilt, sliding
briefly through resistance before hitting bone like rock.
The impact wrenched at his forearm, then at his shoulder.
Hot tears blinded Harper's slitted eyes while his dark
blade twisted against his grip and scraped over the wolf's
skull, peeling skin and an ear from gray-white bone, and
*chunk*ed to rest in the neck vertebrae.

The howling was continuous now, and Harper shouted
into it without thought. The wolf he had struck first was
in the snow at his right, within range of his arm, struggling
to regain its feet. It might be yelping with the others; he
could not tell. Still hunched over, Harper twisted himself
sideways to retrieve his weapon and rotated his wrist to
bring the sword down once more.

The tip of the saber penetrated fur, then continued,
burying itself in the snow. Blood from the animal's neck
cascaded into the thin slot, burgundy dark, then splattered
as Harper lurched backward and the blade came free.

Pain tore at his left side, burning, clinging like napalm.
Weight thrust at his thigh. *Bitten!* Harper pulled down
that elbow, blindly attempting to dislodge the wolf that
was on him—

But the animal was gone. His arm moved past his side
uselessly, helping propel him backward. Then he was
struck on the thigh. He could sense the individual teeth
caving into his flesh. Harper staggered and was thrust
into a pratfall as the wolf slammed its weight into his groin.

On the ground. Snow cushioned the impact and protected his head, but kissed his wounds ungently, the damp
cold searing with an agony he could not tell from fire.

Powder and fluid moved across his body. Pebbles were under his back. Yelps sounded triumphantly from the far side of a crystal curtain.

Everybody get down! he heard within his mind and recognized hysteria in his scream. The sun was glancing off elephant grass and the twisted trunks of splintering trees, and a voice hidden from him by distance and sad darkness was mourning "... he won't be no lifer no more."

A hard exhaustion: There was tension in his right fore-arm. Those fingers were clenched fiercely and Harper pulled that arm to his chest as he curled his legs up and drew his left arm in to protect his face and throat. Black-ness pressed savagely at his eyes, clubbed at him as he writhed upon the ground, while spear points lanced into his shoulder and thrust for his neck. Hot air gusted over his face, fetid and damp.

At the last instant, he thrust with the sword, pushing past his wounded side. The blade struck. That was some-how linked to his own suffering, Harper knew—he shoved and turned simultaneously, unknowing whether he struck at his own flesh or the wolf, but with no alternative.

His throat was sore with gasping. Then a weight was falling upon his chest, warm, with blood-matted fur, limp and unmoving.

Nothing followed. All was silent except for the harsh irregular gasps that came from his own lungs. His heart was pounding, stern and insistent like a waterfall. When he looked, he saw jaws on his chest. Blood was rilling between rotted teeth, dripping over spotted gums to trickle down the green cloth to his neck. A paw pressed gently, affectionately at him, then ceased.

Harper gasped for breath, then reached out gingerly and pushed the dead wolf aside, and stumbled to his feet. The space about him was clear. A whimpering came from nearby, from a wolf with weeping eyes. It opened those eyes to look at him, then bared its throat to the touch of his saber and barked feebly. Harper thrust straight down.

The wolf's head shook, miming coughs, but it was silent as its blood ran over dark fur and soaked into the snow.

The other wolves were gone now, like a bad dream in the morning. There was surprisingly little blood. *Two dead, one dying.*

Never expected I'd ever really use this sword. Then he remembered the stranger. He heard nothing. He turned slowly, reluctantly.

Three dead. The other man was still kneeling, half bent so his face could not be seen. In his lap was the head of a wolf, dead or suddenly tamed. Had he killed an animal that large with his own hands? Now Harper began to feel respect.

The sun was departing, he noted. Pinks and blue-hazed orange—in other circumstances he would think those colors red.

Not now. His attention returned to weaponry. With his fingers, he wiped his sword to clean it of blood and fur, then stooped to sweep it through snow, drying the blade against his pant legs before resheathing it. Later tonight he would plane nicks from the edge, but the sword was once more presentable.

Too bad I can't say the same for me. His wounds were telling on him now, drying blood and stiffnesses hobbling his stride. He had bites upon his shins, he sensed for the first time, and raw knuckles. He would not try to count the scratches, and tomorrow his sorenesses would surely sprout technicolor bruises. There were tears in both sleeves, one pant leg, and down his backside.

Probably I'm not making a good impression, he conceded with amusement. *But I'm alive, for all my embarrassments.*

"We've done all right," he made himself say, conscious of the inanity but feeling a need to express camaraderie. "How are you doing?"

The other man did not answer, did not move.

Shock, Harper thought then. *Wounded.* But he could

see no blood. *Fainted? Not used to having his life on the line.*

But no, the stranger was looking at him now, his thin face turning to track Harper's movement. The light-colored eyes seemed blank somehow, empty. *Spooky.* The red-head suppressed a nervous laugh, then asked again, "How are you doing?"

There was still no answer. Harper grabbed the dead wolf's head at the nape of the neck and lifted it free of the man's legs.

He saw hands then. The left one was bent backward at an awkward angle and rested upon the leather-clad thigh; the right one was white-knuckled, furled about the hilt of a small blood-dripping knife, but still capable of movement. Eyes turned to him, large, melting, green-hued. Long lashes. Full eyebrows. Darkly tanned face.

Indian, Harper thought. *Red skin, high cheekbones, straight pure-black hair, no visible beard on him, and almond-shaped eyes.* But that did not fit with the finely shaped nose, with its liberal sprinkling of freckles, nor with the narrow face. And the eyes were subtly wrong from what he would expect, in some fashion. *Not an Indian.* He could not explain the differences. *Exotic. Well— a new race.*

And very young.

He reached to unfold fingers, gently tugged at the knife blade to snake it loose from the man's grip, and laid it on the snow. Blood was on the sleeve of the heavy cloth coat, he saw, concealed by the darkness of the fabric but plain enough on the snow around the youngster's knees. It might be from wolf or man; he could not say, but the man's rigid air was suggestive.

"Broken arm? We'll get you patched up, guy."

"It is well, all right," the man answered suddenly. "Pleasing is your concern, but not needed. Why are you thinking of mind seers?"

English? Here? Harper could only gape.

"Why do you hate mind seers? Why fear the people

you name Teeps?" the man asked slowly. His voice was surprisingly reasonable, high-pitched but revealing curiosity rather than concern. "You are in love with one. Why?"

Teep! Second Era! One of the Skyborne.

The secret was out! *"No!"*

Then his body no longer obeyed him. His conditioning returned him to combat. His heart hammered within his chest. His breath was loud, deep, panting. His vision contracted, black-rimmed, so that he saw little more than the youth's suddenly frightened face. He could smell his own fear, his own stinking fear—

The dark metal within his sword was bright and gleaming in the evening light, incongruously clean, and it raced the soft rays of the sun as it fell. His target was perfectly positioned for the blow, waiting without tremor, head outstretched as if yearning for it. He had not swung the saber so hard or so skillfully at the wolves as in this moment of madness, he realized dimly.

His arms came down at rocket speed, both hands forcing the blade before him. His heels lifted him from the ground, adding impetus to the blow. His wrists snapped forward at impact, to drive the sword to its stopping point, just below the target.

Shadow veiled the gleaming metal. Darkness hid the sword tip. The head of the man fell into his lap, then rolled onto the snow. It stopped immediately, resting on the nose and one eye.

Mercifully, the raven-dark hair was long enough to hide the other eye. Blood seeped from cavities in the neck, discoloring yellow flaps of fat before it dripped to the ground and melted scarlet trails in the snow. Bone showed, and cartilage—white and gray, where not red-stained.

The body toppled at last, seeming to bow, striking the ground to its front, then falling sideways to lie in fetal position, with its arms cradled before its chest. A knee pushed at the head, making it turn over.

An eye peered at Harper, its brow and lashes beaded

by snow. It was dark now, the green color no longer visible. It accused him of nothing. It threatened nothing.

The man's jacket was hunched up over his chest, Harper noticed, making himself turn away from the exposed eye. Surely that could not be comfortable, and he reached woodenly to smooth the garment down.

The chest was not flat.

A girl. He had murdered a little girl.

Now he had possession of his body again. Harper retched, barely conscious of his tears amid the effort of vomiting. He sank to his knees, careless of the mess that completed the ruin of his uniform, and wept uncontrollably.

He would have died to undo this moment.

"I'll fix this," he sobbed. "Damn the Algherans! Damn them. Damn them. I'll set this right, kid. I'll save you. With whatever it takes. Whatever. Whatever. I'll save you."

CHAPTER FOURTEEN

*N*ight. *Cold.*

He was in bed, nude, with unseen covers sliding off.

His own bed, Harper sensed. *Not in 'Nam. The cabin.*

He sat up with that recognition and stretched into darkness, then tugged at the bedclothes to cover his body once more. He was upstairs in his own room, with his possessions about him and his windows open. His memory was restored.

Kylene had brought him home.

Pleasure stuffed him then, filling him drum tight with a tingling sensation and driving off his cold-engendered numbness. Harper smiled like a suckling baby and fell back into the bedding's embrace, his arms thrown wide, allowing himself to enjoy the present moment.

But thoughts of the outside world returned shortly. Just minutes before, in midsummer, memory told him, he had removed his Teepblind and placed it on the head of a small girl. Now the air that set curtains a-whisper smelled of pine needles and rotten leaves, without flower scents, and bore a glacial chill.

Winter. The minutes had become months, lived through by all but him. *Time travel*, he reflected without irony.

What had happened to Evennle? And to Terocu?

It did not matter, he decided at last. They were still contemporaries, separated by distance rather than by time. By now their lives should have returned to normal, little affected by anything he had done. Perhaps the next time he visited the People, in forty or fifty of their years, he would check on them. But they were not his main concern.

Onnul, he whispered to himself, secretly. *Onnul*. And once more, like a child probing a sore, *Onnul*.

The sharp hurt that produced was fading, he noticed sadly. Too many intruding memories, or simply the process of aging—Onnul's loss no longer ripped into his guts as it once had.

Rescuing her was still necessary. She had been part of the Project, and it owed her that much loyalty for her service, without regard for his own feelings. But there was so much history to be undone, and the Project to which he would restore her could not be the one she had known. How many lives did he have the right to alter for the sake of one woman?

And what would happen even if he did manage to save her? he wondered bitterly. *If she doesn't want me . . .*

But he was diminished by such thoughts. Alone, he could admit private reservations. He no longer knew whether love or stubbornness motivated him. He had once believed that Onnul desired him as he did her; he saw now that his thoughts had traveled no farther than his hopes.

Success. For himself, Onnul, and the Project. What would happen afterward? He could not imagine an afterward.

Not much afterward to imagine. The fantasies that Sweln ha'Nyjuc and Borct tra'Dicovys had spun for him long ago had begun to dispel after the duel with Herrilmin ha'Hujsuon; now he saw them for the spider's web hopes they had always been.

Genetic engineering was possible. It had become reality in the hands of the Janhular; they had killed a quarter of humanity with their plagues.

Mortal men had revived a god's powers and served satanic ends. How often had it happened?

Too often, he reckoned. He was no longer surprised that population had fallen so abruptly in the years after the First Era. He could not believe that either the Algherans or the Chelmmysians would refuse to make biological weapons if it were in their power.

It followed from that that he could not encourage the Algherans to study genetic engineering. It followed from that that he could not hope to have his life extended. It followed from that—

Loneliness. Harper slammed a fist into the mattress.

This diminishes me, he thought again, forcing calmness upon himself. *So things are tough. So what?* No one was entitled to an easy life. At least his had given him adventure, and perhaps he was luckier than most men in being able to recognize duties to perform rather than being the captive agent of undisciplined emotions.

And he would endure. He still had the strength to follow his life road wherever it might lead. He would carry on and trust fate to bring him to a worthy destination.

His body would obey. When he sat up this time, he kicked bed clothing toward the wall and forced himself onto his feet.

The floor was freezing, he noticed unhappily. It certainly was winter. *Get busy on the endurance, chum.*

More than lack of comfort weighed upon him as he stood tiptoe in the darkness. His body bore unfamiliar aches and twinges and some source of tension had drawn taut skin across his upper chest, as if a line of glue had dried upon him. What his fingers traced, however, was scar tissue, puckered along its length and extending to his left shoulder.

An injury. An old injury. Harper leaned with both hands against the bed shelf for a moment, then noticed himself inhaling deeply to counter light-headedness. His body was not balancing correctly, and he was troubled by a sense of lethargy that would not depart. An aftereffect of some drug, he guessed. It should go away with activity. Or perhaps this feeling of being a ghost within his own body came from resting not too little but too long.

He groped along shelves and through the doorway into the next room where, although no warmer, he was no longer in a draft. Through the balcony railing he looked down into the living room. The curtains had been drawn over the great triangular glass wall, but a dying fire cast a sunset glow on the hearth and made silhouettes of the furniture beneath. Harper moved to the railing and stroked the polished wood with uncalloused fingers. Chairs, a cord of wood, the irregular lines bordering the flagstones, Kylene's desk with its stack of teaching spools— All was as it should have been.

His own arms, however, seemed curiously thin, skeletal. Harper gripped balusters with both hands, twisting simultaneously till wood squeaked at him. He relented then, frowning as he massaged creases from his palms. His hands were soft, his muscles weak. *Too much resting. Way out of condition. Oh, hell!*

Fortunately, rebuilding muscle would be more tedious than difficult. Leg extensions, pullovers, chest presses, curls ... *Four Nautilus sessions a ten day*, he told himself, *and work out with free weights on off days till the weather's fit for running*. It would not be the first time he had gotten himself back in shape faster than an Algheran would believe possible. "Bless our ingenious little First Era hearts and physiology."

But inwardly, he sighed. He was thirty-four now, perhaps a year older. Much time remained for him, but pumping iron would not compensate indefinitely for his vanishing youth. Eight years of running around like a teenager, with how many more to come only Cimon knew—what was he gaining from this life?

His lips quirked in a smile as he turned away. "A dacha for retirement. Just like any other secret agent."

And a Russian winter. The windows he investigated had been pulled down, but refused to close until he pushed caked snow off the sills. The panes were decorated by thin deposits of ice in Easter egg patterns. Once he had dissolved holes in the ice with his breath and chilled fingertips, he saw that the ground outside was featureless, dark in the absence of a moon. The nighttime forest made a black wall in the middle distance, and an overcast sky kept the Algheran constellations from his view.

Thick eyebrows, broad bones, a jagged scar on the left temple—his reflected face seemed unchanged. Perhaps the creases across his forehead were more prominent. And if he had the unruly hair of a middle-aged man roused from sleep rather than an adolescent's easily tamed mop, it was still the familiar red-brown, and not yet gray. Nor was it falling out to disgrace him. *Praise Cimon for small favors. Hate trying to explain baldness to the Algherans.* In fact, he noted with some pleasure, he was in dire need of a haircut.

He yawned without further thought, but caught himself. It was worthwhile to be moving again, despite some warning signs of coming stiffness, so he'd dress and not go back to bed. "Coffee'd be nice though," he reflected as he slapped at light switches. "Sure hope my clothes still fit."

His clothing hung a bit loosely, even with two flannel shirts on to ward off the chill, and it took him a while to find clean socks. Kylene had rearranged his wardrobe. But soon he was almost completely dressed.

Almost. Harper frowned. "Where's my spare Teepblind?"

It was not in its storage bin. It was not hanging on the

rack over the bed shelf, nor sitting on his desk. "Damn-italltahell. Where'd Kylene put it?"

In the living room? In the time shuttle? No harm was being done at the moment, but he ought to protect his mind before Kylene awoke. *Search the kitchen and the living room first.*

The boots he was carrying when he went down the stairs were not needed. The Teepblind was near the bottom of the stairwell, dropped over the edge of a step like a forgotten cleaning rag. *Careless*, Harper thought with surprise. *I'd better talk to her about this.*

Fortunately, lack of respectful treatment had not harmed the 'blind. Harper settled it over his scalp, shoving back and forth till hair concealed the fine mesh, then waited stoically while the headband contracted and the vampire needles pricked his temples. Now he felt properly dressed. "That coffee."

At the foot of the steps, he hesitated. The door to Kylene's room was ajar, and he felt an inclination to open it and look at the slumbering girl. But the intrusion might disturb her, and he decided against it. He probably had not been a model patient, and she deserved some rest.

Certainly, it was tempting. Having a young woman asleep in his bed as if she trusted him to watch over her had always given him an inexplicable feeling of peace and contentment. And much to his surprise, the little girl who had caused him so much trouble had become someone of whom he was very fond. Time travel had given him the child Algheran biology would always deny.

She saved your neck, chum, he remembered. She had demonstrated responsibility for more than her own life. That made her an adult.

Yes, but—Harper broke the thought off, smiling at his interior dialog, and left his boots on the stairs. *My little girl, regardless.* And then he turned away, to enter the kitchen.

Coffee down here, cups up there. Fortunately, Kylene had not taken it upon herself to improve his kitchen arrangements and he was able to brew coffee without having to turn on the lights. His good mood lasted while he stirred cream into the Yuban and moved to the living room. The girl's training had gone quite well, he ruminated as he added kindling to the dying fire. She had adapted successfully to a foreign culture and that was the basic requirement; everything else an Agent might need was mere specialized knowledge, which she could obtain as circumstances required. He wriggled sideways in the cube couch, against the resistance of the formfitting plastic, and raised his cup toward Kylene's bedroom door. "You done good, kid."

And what remained to be done was a weight now on his shoulders. Harper sank back into the embrace of the sofa, staring into the crackling fire without seeing, unconscious of the coffee he held to his lips. *Time for Mlart.*

It would have to be a real killing, he decided. Mlart had been too dynamic to stop in gentler ways. That wouldn't please the tra'Dicovys, who had hoped Harper could restrict Mlart's influence while preserving the general's life, but he was not going to waste time trying to protect Fifth Era sensitivities. It might be good Project politics, but it wouldn't work. *Just move history back to where it was, chum, and no one will hand you any criticism,* he reckoned coldly. *The Algherans will accept a fatal accompli.*

Besides, bending history so that the general survived would be incompatible with rescuing Onnul Nyjuc.

So . . . Where? Killing Mlart at the siege of Fohima Loprit was not necessary. It would be esthetically pleasing to restore precisely the history the Algherans had disrupted recently, but since similar historical settings should produce substantially identical futures, he ought to be able to assassinate Mlart at any convenient moment before the city fell.

"Gotta be believable," he told himself. Mlart's death had to appear natural to his contemporaries if it were to be established in the fabric of history. Otherwise, it accomplished nothing.

But that was a secondary consideration. Where and when had Mlart been vulnerable? Harper leaned backward into the couch, shoving his feet straight before him as his eyes closed, shutting out the present while his mind moved forward twelve hundred years. What were the details of that campaign?

Bataillon Carre, he mused finally. Mlart's plans brought back memories of the maneuvers of the Grand Army at the beginning of the Ulm-Austerlitz campaign. Like Napoleon, the Algheran general had split the Swordtroop into easily managed packets kept in supporting distance of one another, relying on the fog of war and the marching ability of his soldiers to keep his opponents uncertain of his intentions and dazzled by his rate of movement. When they were thoroughly confused, he had thrust his units through undefended passes in the Appalachians to reunite on the far side of the enemy defenses...

Mlart was good, Harper admitted, damned good. He understood war. True, from a First Era perspective the Algheran had simply reinvented the wheel, but it had rolled damn well and that was enough to make him unique in this world. And it was execution that counted, not pure originality. Stonewall Jackson had used the same tactics along virtually the same ground during the Civil War.

"Another great captain," Harper growled. "My damned luck. The sonuvabitch'll get a hundred and twenty percent out of his men, and I'll never catch him by himself."

Bigger they come, harder they fall. No wonder Alghera's empire had collapsed after Mlart's death. Ordinary men, with only human vision and wills and personalities, inspiring greed instead of loyalty in their followers, could not recreate the accomplishments of a genius. Preserving Mlart's life had given him time to remold Algheran institutions in a durable form. Killing him before that work was done would leave the Realm hopelessly overextended, natural prey for anarchy. Defeats, riots, coups and countercoups, corruption, tyrants, starvation, law-lessness, unchecked violence ... *Tim Harper, Friend of Progress.*

"So accept it, chum. Get back to work. Where do you make the hit?" He was down to the dregs in his coffee cup. Harper moved to the kitchen and refilled it mechanically, little noticing that the liquid had become tepid. "There. Maybe there."

No. Those ideas wouldn't work. The fire popped apologetically at him, reduced to black and cherry-red embers once more. Harper pushed ashes aside with a quartered log, then blew at the coals till he was light-headed and the wood was wreathed in yellow flames. "Killguide Pass."

Mlart's one sure mistake. Harper closed the screen before the fire and perched on Kylene's desk, remembering.

A direct approach to the Lopritian capital had been blocked, and the two armies had shifted southward into the Blue Ridge, each trying to outflank the other. Killguide Pass, too steep and narrow for the equipment of an army to traverse, had been left undefended. Mlart had moved through it with units of his central division immediately after discovering the error. For two days he was beyond his supply lines and bad weather had kept reinforcements from reaching him.

But luck had been on Mlart's side. The pass had been on the juncture between two Lopritian divisions. Their response was sluggish and piecemeal, and Mlart had survived by holding the central position. When reinforcements reached him, he went over to the offensive, sideslipping the Lopritians with a dramatic night march to the north. Through a miracle of coordination, he fell on the rear of enemy forces blocking Blue Vista Gap while the Swordtroop's eastern wing pressed home its own attack.

Casualties had been light on both sides, and the Lopritians had withdrawn in good order, but Lamehorse Creek had been a major victory for the Algherans. The subsequent battle of the Burning Forest and events during the siege of Loprit had overshadowed it, so only a handful of military scholars had analyzed the early portion of Mlart's last campaign. But Harper had watched that conflict from the time shuttle; he remembered the historians's criticisms.

"Ambush the bastard." Harper's fist pounded the table, making coffee splash onto his hand. He wiped it on his jeans and raised the cup to his mouth automatically. Put a blocking force behind Mlart while he was in the pass, and slow him down till the Lopritians hit him on the front. "Cork him up solid and I'll nail him good."

But where would the troops for that come from? Militia? Locals? No, he needed real soldiers for that. A scratch force of locals would melt like hail in a bonfire before Mlart's professionals. "One chance in a thousand." That was not the way to change history.

So, what else? Partisan forces? Guerrillas? Harper's jaw clinched. The world was better off without that tradition.

But something useful might lie in the idea. Mlart would need supplies, to be found most easily in a town. Soldiers made lousy landlords and there was certain to be opposition to Algheran occupation, even if no more than fistfights and harsh words. Shoehorn the more responsible malcontents into some sort of group—that would provide a framework to work in.

"Or Trojan horse it?" Join Mlart's forces and work up through the ranks till he had access to the general? That would be slow, and it might require Harper to become more prominent in history than would be appropriate. And it would not use Kylene's special talents. "Well, it's a fallback idea."

But first, he would look for a Resistance movement— that would make use of Kylene—and add backbone to it. Tactics, he'd play by ear. Sounding out people, recruiting them, assigning tasks—with a telepath on his side, there would be no errors, no missed opportunities. He leaned forward, considering. The fire crackled, resin sputtering a muted protest.

"Sounds good." He and Kylene would be making no major changes, since Mlart's death had been woven into the fabric of history before the Algherans altered it. An assassination performed by an Agent should stick, since resistance to Mlart was highly probable. Mlart's premature death would become established history once more.

"Real good." Harper moved to the kitchen to freshen his coffee. "Need a role." *But what's obvious.* All right, an aging man with a young wife. It might be useful to claim a military background. A retired soldier then, with some new occupation to explain his presence in the town. Merchant? No, that sounded like too much work and would restrict his freedom. Perhaps a broker of some sort, spending and selling for someone offstage. That would justify wealth, let him come and go as he chose, and give him access to a variety of people.

Don't push too far, chum. Still an employee ... He would have been not too successful nor too low-ranking— a major, say. That was true to life, and majors came from all age groups. Blade Master in Algheran parlance; he'd forgotten what the Lopritian title would be. Harper sipped coffee, staring through the kitchen window into darkness, considering the dim outline of his face upon the glass. *Maybe one rank up, to excuse some of those lines.* Master of Combined Arms. "A promotion. How wonderful. Oh, well."

Someone new, or should he revive an old name? No one would know him. "Make some use of my roistering days?" Harper shrugged. Details of that sort he would worry about later.

What about Kylene? He refilled his cup and returned to the living room. She probably would not master the local accent rapidly, and her exotic looks would brand her as a foreigner in any event. A woman from the opposite side of the continent then, someone the hard-bitten major—no, colonel—had met between campaigns. Nope.

On campaign; even for a professional soldier the rash act of marriage was more understandable during war than after. "My concession to civilian behavior. Ho!"

Only twigs remained in the scuttle. He dropped them onto the fire, bending to blow embers to black-flecked red once more. An old mercenary warrior living with a young woman in happy domesticity . . . He chuckled.

Maybe unhappy domesticity. Play that by ear. *A name for her. Hmmm . . .* She could almost keep the one she had; Waterfall had a Lopritian ring to it, more so than Harper.

He chuckled again. Perhaps he should adopt her name, as a married Algheran would. He'd be madly in love with his new bride, and she'd be bored with him already and shrewish, and he'd be most thoroughly henpecked without realizing it . . . Oh, this was droll! Kylene would be amused.

The fire needed another log, he decided. Unless it had been used up, a small woodpile should still be at one end of the porch. He'd pull on his boots and bring in an armload. *Greet Kylene with a good roaring fire. Fix up a decent breakfast for her and chat.*

The thought sustained him while he pushed aside the drapes and slid open the front door. Almost immediately, extreme cold punched at him. His ears and nose seemed gripped by fiery pincers and breath burned in his throat. Thirty or forty below, he guessed. *A real ice age winter. Never been here during this kind of weather. Now I see what the cabin puts up with, I'm impressed.* Fortunately the porch had been swept, so snow was not drifting down his boot tops. And the pile of logs had not vanished. He knocked several together to dislodge talcum-powder snow, put them under his arm, and turned to admire the landscape before reentering the cabin.

The pond at the foot of the hill was iced over, seemingly just flat land interrupted by the snow-covered mound that was a beaver dam. Nothing of the stream could be seen. The pines were tall and dark on all sides, except for the

gap that led to the corral. His breath was a white plume.
A board creaked beneath him; otherwise the night was
silent.

*Lovely. But I need a moon to make a proper Christmas
card.* Or a Santa, sliding down a chimney. An Algheran
Santa, an Algheran chimney. Harper smiled at the image.
Scent O'Claws, he remembered *There's a sleigh for him!*

But—where was the time shuttle?

It ought to be visible. It was not.

Not synchronized yet. Still in run-time, he decided,
quieting his momentary upset. Kylene must have left the
task to him, rather than meddle with the vehicle's unfamiliar controls. Very well, the task was simple. He would
tend to it later in the morning.

Suddenly he was conscious of the band around his
forehead. The Teepblind. Where had Kylene gotten the
'blind if not from the shuttle?

He saw the footprints then.

One set. Small. Fresh. Leading away from the cabin.

CHAPTER FIFTEEN

Kylene was gone. She was not coming back.

Her closet was half emptied and her bed was cold and much of the bric-a-brac he had given her was missing, along with half the food in the storage lockers. She had left no note. Kylene was gone.

Half a ten-day period passed before he accepted that fully, and even then acquiescence alternated between hope and despair. Knowing that Kylene had left him did not explain why, and Harper raged against uncertainty, feeling hollowed-out inside, his cheeks weighted down by unshed tears. More time passed before he mastered himself, learning not to let his thoughts go beyond obvious faces and forcing himself through the motions of life.

He was straightening up her room, rearranging knick-nacks to fill the empty spaces after changing her bed, when he noticed that she had taken her paints and the art history book. He smiled briefly, amused by a mental picture of Kylene standing before an easel in an artist's smock. But the image changed quickly to a memory: Kylene sitting on a living-room rug with a drawing pad on her knees, her bare feet entwined in the golden shag, hunched forward with concentration while a summer night's rain rebounded from the cabin windows and dropped hisses down the chimney into the fire. Charcoal sticks had left stains on her burgundy skirt and on her fingers and on her lip, and her raven hair had spilled over her freckled cheek and right shoulder so that his fingers had yearned to comb it out, and he had stood behind her and been ignored while Kylene turned jumbled lines into an architect's sketch of a cabin wall...

"Oh, Kylene," he murmured, *I miss you*, he admitted silently, and traced his fingers gently across the lonely pillow on her bed. But he could not say that aloud and finally left the room undone.

He held a private wake that night, intending to become drunk on the Algheran liquor he called pseudo-Scotch. He drank toasts to each of Kylene's good qualities, and one to her bad, then drained a full glass to commend her spirit to Cimon and Nicole and the Agents she would meet in the afterlife and sang as much as he could recall of the Oxen Lament. But he remained perversely sober throughout, as if some sense of decorum kept him from displaying overt loss even without an audience. When he hurled his tumbler into the fireplace, he did not watch the shards withering in the flames but stared instead at his reflection in the glass wall and saw without surprise that he was aging.

In the morning, he went out and killed the horses.

Kylene had left him with three, his palomino gelding and two smaller animals he did not recognize. The six sacks of oats he had found would not last through the winter, nor did the corral provide adequate shelter, so he stunned the animals with his neuroshocker and slit their throats. Afterward, he butchered them crudely but methodically, hanging the meat in an unheated shed. The offal and buckets of bloodstained snow he dropped down a hole chopped in the ice over the frozen stream. Few animals were around to contend with during the winter, but he did not want to fight scavengers for his land in the springtime.

"Wherever I am in spring." Or whenever.

Until this morning, he had seen no alternative to being marooned. The cabin was to have been his lifeboat, keeping him afloat through winter until he could steer his way to another harbor. He would not return to the People, for he was not willing to grow old among them, but farther south were higher cultures, more advanced socially if not technologically. With his knowledge, a comfortable existence should be possible. He might indeed carve out the empire he had once scorned.

But now, his sense of realism was restored. Kylene might return to the Second Era and bend history along a branch that negated the Algheran dream, but she owed no loyalty in this era. He had sworn oaths to defend Alghera. He must hold to them till death or an honorable release from their bondage came to him. Besides, who but him would rescue Onnul Nyjuc?

Onnul. That was the thought that came to him a year tenth later when he finally recognized that he could not build another time machine. His memories of their construction were not enough, even coupled with his knowledge of First and Fifth Era sciences. He lacked the tools necessary to build the tools necessary to build the tools ... One man could not recreate an industrialized world in a short lifetime, and nothing else would suffice to give him the electronics equipment he required. He had searched his library for information and nowhere in the one world at this time was a civilization with the necessary skills, nor any culture that could be readily molded that way. He was stranded.

Marooned. Lost. Abandoned. The realization came hard.

But even then he could sympathize with Kylene's desire to return to her own people. The two of them had been thrown together by accident, he realized. Kylene had finally acted to sever the unnatural relationship and he was now free to continue with his own chosen life as she was with hers. It seemed unfair to criticize her for thoughtlessly leaving her captor inconvenienced.

Would she find her way back? Or would she crash when the Earth's magnetic field reversed in the Fourth Era, or escape the warfare of that time, as he suspected his past comrades had not? No—that was too cruel a possibility to admit. Would she survive conditions almost as bleak during the Second Era?

Who could say? *If You really are up there, Lord—or Cimon, or whatever You call Yourself—please don't let that happen. You let me get back to my world safely. Show an innocent child the same mercy.*

He snorted. "Going senile, chum. You want something to have faith in, get that backhand strike right."

That was another project. Fighting two duels in the space of a year had persuaded him to learn swordplay.

An Algheran book dealing with military protocol served as a study guide. For his salon, he placed a heater in the work shed to make it habitable, then fastened a wooden lath to a strong spring to provide a simulated sparring partner. Ultimately, he cobbled together cams and gear wheels to swing the opposing blade back and forth through an erratic kata. It was a very far cry from facing a genuine swordsman, he realized, but it probably instilled useful reflexes. Besides, a willingness to kill was generally more important than combat skills. Few men are truly skilled with edged weapons, and if he could cope with artificial complexity, perhaps the real world would present no greater difficulties.

In the meantime, the exercise restored stamina to his body, while the elaborations he added to his clockwork opponent kept his mind from atrophying. Both served to bind his thoughts to the present, rather than on fruitless speculations about his future.

The Algherans would not be pleased with him, he knew.

Perhaps if Tim Harper rescued Tim Harper . . . But Agents never managed to meet themselves. "Or never remember it when they do," he had speculated. Evidently some events were too improbable to be allowed, even in a universe that permitted time travel. Very well. He'd save Tim Harper's ass in some more conventional manner.

When his dreams of building another time machine collapsed, he gave the machine a nickname and increased his practice sessions to a full day tenth. That solved none of his problems, but it brought the spring that much closer.

Yet it was fencing that eventually pointed the way to possible salvation. He had changed gear ratios in the machine opponent's driving system, trying to vary the pattern it followed. Watching as the device went through simulated lunges and disengagements, he had guessed idly at the frequency with which particular sets of motions were repeated. Once every two minutes in First Era terms, he had estimated, a hundredth of a cycle per second— ten to the minus eighth megahertz. "Not quite up to broadcasting standards, are you, Rube, old boy?"

Hmmm . . . Broadcasting . . . Radio. Radio beacons. He could transmit a signal for any visiting time travelers, on the off chance that any stopped off in this period. But what frequency should he broadcast at?

No! Any frequency would do. He did not have to rely on chance. His signal would show up in run-time, on the radio-frequency monitors. Any Agent reasonably attentive to his instruments would catch the transmissions and investigate.

Line-of-sight problems? He could put his antenna on a treetop. Or mount it to a moored balloon. Power? He had spare batteries. He could rig up a generator when the stream began flowing in the spring. And use a multipolar antenna to increase directionality. A circuit? That would be the simplest of his worries. He could cannibalize the teaching machine and some measuring instruments to rig a simple VHF oscillator. Modulating it would not be necessary, might even be counterproductive . . .

It really ought to work, he told himself. But it might not. He forced himself to continue with fighting practice, leaving the notion of the radio beacon to simmer in his subconscious. Whenever the idea percolated into his awareness, he insisted to himself that it was only another project.

That did not prevent him from feeling satisfaction a year tenth later when the transmitter was completed and hooked up to its antenna.

He thought that climbing the tree had been his major accomplishment. To do that, he had ruined a pair of boots by pounding nails through the soles, and used plastic webbing in double thicknesses as a climbing loop, inching his way up the trunk with lengths of rope and electrical cable dangling from his belt. The rough pine bark had snagged the heavy cables and clawed at his jeans, and he had been exhausted even before he reached the lowest branches, bathed in sweat that could not escape his bulky yellow parka.

That had been the only dangerous moment. He had wrapped his legs around the trunk, hunching his shoulders to keep the pack near his center of gravity, while he removed his gloves and unfastened the climbing loop with fingers made clumsy by cold. He had reattached it above the outstretched limbs and slowly pulled himself to their level. Only then did he allow himself to look downward at the broken clusters of olive needles and dislodged bark that littered the snow. So far down...

Soon he had been able to store the loop in his pack. Near the trunk the downward-sloping branches had provided support for his weight and he had been able to stand while chopping limbs that blocked his progress. When the hand axe lost its edge, he had stopped. The treetop had swayed with his movements then, and further progress had seemed too difficult to justify the labor.

He had oriented himself by the compass stitched to his shoulder tabs and worked his way clockwise around the trunk, balancing carefully on the snow-laden branches. When correctly placed, he had tugged the pack from his back and reached inside for what seemed a rope ladder with metal rungs. He had broken branches to keep this antenna flat against the tree trunk, then lashed it at top and bottom with strips of webbing.

He had descended carefully, unrolling wire from a spool at his waist, pausing periodically to wind it around branches and anchor it against gravity and wind.

The weather that day had been cold but with little wind. The only sounds he had heard had come from his own breathing and his passage down the trunk. The only smells he had noticed had been from his own body, as if nature had placed other scents in storage until a spring thaw. His breath had been gray-white, like the overcast sky, and the fur on his hood had crusted over with zipperlike beads of milky ice. His toes had become cramped as he neared the final layer of branches but his boots had been too stiff for him to press the kinks out, and he had descended the remaining distance awkwardly, expecting at any moment to slip from his restraining loop.

On the ground once more, he had hammered a crystal nail into the trunk with the flat of the hand axe, then wrapped the end of the cable around it. At his feet, a black plastic pipe that reached to the cabin had held another cable, and the following day he would splice the ends together.

The realization had come then that by using two climbing loops, he could have eliminated most of the risk. But the issue was academic. At the moment, he had been chiefly conscious of the amber resin that stained his clothing and the torn seams that bared his skin to icy kisses from winter air. He had wanted little more than to walk upright and to soak away his sweat and sore muscles in hot water. He had climbed the tallest tree in the block, he had mused as he trudged back to the cabin, and never felt less like a ten-year-old boy.

But he had taken a fallen pine cone as a souvenir.

* * *

His SOS was still being transmitted nearly fifty days later.

Spring was approaching stealthily by then, concealing itself behind the final storms of winter. The snow that fell was dense, gray with moisture, slow to melt. But an occasional pleasant day visited the cabin to belie the evidence of unending cold.

Harper had risen from his upstairs bed this morning under a cloudless sky, dressed in jeans and flannel shirt as usual, and eaten, then busied himself by shoveling pathways to sheds he did not trouble to enter. He had been half bored by the mindless labor, half pleased by the challenge it presented to his rebuilding muscles, thoroughly content to be outside with a bared head and only a light denim jacket.

He did not see the time shuttle land, nor hear it. But unfamiliar footprints showed in virgin snow, rather than in one of his waist-high paths, when he returned to the cabin in the late afternoon.

He did not run. He would not allow himself to show emotion, and he felt a strange reluctance to meet his unknown rescuer. Instead, his pace slowed, until he became aware that he was dawdling and forced himself to step more quickly. When he reached the cabin, he noticed with faint annoyance the snow tracked across his clean porch, then scraped snow from his boots methodically and placed the shovel by the doorway without moving his eyes to the interior. He looked about once more for a vehicle before entering, but evidently it had been left in run-time. He shrugged and pushed open the glass door.

A woman stood before the fireplace, looking at him. Silent. Frozen.

She was taller than average, slimmer than normal. The coal-black hair was long, lying straight without tangles down her back. The sprinkling of freckles across her high cheekbones stood out clearly on her pale skin, and the dark lashes above her green eyes were fluttering. The eyes were almond-shaped, the brows thin. She wore a high-necked blouse of forest green tucked into faded blue jeans that were several inches too short. Water had darkened the bottoms of the pant legs and the plain leather boots that stood on the hearth. Her thin feet were bare on the flagstones and the nipples of her breasts moved up and down with her breath. Her hands were narrow, clasped at waist level. He did not notice a coat.

A beautiful young woman he did not know. Was she an Algheran? Or Chelmmysian? Or yet another culture of timefarers? Then he recognized her and understood that he had suppressed the recognition.

He walked past her as if she were a piece of furniture, to place his jacket on the steps leading upstairs. He tugged his boots off and left them on the steps as well, then returned to the living room in stocking feet, treading carefully as if the heated floor might collapse beneath him. She remained facing the doorway, seemingly still waiting for him to enter.

"I don't—" he began, then broke off. He would not admit to uncertainty. Nor would he resort to sarcasm. He settled for sighing loudly, then moved to flip switches on the wooden box beside the couch. For better or worse, he no longer needed the radio transmitter.

Kylene remained silent through all this. *Damn it, girl! You're the telepath. You talk first.*

But she only watched, turning her head to follow him as he moved to sit on what had been her desk. She swallowed, but her eyes met his unflinchingly when he tried to read her expression.

What's done is done. Harper shrugged minutely, then gestured toward the cube couch. "Sit. Tell me about it, girl."

"May I touch you?" Only the words made that phrase a question. Kylene's voice was without inflection. She did not move.

No need for it. I'm not wearing a Teepblind. "Sure,"

he said, then nodded when that did not seem enough, and stood. Kylene came toward him in sleepwalking steps. Suddenly her arms were around him, squeezing his ribs fiercely. Harper patted her back awkwardly. Her hair was moist, he noticed, and she carried with her the scent of violets.

Her body was ramrod stiff, but she was not crying and she had not broken away from him. Harper choked back the reassuring words that wanted to be uttered and settled for inanity. "Still my little Kylene?"

A head rubbed against his chest. "Are you still my big red bear?"

"Grrrowlll!" Harper rumbled mechanically. "Yup. You should watch me hibernate. Gerr-rowll-rowlll" But that was mere politeness and he could not regret that Kylene saw through the lie.

"I'm sorry," she whispered. "Tayem . . . Tayem . . ."

"Kylene, Kylene," Harper replied evenly. "Don't worry. I did all right."

Kylene shivered within his arms. "You still have Onnul Nyjuc in your mind."

Releasing her, Harper stepped back to the table. "Haven't changed much." He smiled tightly, waiting for an explanation. But Kylene turned away and went to stand at the counter between living room and kitchen, staring in the direction of her old room, so her face could not be seen. Her shoulders were hunched. She picked nervously at a corner of the ledge.

Concealing something, but what? Harper moved behind her, restraining her shoulders with his hands. "Calm down." He massaged her neck with his thumbs, trusting silence to pull speech from the girl, and turned his eyes toward the kitchen window. Evening was coming on, he noticed. It had been a long time since he had cooked a meal for two persons. What would be suitable?

Kylene stiffened, then stepped back deliberately to lean against him. "I went away. Because—because of Onnul.

And because—you killed me." She breathed heavily, seemingly more exhausted than upset.

Harper nodded acceptance, but did not speak. He could not mark the moment when his purgatory had ended, but he knew he had made sufficient atonement. Guilt for that death no longer weighted his soul.

Kylene made a choking noise and shook her head. "I came back—because—I thought I should come back." Wretchedness sounded in every word.

"It's all right, Kylene. You don't have to explain."

She did not heed him. "I stopped. And I came back. And I was lost...but I met you. Right here. You'd put up a big sign, by the pond. 'Kylene, stop now.'"

He had thought of a sign but had never felt it would justify the effort. Harper held his breath, grateful he had not interrupted.

"So I stopped. And I—I talked to you."

Tears were coming, Harper sensed. But he could think of nothing to stop them. Instead, he was compelled to ask, "What did I say?"

Kylene sniffed, but managed to control herself. "It really wasn't you. He was like you, but he was very old. He had gray hair on the sides of his head. His Kylene had left him too, but it was years and years ago. It wasn't—just like this. It was different somehow. I can't explain it."

Harper exhaled noisily. "So don't try."

"He gave me a message for you. Here." She reached in a back pocket and pulled out an envelope that Harper recognized as paper from a writing block.

He took it gingerly between forefinger and thumb. With twilight dwindling, the envelope was opaque, so he moved around the cabin to slap at light switches and held the letter up for inspection in the kitchen. One illegible line and a signature. He did not bother to open the envelope, but crumpled it into a ball and shoved it into the disposal chute. *Take good care of my little girl*, he thought angrily. *How corny can you get?*

"What other pearls of wisdom did I divulge?" he growled. Then his ill temper was checked by Kylene's expression. She was not reading his mind, he understood suddenly. She didn't understand the cause of his anger, and her thin veneer of maturity was beginning to crack. *Take good care of my little girl.*

"Kylene, don't worry," he said gently. "I'm feeling a bit out of sorts with myself, that's all. I'm glad you're back. If you stay . . . Things will be normal again in a while. They—generally turn out for the best." *All right, chum. I hope you're satisfied—Harper.*

"Sometimes they turn out for the best." Kylene tried to smile.

"Uh . . . Yeah. Sometimes."

"That's what you told me. Sometimes. Most of the time, they don't."

Harper put on an artificial smile, and returned to the kitchen to lay plates and utensils on the table. "This other me is pretty cynical." The tone was deliberately light, intended to mask emotion strangely akin to jealousy. Kylene turned away, to face memories Harper could only guess at. "No. He was just lonely. One of his arms had been damaged. A long time ago, he said, before he came to Alghera. But since he couldn't fight with it, he had to settle for being a *bookworm*. He couldn't leave the cabin because—"

"He was afraid," Harper said gently. *I was afraid.*

"No!" Kylene's face twisted with emotions that Harper could not decipher. "He was brave. He hurt so much inside, but he wouldn't go away or let any of the pain die, because—because his Kylene might return. And need him."

Sweet suffering Jesus! Harper thought. *How long?*

Kylene was still speaking. "—wasn't me, he said, but he was very kind. He tried to explain time travel to me. I stayed with him a couple of year tenths. Do you mind?"

Harper hesitated. "I can't—I—well, it's done." He gave a great sigh. "Thank you for your kindness."

After a moment he asked, "What else did he tell you?"

Kylene spoke slowly. "You—he—told me to travel in time again. To go back to the point where I had decided to return to you and as much farther back as I dared. And then I should come forward again. Because time branched like a tree, and coming forward I went out on each limb. I wouldn't find him again, but on one limb I would get to you."

"Yes," Harper said flatly. He pulled frozen horsemeat from a storage locker and sliced off hand-size portions with a crystal knife. "What else?"

Kylene's green eyes moved to his gray ones for a moment, then away. "That was it. He set some instruments in the shuttle so I'd be able to get back to the right times. Then he said he was conspiring with me and that if I did what he told me, I might win my heart's desire. He said that most of the time I wouldn't get what I wanted. Sometimes I would, if I was brave enough to try, and knowing that would have to be my consolation if it seemed I failed."

Take care of my little girl, Harper found himself thinking. *And he threw her into Time with ideas like that! What sort of maniac*—He shook his head, unable to continue down that path of thought, barely able to breathe regularly. The edge of the kitchen counter was hard against his back. *Oh, God! How cruel. No matter what she wants— How could I do such a thing?*

"Kylene." He couldn't look at her. "Kylene, I don't know what this 'heart's desire' business is, but do you know the risks you ran? Look into my head, if you don't. See? No more Kylene." He dumped potatoes and pieces of meat into a stew maker and slammed the lid down to muffle the grinder noise. "Not even little pieces left to remember. If you're going to run away again, don't do it until I tell you how to avoid the risks, please. And if you go away . . . don't ever come back."

The girl nodded abjectly. Then the emotional dam burst behind a flood of tears, and she turned away from him in the kitchen doorway. "I had to, Tayem. I couldn't stand leaving you all alone. With no one. No one at all, not even in your terrible memories. I couldn't, Tayem."

"I don't need pity," Harper snarled. "I'm doing fine."

"It isn't pity. Tayem... Tayem... Please, let me—" Somehow, Kylene managed to preserve her dignity even amid tears.

"I don't need it," Harper repeated. "I don't need it, or you, for anything at all." He threw the knife onto the countertop, then grabbed the girl by her shoulders and forced her to face him. "For the love of God, Kylene, why in the hell did you come back? Why didn't you go where you belong? Damn it!"

But he did not have the hardiness to continue when Kylene collapsed on him and poured sea-water waves of tears onto his chest. "My little girl," he murmured then, and sank to his knees so her head would rest on his shoulder. "There. There. My darling little Kylene. Don't cry, don't cry. Please? Everything'll be all right. Someday you'll meet someone really wonderful, Kylene. And win your heart's desire, and everything else you deserve. Never give your hopes up. Never let your dreams die. Never give up."

Kylene only clutched him more fiercely. "I hate her. I hate her. I hate her," she sobbed, and Harper's face contorted as well with self-hatred and despair.

Kylene needed him and he could not stop thinking of Onnul Nyjuc.

CHAPTER SIXTEEN

True spring arrived at last. The sky was blue continuously and the grass was green enough to make winter memories seem hallucinations. The scent of flowers vied with pine needles in the cool air and a dusky brown bird with a striped breast was calling sweet sweet cheer chillip from the cabin roof when a grim-faced Harper and Kylene left for the future.

As the entrance ramp descended from *Scent O'Claws*, Harper turned away suddenly, to walk around the vehicle's stern and jump the small stream that escaped from the beaver dam. When he returned, yellow and red flowers picked from the hillside were in his hands, bright against the faded green and black of his uniform. He nodded somberly, then handed the bouquet to Kylene. "Peace offering," he muttered.

The ramp retreated after they entered, and swiveled upward, closing flush with the silvered skin of the levcraft so that no opening could be seen. Then the giant axe head shape vanished.

Bare moments later it reappeared. The ramp descended once more.

"Dumb of me," Harper remarked as the airlock opened. "But I have to take care of a few details before we go any further. Be patient." He did not wait for an answer, but ran to a utility shed. The morning sun made a halo of his red-brown hair and glinted on his Teepblind.

He returned shortly with a shovel. "Stay here. I'll be right back."

Kylene bit her lower lip but did not argue, and the man reentered the warship alone. It vanished into run-time even as the entrance ramp was rising.

Kylene stood mutely, viewing the spring landscape as if it were new to her. She no longer carried the dogtooth violets Harper had given her, and soon she skipped across the stream to pick herself another bouquet.

Perhaps one minute, perhaps two, passed before the *Scent O'Claws* reappeared. Kylene was at the foot of the ramp when the airlock opened.

Tim Harper stood there in mottled red and brown battledress. He carried a muddy shovel, which he pitched with both hands into the pond. A startled beaver slapped water frantically with his broad tail till he recognized his eccentric upright neighbor, then submerged.

Harper laughed, then bounded down the ramp to extend a hand to Kylene. "My lady, shall we go?"

Kylene smiled and held out the bouquet. "For you."

Hand in hand they reentered the vehicle.

The time machine vanished.

Here ends Book Two of *The Destiny Makers*.
The tale will continue in Book Three,
Soldier of Another Fortune, in which the mission to
assassinate Mlart is endangered by the arrival of an
enemy telepath—and fellow time traveler.

ABOUT THE AUTHOR

Mike Shupp is a thirty-nine-year-old aerospace engineer living in Los Angeles. This is his second novel.

There's an epidemic with 27 million victims. And no visible symptoms.

It's an epidemic of people who can't read.

Believe it or not, 27 million Americans are functionally illiterate, about one adult in five.

The solution to this problem is you... when you join the fight against illiteracy. So call the Coalition for Literacy at toll-free **1-800-228-8813** and volunteer.

Volunteer Against Illiteracy. The only degree you need is a degree of caring.

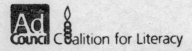

Ad Council · Coalition for Literacy

LV-1